OLEA
IN JUNE

Whitney Vandiver

OLEANDERS IN JUNE

A NOVEL

———— •• ————

WHITNEY VANDIVER

NORTHERN PINES PRESS

NORTHERN PINES PRESS

Oleanders in June

Publishing support by The Self Publishing Agency
Book designed by Liana Moisescu
Book interior designed by Laura Wrubleski
Author photograph by Stacy Anderson

Library of Congress information available upon request.

Print ISBN 978-1-7339316-0-1
eBook ISBN 978-1-7339316-1-8

NPP 1 2 3 4 5 6 7 8 9 10

MAY

*T*he gentle tap of water against the window pane woke Alfred from his sleep. He had been on the island less than twenty-four hours, and thus far the hours had scented the air with summer rain. The morning tasted of salt and sweat. He reached stiffly for the side table where the cool brass of his pocket watch sat beside the dark oil lamp. The second hand ticked thickly in the quiet of the early morning, and he could just make out the time. Nearly six o'clock.

Alfred's eyelids itched in the morning light as he rose. There was something foreign about the way the air clung to his undershirt, but he pushed the thought away as he looked out the window at the front of the boardinghouse. He'd slept soundly through the night, but it had done little to make up for the two days he'd spent traveling to the coast.

He licked his chapped lips as he watched the soft early-morning glow bloom over the gulf waters. Cast in the fragile light of a city waking along the shore, the frail hues of pink and purple lingering at the front windowsill gave him a glimpse of the world he'd stepped into. He stood wholly in the window, taking in his first morning on Galveston Island. It was tremendously exhausting.

The brass of a barometer shimmered on the windowsill, and he gave it a tap. The mercury had risen through the night, ushering the storm north of the island and signaling cooler temperatures for the day. It was a refreshing thought. What few items he owned hadn't filled his suitcase, and he was in no shape to be buying summer shirts any time soon.

All was quiet as he made his way along the hallway and set his toiletry bag down in the washroom. He had pulled himself together and was mid-wash, the previous day's travel slipping from his skin as he shaved over the wash basin, when the door rattled with a solid knock. He pulled at the nearest towel to clear his eyes and opened the door in a partially blind grab, leaving shaving soap on the handle. The man on the other side was slim and dressed in a pressed shirt with the collar open, perfectly measured suspenders, and a smooth black tie. A towel was draped over his arm.

"The new boarder, is it?"

Alfred wiped absently at the remaining soap on his face as he stuck out a hand. "Alfred Ridgeway."

"John Briggs." The man eyed his hand before scanning the whole of Alfred's upper half. "A pleasure, I'm sure."

Alfred straightened a touch as he caught the scent of gin. From downstairs the clink of dishes carried up the stairs as the sun brightened the hall behind the man.

"Perhaps if you'd arrived like a gentleman," John continued, "you'd be aware that my shift is from six to six-twenty."

"Your shift?"

"I'm not certain how they wash themselves in the Indian Territory, assuming they take the time to do so, but sharing a washroom with another man will lead to rumor in civilized cities."

Alfred tightened his jaw.

"You'll find Mathias an early riser and in the washroom by five-thirty," John continued. "I wash from six to six-twenty. You'd do well to find a time that doesn't disrupt the entire household for the sake of a shave."

"Is there a schedule for other ablutions outside of morning grooming or shall I see the proprietor to be assigned a time to read the newspaper as well?"

John glanced at Alfred's shirt as a smirk pulled at his mouth. Alfred followed his gaze to see a patch of darkened cotton spread from the buttons of his shirt. He wiped the water from his chin with the towel and looked up to see the man's shadow moving down the hall. He clenched his teeth as he shut the door. The mirror above the wash basin showed a freshly washed man, but his origins were still visible. A corpsman by training, he was traveling by assignment, the wrinkled shirt and dull tie giving away his vulnerabilities. He rewet his face and applied the last of the lather before finishing his shave. The tie gave a slight bend at the bow as he worked it into place and affirmed what he already knew: he fit in neither world. He was too worldly for the farm and by no means a gentleman. He was somewhere uncomfortably in the middle—a traveler perpetually in someone else's land.

Alfred pulled at his cuffs as he entered the dining room. Another man was already seated at the table, reading intently from a newspaper. His olive skin glowed in the sunlight streaming in from behind him, with the paper leaving only his forehead and a head of thick black hair exposed. Alfred's entrance was cut short by a woman's cheerful salutation.

"Good morning, Mr. Ridgeway," she beamed as she came in from the kitchen. "I trust you slept well after such a long trip."

The man lowered his paper at her words, and Alfred gave him a nod as he took the seat across from him.

"Yes. thank you, Mrs. Poplar."

"Very good." She set down a basket of day-old rolls and a saucer of cut melon. "I don't believe you've met Mr. Ortiz."

"Mathias," the man corrected, offering him a section of the newspaper that had been discarded on the table. Alfred shook his head with a tight smile.

"Fresh poached eggs on toast," Mrs. Poplar carried on as she returned from the kitchen and set a full plate in front of both men. "And spicy potato hash."

"This smells divine," Alfred noted.

He filled his plate until the sharp scent of jalapeño peppers mingled with the buttery toast, the juice of the pickled cucumbers running into the fried potatoes. He swallowed in anticipation.

"Do eat, dears. Oh," she started with a little hop toward the kitchen, "the coffee."

She returned with a pot that steamed from its spout. Mathias quietly folded the newspaper and set it on the corner of the table as Alfred cut through the skin of his egg and watched the yolk run over the toast.

"It was quite a storm that came through last night," Mrs. Poplar commented as she returned to the table with a third plate and set it in front of an empty chair next to Mathias. She poured a steaming stream of coffee into both men's mugs. "The roads will be quite muddy in some parts of town. So do be mindful when you return this evening to remove your boots before taking the stairs."

"Mrs. Poplar likes to imagine that we are the messiest of our little family," Mathias announced.

She scoffed and made her way back into the kitchen before joining them with her own plate of melons and toast with cream. "Not true in the least. I've never had cause to lecture him on minding his boots or keeping a proper gentleman's bed, but there is always at least one in every lot that needs tending to."

Mathias smiled wholeheartedly with a cheek full of food, and Alfred felt the atmosphere of the room fill with the subtler comforts of home, a lightheartedness that put him at ease.

"It is most unlike Mr. Briggs to be late to the table," Mrs. Poplar commented as she took her seat.

Alfred swallowed a bit of egg and toast and wiped at his mouth. "I am afraid his tardiness is my doing. I was unaware that we were assigned shifts for the washroom."

Mrs. Poplar raised her eyebrows as she sipped from her cup.

"I did the same when I first arrived," Mathias remarked with a nod. "I assume he insulted your gentry and made it clear when you should observe your twenty-minute shift?"

"Six-twenty."

"The last shift. You'll want to watch your time or you'll miss breakfast altogether."

Alfred glanced at Mrs. Poplar, who was shaking her head.

"No need to rush, Mr. Ridgeway. I never let a boarder go hungry, though you might find the hash a little cold."

She passed a white porcelain bowl of warm syrup toward him, and he drizzled it across his hash. White light streamed in through the window, slicing through the plate of remaining eggs, and a sense of comfort settled in his mind. It was a simple scene that contrasted sharply with the earlier tension of the morning.

"Good morning, all."

The air sizzled across the table as John rounded the corner and took his seat next to Mathias. Mrs. Poplar gave a pleasant smile as her final boarder set about cutting his toast. He poured himself a cup of coffee and began eating without another word.

"Sugar, Mr. Briggs?" She held up a sugar bowl that matched the coffee pot. A small spoon handle stuck out, clinking with her motion.

"Oh, yes." He motioned to Mathias, who passed the bowl to him. "You know, Mrs. Poplar, doctors are beginning to prescribe a daily dose of sugar in diets to help women with fatigue. Perhaps you should consider adding it to your own coffee to give you a little pep in your step."

Mrs. Poplar kept her eyes on her toast. "I believe I have plenty of pep in my step for my day, but thank you, Mr. Briggs." She looked at Alfred as she tore off a piece of toast. "This is what I get for boarding medical students."

"I quite agree," Mathias replied, washing over her off-handed comment. "You've plenty of energy, Mrs. Poplar."

"Oh, come off it, Mathias," John shot back.

Mathias wiped his mouth with his napkin and reached for the coffee pot.

"I simply mean to reassure her that a recommendation of a novel study does not warrant a change in diet, especially for a woman of a certain age." Mrs. Poplar shot him a look, and he held up his hand. "My apologies, Mrs. Poplar. I am referring much more to your physical age than your disposition."

She returned to her toast.

"It is much more than a recommendation," John countered. "It was published in the Journal of Physical Medicine for God's sake."

Mrs. Poplar dropped her fork loudly on her plate with a clang that caused all three men to jump.

"My," she laughed with a look toward Alfred, "I must have clumsy fingers today."

"Perhaps a symptom of your certain age," Alfred joked with a smile that she returned.

The room settled into a subtle symphony of utensils on ceramic, lips wet with coffee, and birds singing from just beyond the window. Mathias was the first to break the natural melody of the meal.

"Mrs. Poplar says you're from up north."

"Indian Territory."

Mathias chewed on a bite of melon with a crinkled brow. "Is it as terrifying a place as they say?"

"That depends." Alfred scooped another spoonful of hash onto his plate. "What do they say?"

"Natives running amuck. Towns sacked. Disease spreading from town to town."

"I'm sorry to disappoint you, but it's nothing of that sort," he said with a grin. "Some areas deeper into the territory might be hostile to visitors, but not on the outer edge where I lived."

"The territories sound like a God-awful place for a man to make a home," John inserted. "No electricity. No plumbing . No civilization."

Mathias took another bite of melon and rested his arms on the table. "I've always been interested in the medical treatment that tribes use," he said. "Do you know any tribesmen?"

Alfred grinned at the table's utter disregard for John's comment. "A few. I worked the fields with a young Cherokee on my father's farm."

"Did you ever talk medicine?"

"I'm afraid not."

Mathias's face fell as he took another drink of coffee. Mrs. Poplar's voice was a light breeze across the table as she tilted her head toward the newest boarder.

"What drew your family to farm there, dear?"

"Price."

"The land is cheaper?"

"Terribly cheap."

Mathias speared the last of his hash. "Why is that?"

"Because it's a God-awful place to live," he replied flatly.

Mrs. Poplar erupted with laughter as Mathias struggled to keep a straight face. Alfred threw a glance at John who seemed to find the comment at his expense and pursed his lips as he picked up the newspaper. Alfred cleared his throat as the table quieted.

"Not to discredit the land, but it's not ideal for crops. Wheat grows in some areas, and cotton is beginning to take in the southern half. But overall it's not an easy place to make a farm."

"I've heard it's hot," Mathias added.

"And dry," Alfred commented with a sip of coffee.

"Well, you'll not find the island dry," Mrs. Poplar added, "but you'll be well-prepared for our late summer heat if you're already accustomed to hotter temperatures."

"I'm hoping to find it more than bearable," Alfred replied with a glance out the window. "I'm interested in studying the climate of the island. It's so unlike anything I've ever experienced."

Mrs. Poplar folded her napkin and laid it across her plate. "Mr. Ridgeway has accepted a post with the island's weather office."

He perked up at the words, feeling their weight as they settled on the table. He had been training for months for the post, and now he was only a few days away from meeting the island's renowned climatologist. Alfred had traveled to the edge of Texas and was poised on the edge of his future.

"Fascinating," Mathias commented. "You'll be working with Isaac Cline, then. As a climatologist?"

"An Assistant Observer."

John sniffed at the comment. "And what is it that the bureau does," he asked as he popped the paper to stiffen its lines, "aside from misreading the skies and issuing inaccurate forecasts?"

"They're not always inaccurate," Mathias argued.

John shot him a look and returned to his reading.

"Forecasting is quite difficult work," Alfred ventured.

"Yes," John assured them as he folded the newspaper. "I am certain it compares to the intellect required to save lives that we perform at the hospital daily."

Mrs. Poplar straightened, dropping her hands into her lap, as Mathias leaned back against his chair. Alfred watched John stand and brush the crumbs from his shirt.

"Well, I'm off to assist a guest lecturer. We have a Dr. James Barton visiting from Uganda who is addressing the select few who are brave enough to tackle the challenges of international medicine, and I'll be assisting the poor man in preparing his notes before the talk tomorrow."

"Very good, Mr. Briggs," Mrs. Poplar pined. Alfred sensed a rehearsed tone, a feigned interest, but John seemed to either not notice or not care. "That must be quite an honor to assist a doctor studying disease overseas. And in Africa of all places."

John stood and looked past them at the back wall as if seeing far into the distance at some great wilderness. His hands settled on his hips as his chin tilted slightly upward, and Alfred smirked at the stance, trying to imagine John tackling any form of nature. His mind wandered as he took in the future savior of the ill. He wondered if being at death's bedside created a similar natural instinct for survival: the hunter ever-pressing forward for fear of becoming the hunted.

"A horrid place to live, isn't it," John asked thoughtfully. He squinted his eyes as if an imaginary desert sun were bearing down on him. "I can't imagine what would draw a man of his caliber to leave civilization to tend to the uncivilized."

"Rejoice with those that do rejoice and weep with those that do weep," Mrs. Poplar replied as she stood and started toward the kitchen with the coffee pot.

John looked at her blankly before returning to the dining room. "Yes. Right. Well said." He took his leave from the table and made his way toward the front room. After a moment, the door shut and the house fell silent but for the clink of dishes in the next room.

"Here we go," Mrs. Poplar commented, returning from the kitchen. "A fresh pot to start the day."

Mathias brightened as she set the coffee pot on the table and took his empty plate. He smiled at Alfred as he poured him a cup and slid it across the table.

"Welcome to Galveston, Mr. Ridgeway."

Alfred returned the toast and took a drink as Mathias watched him with a knowing grin. The liquid had barely made it down when Alfred coughed and drew in a deep breath. When he looked up, Mathias was laughing, his bright eyes greeting the morning in veritable amusement. Mrs. Poplar chuckled from the doorway of the kitchen, a tea towel over her shoulder.

"Turkish coffee is only for the strong-hearted," she commented. "Give it a few weeks and you'll be asking for it after every meal."

She disappeared into the kitchen followed by the sound of water sloshing and plates clinking in the open basin sink. Mathias sipped at his cup and gave a smack of his lips.

"It got me the first time as well. Mrs. Poplar's little trick on new boarders."

"I've never tasted coffee this strong before." Alfred cleared his throat as he sniffed at the bitter coffee and looked into his cup before taking another sip. It was brash and the metallic taste stayed on his tongue long after his cup was empty. Energized and refreshed, he quickly came to understand why Mathias had only given him a third of a cup.

"Have you learned the city yet?" Mathias stood and stretched his back.

"No, just the sections I viewed from the carriage on the way from the station."

"Mostly houses and the business district then?"

Alfred nodded, his head buzzing from the coffee.

"Well, while John busies himself with foreign doctors, I am spending my Saturday on the Midway. I've planned to meet a few colleagues for a small scandal on the beach." He smirked. "Care to join me?"

"What sort of scandal?"

"Nothing serious," Mathias acquiesced, downing the last of his Turkish coffee. "There's a small fair in town down by the piers. It's a dime to get in and a few nickels for the games. I heard they have a moving picture box, the kind with the crank."

Alfred hesitated as he considered the cost, knowing his pockets had nothing more than worn cotton between the seams.

"Come along," Mathias prodded. "I'll pay your way in as a welcome. It's the least I can do to show you around and introduce you. Besides that, when will you have time to flitter about an island fair again after starting your post?"

His point was well-founded. Alfred gave a nod as he stood. He didn't report to the bureau office until Monday morning, and aside from learning the island and checking his barometer, he had little to do. If nothing else, the walk would stretch his tight calves and work the last of the train ride's stiffness out of his muscles.

"Where's the Midway?"

"About a forty-minute walk if you're inclined. It's not worth hiring a carriage." Alfred gave an agreeable nod as Mathias made a last wipe at the corners of his mouth. "Superb. I need to do a bit of cleaning and promised I would help Mrs. Poplar with her garden before the day grows too hot. Let's meet down here around ten." Mathias scrutinized Alfred as he rounded the table. "Do you have a straw hat?"

"No."

"I'll lend you one of mine," he said as he turned toward the front of the house.

Alfred stepped into the entryway of the dining room to watch him walk through to the sitting room. "A bowler won't do?"

"Not in the summer. Let that be your first lesson in life on Galveston," he called out as he turned and started up the stairs. "Dress for the heat and be thankful when you're wrong. It's the only way to avoid disappointment."

He had no idea what Mathias meant, but after the way his morning had already gone, he was inclined to believe practically anything the man told him. Alfred started up the stairs, cupping his neck with his palm. He was going to an island festival with a man he barely knew in an unfamiliar city—and the top of his priority list, apparently, was his lack of a straw hat.

CHAPTER TWO

*M*rs. Poplar was sitting on the love seat at the front of the house when Alfred came downstairs a little before ten o'clock. Her hands moved up and down with thin green thread as she embroidered a tea towel. Her eyes twinkled into a smile when she looked up at him.

"Off to the festival, dear?"

"We are." He took his jacket from the rack near the door. "Will you be joining us?"

"No, I'm afraid my day is better suited to staying around the house. My hip would only slow you down."

Footfalls echoed as Mathias came down the stairs. He was in pressed clothes with a fresh shave, and his hair was slicked back with thick curls pulled into place. He looked between Alfred and Mrs. Poplar.

"Ready to be off?"

Alfred held the door open as Mathias took his jacket from the coat rack. The day had already grown warm and left the air heavier than the night before. Alfred made to slip on his jacket but thought better of it as they stepped into the sun. A light breeze met them on the street, and honeysuckle seduced his nostrils as they crossed the nearest intersection to make their way south toward the ocean. Mathias appeared to be more at ease in the heat despite his shirt fitting snuggly across his chest.

"I had the suit tailored for my induction into the medical society at the university," Mathias explained. "It's one of my better shirts."

"How is one inducted into a medical society?"

They passed a house where children played a game in the yard. He watched them jump and shout as the ball flew from one side of the fenced space to the other.

"The society only accepts top scoring students. It's all a matter of exam scores and clinical performances. It's quite a difficult process to apply, but it reflects well when applying for positions after graduation."

"Is John in the medical society?"

"John is in everything," Mathias snickered, "but not in the way he should be."

"How do you mean?"

"John is the sort that doesn't give much thought to the purpose of societies and organizations. To him they are just standard credentials that every student should have behind his name. He wants his name to be attached to them all without any real effort in association."

"Like a collection."

"Precisely."

They let a young couple take the sidewalk in front of them. Down the street a line of pedestrians crossed at the next intersection, women's parasols bobbing above them as they walked, shading them from the late May sun.

"Why do you study medicine?" Alfred asked as they fell back into pace.

"I want to be a pediatrician."

"A pediatrician?"

"To treat children."

They caught up to the group of pedestrians and slowed as they crossed the next intersection. The morning continued to heat up around them.

"Is treating a child so different than treating a man?"

"They are quite different. I believe they are much more susceptible to certain illnesses."

"Because they are so small?"

Mathias laughed wholeheartedly at the simple question and shook his head.

"It's more a matter of their development. Their bodies haven't reached the capacity of an adult's body. Consider a yearling tree. In the wild it has planted roots and acclimated to its surroundings, but it is still not as strong as the seasoned trees around it. Winds, floods, disease, nearly anything could affect it."

The crowd thickened as they continued down 16th Street.

"Likewise, consider the same yearling if uprooted and replanted in a yard. Its body is now introduced to new soil and with that comes new enemies—different insects, an altered soil chemistry, perhaps various new weather phenomena. Until it has taken root and become acclimated to its new environment, it goes through a period in which it is vulnerable to anything new. Everything it experiences for the first time is unprecedented until it learns how to respond for self-preservation."

"Children don't have that sense of self-preservation?"

A breeze carried the salty scent of the ocean through the crowd, and the fronds of palm trees rustled overhead.

"Perhaps it's learned. The sea air does women good for vapors and nervous tendencies, but it seems to bring about issues for young children."

"Such as?"

"Headaches, runny noses, sore throats. It's a growing phenomenon that we can't seem to place well enough to diagnose consistently. The truth is we never know for certain with children if it is a more tender reaction to what men pass off as minor irritants or something altogether different."

"You mean it's a matter of interpretation?"

Mathias smiled at his words.

"Yes, to some degree I would say children are up for even greater interpretation."

Having been caught up in the current of the crowd, they crossed Avenue O and saw the first signs of the festival: flags flying overhead, their red, green, and yellow colors small sails flapping in the wind. As the people in front of him mingled and moved about, Alfred remained distracted by the gathering of locals until they reached the other side of the street and the group thinned. He halted at the edge of the walkway and found himself looking out beyond the faces of passersby and into the rushing waves of the Gulf of Mexico.

Alfred stood entranced. Waves began far out at sea and grew in complexity as they neared the shore, breaking as they met the shallows before reaching up the sandy beaches like tendrils and pulling what they could back out with them. Before him was the beach, an uneven landscape of light brown sand that blended tenderly into the water's edge. The sky was a bright blue, and over the waterline wisps of slender clouds pulled like taffy across the smooth glass of the sky. The force of the ocean wind rushed upon him. A sensation started in his forearms and spread up his biceps and across his shoulders until goosebumps covered his skin. The warmth of the ocean wind was fresh and different from the balmy air that circulated the island. It was sweeter somehow. The fruit of the scene was brighter than what he had experienced farther inland: all along the beaches were swimmers in their swimming suits and bathing trunks splashing in the water. Sunbathers rested in the shade of large umbrellas that had been nestled in the sand.

It captivated him.

Mathias called to him from farther down the row. Alfred pulled his eyes from the water and made his way toward the gate. He glanced once more at the ocean's colors over the water as they moved with the crowd. Mathias led them into a line of young couples and excited children.

"First time seeing the ocean?"

"It's magnificent."

They scooted forward with the crowd, the smell of popcorn wafting on the ocean breeze.

"It's not always this peaceful," Mathias noted. "You should see it when it storms."

A small gate came into view, dwarfed by the oversized flags that whipped and popped overhead. Mathias paid their way in, earning them each five game tickets. Mathias pocketed the tickets and threw on his jacket, straightening it a little at the collar but remaining unfrazzled as the wind flapped the material around his waist like a cape. His brown eyes were bright with excitement and he bit his lip as he took in the festivities. All around them the carnival bustled with children running from one game stall to the next, parents paying for amusement, and vendors selling popcorn, cotton candy, and roasted peanuts. It was a spectacle of color and motion, inundating them from every direction. Alfred's head spun with it all.

He felt Mathias nudge his arm and followed his gesture to a row of games. "Let's have a go at them!"

Alfred followed him past a popcorn vendor to the first booth, where a wooden table supported several milk jugs at odd distances, some on the table with others on blocks of varying height so that none were exactly the same. A young boy tossed rings at the jugs, missing the first four and clipping the spout of a fifth with his final throw. The boy stomped his feet as his father pulled him away toward a man juggling bright green balls.

"What's the aim?" Alfred asked, scanning the table of milk bottles.

"To get rings around as many bottles as you can." Mathias traded one of his tickets for five rings and weighed them in his hand. "The key is to focus on just one jug and perfect the throw."

He threw his first ring with a loose wrist. It bounced off a bottle and rolled off the table. He threw a second one that nearly missed the spout altogether but clipped the top. His third throw was lighter and steadier, the ring whizzing through the air and landing perfectly on the spout with a ting as it fell onto the neck of the bottle. He gave a broad smile and puffed his chest at the vendor, who shook his head in defeat. Mathias squinted and tossed the last two rings, missing with the fourth and ringing the neck again with the fifth.

"See? Easy." He turned to the vendor. "What do I get?"

The man stretched up and pulled a tomato-red pennant from a peg board. Mathias waved it triumphantly in the air, and Alfred found his enthusiasm contagious as his housemate gave him a challenging grin.

"Care to try?"

Alfred bit his lip as he considered the game, but felt a pull to see the rest of the festival. "Let's explore first."

Mathias gestured down the aisle where a row of games filled both sides. Beyond that, a small octagon pen of wooden planks sat in the middle of the street, making the fence just high enough for a goat to lift its head over the wood and nibble at a child's hand. Sheep wandered inside the pen with a saddled donkey. An older man with a thick grey beard shouted over the crowd advertising an adventurous ride around the pen, while a younger man that Alfred deduced was his son hoisted a small girl onto the saddle and began to lead the animal around the wooden border, scattering sheep and goats as he walked. Another man in a yellow vest held a large snake, its body wrapped around his shoulders and arm, next to a brightly painted sign that promised exotic animals like the city had never seen before.

Mathias led them toward a vendor cart that offered roasted peanuts and bought two bags, handing one to Alfred with an eager grin. All around them the festival was alive with color and noise as Alfred cracked open a peanut shell and tasted the salty bitterness of the treat. Looking back toward the gate, Alfred lost sight of the edge of the carnival as the crowd blended into the maze of booths and the sounds of the petting zoo; the city buzzed in excited tones as a deep voice came from the crowd.

"Mathias."

An older gentleman approached them. He was slender and nearly eye to eye with Alfred, only his thinning grey curls losing what little height the younger man had on him. A confident nose preceded his bright blue eyes, and he carried himself patiently, as if years of thoughtful living had taught him to consider his path before misdirection led him into inescapable conversations. He paused at the peanut cart and paid the man a nickel in exchange for a bag.

"Ah, good day, Mr. Jeffries," Mathias greeted him.

"That it is," he replied flatly, cracking a peanut shell over the ground and letting his eyes fall on Alfred. "And who might you be?"

"This is Alfred Ridgeway of the Weather Bureau."

The man stuck out his hand and gave a tight grip as Alfred shook it. "Daniel Jeffries."

"Mr. Jeffries owns a tailor shop on the Strand," Mathias explained.

The man ignored his introduction as he popped a peanut into his mouth and kept his eyes on Alfred.

"The Weather Bureau, you said? You'll be working with Isaac Cline then."

"Yes, sir, as an assistant observer."

"It seems the government should invest a little more time in their equipment if they want to boast a bureau that does more than predict the weather. It appears we're no closer to seeing a hurricane before it arrives than a decent summer day to swim by."

He pulled out another peanut and watched the shell crack between his fingers. Alfred kept his voice in a kind tone, working carefully not to appear to smart at his words.

"I'm sure you can appreciate the difficulty we have in forecasting. The winds seem to make up their own minds on whether they're more suitable for flying kites or creating swells. Science has leaps left to make before investments in equipment are the equalizer for accuracy in forecasts."

The man stared at Alfred with small eyes and a stern brow. After several seconds of silence, a small grin crossed his mouth.

"Alfred, my boy, you'll fit in perfectly on this island."

Mathias chuckled as he popped a peanut into his mouth and looked about the crowd as if searching for someone. Mr. Jeffries looked out beyond the Midway at the waves crashing onto the beach. Swimmers danced in and out of them in miniaturized waltzes.

"That little hospital of yours is growing quite nicely, Mathias."

"We're at thirty-two students this year already."

"So many," he mused. "It'll be a full-fledged attraction within a few years, I'd wager."

"The first medical school in Texas has got some draw to it," Mathis replied.

Mr. Jeffries looked off into the crowd and squinted his eyes in the midday sun. "There they go, off for another ride on that damn donkey." He gestured toward the petting zoo. "Have you ever heard of such a ridiculous attraction as donkey rides?"

"I'm surprised to see you here," Mathias observed. "You don't strike me as the sort to find amusement in a traveling fair."

"My grandchildren." He pointed at the small corral where three donkeys were being led by rope. "They said they wanted to see the peacocks."

"I didn't realize there were peacocks here."

"There aren't." He stuck his hand out once more with a sigh. "It was a pleasure, Alfred."

"Likewise."

"Mathias, I've got a new shipment of silk that Mrs. Poplar would like to see. You'll pass along the word for me?"

"Of course," he replied with a nod. "I hope your grandchildren enjoy the peacocks."

The man rolled his eyes and sauntered away. The smell of popcorn entreated Alfred's senses as the warmth of the day continued to permeate through the crowd. Behind them a man cursed at a game vendor, and Alfred turned to glance at the commotion before seeing Mathias glance at his pocket watch.

"Keeping the time?"

Mathias dropped his watch back into his pocket. "I was hoping to run into someone but hadn't agreed on an exact time."

"We're not in a hurry," Alfred coaxed as he looked about the crowd. "Shall we walk around and give the festival a look?"

The roasted peanuts were a treat to Alfred's palate as they wandered through the festival, walking past a tent showing off a man juggling melons alongside a woman who challenged them both to try for the title of the strongest man in the city. Despite the cool blue of the water just a few hundred yards beyond the festival, the air was thick and pulled at his collar and undershirt with moist fingers.

As they neared the petting zoo, Mathias was caught by the arm and pulled into a conversation with a young man about the week's clinical rounds. Alfred removed himself from Mathias's side after several minutes of eavesdropping and busied himself with a small goat that was rubbing against a fence post on his impromptu enclosure. He petted its head, feeling the bony angles of its skull and floppy ears with his rough, calloused hands. He glanced back at Mathias, who stood with his hands just inside his pockets and his jacket pulled open slightly to reveal the shimmer of his pocket watch chain. Alfred reached into his pocket and felt the outline of his watch where it floated without attachment. He compared so little to the men around him. Standing still with a brown and white goat nudging his pant leg, he watched the gentlemen move about him as if he were a poster, something at which to glance and take in but not to study or remember. They wore clean bowlers and pressed shirts with crisp jackets; he fingered the worn hem of his jacket and turned back to the goat, squatting to give it an aggressive rub between the eyes as it chewed on a mouthful of hay. He might not have made the same acquaintances as Mathias, but he had managed to find at least one soul that he could understand.

"Aren't they gorgeous creatures?"

A thin-framed figure stood over him, her face covered in the shadow of a parasol. He stood carefully to his feet and met her hazelnut eyes. Her brunette hair was pulled up from her neck, but the breeze had blown several strands loose so that they buoyed at her collar. A delicate nose tilted up to look him in the eye, revealing an open smile that brightened her expression. Contrasting the scene around them in a white dress, she looked every bit the part of the city as he had come to expect it but something about her stood out from the others. He studied her eyes as he caught his breath.

"They are the most mischievous things, though" she continued. "Always getting into something and wanting attention when it's not due."

Alfred found his voice. "Goats?"

She gave a chuckle and bent to pet the animal.

"Of course!" She rubbed at the animal's chin as it gnawed on a sprig of hay. "Unless asses are just as roguish, but I don't imagine they care much for eating my Papa's honeysuckle."

Alfred tilted his head to look more closely at her. "You have goats?

"No. Do you?"

She stood and shaded her face once more with her parasol. He furrowed his brow and shook his head, the noise of the festival returning to his ears as someone slammed the hammer down on the scale across the way and the copper ting of the bell filled the air. She smiled at him warmly, which unnerved him. He took in a breath of salty air to ask her name when another young woman joined them, her parasol drifting behind her.

"Florence, how ever do you keep your reputation, running off on your own so carelessly as you do?"

Her companion squinted toward the water and let her head tilt to the side, her loose strands rolling over her neck and onto her shoulder to reveal a smooth jawline. Florence gave the woman a quick glance.

"Who says I do it carelessly? Perhaps I've put a great deal of thought into each rendezvous."

"They'll be saying scandal before the summer."

"There's nothing scandalous about a festival, Evelyn," she commented lightly. "It's little more than roasted peanuts and men throwing away money on a ring toss. How would I ever stir up a rumor here?"

"I haven't the faintest idea as dull as it all is." The woman looked longingly toward the gate before releasing a deep sigh. "We've done our duty. No doubt William will be entreated to return us home after so long in the sun. We should go."

Florence took hold of her friend's arm and turned back to Alfred.

"How rude to suggest a lady leave a conversation with a gentleman without proper introduction, Evelyn." She met his eyes once more and jutted her chin out slightly, her sun-kissed skin revealing faint freckles along the bridge of her nose. "I was rather enjoying a thoughtful conversation with Mr.—"

She shot an eyebrow up, and he took the cue.

"Ridgeway." He cleared his throat and let the bag of peanuts fall to his side. "Alfred Ridgeway."

"With Mr. Ridgeway," she finished with a smile.

Evelyn kept her body turned so that she continued to face the gate but let her eyes roll down to his shoes and back up along his jacket.

"And what were you so thoughtfully discussing, might I ask?" Her words were directed at Florence, Alfred noted, despite her eyes remaining on him.

"Goats," Florence replied.

Evelyn shot her a rigid look. "Goats?"

"Yes, Mr. Ridgeway was about to tell me about his goats, I believe."

Evelyn turned her body toward Alfred as if to join their conversation. Her mouth twisted into an amused smile. "Raised on a farm were you, Mr. Ridgeway?"

Alfred caught her tone but engaged in the banter carelessly, keeping his attention more on Florence than her counterpart. "Yes, as a matter of fact." The corners of his lips pulled upward into the beginning of a smile as Evelyn's face flattened. "My family farms quite a large set of fields in Tahlequah."

"That sounds wonderful," Florence replied, her voice sultry in the heat of the day. "Is it in Texas?"

"Indian Territory."

"Oh, my," Evelyn erupted, bringing a gloved hand to her chest in what Alfred took to be a rehearsed flare. "You live in Indian Territory?"

"In the northern corner, very near the Arkansas border."

"How fascinating," Florence commented, her eyes sparkling as she spoke.

The two shared a smile.

"Indeed," Evelyn cut in, her voice low. "I didn't realize civilized men existed in the territories."

He tightened his smile as he caught her eye.

"You are not the first to make that mistake."

"Do tell us about it," Florence interrupted.

She let her parasol fall onto her shoulder, the edge falling back as the sunlight washed over her, painting her white dress like snow on the prairie. She ignored Evelyn, who huffed mildly and searched the festival for something more interesting.

"It's very similar to Texas but with flat fields and prairies. Of course, we have nothing like the coast and even Galveston has already outgrown some of our larger cities."

"With colorful sunsets, no doubt."

"Please, Florence" Evelyn remarked dryly. "The Indian Territory is no place for a woman."

"There is actually a good bit of talk of declaring statehood in the coming years," Alfred replied.

"Statehood!" Evelyn gave a dark chuckle as she pulled uncomfortably at a glove on her hand. "What will they think of next?"

"I think it would be a thrill to see the Indian Territories," Florence commented, her eyes still on Alfred. "I imagine it's quite beautiful to see nature so unrestricted with so few men far and between towns. Is the land mostly unsettled?"

"Oh, yes. It's a breathtaking landscape. The plains are gold in the late summer and the flat land pulls the winds through the trees. And the sunsets in the summer paint the skies red just over the wheat before harvest."

She continued to smile at him as a small silence settled. He felt his chest grow warm.

"You are quite the poet, Mr. Ridgeway."

"Please, call me Alfred."

"Alfred." She kept her hands lightly on the handle of her parasol, as if preferring their informal exchange despite the circumstances. "I am Florence Mae Keller."

Her lips parted as if to ask a question when Evelyn swatted her arm with a hollow white glove.

"William is here."

Three men approached their little group along with Mathias, who took his place across from Alfred and quickly began introductions, gesturing to each man in turn.

"This is William Goodman, Elijah Baker, and Thomas Brighton. Mr. Ridgeway has come to study the weather. He recently arrived in Galveston for a post with the Weather Bureau's office."

The tallest of the three who had been introduced as William pulled a pack of cigarettes from his jacket, offering them to the men around him. All but Mathias and Alfred accepted the offer.

"The Weather Bureau, eh? Here in Galveston?"

Alfred nodded and watched as Mathias took a step away from the group and began a private conversation with Mr. Brighton, the only man who went without a tie.

"Are you working with that chap who takes the measurements on the roof downtown?"

"Dr. Isaac Cline."

"Yes, he's the fellow. An interesting man. We met during a lecture of some sort." He let loose a puff of smoke that mingled in the air between them like slow moving honey fresh from the bark. "What is it you intend to study? A place like Galveston can't provide that much to observe. More often than not, it's an overly humid sandlot with rainy mornings and balmy evenings."

"There is actually a great deal to study. Take the oceanic currents for an example. We still do not understand the exact role they play in the development of storms at sea. They could be a primary factor in how tropical storms are formed yet we have no way of observing them for predictions."

"Do you think we could learn to do that in the future?"

"Weather forecasting is a vast field and still in its infancy in many ways, but the Weather Bureau's primary objective is to develop tools to forecast weeks in advance."

"Weeks in advance," William mused with a draw of his cigarette. "You'll rival almanacs." He gave Alfred a nudge with his elbow. "Do tell me, how does one go about measuring something like that? I mean one can't go into the water and see it, can he? What types of instruments would you use—"

"William," Evelyn cut in with mock sincerity, "I do hate to interrupt your interest in Mr. Ridgeway's profession, but we really should be returning home. Mother will not take kindly to us missing tea with her friends yet again."

The man raised his eyebrows in agreement.

"Right. As my dear sister has noted, we must be off then." He extended his free hand to Alfred. "I do hope we have an occasion to chat about your profession at length. Perhaps you could join us for drinks one afternoon next week?"

"I think I would rather enjoy that."

"Excellent! Where shall I post you the time and place? We change week to week, I'm afraid."

Alfred's expression was blank as he realized he had not yet memorized the address of the boardinghouse. He wondered if Mrs. Poplar was well known enough to simply give her name, but he felt himself begin to blush at the thought of stating his proprietor's name in lieu of an address. He cleared his throat and glanced at Mathias, who was still chatting with his Mr. Brighton where they had wandered several yards away from the group.

"I've not yet committed the address to memory. Perhaps Mathias can better answer your question."

William cupped Alfred's shoulder with a strong hand.

"Ah, what a grand idea! I'll invite you and Mathias both." He took another draw on the cigarette and looked toward the petting zoo where the women and Mr. Baker were walking the perimeter and flirting with two talkative sheep. "Evelyn! Time to go."

He glanced toward Mathias and Mr. Brighton before giving a sharp whistle. The two men turned to look at him, keeping their voices low as they finished their conversation.

"I'm always having to break those two up," he confided.

"William," Mr. Baker called out as they neared, Evelyn's laugh trailing, "what was the name of that poor man that came in for a loan to breed his sheep? You remember, the one that talked incessantly about his wife knitting them hats to keep them dry in the rain."

Evelyn snorted and covered her mouth with her gloved hand before slapping his shoulder playfully with her free glove.

"Really, Elijah! You must stop!"

"The poor man had a knitted sheep cap in his pocket!"

Evelyn continued her laughter as William dropped his cigarette and snubbed it with his shoe.

"Really, Evelyn," he rebuked. "And the man wasn't poor by any means. He owned two farms and had a rather lucrative stock that had earned him a small fortune."

"Oh," Evelyn declared as she recovered from her laughter. "Perhaps Mr. Ridgeway knew him then."

She giggled as Mathias returned with Mr. Brighton and clapped William on the shoulder.

"Leaving so soon?"

"I'm afraid so. We've dinner before returning home."

"We're dining at the Tremont House," Evelyn replied, leading the entire group to nod as Alfred looked on, completely out of touch.

"But I've roped Alfred into joining us for drinks next Tuesday," William commented. "You'll join us, too?"

"Of course," Mathias replied with a nod toward Mr. Brighton.

"Excellent!" He motioned toward the gate. "Ladies, shall we?"

Evelyn reached for Mr. Baker, who offered her his arm, and William started to follow them. He gave them a tired smile as he departed.

"Good evening, gentlemen."

Mathias lifted a single hand and let it fall on Mr. Brighton's shoulder as the man joined William and their words disappeared in the bustle of the crowd around them. Alfred let his eyes drift from their backs to Florence, who walked slowly beneath her parasol. She turned toward him and paused at the back of the group.

"I do hope to see you again, Alfred."

"As do I, Ms. Keller."

Alfred felt his heart pound against his sternum as she lifted her parasol over her head with a grin.

"Do call me Florence."

Her steps were airy as she sashayed toward the gate. He watched her go, her dress flowing in the breeze, a wave of lace and cloth billowing above her boots. He heard Mathias speak but his ears were deaf to the world. Only his eyes registered the scene before him and he let his mind take over, straining to remember the look of her body as she disappeared into the crowd, a wisp of prairie primrose in a sea of cordgrass.

His senses flooded back as his hand jostled at his side. He looked down to see the bag of roasted peanuts, a section of paper torn off and dangling from his hand. Two goats quickly ate the remnants of his roasted peanuts from the ground, their mouths smacking and their heads bobbing with each mouthful. Mathias held up his own bag, and Alfred took a peanut without a word, both men silently watching the goats eat their free fare.

CHAPTER THREE

The morning light was already beaming through Alfred's windows when he let his feet touch the cool floorboards, a sensation he welcomed after another night of sweaty sheets. He stretched and felt his muscles resist the movement. Letting his feet rest on the floor a few moments longer, he checked his watch and took a deep breath. Sharing a washroom with John and Mathias felt more rigorous than doing so with thirteen other platoon members in Virginia as he trained for the Signal Corps. Perhaps John had gone into the wrong profession.

When he opened his bedroom door, the air turned a touch warmer and his nostrils flared instinctively at the smell of fresh biscuits. He appreciated Mrs. Poplar's southern style in cooking and, though he was hesitant to tell her for fear of bruising propriety, she reminded him of his grandmother in the way her smile pushed at her eyes. If he had been comforted by anything thus far, it was Mrs. Poplar's company.

The washroom door was shut, which was not unexpected. Mrs. Poplar provided them a great many comforts, but she kept a well-structured household—and expected the same of her three tenants. Alfred opened the door, a towel tossed over his shoulder, and caught himself in the doorway. John cursed and turned toward him with his body bent over the sink and a razor in his hand. Despite half his face hidden behind a thick coating of shaving soap, Alfred could see that he was unhappy.

"What the hell do you think you're doing?" John's voice boomed within the small space as Alfred checked his pocket watch.

"It's six-thirty," he replied, letting his eyes linger on the speck of blood that had begun to show at John's jawline.

John dabbed at the nick and dipped the edge of the razor in the basin of water before resuming his shave. His voice was quieter but held the same authoritative tone that Alfred was certain was second-nature.

"I've been assigned a new shift at the hospital for summer hours."

Alfred's ears grew warm. Even beneath a partial mask of shaving soap his face was smug and taut. "What of the washroom schedule then?"

John made a contorted face as he shaved beneath his nose. "You and Mathias can sort out when you use the washroom, but I'll be grooming and dressing from six o'clock to six-thirty now." He shaved the last few sections near his hair line. "Outside of that, I couldn't care less about what you do or when you do it."

He glanced at Alfred with raised eyebrows as he wiped at his face to remove the remaining shaving soap.

"Now if you don't mind," he said briskly.

The door slammed, and Alfred let out a deep breath, feeling it bounce against the door and back onto his face. A squeak of the faucet announced John's lack of preoccupation with the encounter, but Alfred felt his face burning as he crossed the hallway toward his room. He felt certain that what civility John did have was only for Mrs. Poplar's benefit, and, were the poor woman to die or suddenly be taken ill, morning exchanges regarding the washroom would turn into little more than wrestling matches over the cleanest towel. The yelp of swollen wood rubbing on the doorframe caught his attention, and he turned to see Mathias standing in his doorway, his collar open and his thick black hair brushed loosely to one side.

"What's with all the ruckus?"

"John. He's taken the liberty of changing the schedule without informing me."

Mathias nodded with an exaggerated motion and turned back into his room. Alfred crossed the hall and stopped outside the doorframe, looking into the room after him. What part he could see without giving away his interest was sparse. A thin crucifix hung over the bed and a book sat on the table next to the oil lamp along with a half-full glass of water.

"You don't find that odd?"

Mathias sat down on the bed and began tying his shoes. From where he stood, Alfred could make out the corner of a bureau, a single drawer pulled out and the top doors swung open to reveal several shirts and ties.

"Not really. He does it every few months." Mathias gave a small laugh at Alfred's expression as he stood. He hooked a tie around his collar with ease. "Come on. Leave your towel in your room and grab a tie. Mrs. Poplar doesn't mind if we aren't freshly shaven so long as we're dressed appropriately. And waiting for John is likely to ruin your appetite."

Mrs. Poplar, dressed in a subtle blend of grey and blue hues, met them at the table with plates of scrambled eggs, sliced melon and warm biscuits. Next to each one was a bowl of oatmeal topped with brown sugar and nuts.

"Good morning, gentlemen. Coffee for either of you?"

Both men nodded and she poured from the metal pot before carrying it to the kitchen to brew a new batch. She returned with a smaller plate for herself and took her seat at the table. Her cheeks were a rosy shade as she spoke, her movements wafting the juicier smells of the kitchen toward the men.

"It hadn't dawned on me until this morning, Mr. Ridgeway, as I was preparing a chicken for supper, what a blessing it will be to have a gentleman of the Weather Bureau joining us regularly for breakfast."

She poured a spoonful of syrup onto her scrambled eggs as she rocked from side to side to settle into her seat. Alfred looked at Mathias, who shrugged and took a bite of his biscuit.

"How is it that a chicken reminded you so vividly of my occupation?"

"Oh, my!" Her laughter bellowed over the table and she drew a hand to her chest, catching Alfred's arm with the other one. "How indecent that must have sounded!"

Both men laughed, caught off-guard by her giddiness, and her face flushed at their amusement. She dabbed at her eyes with her napkin as she caught her breath.

"No, dear, not the chicken but the planning of my day." She returned to her scrambled eggs. "Surely you will be privy to the forecasts of the day?"

"That's a fair assumption."

"Any idea of today's weather by chance?"

"Give the poor man a chance to find his desk first, Mrs. Poplar," Mathias teased.

"I only know what I've read in the paper," Alfred noted, "but it looks like clear skies beyond the window."

"A fine day for a women's meeting then. Lorraine Bachman is hosting a reading at the library for our group. I'm sure it'll be a small affair but well worth the trouble."

"What sort of reading?" Mathias asked.

"A collection of Wordsworth poems followed by a discussion of the significance of nature. There has been a great deal of talk that perhaps the development of the island has exceeded its resources and that we should be looking to preserve the natural state rather than construct more buildings."

"That sounds like poppycock."

John's voice carried over his footfalls as he entered the dining room. He took his seat next to Mathias and popped his napkin in the air with flair before letting it fall over his lap.

"You have your interests, Mr. Briggs, and I have mine." She took another bite of egg as John poured himself a cup of coffee, ignoring her cool tone. "Now tell me, gentlemen, how was the festival yesterday?"

"Quite spectacular," Mathias replied. "They had games, a petting zoo, vendors with treats of all sorts."

"Mrs. Buchanan and I talked of visiting it today. I would hate to miss something so entertaining, and I hear they will be leaving soon."

"The day after tomorrow."

"I do hope they have roasted peanuts."

"I happen to know for a fact that they do," Mathias assured her.

She raised her eyebrows in satisfaction. "That is, of course, assuming that two unescorted women of our age is not so salacious a sight as to set about rumors."

John's fork tinked as it fell onto his plate, causing the others to jump; he chewed quickly at his eggs and flipped to the next page, skimming the article titles without much attention. Alfred cleared his throat as he looked toward Mathias.

"The gentleman we met at the festival, Mr. Goodman—how do you know him?"

"William is a banker. We were introduced at a fundraising dinner for an expansion of the college."

Mrs. Poplar gazed over her glasses. "Evelyn Goodman's brother?"

Mathias nodded.

"He was a very sociable fellow," Alfred continued, poking at the last few pieces of melon on his plate.

"That he is." Mathias let his spoon drop into his nearly empty bowl. "And that is likely why he is such a good banker."

Mrs. Poplar took the liberty of pouring them both more coffee and eyed John's cup, which was still full.

"His sister, on the other hand," Mathias continued, "has an innate talent for attracting brash conversations and inelegant lighting."

"Mr. Ortiz!"

He straightened and cut his eyes at Mrs. Poplar. A long moment passed before she bent down to continue her breakfast, as if drawing out the reprimand before the men could continue.

"What I mean to say," he continued, keeping his eyes at the head of the table, "is simply that Ms. Goodman did not acquire the amenable nature that her brother so commonly exhibits."

His eyebrows sparked upward as he caught Alfred's gaze and took a drink of his coffee. Alfred ventured another thought on the topic.

"Ms. Keller, however, was quite refreshing."

"She usually is," Mathias replied with a nod, emptying his cup.

"Who is this, dear?" Mrs. Poplar asked.

"Florence Keller."

"Oh, that she is. A kind soul with a wild spirit."

Alfred leaned back in his chair and folded his napkin on the table. "How's that?"

Mrs. Poplar shook her head to clear the air of any indiscretion at her words. "Florence is a dear woman, but I find that she occasionally yearns for more adventure than a woman's life is meant to hold. But that is the mindset of this younger generation. Marriage does not suit all women as it did in my day, but I do believe we were made the better for it."

Mathias caught Alfred's eye and gave such a nearly imperceptible shake of his head that Alfred wondered if he had imagined it, but he let the conversation fall nonetheless. Mrs. Poplar was not apt to give undue criticism, or any at all, at her own table, but her words had clearly had an intention that Alfred was not keen to question.

Mathias eyed the front page of the paper as John held it practically between them. He pointed at a headline near the bottom of the page.

"It says that Mr. Eller's shoe store caught fire yesterday."

"Oh, what awful news," Mrs. Poplar exclaimed, the previous topic all but forgotten.

She softened as she leaned closer to Mathias and searched for the article. Mathias pointed, drawing her attention to the bolded print. John pulled the paper in toward himself to read the headline and then gave a small noise as he returned to the financial section.

"I do hope he is alright. He is such a kind man, that Mr. Eller," she continued.

"He may be kind," John interjected, "but he's a poor cobbler and an even poorer businessman." He folded up the newspaper and dropped it next to his empty plate. "In both senses of the phrase."

"Oh, hush, Mr. Briggs," she reprimanded. "Mr. Eller does the best he can with what God has given him."

"I suppose you're right. There is only so much a man can do with local leather and crippling arthritis."

He took a final drink of his coffee, and with little more than a quiet farewell, excused himself from the table.

"Will you be joining us for dinner, Mr. Briggs?" she called after him.

"Not this evening," he replied from the hallway.

The house grew quiet as the front door shut and soon a familiar informality returned as Mrs. Poplar offered Alfred a third cup of coffee, which he politely declined. Mathias scooted his chair back from the table.

"I must be off as well."

"Roasted chicken with carrots and onions in brown gravy," Mrs. Poplar commented with a small lilt on the last word, as if asking a question.

"I will catch an early trolley to ensure I won't be late," Mathias replied with a knock on the table.

He excused himself from the table, the scent of his soap from the previous night's bath wafting through the air as he passed. Alfred breathed in a mingle of glycerin and brown sugar. After Mathias's footfalls faded overhead, Mrs. Poplar broke the silence.

"I do hope John did not set you back too much this morning."

He shook his head as he swallowed the last bite of biscuit.

"Only a bit. I was surprised was all."

"You'll have missed the trolley, I'm afraid."

He let his shoulders slump as the realization took hold. It was his first day reporting for duty and he was already off his intended schedule. Hiring a coach should the next trolley run too late was a waste of money he didn't have to spend.

"I can call a carriage for you," she offered. "Unless you prefer to bicycle."

"I would, but I don't have a bicycle just yet."

She took another biscuit, set her elbows on either side of her empty bowl, and began to pick the fluffy pastry apart, placing small bites of the crumbly mixture in her mouth like a crow pecking at a leftover meal.

"My husband was keen on seeing about new things and found carriages dull. He said there was nothing to be seen from something so far removed from street scenes and where one had little control over his own direction. He preferred to take himself to work." She pulled off a larger bite. "He bicycled whenever he could."

He took another biscuit from the basket, mimicking her motions.

"You still have the bicycle?"

"I was going to learn to ride it after he passed, but the urge never truly took hold. I'm afraid my hip protests too much now to manage it, but it seemed wasteful to simply toss it. It's a bit rusted, but it should work all the same as long as you mind your pant legs."

"That is very kind of you, but I wouldn't want to risk damaging it."

She waved him off with a flick of her wrist. "That old thing isn't worth the trouble. Henry loved it when he was alive, but it does me no good. Before Mathias, it sat in the carriage house untouched for three years."

She let the rest of the biscuit fall into her empty bowl. The thought of being so free to explore the island thrilled him, but he felt disproportionately conciliatory in accepting her offer, as if he hadn't yet earned the right to use something so personal, having lived in the house for so short a time.

"Of course, the seat might need a bit of adjusting. Mathias is much shorter than you, and I'm sure you would need to raise it slightly to make it more comfortable."

"A small price to pay for such a luxury," he said with a chuckle.

She gave a broad smile that lifted her eyes.

"Shall I retrieve it?" He scooted his chair back.

"No need, dear. I've already pulled it to the front of the house for you."

"Oh, that was kind of you."

"And," she continued as she rose from the table, "I put something aside for you."

She disappeared into the kitchen and soon returned with a small parcel wrapped in a kitchen towel and tied with string. He took the package, his hands warm beneath it as fresh bread met his senses.

"A few biscuits for the day." She gave a warm smile. "In case you forget about lunch."

CHAPTER FOUR

*A*s Alfred pedaled down the street, the day was breaking in a brilliant blue that washed the island in bright light. The morning wind came off the ocean in gusts that smelled of saltwater and seaweed as the tops of buildings caught the early-morning light with their peaked cornices. The bicycle was rusted as Mrs. Poplar had said it would be, and the pedals stuck each time Alfred tried to get going again after slowing at intersections. As he pedaled along the last block of 23rd Street, passing a leather goods store and small deli that promised fresh bread and biscuits, he slid into an effortless idle at the center of the shipping district. The front wheel gave a long squeak as he slowed, and he hopped off to walk the contraption to the front of the E.S. Levy Building.

It was five stories of tan stone, with a first floor of windows displaying the latest in fashionable men's clothing. Large mannequins wore fitted men's suits and tops hats while smaller versions donned black velvet jackets and leather shoes for boys; a shallow awning extended over the sidewalk to shade potential customers as they peered into the clothing store. The fifth floor of the building was set apart and outlined in red stone, making its lines exaggerated and bold in contrast. Six sets of windows looked out onto Market Street from the top floor. Businessmen and early morning shoppers passed in front of the glass, occasionally stopping to examine a new petticoat or bowler hat, despite the store's doors remaining locked until the following hour.

Alfred leaned the bicycle against the brick and straightened his shirt, ensuring it was tucked in on the sides and back and then tightened his tie and swatted at the light dusting that had coated the bottom of his pant legs. The humidity of the island was aggressive, and he was already sweating beneath his shirt. It was an odd sort of oppression that hung about and tickled at his stubble like a persistent gnat.

The private foyer was tiled with pale pink squares and wallpapered with simple mauve and silver stripes that stretched up with the staircase to his left. A metal-framed board hung on the wall just inside the door, announcing businesses and suite numbers. He scanned the list of tenants—which included a lawyer for private affairs, a carriage service, and some sort of importer—until he found the one he sought: *Dr. I Cline, Weather Bureau.* He had contemplated leaving the bicycle in the entryway, but the door opened to the street. Leaving it to the elements seemed irresponsible, and he gazed up the narrow stairwell with tight lips. What a first impression to make: dusty hems and a rusty bicycle. He gave a huff, careful to keep the dirt from rubbing against his jacket, and attempted to roll the bicycle up the five flights of stairs, lifting it on every other step to give it more traction and minimize the noise.

The suite was on the fifth floor, the first door to the right on a long hallway that appeared to stretch the length of the building. He dusted off his sleeves once more before opening the door and walking the rusty bicycle into the office. The room was well lit from the tall windows that overlooked the streets, with particles of loose dust filtering through shafts of golden light, the remnants of someone shifting books or maps. A figure stood at the sparse bookcase against the far wall of windows. He was tall and let his shoulders fall slightly forward as he skimmed a book. Alfred shut the door, balancing his bicycle by his side, and the front wheel gave a small metallic groan by way of introduction as he moved farther into the office.

The man turned with a stiff expression. It was made intimidating by his sharp jaw and tight curls of black hair that were slicked away from his brow. Alfred felt small despite his six-feet of height, all the more so when the man's voice came smooth like water.

"Yes?"

Alfred pulled his shoulder bag over his head and let it fall to his side. He gave a smile as he offered his hand. "Alfred Ridgeway, the new Assistant Observer."

"Ah, yes." He returned the gesture with a firm grip and took in Alfred's appearance, letting his eyes settle on the bicycle behind him. "Isaac said you would be reporting today."

"I apologize for being a bit tardy. I missed the trolley."

The man gave a curt nod as if assessing if it as a viable excuse. He set his book down on the desk behind him.

"I trust you've found proper living arrangements?"

"On Postoffice Street and 14th Street."

"You're boarding?"

His hands slid easily into his pockets as he casually closed the distance between them. His thick locks were trimmed and calmed behind his ears.

"With Mrs. Gretchen Poplar."

"A dear woman," he replied with a small smile that pulled at one side of his mouth. "Well then, proper introductions are in order. I am Joseph Cline, Isaac's brother."

His breath carried a hint of strong coffee, and Alfred glanced beyond his shoulder to see a small unwrapped parcel, the remnants of a croissant atop it.

"We've been waiting months for the bureau to send us an adept assistant. It seems they can't find someone capable of even the simpler tasks."

"You've had other assistants?"

"A few." His grin became tight. "We're quite pleased that the bureau has sent us another one to try out. It's become difficult for the two of us to keep up with it all between the maritime reports, port inquiries from ships, local forecasts, and so on. It will be a relief to have someone helping with the smaller things about the day."

Alfred nodded and let his eyes flicker about the room as the statement took hold in his mind. So settled was it that Alfred would be the lesser of the three that he felt it grow on him like moss, crawling up his sides and onto his face like a new skin. An assistant was a respectable post to start, but his position was clear—what room there was to grow was not his to claim. Joseph's voice was deep in the hollow space.

"You've not met my brother, then?" When Alfred shook his head, Joseph nodded and crossed his arms. "You'll find he is not terribly conversational except when he is overly instructive about duties in our office." The man's expression appeared to darken, but Alfred was uncertain if it was his eyes or the shifting shadows of the light that had created the illusion. "I'm sure he will explain your duties in detail when he returns."

"I've read a good deal of Dr. Cline's work," Alfred noted. "I'm keen on assisting in any way I can be of service."

When Joseph gave little expression in way of a reply, Alfred searched for the office for a new topic, but his effort was unnecessary. Joseph let out a breath. It was small but perceptible as he leaned back against the edge of his desk.

"Isaac is the Chief Climatologist, mostly by years, but he has grown accustomed to filling his days with data analysis for publications and approving forecasts. He occasionally gives lectures when he's not busying himself with writing his book on climatology. The majority of the work, however, is done on the roof and in the field." He narrowed his eyes a touch. "That is where I tend to work the most. I do the majority of data collection as well as the technical side of things. Ensuring data is consistent, assessing what data should be collected, and so on. What analysis Isaac does is often in terms of trends, weather patterns, the science behind how the weather comes together. Higher-order considerations that most of our inquiries could care less to understand." He stared at Alfred for a long moment. "Farmers don't care how a tropical storm is formed. They only want to know when it will stop raining."

Whether Joseph expected a reply was unclear, so Alfred treaded lightly.

"Doesn't understanding the motivation behind weather improve our answers to even the smallest queries, such as when it will stop raining?"

"Perhaps," Joseph replied, "but our primary function in this office is to provide reliable forecasts. Whether or not that is tied directly to the trends across the country is yet to be seen." He let out a loud breath. "And your job is to ensure that our equipment is well-maintained and up to par with the task. I've been doing it for quite some time and can say it is not an overly-complicated task. I'm sure a man of your caliber can handle the work on your own."

Alfred felt himself stiffen at the remark. The statement lingered between them, and Joseph pushed himself up, making his way toward a shelf lined with instruments. He pulled a large notebook from the shelf.

"When Isaac is out of the office, which he often is, you will report to me." He turned and set the notebook on the small table in the center of the room. "I will monitor your progress and check your readings until we are satisfied that you understand everything sufficiently. As my assistant you will also be running errands such as delivering reports and telegrams or personal inquiries when I am unable to do so. Understand?"

Alfred gave a deflated nod. The room was stuffy, but that was only a small cause of the discomfort he was feeling.

"Your break will be from noon to one o'clock. I suggest if you have any personal errands to run, you do so during that hour."

He opened the logbook and scrutinized the dates as the top. He pointed as if to continue the training when a reserved voice came from the doorway.

"Ah, Joseph." A similarly slender but shorter man entered the office with two packages and a handful of telegrams. He gave a short but warm smile to Alfred as he passed toward the desk on the far wall that looked out onto Market Street. "I see you've met our new charge."

"Yes." Joseph eyed the packages as he passed. "I was explaining the expectations of the post."

"A good initiation," the man replied, speaking more softly than his brother had. "But there's no need to overwhelm him from the start. Although, I'm sure it is a relief to you to have another assistant in the office."

Alfred saw Joseph bristle at the remark in his peripheral vision and felt the room expand with tension.

"Joseph was clarifying our responsibilities for me," Alfred commented lightly. "The differences in duties and such."

The slender man looked up from a telegram and let his eyes shift between the two.

"Good." A grin tugged at his mouth without taking over his expression, as if he were reserving some emotion for a more suitable exchange. "I'm Dr. Isaac Cline, and as I'm sure my brother has explained to you in his own way, I am the Chief Climatologist for the island."

Alfred shook the man's hand and waited for the room to breathe.

"Well, if Joseph has given you a proper introduction," Dr. Cline continued, "perhaps you could start the morning by sorting through these inquiries we've received and then running a report to the telegraph office for me before noon." He held out the stack of telegrams. "Joseph, why don't you walk Alfred through the process and begin training him on communications. We can visit about the formalities of the post later this afternoon, a good portion of which I'm sure he already learned in training."

Joseph remained at the table.

"I need to take measurements on the roof."

Dr. Cline looked over his glasses at his brother.

"I'll see to the observations. It will only take an hour or two for you to walk him through the telegrams." He kept his arm extended, pressing the task on the man. "The sooner, the better."

After a moment of silence, Joseph reached out and took the telegrams, turning his back toward his brother as he pulled a stool closer to the table. He sat and began sorting them in silence.

"Alfred, I recommend taking notes as you go," Dr. Cline instructed quietly. "I'm sure you learned the bureau's code for forecasting, but it will do you good to practice before taking it on by yourself." Alfred nodded and started toward his pack to retrieve his notebook. "And if you have any questions," Dr. Cline commented, pausing to look at his brother, "ask me."

Alfred pulled a stool up to the table, careful to sit near Joseph but grant the man enough space to fume silently as he sorted telegrams.

CHAPTER FIVE

*T*he morning dragged on as Joseph combed through seventeen telegrams, some from bureau officials, others from ship captains putting out to sea or from nearby weather stations. A few were handwritten inquiries that had been left in the telegraph office by locals. All were inquiring about the weather trends and forecasts for the upcoming week. Joseph took little care to properly explain the process by which certain telegrams were answered with technical forecasts and others with more common language, but Alfred was able to discern that the content of the replies was based on the recipient's knowledge of weather and their reason for needing a forecast. Captains were concerned with wave height, winds, and the possible formations of tropical storms; farmers were concerned about the amount of rain, temperature, and longevity of patterns. While it seemed the Weather Bureau preferred technical answers more often than not, the sort Dr. Cline and Joseph readily spouted off to each other in everyday conversation, some care was taken to ensure each recipient could understand the reply regardless of the content.

After he instructed Alfred on the majority of the telegrams, Joseph excused himself from the office to check the instruments on the roof. Dr. Cline appeared lost in his reading, and Alfred was left to answer the last five telegrams on his own. He was annoyed with Joseph's urgency to move through the process and the lack of detail he provided, but the task was energizing nonetheless, especially when he considered that his time could have just as easily have been assigned to cleaning instruments instead. It took him twice as long to complete the replies as it had Joseph, but he found a second wind as he read through the observation log of instrument readings and reconciled them with reports from ships at sea. When he had finished, he had written replies to two seamen, a shopkeeper with visiting family, and a weather station in Abilene.

He checked his pocket watch and was surprised that his break time had arrived. He stretched his arms into the air, feeling his back muscles resist after being bent tightly over the table, and collected the replies in a neat stack. Dr. Cline was reading a manuscript at his desk, his shoulders hunched over so that he could follow his reading with an index finger while he jotted notes on a separate sheet of paper.

"I've finished the telegrams. Would you like me to take them to the Western Union office?"

Dr. Cline looked at him blankly over his glasses.

"Oh." He looked about his desk as if the world had returned to him in a flood of consciousness. "Yes, and this report as well. It's for the bureau. It takes priority over the others."

Alfred placed it on the top of the stack as Dr. Cline turned back to his manuscript, his voice slightly muffled as he spoke.

"Did Joseph clarify everything for you in the way of inquiries and telegrams?"

"I believe so."

He hummed a pleasant note and began to skim the paper to find his place amid the handwriting. Alfred hesitated a moment before he spoke again.

"May I leave now to deliver the telegrams and take my break after? I know it's a little earlier than scheduled."

Dr. Cline turned to look at him and removed his glasses. "Your break?"

"My dinner break, sir."

He held Alfred's gaze for a long moment and then glanced toward the closed door at the end of the room, his brow falling.

"Did Joseph instruct you to take your leave at a specific time?"

"Noon to one o'clock."

Dr. Cline nodded slowly, keeping his eyeglasses suspended in the air in front of him, his forearm resting on the back of the chair.

"I see. Well, it is good to have a schedule, especially when it comes to taking observations. Those cannot be neglected. I prefer to keep a schedule that allows me to take my meals at home with my wife. She's pregnant, you see."

Alfred gave a small nod.

"Our protocol dictates that one of us is present in the office between the hours of seven and six." He paused a moment before continuing. "However, that does not mean your movements are entirely dictated by your schedule. We can be flexible when needed. I occasionally return home in the afternoons when my wife is sick from the heat or her condition, and I would expect that you would require the same courtesy should something urgent arise for you as well."

The man's voice was soft but firm in a way that betrayed a life experience that Joseph appeared to lack, and Alfred was perplexed as to what to make of him. In some ways he came across as a gentle soul with understanding eyes that pleaded to be considered, but that conflicted with the measured and matter-of-fact tone he used when directing the other men. His rigidity spread from his jaw through the way he held his glasses just beyond his chin when he spoke, but Alfred felt a kinship with him in the moment, as if his rougher edges were smoothed by his solitude with the books and instruments.

"Thank you, sir."

Dr. Cline replaced his eyeglasses, and with that simple gesture the kinship ceased and Alfred was once more staring at the man who was known for having earned his medical degree out of sheer boredom. He turned back to his manuscript.

"Just be certain we don't all leave the office at the same time unless absolutely necessary. I often break between one and three."

"Of course." He teetered on the decision to go, but found his feet firmly planted to the floorboards. "If it wouldn't be too prudent, I was wondering if I could start researching influences on the local climate."

Dr. Cline turned in his chair, repeating his routine of sliding his glasses down his nose with a quick blink of his eyes. He stared up at his assistant expectantly.

"I've read some of your publications on the influence of climate on medical conditions," Alfred continued, "and Joseph mentioned that you are working on a book that I presume is on the same topic. I've given a lot of thought as to my own research and am eager to get started, preferably looking into oceanic winds." When Dr. Cline remained quiet, Alfred swallowed dryly. "That is, if it's acceptable to do so when I have spare time."

"I see." He set his glasses down on his desk and rose to his feet. "Pardon my hesitation. We've not had much eagerness in our office as of late."

Alfred sensed the change in tone and braced himself.

"However, I think it is important to emphasize that, while you will undoubtedly find time to spare during certain seasons, the experience that comes from this post can be overwhelming at times. Experience that is necessary to be successful in the bureau."

"I understand that I have a great deal to learn, but I—"

Dr. Cline lifted a hand to cut him off. Alfred quieted and tried to keep his composure.

"It's not that I doubt your abilities as a climatologist, Alfred. I doubt your ability to balance yourself in this climate."

"On the island?"

"And in this post. It is easy for a man to become lost in his work, but that is not a healthy way to live. You must seek interests beyond the office, something else to bide your time. For me it was pursuing a medical degree."

The example was humorous, and Alfred struggled to conceal his laugh. It shined through his expression, and Dr. Cline acquiesced with a nod.

"What I mean to say is that you will have plenty of time to work on your own research when the time comes. In the meantime, I think it best to keep your head in your training and look for ways to entertain yourself outside of your work. Books are good, but love is preferred."

He turned back to his desk, leaving the young observer staring at the open window over Market Street. Alfred sighed as he crossed the office and slid the telegrams into his bag along with the parcel of biscuits Mrs. Poplar had packed for him. Nothing was going as he'd planned with this new post. The tension with Joseph. His rank below the other man. The expectation to do a simpleton's work before working on his own research. It all felt as if the air had gained weight throughout the morning and was slowly collapsing against him. Deciding that the walk to the telegraph office was preferable to taking the bicycle down the stairs, Alfred stepped out of the office without another word and left the rusty relic leaning against the wall.

The air beyond the stairwell was burdensome and tugged at his shirt when he stepped onto the sidewalk. It filled his lungs with hot breaths, but it relieved the tension that had grown within his muscles on the way down. The street was bustling with men in suits and bowlers and carriages rolling down the dirt road as monstrous clouds glided overhead.

The telegraph office was two blocks north of the Weather Bureau on the Strand, the hub of the island's industry that sat a block from the wharves. The horizon was full of piercing masts and billowing clouds of steam as ships moored at the harbor and unloaded their freight. His body was already growing warm as he turned the corner onto the street. The Western Union office took up a single storefront in the middle of a block on the Strand with a cooper on one side and a drug store on the other.

The clickety-clack of telegraphy rang throughout the office as Alfred stepped into a small waiting area. A polished wooden counter separated him from the synchronized ballet of clerks who worked their hands together in a seamless dance with their machines, hands tapping at knobs and sending clicks into the air. The cacophony rang like a discordant orchestra to Alfred's ears, one in which only the performers could find the melody.

He waited behind a woman in a tightly fitted blue dress with a parasol leaning against her leg. She wrote carefully on a small square of paper, drawing each letter with precision, while the front desk clerk stared casually out the nearest window. When she had finished, the clerk walked the woman's telegram to a messaging station at a leisurely pace, taking long, steady strides that allowed him to look in on each transmitting clerk as he passed. When he returned, his dark eyebrows jumped as he spoke.

"Dispatch?"

"For the Weather Bureau Office." Alfred pulled the stack of telegrams from his bag.

"How many?"

"Eighteen."

"Any to government offices?" The man pulled a small form from beneath the counter, his tone suggesting a familiarity with their daily load.

"Only four."

"Separate those out. Any personal?"

"No."

Alfred separated the telegrams, and the clerk took the two stacks and quickly skimmed them, counting the words and jotting the numbers down on a receipt. After several minutes, he put the last one aside and totaled the words to be transmitted.

"That'll be two dollars and twenty-four cents," he commented as he signed the bottom of the paper.

Alfred stared at the man. The sounds of the machines clicked in his ears as he opened his mouth to speak but found it dry.

"Shall I charge it to the bureau's account?"

Alfred let out a small chuckle and felt a warmth take over his face as he gave an appreciative nod. The clerk made a small note at the top of the form and handed it to Alfred. He blew out a long breath as he left the telegraph office, the moment's anxiety slipping away. He'd been so wrapped up in doing what was needed that he hadn't thought through the process—and getting caught bare-pocketed would have been an embarrassment he couldn't have easily shaken.

The air grew heavy as the sky began to darken. The clouds melted into mercury, still letting some light penetrate their edges, before they expanded with moisture and floated slowly overhead like balloons threatening to burst. The shadows had crept into the office by the time Alfred returned from his midday break. Dr. Cline was absent from his desk, which glowed in the dim electric light of the wall sconce. Joseph was bent over a map at the table, carefully marking wind patterns with a ruler. It was a proof, Alfred realized as he neared, that would be sent to the printer later in the day. Joseph glanced at Alfred.

"Isaac has asked that I train you in taking observations on the roof." He made a final correction before letting the pencil fall onto the desk. "I suggest we do it sooner rather than later. It looks like rain is moving in, and it's much easier to learn when you can see the tube markings."

"Alright." Alfred rolled up his sleeves in an attempt to cool his skin as he watched the man stand and stretch his back. "On that subject, how do we correct forecasts?"

Joseph furrowed his brow. "How do you mean?"

"When we've given inaccurate forecasts like today. The official forecast called for clear skies with rain stalling out until tomorrow." A hard but solitary raindrop struck the window above Market Street. "How do we correct the forecast?"

"We don't." He pulled a logbook from the shelf near his desk and handed it to Alfred. "We can't retract a printed forecast."

"That must put us in an unfavorable light at times."

"I'm certain it does, but forecasting is not an exact science. It is significant that you remember that. We never guarantee our work, only our efforts. It is called forecasting for a reason."

As he followed Joseph down the hall and to a door hidden around the corner from the top of the staircase, Alfred wondered if Dr. Cline shared his brother's outlook on the definitiveness of their field. Considering they were brothers, they were misaligned in ways that left Alfred unsure of his own footing when he was among them, all the more so when his role was the topic of discussion.

But he put the thought out of his mind as they stepped out onto the roof. The winds had picked up and were gusting from the gulf as he followed Joseph over to a station of instruments that had been installed to measure every aspect of the local weather. A wind vane spun unevenly overhead beside a rain gauge that was screwed into the top of a wooden stand. A hygrometer measured the humidity level, a barometer indicated the pressure, and three or four other instruments sat on similar stands, all measuring the atmosphere around them as mercury moved up and down in tubes.

Joseph took the logbook from Alfred and settled it between two stands to protect the open pages from the wind. They stood well above the other buildings around them, granting him an unobstructed view of the city in every direction. The harbor bustled with activity to the north. The masts of ships jutted up into the sky, their hulls rocking in the choppy water as tiny figures hurried to load cargo. The streets looked like a living map as people walked in and out of stores and carriages rolled down the avenues. He turned a slow circle, taking in the view. Beyond the beach, where the water stretched into a perpetual abyss of wonder, he could see a deepening grey that painted the horizon like the cusp of midnight. It had no distinct edge, only a blurred front where it ushered rain and wind across the water and toward the shore.

Even as Joseph spoke to him, calling him back to the station, Alfred's ears were deaf. The entirety of his senses was focused on the view from the rooftop, a scene that he knew only a handful of men had taken in. He felt lost in the utter rawness of the nature that encircled their little camp on an island that might as well have been in the middle of nowhere. And in a quiet voice he heard Mathias whisper what he now knew to be one the greatest truths of the island: "You should see it when it storms."

CHAPTER SIX

The rain had let up from its afternoon deluge when Alfred came down Market Street just after six o'clock. The fading remnants of the workday hustle were scattered along the street as figures dodged puddles and horses' hooves sucked at the mud. The clouds had begun to disperse, leaving behind shafts of light that painted women's dresses the color of summer peaches, and the warm evening air hung on the eaves like wet leaves. He had removed his jacket after the first five blocks of pedaling and welcomed the breeze that tickled his uncovered arms. When he arrived at the house on Postoffice Street, a coach waited in the street and the front door was propped open with a jar of pale sun tea.

Voices carried from upstairs as he hung his jacket on the coatrack. He stood at the landing for several minutes, listening to the muffled voices of Mrs. Poplar and a man he didn't know, before a wooden pop in the parlor made him jump. He turned to see John standing from one of the wingback chairs. He eyed Alfred darkly.

"Catch a little mud in the street, did you?"

Alfred ignored the comment and motioned his head toward the second floor.

"What's going on?"

"Mathias has the flu," John replied flatly. He dropped a small book onto the round marble side table between the chairs.

"Has the doctor come?"

John reached into his vest pocket and removed his pocket watch. "He's up there."

The voices became muted as they stepped beyond the hallway. Alfred looked back at John, his brow set. "Why aren't you up there?"

John's eyes looked up but his head remained cocked toward the window where large droplets began to beat against the porch railings.

"With a man who's got the stomach flu?"

"You're a doctor."

"And the first thing a good doctor learns is that risking infection unnecessarily is a simpleton's error."

"Unnecessarily?"

John let his head fall back so that his chin stuck out. He slid his hands into his pockets as he watched Alfred, the faint pink glow of the evening sun tinging his white collar. He looked the part of the medical student, but Alfred studied his face carefully. His eyes were small and set with a smooth brow, the antithesis of the emotion that rushed through Alfred in the moment.

"He's your housemate," Alfred contended. "You couldn't even tend to him until the doctor arrived?"

"The man has the flu. What would you have me do? Read him a bedside story?"

"Maybe if you would show a little compassion to someone other than yourself—"

"Compassion?" A hearty laugh erupted from John's throat before his tone took on a note of sarcasm. "And pour my heart into something to help the better good? I wonder which would suit me better, feeding the poor or predicting the weather."

The floorboards creaked above them and the clack of heels carried quickly overhead. Mrs. Poplar appeared at the top of the stairs and stared down at Alfred as she took the steps carefully. She came to a stop on the last step, one hand resting on the banister and the other lifting her skirt above her boots.

"Gentlemen."

Alfred lifted his chin and gave a curt smile in her direction. "Mrs. Poplar."

She held them in silence as Alfred bit the inside of his lip and John faced the parlor window. The air in the house was sticky and smelled of roasted potatoes and shoe polish. Alfred swallowed and felt his stomach churn with the sickly sweet taste of anger. He avoided Mrs. Poplar's gaze, looking out the open door instead where the rhythmic beat of fresh rain filled the silence of the room. After several moments of silence, heavy footfalls came from upstairs, and a man joined Mrs. Poplar on the landing.

"Mr. Briggs," she started, her voice back to its light tenor, "if you would be so kind as to show Dr. Collins to his carriage."

John made his way to the coatrack, as she made room for the doctor to pass.

"Thank you again for coming, Stanley."

"Not at all, Gretchen," the man said with rosy cheeks. "It must feel odd not having a doctor in the house at times like these." Her cheeks budded into a smile, as he snapped his medicine bag shut. "Of course, having doctors in training as your boarders are bound to be as good as any."

He noticed Alfred and offered his hand. "Apologies! Dr. Stanley Collins."

Alfred took his hand with a curt nod. "Alfred Ridgeway."

"Mr. Ridgeway," she cut in, "is my newest boarder. He works with Dr. Cline in the Weather Bureau."

"Ah! Another weatherman has come to the city. It seems we need one more to handle the fickle temperament of our island. We never quite know what is coming our way off the water."

"Today being a prime example of how poor of a science it has become," John cut in as he settled his bowler on over his hair. "The forecast was for clear skies today, was it not?"

"The storm was slated to arrive tonight if I'm not mistaken," Dr. Collins added.

"But not today," John remarked. He gave a smirk as he stepped out onto the porch.

Mrs. Poplar put a gentle hand on the doctor's shoulder as she walked toward the door. "Do give Rose my best and my apologies for calling you away from dinner."

"Oh, not to worry. She is used to it by now, as I'm sure you were as well."

"It is the way of a doctor's wife."

"Call if he worsens in the night," he said as he joined John on the porch, popping open an umbrella.

Mrs. Poplar watched the two men step out into the rain. After a short exchange, John joined the doctor in the carriage, and the driver whipped the reins to start the horse on its way. Mrs. Poplar removed the jar of tea from against the door and shut it with a small click of the latch, swatting at a mosquito as it buzzed about her. The door sealed them into a sticky silence with the low hum of rain on the roof.

"How is he?"

"Dr. Collins says he has the stomach flu," she replied as she looked up the stairs.

"Is there anything we can do for him?"

"Nothing to do but let it pass. He needs to rest." She let out a small sigh and looked at Alfred. "And we'll need to keep him hydrated."

A noise came from above and she started up the stairs, lifting her skirt as she hurried. She rushed into the bedroom across from Alfred's and put her arms around Mathias' bent figure, easing him back into bed. She took a bucket from his shaky hand and set it beside the bed. Alfred watched from the doorway as she settled him back onto his pillow and dabbed at his forehead with a wet cloth from the side table. After a few minutes, Mathias' breathing slowed and she left the room quietly with the bucket, leaving the door open. Alfred heard the faucet start and water splashing in the washbasin. She returned the bucket to his bedside before standing with Alfred in the doorway, wiping her hands on a towel.

"He's been sick since lunch," she whispered.

"It was wise of you to call on Dr. Collins."

"I didn't call on him."

He looked at her, but she kept her eyes on the young man in the bed.

"Then how did he know?"

"Thomas Brighton sent him. It seems they were dining together when he became ill."

Alfred looked back toward his friend. "Did he bring him home?"

"No, he came home alone, the poor dear." She let out a soft breath and crossed her arms. "He went straight to his room. I found him like this after hearing him make a ruckus as he made his way back from the washroom."

The floor creaked with Alfred's weight as he shifted to lean against the doorframe. Their movements were amplified in the quiet of the empty house. With John out and Mathias asleep, the space felt hollow.

"You look tired, dear."

He kept his gaze on Mathias's thin figure. The sheet heaved and fell with each breath. "It's the heat, I'm sure," he argued, his stomach tightening at the excuse.

Mrs. Poplar made a small noise of recognition and turned back to the room.

"Well, no use both of us watching him," she argued quietly. "I have some roasted chicken and potatoes in the oven. We will both need to eat if we are going to care for him."

"Will he be alright alone?"

"I should think so. Dr. Collins administered a small dose of laudanum."

Alfred thought back to his mother's medicine cabinet. "Opium?"

"In a syrup. It's mixed with wine to help him sleep."

"Will that help his flu?"

She shook her head as she made her way toward the stairs. "No, for that he gave him a remedy of sugar and arsenic."

CHAPTER SEVEN

The floorboards creaked in protest as they sat down at the table. With only the two of them dining, Mrs. Poplar fixed their plates in the kitchen and left the meal in the oven, bringing only a basket of rolls to set between them. They took their usual seats despite being the only ones in the room. Returning with two glasses of tea, she motioned for him to eat as she took her seat; he picked up his fork and watched her, letting her take the first bite to ensure she was indeed forgoing her ritual of saying grace. Overhead a rumble of thunder vibrated the china in the hutch behind her.

"How did you get on with your first day at your post?" She pierced a piece of chicken with her fork and scooped up a slice of softened potato.

"I'll have plenty to keep me occupied."

"A good sort of work?"

He chewed silently and considered his answer. "I suppose. It is very much an assistant post, more so than I had anticipated."

She nodded as she looked out the window at the shrubs beyond the pane. They bounced and swayed with the rain as the evening wore on. The pink petals of the oleander bush were bent back and tucked between the sharp leaves. Alfred followed her gaze as he bit into a roasted potato, the rosemary and basil tickling his taste buds.

"You're ready for bigger mountains, as my father used to say."

"Pardon?"

She glanced back at him with a smile. "Perhaps prairies are more appropriate for you. Something more than—" She lifted her chin with a quizzical look. "What is it they have you doing?"

"Sending telegrams."

She nodded. "Yes, there are certainly bigger things to do in the world than sending telegrams. Forecasting is a sharp science, though. Not something for the inexperienced, I would imagine."

"How is it you know about forecasting?"

Another rumble came through the window panes.

"Dr. Cline's wife often attends my bridge club. I've had the occasion to speak with him a few times." She gave him a tender look. "Trust me when I say you are not the only one who has yearned for a better view of the world."

He stabbed a piece of chicken and a carrot as she took a roll from the basket and began tearing it apart as she had at breakfast.

"I met Dr. Cline when he first arrived on the island." She lifted her eyes to the ceiling as she thought. "That was over ten years ago. He was a young, enthusiastic man, but I suspect that is difficult to imagine seeing him as he is now."

Alfred chuckled as he took a roll from the basket.

"He once explained the concept of barometric pressure to me," she continued, "and how it affects the development of storms. I recall him describing how the pressure keeps moisture on the surface of the earth. The less the amount of pressure, the more that warm air and moisture rise, which leads to vapor being formed in the clouds. Am I getting this right?"

He nodded, impressed.

"Good. He explained that if the pressure is too high, deserts are created, but if the pressure is too low, storms occur. That's what causes our hurricanes to form. It seemed to me that he was saying that weather forecasting is a science of reading what has occurred and is occurring to predict what will be the result."

"It is precisely that."

"However, I believe he had a broader meaning in his explanation. Life is a lot like weather. We do not know what is forming elsewhere in our lives, what is to come. We can read the observations and guess at what lies ahead, but we never truly know what is developing just over the horizon. Just the same, a simple aspect such as pressure can make all the difference. Too much, and we find ourselves in a desert, void of life. Too little, and we become castaways in a storm. Life, it seems, is all about balance."

Alfred took another bite of his potatoes. Rain beat at the window across from him as the oleander petals disappeared in the shadows of the storm, an early onset to night. He let out a small sigh.

"It's just rather exhausting, the constant negotiation of it all. It's a new post in a new city that has a different way of life."

"It has only been a few days, dear."

"It's the unexpectedness of it all that's thrown me. Dr. Cline has advised that I find a hobby to busy my mind should I find my work too mundane to keep me occupied."

"Is that so dangerous an idea?" She took a sip of her tea as he let his mouth pull up in a surrendering grin.

"I'm sorry. It's not right that I'm filling dinner with my complaints."

"No harm in being disappointed," she replied warmly. "I can assure you that life is full of disappointments. The key is to not dwell on them."

"Good advice."

"Yes, well," she paused a moment, "my husband was a wise man."

Her tone was gentle and he sensed a softness in her words.

"I caught Dr. Collins's comment about your husband. He must've thought highly of him."

"Most people did."

He gave her a knowing grin that she returned. "Hence the boarders?"

"Yes," she mused, "I've found it best to keep doctors in the house since his passing. If they're solid at their craft, they'll need boarding for a long while. I also miss the talk of medicine and diagnoses from time to time."

"He shared his work with you?"

"Oh, yes, Henry shared his profession with nearly anyone who would listen! Me, friends, the pastor. Everyone knew about his work whether they wanted to or not."

"Do many medical students require boarding?"

She nodded vigorously as she chewed on another bite of chicken. "There are always a few needing to board. I had seven applications within a week of posting my first advertisement, and my house has been full since then."

A lull in the rain quieted the world beyond the room.

"If there are so many medical students needing a room," he asked quietly, "may I ask why you accepted my application to board?"

She considered the question and finally shook her head slightly, returning to her biscuit.

"Something about your letter stood out to me. I felt it would be good to have someone like you in our little family this year. Someone different."

"You mean not a medical student?"

"You talked of your finances and the post you would taking, as all applicants do, but most of them simply leave it at that. As if that's enough by which to judge a person I am letting into my house. But you gave me more. You mentioned your home and your ambition to work as a climatologist. I could feel an energy in your letter that I found appealing." She finished her biscuit and reached for her glass. "It was a pleasant change from the astute personalities I've come to expect year after year."

He watched her take a drink and noticed the shadows beneath her eyes. The day had already been long for her. All the more so without John's trained assistance.

"I don't think I've said how much I appreciate your confidence," he remarked. "And your hospitality. You've already eased today's troubles."

"It's nothing a good cup of tea wouldn't do," she said with a quick smile, her voice ringing with a brighter note.

He stretched his neck to loosen the collar and feed what air he could into his shirt. "The air here is so humid, like it's wet all the time. I can't ever quite catch my breath." She gave a small hum of agreement as he continued. "You must think quite fondly of the island to remain here after losing your husband."

"I do. It has a sort of beauty to it that I've not found elsewhere. I was born in Louisiana, the land of swamps and alligators, which has its own sort of elegance but in a much less sophisticated manner."

"What on earth possessed you to move here?"

"The same as most people." Her cheeks lifted to brighten her eyes. "Love." Alfred pushed his chair back slightly from the table, pulling his tea glass closer to him, as she rested her chin on her hand. "I married my husband shortly before he took his assignment in Texas, and we migrated south until we reached Galveston. That was nearly thirty years ago. He taught at the hospital, you know, when it first opened."

Her face shone brightly in the electric light as her eyes drifted beyond Alfred's face.

"He was a fine teacher. And a good surgeon." She let her eyes wander back to the table. "I miss him terribly."

They sat quietly for a few moments, the sound of rain returning to the windowpane before Mrs. Poplar excused herself quietly and took their plates to the kitchen. She returned with saucers of cake topped with baked pears.

"Thank you for dinner," he said. "I know this was likely an inconvenience with Mathias being ill."

She waved off the comment with a scoff.

"No trouble at all, dear. I had to eat as well."

He cut into the cake and watched the sugary glaze of the pear seep into the fresh crevice. "Mr. Ortiz and Mr. Briggs will be fine doctors," she announced as she arranged a bit of cake and pear on the end of her fork and then looked at him candidly. "And what shall you become?"

His eyes looked up at the firmness of her question. It was so matter-of-fact, as if she had no doubt that he had a plan and a future that was solely his, but he faltered in owning the confidence. He knew what he should say, what he would have said nearly half an hour before, but the force with which she had asked the question made him doubt his existence on the island. He hadn't given any possibility to the idea of being anything other than what he had come to Galveston to be. He took a bite of pear and chewed slowly.

"Perhaps a less pointed question," she suggested, "would be why you are interested in studying the weather at all."

That much he knew.

"To better understand what is thought to be unexplainable."

"This applies only to weather?"

"I suppose so. I hadn't really given it much thought to consider anything else."

"That's good," she replied, scooping another bite of pear onto her fork.

Her tone was confident and it put him at ease despite their return full-circle to the original topic. He was reflective for a moment.

"Did your husband have any hobbies?"

"Hobbies?" She raised her eyebrows at the question, giving it some thought. "Well, yes, he played cards quite often. In the clubs only, mind you. Never privately as some men do. And he was a great painter. He didn't paint as much in his later years, but he was once fine at it." She pointed causally toward the front of the house with her fork. "He painted the portrait of me in the front sitting room after we were first married."

"Did he really?"

Her head moved in small nods and she looked up at him with bashful eyes.

"Most don't recognize me behind the oil." He went to respond but she cut him off with a wave of her hand. "It's the grey hair."

He took a last bite of his cake as she continued.

"He was a very talented individual. But he kept more to his books in his later years. It was just easier, I suppose. That's the curse of doctors, you see. They know their own diagnoses before they ever step foot into another man's examination room." The small silence that followed tugged at Alfred's chest Her voice softened. "He died of lung disease five years ago."

"I'm very sorry."

She smiled broadly as if to push away the sentiments and speared a piece of cake. "Why do you ask, dear? About the hobbies?"

"Dr. Cline encouraged me to find an interest outside of work. He said it would do me well to keep my mind engaged elsewhere when I am feeling as though the work is too slow."

"I don't think it will be difficult for you to do. To be quite honest, I envy you, dear."

"How's that?"

"You are fresh and full of spirit. There is little that can keep you from going wherever you wish to go."

He nodded as the thought took hold. "I'll work to keep that perspective in mind."

She gave a solid nod as they stood and came around to finish clearing the dishes, pausing to reach for the folded newspaper in the seat next to him. She hesitated, making a tight face as she took hold of the paper. He took a step closer.

"Are you alright, Mrs. Poplar?"

"Oh, yes. Just a little age creeping in." Her expression eased, and she hit the newspaper against the table. "Mr. Briggs might be an intelligent man, but he has yet to learn how to refold a newspaper."

"Actually," he extended his hand with raised eyebrows, "may I read it?"

"It's wrinkled," she said with a frown. "And Mr. Briggs never replaces the finance section."

"That's quite alright," he replied, taking the crinkled newspaper. "I'm not one for finances."

———•●•———

Mrs. Poplar had insisted on watching over Mathias on her own but had retired to her room after more than three hours of bringing him water and giving him spoonsful of Milk of Magnesia, which her late husband had sworn by for poor stomachs. Alfred had been left to peruse the classifieds of the newspaper before starting in on a book from the office. As his pocket watch ticked past eleven o'clock, he rose from his chair and stretched his arms over his head. A pinprick of a pop came from his neck, and he rubbed at it instinctively. His body was slow to respond as he turned toward the door and trudged through the air as if it were water. The door might as well have been a mile away as drained as he felt.

Mrs. Poplar had extinguished the oil lamp in Mathias's room and left it dark for him to sleep. Alfred peered toward her closed door before crossing the dark hallway and stepping into his friend's room. The rain ticked at the windows in a steady rhythm as the sheets buoyed up and down with Mathias's breathing.

A sound came from below Alfred, muted but solid. He pricked his ears and turned his eyes to the floorboards of the stair landing, which was partially lit by his oil lamp across the hall. In the relative quiet, he was certain he had heard a rush of rain as the front door opened and then slowly shut. He searched his memory as he tried to recall if he had seen Mrs. Poplar lock the door, but he had been upstairs washing up when she would have closed up the house. As a creak came from one of the first few stairs, Alfred gingerly stepped back to submerge himself in the darkness of Mathias's room, just out of the muted stream of light.

The tell-tale creak of weight on the stairs shot into the quiet of the house as a figure appeared on the top landing. Alfred could only make out the man's right side—a wilted red rose stuck inside a suspender, a jacket over his arm, and a bowler askew on his head—but he recognized the arrogant posture even in so little light. As John reached up to remove his hat, he caught sight of Alfred's cracked door and froze, his body perfectly framed on the top step. Alfred could see the reflection of the pale lamp light in his eyes as he searched the room with frantic, squinted eyes, as if searching for a spy in unfamiliar territory. John glanced at Mathias's room and then back to Alfred's doorway, scrutinizing the scene, before taking a slow step onto the platform, the stairs creaking once more as he lifted his weight onto the floorboards. From his curled fingers hung his shoes with shoestrings dancing to each step. Keeping an eye on Alfred's doorway,

John moved carefully down the hall beyond the washroom, taking well-placed steps until he was out of Alfred's vision. A small click came down the hall as he shut his door.

Alfred stepped out into the hall. A sliver of light flickered to life beneath John's door, and a shadow moved about inside the room. The storm had moved in hours ago, much more strongly than Alfred had expected, and the streets had begun to flood well before sunset. Perhaps John had been stranded at the hospital, waiting for a carriage to brave the streets. Alfred considered the alternatives and groggily shook his head to clear them from his mind. Despite not caring for the man, he preferred not to think so lowly of a man with whom he was sharing a boardinghouse.

Alfred clutched his book to his side and made his way quietly back to his room. He fed more oil to the lamp, which had begun to flicker, and settled heavily back into his chair. He opened the book and tried to concentrate on the words, but the world continued to pull at his senses. The wind rattled the window panes as the rain beat against the glass in an odd sort of melody. When gravity began to tug at his eyelids, he gave into the sounds of the night, skipping his nightly ritual and falling onto his bed fully dressed, the rain ticking softly at his windowpane, the rose at John's chest the last fading image in his mind before sleep overtook him.

CHAPTER EIGHT

The storm had continued through the night and left the streets dank and sullen, dying Alfred's morning a lonelier hue than before. Now taking the earliest of morning measurements, Alfred was the first in the wash room and the only one at the breakfast table as he ate. Mrs. Poplar had insisted on cooking him breakfast despite the much earlier hour, and he hadn't had the energy to argue. His stomach was full and his body buzzing with caffeine as he bicycled toward the business district, crisscross dirty avenues and smeared sidewalks that were coated with the silt of flooded landscaped gardens and work yards. The earliest trollies wouldn't run until closer to six-fifteen, which sped up his commute as he whizzed down Church Street and took a sharp turn onto 23rd Street. With only a few coaches clopping for fares so early in the morning, he had little traffic to contend with and found himself wheeling the bicycle up to the side entrance of the Levy Building well before six-thirty. The sun had already begun to paint the sky a pale violet that was blending into pink as he unlocked the office and settled his things near his desk. The office was quieter than he'd yet experienced it, and something about the silence thrilled him. He found the logbook Joseph had shelved by the windows and made his way toward the roof entrance near the stairwell.

When he returned with notes on comfortable winds and an analgesic temperature, he found Dr. Cline had arrived during his absence and was standing over two maps he had rolled out onto the table in the center of the room. He looked up over his glasses when Alfred entered and gave a curt nod.

"How were the morning's observations?"

Alfred let the logbook fall open in his hands.

"Eighty-three degrees, pressure at twenty-nine point six two, and humidity at eighty-four percent. Winds are out of the southeast at four miles per hour with a small gathering of cumulous clouds over the shore to the east, about six miles out."

Dr. Cline gave a satisfied hum, pleased with the day ahead. "We'll need to have the local observations sent to D.C. by seven-thirty."

"Joseph walked me thought the process," Alfred nodded. "May I try?"

"Can you do it in time?"

"I can," he asserted, his pulse quickening with the words.

Dr. Cline returned to his map as Alfred took a blank telegram card from his drawer and addressed it as Joseph had shown him, indicating the highest priority next to the office's regional number from his notes. He carefully printed the morning's observations in the blank square at the bottom of the card, but the translation into the bureau's code took longer than he expected. *Oxford* for the temperature if it was eighty-four degrees, *buffalo* if it was closer to eighty-three. He strung the words together in a nonsense sentence to save on letters when it came to the daily report, crafting a message that only another climatologist would be able to decipher. *Gulf train oxford vincent bullrush arrow saint molasses.* Each stand-in word carried so much information that he triple-checked his encoding before feeling confident in his work.

Dr. Cline verified the telegram before dropping his glasses onto his desk. "I have an additional map for the printer to mark the moving fronts. I'll take you." He rolled up the two maps on the table and handed them to Alfred. "Best we start off now before he pushes them of until tomorrow. Only our daily map for forecasts in the papers is guaranteed within half an hour." He took his bowler from atop the coat rack. "We'll deliver the telegram to Western Union first."

The Clarke & Courts Printing took up the southeast corner of 24th Street and Ship Mechanic Row, less than two blocks from the weather bureau office. The streets were growing as the city came awake, and Alfred's stomach growled at the smell of fresh bagels as they passed a deli. Inside the printing office, the clerk desk stretched the length of the lobby with a swinging wooden gate at the end. An elderly gentleman in a tight brown vest looked up from the desk, the wrinkles from his brow spreading into his thick, white hair.

"Time already?"

Dr. Cline gestured for Alfred to put the maps on the desk.

"These are for a lecture later this week. We'll have the national forecast map to you by seven-thirty."

"The usual format?"

The man unfurled the maps and scrutinized the hand-drawn lines with a monocle that was chained to a vest button. His blue eyes poured over the details with magnified intensity. The climatologist gave a nod that Alfred was certain the clerk had not seen, but he continued the conversation as if he had.

"You're in before the rush today," he commented as he rolled up the two maps. "I should have them finished by evening. How many?"

"One of each," Dr. Cline replied.

The man nodded as he scooped up the maps and deposited them onto a large oak table behind him where several manuscripts and loose papers had been stacked and sorted.

"I've also come to introduce our new assistant," Dr. Cline continued, laying a light hand on Alfred's shoulder. "This is Alfred Ridgeway."

The man squinted as he took in Alfred's face, causing his own to shrink into a scramble of wrinkles with a sharp nose pointing out.

"Another climatologist on the island?" He held out a small hand. "Buttons."

"Pardon?"

"Buttons," the clerk repeated with a sturdy handshake.

Alfred looked to Dr. Cline and then back to the clerk, neither of whom spoke. After a moment, Dr. Cline let out a chuckle.

"Buttons is Robert's nickname."

Alfred's head moved into a slow-motion nod as he retracted his hand.

"I haven't always printed maps," the man explained.

"You used to make buttons?"

"Nope."

Buttons scribbled onto a small payment card and signed the bottom line with a flare of his pen before handing it to Dr. Cline with a satisfied smile. The climatologist pocketed the card while Alfred squinted at the clerk in confusion.

"Alfred will be assisting with the morning maps from now on, likely making each day's run."

"I'll have to find you at the Tremont to catch up on my gossip, then."

"I look forward to it."

With that, both men nodded and turned to go their separate ways, Dr. Cline toward the door and Buttons back to his office. Alfred followed his supervisor into the street, his mind fuzzy from the exchange. He neither understood the man's nickname nor how Dr. Cline's persona could engage in any sort of gossip, but whatever he had just witnessed, he felt it was an intimate moment between the men. And for that he was grateful, feeling as though he had been introduced into a circle rather than brought along as a spare cog.

They intercepted a delivery boy from Western Union on the stairs of the Levy Building, and Dr. Cline walked Alfred through the telegram's description of the national forecast for the next twenty-four hours. Combined with the regional forecast Alfred had written up less than an hour before, it painted a picture of the nation's forecasted weather, something that Alfred still found impressive after more than a year of anticipation at seeing it firsthand. Within minutes, his mentor had a full forecast ready for a map to be drawn, and Alfred was sent back to the printer to wait for Buttons to draw up the forecast map so it could be delivered to the *Galveston News* office before the eight-thirty deadline.

The day was turning bright and blue when he returned to the office.

Joseph had not yet arrived, his early hours relieved by Alfred's shift, and Alfred found the relaxed silence encouraging as he sorted the day's telegrams. The hours sailed by quickly as he drafted replies and looked at reports of nearby weather—telegrams from Austin and Dallas, a note from Dr. Cline on the onset of the storm season, and a letter from a captain discussing his encounter with rough seas offshore three days prior. When his stomach interrupted his thoughts with a grumble, he glanced at his pocket watch. It was nearly noon and he was famished. Another parcel of leftover biscuits was nestled in his bag, but he wasn't keen on eating in the office. Joseph had eaten his breakfast at his desk the previous day, but Alfred had to admit that pulling out a basket-worth of cold biscuits for the noon meal left an altogether different impression. He finished the last two telegram replies distractedly and scooped them into his shoulder bag.

"Sir?"

Dr. Cline looked up from the center table where he was comparing maps of ocean currents with a logbook of dates.

"If it's alright, I'd like to deliver the telegrams and start my break." Dr. Cline nodded and replaced his glasses on his nose. "I need to run a personal errand during my break, but I'm not familiar with the address."

"Where is it?"

Alfred retrieved the handwritten note from his pocket. "Twelve-oh-three Twenty-Fifth Street."

"That's the other side of Broadway, not far from my house. That'll be near Avenue L, quite a way to bicycle." He pursed his lips in consideration a moment. "I'd suggest taking a trolley. Depending on the errand, you can make the trip in a little over an hour if the stops are timed well."

Alfred gave his watch a glance as he made his way down the staircase and out into the humid day. The trolley was arrived a few minutes after its scheduled time, and he jumped onboard, praying that he knew what he was getting himself into.

CHAPTER NINE

Alfred had almost missed the post in the corner of the newspaper, but something about its simplicity had caught his attention. Being a notetaker sounded simple enough and hardly a hobby, but he needed something. Dr. Cline had been clear about that. The trolley had let him off at the corner of 25th Street and Avenue L where a lush median of palm trees and large-leafed ferns lined the route in shades of green and yellow. The smooth avenue of 25th Street led toward the oceanfront to the south, and the long, metal footprints of trolley tracks divided the street, which looked nearly twice as wide as the one outside of the boardinghouse. Unlike the neighborhood he slept in, this block boasted tall, stone constructions with lacy porches and luxurious gardens. Taking stock of the street, Alfred took a moment to roll down his sleeves, slip on his jacket, and adjust his tie before making his way down the row toward the address he sought.

A wrought-iron fence encased the lot, and a wide porch stretched the wingspan of the house's facade. Dark green bushes were trimmed against the front of the porch with citrus-colored buds trumpeting from the shrubbery. The manicured grass cushioned a single tree in front of the house. Its red trunk caught his eye, and he stopped to admire the flattened, feather-like leaves made of pointy needles. As the branches shifted in the breeze overhead, he rested his hand on the smooth bark and caught the scent of evergreen. The smell reminded him of holidays back home, flooding his mind with memories of sledding and singing hymns by firelight, misfit thoughts in the balmy midday of the coastal island.

A door shut at the house and he snapped his attention back to the porch, letting his palm fall from the tree. A middle-aged man stood there with his hands clasped in front of him; his clothes were immaculate, and Alfred knew even from a distance that he disapproved of him touching the tree.

"May I help you?"

Alfred made his way onto the brick path and up to the bottom step of the porch. "So sorry. Are you Mr. Carson?"

"No."

The man stood motionless and stared down at him.

"Oh," he replied, taken aback by the man's tone. "Well, I've come to call on Mr. Carson."

The man stared with little expression until Alfred retrieved a scrap of newspaper from his pocket, holding it out for the man to take. When he didn't move, Alfred lowered the clipping and spoke again in a firmer tone.

"I've come to apply to his post for a notetaker."

The man let his eyes cascade down Alfred's suit, as a smirk crossed his lips. "Do come in."

He turned on his heels and Alfred followed quickly. He brushed himself off as he made his way up the stairs and took a single long step through the open door and into the cool shade of the foyer.

"Your name?" The door shut with a pull at the air that made Alfred shift on his feet.

"Alfred Ridgeway," his voice boomed in the open space.

The man disappeared into an adjoining room, leaving Alfred to stand in the silence of the house. He breathed in the smell of wood polish and pine. A grand staircase traced the line of a large painting of an older woman and her hounds and a chandelier hung overhead. He felt tremendously inappropriate in the space and began to wonder if he had misjudged the advertisement. As he looked up at the electric sconces on each side of the front door, he concluded that he was not at all the sort this Mr. Carson would need. He turned toward the front door and reached for the engraved doorknob.

"Mr. Carson will see you now."

Alfred looked back to see the man's eyes dart to the doorknob, and he instinctively pulled his hand back. He smiled nervously and motioned toward the decorative brass knob.

"Is it a deer?"

"A gazelle."

Alfred gave an exaggerated nod, glancing about the room as if suddenly interested in the architecture. The man led him through the house to a wood-paneled room. Light poured through open windows and lit up floor-to-ceiling bookcases, a puffy sofa, and a large desk at the end of the room. An elderly man with thin eyeglasses and an unbuttoned collar was bent over the desk. Alfred's eyes wandered, leaving him completely unnerved.

Every single surface—the sofa, the chair, the coffee table and side tables, the desk, the bookshelves—held some form of a book or paper. Loose sheets were casually laid on flat surfaces, and rolls of thicker parchment were haphazardly stuck into shelves between books and together as collections in the corners of the room. Alfred tried to take stock of himself before clearing his throat. The man looked up from his desk and gave Alfred a warm smile.

"Ah, Mr. Ridgeway!"

The man stood stiffly from his seat and shuffled around the desk and toward the front of the room, extending his hand. He was nearly six inches shorter than Alfred, his small stature exaggerated by his slightly hunched shoulders and raspy voice.

"Thank you for applying to my post."

"Thank you for seeing me, Mr. Carson."

"Please, call me Hilary. Sit?"

He motioned toward the sofa and made his way over to the chair, brushing together the papers that covered the seat and setting the stack onto a table. He sat down with calculated movements, easing into the chair with his elbows straightened against the chair's arms and an irritated expression.

"My knees," he commented, rubbing them with bony hands, "They're not what they should be at my age."

Alfred smiled and cleared a seat on the sofa as Hilary had done, adding his papers to the stack.

"How should they be?"

"I would like to think less grumpy."

The man leaned back in his chair, admiring the fireplace as if it were ablaze with flames and popping timber. Alfred watched his eyes scan the marble mantle and down the side planks before investigating the white tiles beneath the metal grate that held the imaginary logs.

"A terrible design really," the man commented to the fireplace, "putting the warmest part of the room so far from my workspace."

It looked odd, a seasonal piece sitting voicelessly in the heat of the summer, unwanted. Its silence made the room feel hollow, unfinished somehow.

"Perhaps you could move your desk closer."

"No good." He shook his head and kept his eyes on the metal grate. "I prefer to be near the windows for the light. But I hardly use it anyhow. It's a thing one rarely needs down here, something to keep warm."

Another moment of silence followed, and Alfred began to wonder if he were meant to carry on the conversation. The door to the room opened and the butler stepped in with a tray. He set it on the table between them, ignoring the loose papers beneath it, and poured two glasses of water. Alfred gladly took the tall glass and paused to examine the bits of sliced lemon and strawberry that floated at the top.

"Thank you, Ernst," Hilary commented as the man retreated quickly from the room.

Both took long drinks from their glasses, and Alfred began to relax despite the warmth of the room. Hilary held the glass in one hand and let the other fall carelessly over the arm of the chair. He sat quietly, smiling at Alfred between sips of water and admiring his fireplace. After what felt like an uncomfortable stretch of time, consumed by a growing worry that the majority of his break would be spent silently drinking water, Alfred leaned forward.

"If I may, sir, what sort of notetaker are you needing?"

"Ah!" Hilary shot an index finger toward the ceiling. "That is a most appropriate question. I suppose neat penmanship should be required, as it will involve a great deal of note-taking in the field. Good eyesight as well. My eyes are nearly as bad as my knees." He lifted his eyes in thought. "And preferably one who isn't afraid to face his own morality when it dawns on him, as it inevitably does."

"Morality," Alfred asked with narrowed eyes, "or mortality?"

"I should think both would be suitable for the post." He took a drink of water to signal the end of his answer and smacked his lips at the piece of strawberry that stuck to his lower lip. Alfred stared. He had never met an asylum patient, but he was beginning to suspect that Hilary would fit the bill nicely.

"This note-taking in the field, will you be dictating to me? Or will I be observing as I go along and taking notice for you?"

"Both, I would imagine, but birds can be tricky at times. Especially ones like the *Piranga rubra*. Telling the male and female apart is a simple matter of yellow patches, and it all blends together after fifty feet or so." He leaned forward and squinted his eyes at Alfred. "You can always see him, but the trees and limbs absorb her right into the overgrowth. A wonderful camouflage, you know."

"Pardon?"

"The Summer Tanager. It's small but quick. You'll know it when you see it, just as it's named, a vibrant red mixed with a brown undercoat and all yellow spotted throughout its belly and neck." He moved his fingers quickly in the air. "The male looks like it's been dipped in strawberry punch. I've seen plenty of him, but I haven't been as lucky with the female. Of course, the Roseate Spoonbill is my primary study. But my eyesight tends to get in the way. Hence my advertisement for a notetaker."

He leaned back into his chair with a wink, as if all of Alfred's questions had been answered.

"Birds?"

"Of course. They're the most spectacular things on an island like this."

His peculiar words inspired Alfred to try to tease from the man some form of explanation. He'd wasted his entire dinner break to travel across the island, and he didn't plan on making the trek twice.

"And how is it that you'd like me to help you?"

"As I said, my eyes are as bad as my knees. I can still see, mind you, but between the fading light and my slow hands, noting the time and whereabouts of my birds has grown difficult on good days. Some notes I take myself when I am up to it, but even those must be transcribed into my ledger. I need a younger man with steady hands and sharp eyes to catch what I miss."

"I see."

"Oh, that's good. You're qualified then."

Hilary stood with a wobble as Alfred shook his head.

"No, Mr. Carson, I meant—"

The man put up his hand as he made his way around the sofa. "Hilary, please."

"Hilary, I'm afraid I've misjudged the depth of detail in this position. I have a full-time post with the weather office. I would not be available for regular outings."

"I am certain we could agree to a schedule that accommodates this weather work of yours," he replied as he adjusted his glasses, searching the bookcase.

Alfred stood and walked around the sofa. "That's very generous of you, Mr. Carson, but I'm not sure I'm the right fit for the type of note-taker you need."

The old man continued to search the shelves, moving carefully from one book to the next and occasionally shifting a scroll or set of papers to better read the titles.

"Oh, I think you are, Alfred."

The comment caught him off-guard, and he glanced about the room for anything to make sense of the exchange he had found himself in. The man was comical, no doubt—to what degree Alfred could take him seriously, however, he was unsure. Aside from the red-headed woodpeckers that knocked at the trees back home, Alfred knew nothing of birds, especially on an island where he had yet to even learn the street names.

"Ah, here it is!" Hilary pulled down a small leather-bound book. "This will help you learn some of the most common birds in these parts. It was my first field guide."

Alfred took the book and turned it over in his hand, feeling its weight as frayed edges tickled his fingertips. He let it fall open in his palm and a crisp pen drawing of a large bird in flight filled the page; its wings were spread open over its body with its neck pulled back and tucked in against its frame. A long beak jutted out from its head. He read the neatly printed name below the picture.

"The Brown Pelican."

"They're massive," Hilary replied with wide eyes as he made his way around the desk. "Wait until you see one up close. You can fit a grown man's arm inside that beak."

Alfred looked at the drawing and then back to Hilary as the man began to organize loose papers into stacks. Alfred ran a finger along the page and felt the impression of a pen along the fibers. He looked up with a cocked eyebrow.

"You wrote this?"

Hilary nodded as he continued to shuffle papers about his desk.

"As I said, it was my first field guide."

Alfred flipped through the book with both hands, skimming over sharp drawings and rough sketches of birds in flight. The pages were full of small Sanderlings and Terns and the exaggerated form of the Great Blue Heron. Notes were neatly printed with names, descriptions, and lists of observations such as suspected migration patterns, mating rituals, and nesting preferences. After several entries, he snapped the book shut and set the book down on the desk.

"Mr. Carson—"

"Hilary."

Alfred took a deep breath.

"Hilary, I do apologize for intruding unannounced, and I greatly appreciate your hospitality in light of it. But there must be a better man for this position. I simply know nothing of birds or sketching for that matter."

"You'll learn easily enough." Hilary's eyes softened as he smiled. "As with everything else on the island."

Alfred straightened. "How did you know I'm not from the island?"

"You couldn't have been here long with a shirt like that." He gave a quick wave toward Alfred. "You'll learn that there is a fine balance between fashion and comfort in this part of the world. And summer shirts began to fill the Strand last month."

Hilary rounded the desk and picked up the book, handing it to him with a confident gesture, and spoke matter-of-factly.

"I suggest one evening a week and two Saturday mornings a month to start. I can notify you by post when an outing is arranged. No need to reply unless you need to reschedule." Alfred was too slow to reply before Hilary continued. "I trust a dollar and a half would be suitable wages for each outing."

Hilary made his way back toward the fireplace, a small stack of papers in his hands as Alfred watched the man settle back into his chair with a grimace. Alfred followed the man's steps in disbelief.

"Pardon?"

Hilary looked up. "You require more?"

"No. Of course not." He swallowed and found his throat dry. "That's a generous sum."

"Brilliant! Now, the best place to start is with a quick lesson in bird-watching etiquette to get that over and done with. It will make our first outing go much more smoothly. You'll find a few pages on it at the start of the guide." He scrunched his brow tightly. "You're on your noonday break, yes?"

Alfred nodded.

"Right, you'll have ridden the trolley then. Let's start there."

"Where?"

"On the trolley," Hilary replied as he stood to his feet.

He worked at his balance before taking off toward the door, grabbing his hat and jacket on his way out the door. Alfred stared after him with an open mouth until the old man's voice came gruff but loud from down the hallway.

"Don't forget the book!"

Alfred tossed the book into his sack. The man was nearly to the front door by the time he caught up with him, mid-sentence about the significance of proper lenses in binoculars as he swung the door open dramatically and let in the hot air of the afternoon.

Chapter Ten

The following day was overcast with wind that gusted headlong onshore. The forecast had called for light rain, which Alfred had noted on telegrams and the regional forecast, but the forceful winds had taken the entire bureau by surprise. It had been a constant source of annoyance as the window panes rattled with each gust and the drafts at the sills whistled throughout the day until the front moved offshore and left the island with a light, warm breeze. When Alfred left the office, a headache was raking his mind raw, growing steadily worse as he bicycled back toward the boardinghouse more than ten blocks away. When he finally made it to his bed, he debated whether he would join the house for supper or skip the meal altogether and sleep through the evening. His body was giving in to sleep when a knock came at his door, ringing in his ears. The door creaked open and Mathias's head popped into his room.

"Ready?"

Alfred squinted his eyes, his fingers squeezing at his temples. "For what?"

"Drinks at the Tremont House, remember? I told you the invitation came in the post yesterday."

Alfred stood slowly. "I'm sorry. I completely forgot." He reached for the tie that still swayed in his bureau. "Do we need to leave now?"

"Yeah, I was going down to find a coach. I reminded Mrs. Poplar this morning so she wouldn't expect us for dinner." He scrutinized Alfred's face. "Are you alright?"

Alfred worked at his collar as he tried to rebutton it, his tie hanging loosely over each shoulder.

"Not really. I've had a monstrous headache all afternoon."

"Too much work?"

"Or too little sleep."

"I'll take the blame for that," Mathias replied with a grimace. "Wait here."

Mathias disappeared into the hallway as Alfred grabbed his pocket watch and wallet from his side table, feeling the weightlessness of the leather. He opened the doors to his bureau and pulled a small cigar box from the bottom shelf. The lid squeaked as he pulled it back, careful not to let it fall back on the hinge of paper that attached it to the box. He thumbed the few bills that lay along the bottom before removing two and palming a few nickels. He folded the bills into his wallet, dropped the change into his pocket, and shut the bureau.

When he stepped into the hall, Mathias greeted him with a smile, rolling onto the heels of his shoes.

"I have just the thing for you." He handed Alfred two small pieces of wrapped candy. "Medicine drops."

"For a headache?" He examined the paper wrapping as they came down to the first floor.

"Yes, they are wonderful! Dr. Collins gave them to me to help with my fatigue. I'm telling you, take one of these and you'll feel right again in no time."

He unwrapped one and sniffed it, taking in the medicinal scent and a hint of sweetness.

"What's in it?"

"A remedy of honey and aspirin." He shut the door behind them.

"That's it?"

"And cocaine. It'll help with the headache and wake you up a bit."

Alfred looked at Mathias, realizing for the first time that he was quite energetic for having just recovered from a stomach flu. They started toward the street, and he popped the medicine drop into his mouth.

"I guess I can't argue with a doctor."

———•●•———

The Tremont House was a statement piece in the business district, a hotel that sold grandeur and opulence to wealthy visitors and boasted an upscale restaurant that attracted those looking to be in the know when it came to the newest trends in fine dining. The restaurant took up a section of the bottom floor welcomed diners into the lobby with a tall vase of orange tulips and a tray of mints. Alfred followed Mathias into the dining room where crisp cream-colored walls stretched up to a paneled ceiling that held a chandelier of cascading crystal. Oil paintings of ships at sea and harbor sunsets hung over elaborately set tables, the air thick with hushed tones and the clink of silverware. Alfred drank in the elegance, tipsy with awe.

"Ah!" William called to them from across the room, raising a hand to catch their attention.

Two chairs had been reserved for them, and Mathias left Alfred the one nearest William, giving him a full view of the room with the windows to his back. Mathias took the seat next to Thomas Brighton, as William snapped at a nearby waiter and turned back toward the men as he spoke.

"What'll it be?"

"Mint julep," Mathias ordered.

William pointed his finger toward Alfred.

"The same," he replied.

"Two mint juleps and an order of boiled shrimp for the table."

"No shrimp for me," Thomas interrupted. "I'll take Oysters Rockefeller."

The waiter took a menu from William, who clapped his hands together as he turned back to the group.

"Now that we're all here, we can talk about a truly serious matter I've had on my mind for quite some time now."

The table grew silent, a quiet eye amid the talkative storm around them, and Alfred glanced at Mathias and then back at William, who raised an eyebrow.

"The Epsom Downs Derby."

The silence carried for a second before the men at the table laughed.

"It was a travesty," Elijah Baker prompted, "the lot being pulled along as they were. The rest of the brood didn't stand a chance against him."

William nodded. "Well, that's what one gets when the Prince of Wales is paying for the training. That horse's breed is probably better than all of ours combined."

"Was it Albert's horse?"

"Rightly Victoria's horse," Thomas cut in.

He looked to Mathias, who gave him a nod of agreement and scooted his chair a bit closer to the table to position himself nearer the man and break the evenly split circle around the table. He glanced at Alfred with squinted eyes and leaned over with a whisper.

"The sunlight is bright to be so late, don't you think?"

Alfred twisted to look behind him and out the windows onto 23rd street, where a carriage offloaded two well-dressed women, their parasols the color of peach sherbet as they made their way toward the front of the restaurant. When he brought his attention back to the group, Mathias was talking with Thomas, their conversation of sailing drowned out by the continued talk of the British horserace.

"I don't see why the government should be paying for any of the monarchy's living expenses," a hefty man asserted, "especially their horses when they keep the winnings."

"Alfred," William announced. "This is Charles Bendrick. A local importer."

The man gave Alfred a curt nod before continuing his tirade, taking a drink of whiskey between arguments.

"They have parliament now, who does a good deal of the government work, and Victoria's a wealthy woman. I say let her pay for her and her own and see how the royal family starts to live. Like the rest of us, I'd imagine. Teach them to tighten their purse strings a little."

Alfred's mouth pulled into a grin, and he cleared his throat, feigning an itch, as he tried to hide his humor at the men talking of themselves as if they represented the common people. Charles tapped a pudgy finger against his glass and ignored the hollow sound it elicited as a large gold ring ticked against the rim.

"The government is not paying her from taxpayers' pockets," William explained. "Most of the money she sees is a result of her predecessors relinquishing ownership of estates to parliament. The monarchy has given over the Crown Estate, worth millions more than what she sees in payments, for the benefit of the nation. For God's sake, Charles, the empire would be broke if the monarchy hadn't, as you would so poorly put it, loosened her purse strings a little and shared her wealth with the people."

Charles balked at the statement as William diffused the tension.

"Let's turn this back to the race, shall we?"

"My wife thinks it so endearing that he named it Diamond Jubilee in honor of his mother," Charles remarked, assenting to William's request. "A fitting tribute, eh? Naming a horse in honor of the Queen of England."

"Dear God," Elijah protested, his voice rising slightly above the rest. "That woman has ruled for long enough. Sixty years is far too many, and a woman her age can't be enlightened enough to know what is best for her kingdom."

"Queendom," Charles interjected, as he raised his glass in mock support.

"Yes, well. It is time for Albert to take the throne."

"Senior or junior?" Charles inquired.

Two waiters arrived at the table as the men laughed at the remark.

"I'd take either," Elijah commented.

The taller of the waiters set a mint julep in front of Alfred. The perfume of the man's soap mixed with the scent of the mint leaves made Alfred's head swim with intoxication. The life around him pulsed with an otherworldly energy. It was surreal to be seated in the middle of it rather than peering in from the other side of the glass.

"Say, where's Briggs?" Elijah added. "This is his second dinner to miss this month."

"Preoccupied," Mathias replied.

"Likely swindling someone," Charles commented.

"At the hospital actually," Mathias corrected, ignoring the man's scoff as he leaned over to Alfred, his eyes cutting sharply across the table. "He excused himself rather quickly," he whispered, "when he heard Charles would be joining us."

The shorter waiter replaced the vase of fresh flowers at the center of the table with a silver tray. It held a large bowl of boiled shrimp, their tales hanging over the side, and small cups of red sauce. He set a smaller tray of oysters in front of Thomas and then walked around the table placing an appetizer plate in front of each man. The men loosened their napkins before taking cups of sauce and pieces of shrimp from the tray. Alfred followed suit.

"You like mint julep as well?" Mathias asked quietly.

"No, I've never tried it before," Alfred admitted. "It sounded too good to pass up."

"Give it a go then."

He sniffed the drink, catching a strong spirit beneath the mint, and took a sip. It was smooth and weaker than he had expected. The mint lightened the burn as it slid down his throat and left a refreshing taste in his mouth. He nodded to Mathias, who returned a smile.

"They make it with bourbon here, but they don't always have it. If they've run out of ice, they pull it off the menu until a new shipment comes in."

Alfred took another sip, feeling the rush of the evening as it elated his mind. The mint leaf sank beneath the ice as he set the cocktail next to his plate.

"Well, now that the drinks and food are here," William started, "we can start this evening off right. In good spirits!"

Alfred chuckled as Mathias gave a generous bark of laughter. Elijah groaned. A smile took over William's face as he looked to Alfred.

"It never gets old," he stated proudly.

"As a matter of fact," Charles replied, "it does."

William waved him off and motioned to Charles as he used his smallest fork to pull the tail off an oversized shrimp. "Charles owns a store on Market just down a way. He's invested in the economy for imports and exports, so I'm afraid you'll have to forgive his rather liberal views when it comes to the monarchy."

Alfred lifted an eyebrow as he took another drink, his confidence accentuated by the buzz around him.

"Cheeses, liquors, and cured meats. A whole assortment," Charles pitched. "Whatever you need, I've got it."

"But don't expect a discount for being an acquaintance," Thomas commented as he pointed at Charles with his shucking knife. "He doesn't take a cut, even for his best patrons."

Charles held his hands up innocently. "A businessman has to stay in business." He winked at Alfred. "But I'm not above giving a first-time customer a break to try my goods. Best in town!"

Thomas loosened an oyster from its shell. "Nonetheless, you should be looking to expand. Julius Runge took his store to three floors."

"And then folded."

"Now, now," William commented. "We can't always predict the market."

"He very well should have," Charles contested. "He had Kauffman to back the other half of the business. It's a pity the old man's name was removed, what with all the money he put into that business."

"Julius ran his store quite well," Elijah noted, waving at the waiter for another scotch. "He was the only one to import certain goods. It's a smart tactic."

"What? South American coffee?" Charles spoke with a mouthful of shrimp. "It certainly didn't keep him afloat, did it? Soon enough every store in Texas will be importing once taxes go down and the cost is less prohibitive. I'm telling you, longevity is not won with the exotic."

"Nonetheless," Thomas added. "Having had the largest stock on the island of European labels is not a simpleton's tactic. It took some legwork."

"Well, what do you expect? He had a constant throng of Europeans coming abroad on his ships, filling the island with immigrants. He had a monopoly on the trade, didn't he? Liquors and workers, they were all the same to him. An import is an import."

"Let's be civil now, Charles," William remarked.

Charles waved a dismissing hand toward William as he swallowed a bite of shrimp.

"I only meant that Julius had the perfect arrangement to import such luxuries. The rest of us can't compete. There's simply no use in trying to bring such foreign goods to the market as long as men like him have their hands in it."

Having watched William's quick motions with his knife, Alfred mimicked his cleaning of the shrimp, clumsily pulling a dark vein from the back, and then pulled the meat from the tail. He took his first bite and tried to keep his expression calm as he worked at the chewy texture.

"Personally, I think his work overseas does a great service to the island." Thomas was shucking another oyster as he spoke. "What harm can come from improving foreign relations? He's consul to the German Empire, for God's sake!"

"An excellent point," William added. "There are very few opportunities for immigrants to come to America. Can we really fault the man for using his own money to provide them opportunities? They work just as hard as any other man."

"When there are jobs to be had," Elijah remarked.

"Are you implying that we have a shortage of jobs?"

"Not in the least. It's only that there are a finite number of positions a European immigrant can fill, especially one who does not speak English. You can't imagine that those should be available indefinitely."

"Perhaps not but that seems a rather conservative way of looking at it."

"It's all a matter of control," Charles interrupted.

The party looked at him as they deveined their shrimp, shucked their oysters, and finished their first round of drinks.

"And it is imperative that we maintain control of the market, of the jobs. It does no good to let the island become inundated with workers for whom there is no work to be had. I say it's high time someone put his foot down and had some control over who should be allowed onto the island."

"Who should be allowed?" Mathias's voice was quiet but crisp. Charles lifted his head from his plate of shrimp tails and caught the man's expression.

"Right," he replied, glancing around the table for agreement. "It's not as if the island can continue to grow indefinitely. We are an island. We have limited resources by definition and one of those is land. If every polack and herman is given the right to make a name for himself, as the saying goes, and buy up land left and right, there'll be nothing left for the rest of us."

A small silence pulled at the tablecloth as the murmur of voices and clinks of silverware filled the leftover space. Mathias stared at the man as William broke the silence in a well-punctuated tone.

"That is a very narrow-minded view, Charles. I doubt any of us here will share your opinion of Galveston's progress in providing opportunities and refuge to those from countries that are less opportunistic than our own."

Charles lifted his chin and let his eyes dance from face to face until they fell on Alfred.

"What about you, Mr. Ridgeway? I understand you're quite fresh to the city. I doubt you've had time to be tainted by the majority's views. How do you take all of this mingling of classes and new-century talk?"

Alfred set his glass down and cleared his throat. His heart had been racing throughout the conversation, though he wasn't entirely certain it was from the excitement of the meal. His limbs buzzed with energy and his mind was whipping from one comment to the next, waiting for the perfect moment to join the conversation.

"Actually, I find it quite refreshing."

His own tone surprised him. It was sharp and witty in his ears, and he found himself smiling at William as he spoke.

"The city is like nothing I have seen before. The island is a confluence of culture and energy. Restricting the influences, seeing them as encroachments rather than improvements, would only hinder such progress. It seems a rather immature way to look at it all if you ask me."

He finished his mint julep in one gulp. Whether it was the drink or the pill Mathias had given him, he wasn't certain, but his confidence soared like a bird overhead. He glanced around the table. All of the men were smiling at their plates with tight faces and averting their eyes. All but Charles. The man's face had grown bloated as he pulled his head back, the loose skin beneath his chin bunching around his face. With his cheeks turning a bright red, he looked like a viper preparing to strike, but Alfred didn't feel any remorse at the man's expression, though he knew that such a reaction would likely have been the most prudent response after an apology. William spoke before either of the men could continue.

"Another round for everyone?"

He caught the waiter's attention and signaled for him to come to the table as the room crescendo around them. Charles cleared his throat and pushed himself from the table.

"Not for me."

"Oh, Charles, don't take this all so personally," William pleaded.

"I didn't mean any offense," Alfred added.

"None taken, my boy," he replied to the table, his face still florid as he avoided glancing across the table. "I simply must return home. My wife is not well this evening and my duty is to her tonight. You'll have them charge to my account?"

"Of course," William replied. "I do hope Gwendolyn recovers."

He gave a curt nod as he stepped around the table. His round figure moved through the room with determined steps and disappeared beyond the towering vase of orange tulips.

"I sincerely apologize," Alfred started.

William lifted a hand to cut him off. "We all know Charles is very opinionated, which makes him a shrewd businessman but a terrible socialite."

Elijah gave a snort.

"And I have never heard him put his wife's wellbeing over a drink in the six years I've known him."

They all nodded with quiet murmurs as a second round of drinks was set on the table. Soon the conversation turned to rugby and golf, and on this matter, Alfred found, he and Thomas had absolutely no opinions. As the evening progressed, they discussed the market, fashion trends, fellow bankers and storekeepers, the upkeep of the bathhouses, and what little comparison could be found between fresh shrimp and what was served half-heartedly in Houston.

After another round of shrimp and oysters had been ordered and picked through, Mathias offered Alfred an oyster and dropped an oval shell onto his plate. He handed him Thomas's shucking knife and showed him how to separate the meat from the pearly interior of the shell, keeping the toppings on the slick meat of the mollusk.

"Now, don't chew," Mathias instructed. "Just swallow it whole. Some of the cream and bread will stay for flavor."

"What happens if I chew it?"

Mathias grinned. "You'll only do it once. I promise."

With a tapping of the shells over their empty glasses, the two tilted their heads back and poured the oysters into their mouths. Alfred swallowed the meat and felt it slide down his gullet, leaving behind the taste of a heavy cream and toasted bread crumbs. The contrast of textures was intoxicating, and he decided almost immediately that he preferred the flavors.

"Another?"

He finished the oysters with Mathias as William drew the night to a close, discussing the shrimping industry with Thomas and Elijah. The restaurant quieted as the last rays of daylight carried over the rooftops and left the street beyond the windows in shadow, lit only by the flickering glow of the gas lamps along the storefronts and the electric lights that hung over the intersections. The flavors of the night mixed in Alfred's stomach as his head swirled from the experience. The extravagance of the evening had been wonderfully overdone. As the men parted, the other three making their way toward William's waiting carriage, Alfred and Mathias began walking toward Broadway, the warm evening at their collars and the late dew of the day sticking to their heels.

"How is your head?"

They stepped aside to let an elderly couple into their carriage.

"Much better. I see how you recovered so quickly. For such a small pill, it packs a punch."

"No doubt."

"The two mint juleps probably didn't help, though."

They crossed onto Postoffice, and Mathias lifted a hand to wave down an approaching cabbie.

"But you'll want to get plenty of sleep tonight," Mathias replied as he held the door to let Alfred step up into the carriage. "With as much drinking and talking as you did tonight, you'll be exhausted when it wears off."

Alfred could only smile at his remark as he settled onto the seat and let his eyes look out onto the street. Whatever he felt when he woke the next day, it would surely be better than the mornings before. He had spent the evening drinking and dining with some of the island's finest men, discussing business and gossiping about people as if he belonged at the table. His week had been a whirlwind of changes, pulled to and fro on the wind, but as the carriage made its way toward the boardinghouse on Church Street, the last semblance of evening fading from a deep violet to a heavy night, he looked out onto the city lights as if they were his own. And somewhere in the rocking motions of the ride, he fell asleep to the sounds of the occasional passerby and the hooves of the horse clopping rhythmically on the worn surface of the street.

CHAPTER ELEVEN

*S*ee it there?"

Alfred gazed across the marsh, following Hilary's bony finger to a patch of saltmarsh cordgrass that rose like wheat stems over the water.

"The shiver above the black needlerush grass."

The slender stems shuddered from deep within the patch, and Alfred watched the grass intently. It stilled as a long, pointed beak emerged in the morning light, followed by a small head of black and white feathers with a yellow crown. The heron stepped out of the grass and strutted along a plat of raised soil that lifted out of the marsh water.

"It's a male," Hilary commented.

"How do you know?"

"The colorful crown." He handed Alfred a pair of binoculars. "Females have grey and white heads. No crowns."

The bird's stalking gait filled the lenses as he observed its movements. It had a slender build with lanky legs that stretched expertly along the marsh floor. Hilary removed a sketchbook and leather pouch from his canvas bag and began to settle himself on the stool behind Alfred. Its stumpy legs had sunken into the soil and he fell onto it in a squatting motion that left his knees close to his chest.

"How long is the crown?" Hilary asked.

Alfred stared at the bird as he considered its size. "Perhaps three inches."

Hilary's crooked fingers moved in loose motions that dragged his pencil across the paper in quick, rough scratches.

"What about the proportion?"

"To its head?"

Hilary nodded, lost in his sketch. Alfred stalked the bird with the binoculars as it edged into another stand of marsh grasses, its legs disappearing.

"About a third of the head length."

The shape of the bird's head filled the top of Hilary's paper as the live specimen waded in the water, moving in and out of stands with light steps and creating the smallest of ripples with its feet. It paused and held its head motionless for a moment before striking at the water and emerging with a flat fish in its beak.

"It caught a fish!"

Alfred's hushed excitement was odd in the quiet hum of the bayou. Hilary took the binoculars and adjusted the lenses. The scene came into focus, the outline of a white, flattened fish with black stripes wriggling in its beak.

"Sheepshead."

"The fish?"

Hilary nodded and handed him the binoculars. "Ugly things. Their teeth are square like ours. Looks like they're smiling at you." Alfred watched the man return to his sketch, contemplating how much truth there was to the description. "I've got the neck all wrong," Hilary continued as he took up his pencil again and redrew the neck in an exaggerated curve.

"It swallowed it whole," Alfred narrated to the water.

Hilary was silent as he continued to sketch the long-billed heron with knobby knees and an oblong body. His hands moved quickly and smeared the darker lines as he dragged the sharpened pencil tip across the image. Alfred glanced at the fragmented sketch and then back at the bird as it swallowed its prey.

"The wing feathers are longer," he corrected. "They're more pointed."

Hilary moved his pencil tip to the center of the paper without hesitation and stretched the wingtips along the body with quick, uninterrupted strokes; Alfred returned to birdwatching.

Hilary had sent a post the previous week informing him of their first outing the following Saturday. No reply had been needed, and a squeeze horn had announced Hilary's arrival at the boardinghouse. Alfred had stepped off the porch in his thinnest shirt with an unbuttoned collar to find Hilary bedecked in tan corduroy pants with mud-brown suspenders over a white linen shirt. Alfred's entire body had trembled with the rumble of the massive Benz Motorwagen beneath him. The ride had had Alfred gripping the metal frame and the brim of his straw hat as the man had careened down Broadway at more than ten miles an hour, turning heads and puffing smoke into the air. Alfred could see why it was the only one of its kind on the island. How anyone would prefer that to the quiet of a bicycle was beyond him.

Within minutes of parking it next to a field, Hilary had unpacked his birdwatching kit and marched into the black needlerush that edged Buffalo Bayou at the center of the island. They had been watching for long-billed herons and Roseate Spoonbills for barely ten minutes before they had spotted their first catch, a young male who had flown into the stand of grass.

"Now," Hilary declared, as he turned the page in his sketchbook, "this is the hard part: sketching it in flight. I'm going to start sketching it, and I want you to watch the bird and tell me when it takes flight."

"What am I to do?"

"Commit the details to memory. Then look at my sketch and tell me what needs to be corrected."

Alfred let the binoculars fall from his face as he resettled himself onto his haunches. "Wouldn't it be simpler for you to observe the bird and then draw it afterward?"

"It's just a blurry body of fluff to me from this distance. I need your eyes to do the work."

Hilary's hand began to jerk and slide with quick motions, and Alfred returned to the binoculars, the lenses scanning the horizon. Stands of grass and weeds populated the bayou in tufts of stems and seed pods. The cordgrass waved heavily in the breeze while an overgrowth of bushgrass tickled at the fans of palmettos. The undergrowth beneath a palmetto gave a tale-tell shudder, and Alfred focused the binoculars on the plants as the small body of a marsh rabbit emerged. Its brown and grey fur kept it precariously on the edge of camouflage with only the occasional movement giving away its full size. A splash sounded in the bayou, and Alfred slid the binoculars back to the center of the water where the heron was shaking his head and taking large gulps that exaggerated the length of its neck.

"It caught another fish."

Hilary made a noise of amusement that blended with the scratching of his pencil.

"It'll be leaving soon then."

As if on cue, the heron jutted its chest forward and rocked back onto its feet, straightening its legs and lengthening its entire body. Long white wings extended as they pushed a rush of air against the water and the bird took flight, its feet tucking upward and hanging slightly from its plush underbelly. The entire scene unfolded in less than a second.

"It's flying!"

The bird was out of the water in a single motion and rising above the bayou quickly; its form melted into a smooth shape as it began to fly southward. After several flaps of its wings, it began a graceful soar, a single island specimen disappearing into the blue of oceanfront sky.

Hilary turned his sketchbook in his lap so that Alfred could see the sketch of the bird in flight. It was a rough outline of the bird's body with its head tucked back and its wings in mid-flap. Hilary's eyes roamed the bayou water as he waited on his student to begin correcting his drawing. Alfred drew in a breath of grass and stagnant water.

"Its feet hung lower."

Hilary's hand slid across the paper in short strokes as he extended the length of the legs and redrew the feet so that the knees were tucked against the body. Alfred watched him alter the drawing by pulling back the neck, extending the length of the wings and narrowing the tip of the tail. He completed the sketch by adding a few areas of shading to give the bird depth and girth. When he was finished, he rotated the sketchbook on his knee so that Alfred could see the image more clearly.

"That's it."

Hilary flipped the thick paper of his sketchbook and sat it comfortably on his legs with a clean page beneath his pencil. He looked out over the water and squinted at the brightening sun, his wrinkles deepening into crevices at the corners of his eyes.

"Now, we wait."

"For what?"

"The one I'm after today. A female rosette spoonbill."

He opened a small wooden box he had set at his feet and pulled out a metal cup, a single paintbrush, and a long metal case. He handed the dented cup to Alfred and motioned toward the edge of the water.

"I'll need water."

Alfred stood and stretched his back before dipping the cup into the bayou water. It was tinged brown as he brought a cupful up from the surface. Hilary balanced the cup on the ground against his feet, the bottom of the copper sinking slightly into the soil. He sat a metal case of watercolors along the top of his sketchbook and took up his pencil. Loosely defined lines filled the page with sharp angles as the very rough outline of a bird came to life between them.

Alfred looked out over the water to see the sky losing its peach skin, melting into blue as day arrived in full. The bayou's morning ritual began to fade. The chirps of frogs drifted away until only the buzzing of insects and the occasional splash remained, like the last notes of an orchestra tuning for opening night. The music carried him into a meditation that was broken by Hilary nudging his arm, his thoughts falling like coins in the grass.

"Look."

Alfred followed a knobby index finger across the water and searched the stands of grass. Patches of pink duckweed floated in pinprick-size buds along the surface of the water, hiding the depths, but nothing moved.

"I don't see—"

Hilary was on his feet before Alfred could turn and clasped his palm over Alfred's mouth with a hardy smack. Alfred's head rolled but Hilary kept his grip as he squinted out over the water. His skin smelled of graphite and sweat as Alfred breathed heavily through his nostrils. Keeping his eyes trained ahead, Hilary let his hand drop from Alfred's face and pointed into the distance.

"In the water," he whispered, "beside the tallest palmetto."

Alfred's ear tickled at the man's breath, but he kept his attention on the water and strained his eyes to see something, anything, out of place. He shook his head, growing concerned that the man's vision had failed him entirely, but then it moved, a small break in the water. It was covered in duckweed from skimming the surface, a vibrant rosacea on dark scales, and Alfred's mind jarred when the tail came into view, a thin wake just beyond the duckweed hump that swept gently from side to side. When he found the head, nearly four feet in front of the traveling duckweed, his heart slammed against his chest.

His arms shot out to his sides when Hilary clasped his hand back over his mouth and pulled him slowly down to a squatting position.

"Don't move," Hilary instructed in a husky voice.

Not twenty feet away, the alligator had slowed his swim at their movement and turned his snout toward them like a compass. He seemed to float in the water effortlessly as the surface rippled gently against his body. Both men sat quietly, but Alfred's muscles tensed as he began to calculate how little it would take for the predator to cross the distance between them. His mind raced as he lived out the scenario in his head, the newspapers lamenting the tragic deaths of a young man, newly arrived on the island, and an eccentric old birdwatcher.

A frog was the first to break the tension, chirping from somewhere nearby. The animal's body rotated in the water with the slightest of movements. His snout and tail in a perfect line, he created a small wrinkle in the surface as he shifted his attention to another line of grasses. Alfred let out a quick breath.

"We should go."

He pushed himself up to a squatting position and glanced back to see the old man poised over the paper with the pencil loosely between his fingers, his eyes watching the water. Alfred scooted clumsily backward until he was beside him. His words were hushed but made urgent by his tone.

"What are you doing?"

"What we came here to do."

Alfred looked from the man to the bayou as he processed the words. The alligator was turning back toward them as they whispered behind the short grass at the water's edge.

"You're going to sketch it?"

"Him."

"What?"

Alfred's voice rose in agitation, his muscles burning from his squatted position.

"I'm going to sketch *him*." Alfred shook his head as if to argue, but Hilary cut him off. "It might seem droll to you to think I would consider such a minor detail significant in this moment, but these are the sorts of observations you are here to learn."

Alfred's tongue felt swollen as he swallowed.

"Hilary, this isn't safe. That thing could attack us."

"It could." His pencil tip skimmed the surface of the paper in faint lines as he judged the distance between the snout and the tail. "It might."

Knowing he couldn't leave the man alone on the shore, Alfred gave into his shaking calves and let his body collapse onto the soil with a soft puff of dirt. He drew his knees up to his chest, keeping them ready to fly beneath him if needed, and drew in long, intentional breaths. After a minute of only the click of insects and the quiet scratching of Hilary's graphite against the paper, he felt his agitation wane.

"Alright," he finally conceded. "How do you know it's a male?"

"It's size." The long scratches turned into short spurts as he began to shade the snout.

"The male is larger?"

Hilary nodded as he glanced from the paper to the alligator and back again. Alfred noted how much more often he looked toward the water during this sketch; his attention had been only half devoted to the heron, but now he was slowing his pencil and criticizing the alligator every few seconds. Alfred would have bet his day's earnings that it was more out of curiosity than caution. He raised his head slightly as if to gain a better perspective and took in the distance between the alligator's snout and tail.

"How big is this one?"

"A naturalist once taught me a way to measure one without ever nearing it. The distance from its snout to the back of its head is roughly a fifth of its total length."

Alfred considered the motionless head. "His head is a little over two feet." He saw Hilary nod in his peripheral vision and felt his chest constrict. "It can't be that large. Ten feet? That's larger than a man is tall."

"Males usually are. This one is well-fed, but I have seen larger ones in this bayou."

He drew a few dark lines to emphasize the edge of the water against the reptile's scales and then let his pencil fall to the earth before fingering his paint case.

"And you come here anyway?"

"Well, that's the point, isn't it?"

Alfred struggled to disguise his irritation. "I thought the point was to sketch birds."

Hilary dipped the tip of his paintbrush into the cup of water and lathered the wet camel hairs onto the brown oval of paint. "We're sketching nature, my boy. Why would we stop at birds?"

"I can think of several reasons I would stop at birds." Alfred gestured toward the water. "He's the first one."

Hilary chuckled as he filled in the sketch with the faint tan of deer hide.

"I envy your innocence." He wet the green paint and created an overlap of the colors as the head began to push out from the paper. "You have so much left to learn and so much time to learn it. This entire island is a new canvas for you. I only have as much time as I have, and there is so much left to sketch and paint." He quieted as he scrutinized his blend of green highlights. "I will never see it all no matter how much I try."

A new sense of sympathy overwhelmed the scene as Alfred watched the old man master the colors of a reptile blanketed by duckweed blooms. The image was suddenly remote and intimate in a new way, and he let out a breath that swirled the colors of the day in his mind. He looked back at the snout in the water, scooting up the bank quietly so that the back of Hilary's head was in the foreground of the scene. The old man was framed between a young sapling and a set of aged palmettos, Alfred's own take on the moment.

After a few more minutes of flicks and drags of his paintbrush, Hilary began packing his supplies back into his daypack. He moved to his feet with a quiet groan and stood bent over for a beat before straightening as much as his back would allow.

"A good's day work that was."

Alfred dusted off his pant legs with his free hand as he rose but kept his eyes on the alligator as Hilary packed up his stool.

"What about the Roseate Spoonbill?"

Hilary chuckled, holding onto Alfred's arm to keep his balance as the bank inclined slightly away from the water.

"No less than a half hour ago you would have run to Mudville if I'd let you. Now you want to stay?"

"I thought better of the scenery," he replied as he followed Hilary away from the shoreline, glancing back to the water every few seconds.

"It will grow on you, my boy. No doubt. But don't let it fool you." He took arthritic steps as the ground slanted to the right and then jutted up at an odd angle. "Many of the most beautiful things on this island are the deadliest. If you learned anything today, I hope it's to not trust too completely what you see in front of you."

As he neared the edge of the taller grasses that had hidden them among the bayou's flora, he teetered and reached out with his left arm. Alfred caught him by the forearm, the daypack slipping from his hand and clattering to the ground as the copper cup sprang free and bounced against a rock. The air rang metallic with the ting of hard metal as the two regained their balance, the noise sending a flock of ducks into flight overhead. Their sudden flutter from the grasses reached the men's ears like a thousand paper fans as frantic quacks joined the rustling stems of cordgrass, and both men instinctively ducked as the bayou took to the sky around them. The birds' bodies scattered until hundreds of forms filled the blue morning and a shadow covered the men, blotting out the sun, a cloud of mallard wings moving westward like a small storm overtaking the island. As Hilary continued toward the motorized wagon, Alfred ventured a glance back into the bayou where the small but dark snout of the alligator had crept up to the shore and watched them from the water's surface, a blend of black scales and pink duckweed stalking them over the hill.

CHAPTER TWELVE

*I*t didn't take long for Alfred to realize that Sunday service was a full affair on the island. Crowds of coaches deposited church-goers on corners and in front of church doors while pedestrians flanked the streets. The pews were dotted with blue and yellow hats as women fanned themselves against the heat, filling the rows to the brim, but Mrs. Poplar had a reserved seat for him, a benefit of longevity as she described it. Keen on treating her boarders well even beyond the kitchen, she'd found Alfred a spot beside her after negotiating the rest of the group down the pew.

The service at St. John's was lengthy, a heavy-handed lecture that the reverend dragged through the humid chapel, and Alfred struggled to keep his attention on the words. He was used to the shorter services back home. Simple and to the point, they were applicable to farmers and field workers. This reverend, however, was much more interested in speaking to the socialites, a group from which Alfred quickly discounted himself. When the service finally ended, the welcomed silence that followed pulled at Alfred's ears like cotton.

Reverend Bradfield walked into the aisle to greet his nearest parishioners. Alfred replaced the hymnal in the pew pocket in front of him and waited as the well-organized pews muddled into a throng of mingling handshakes and voices as everyone scooted toward the doors at the front of the church. Mrs. Poplar's voice carried behind him as she cooed over a young lady's hat. Beyond the doors, the mid-morning air had grown stale, the coolness of the night lost entirely. With no clouds for cover, the island radiated heat from the ground up, and the weakest of the lot stood beneath the larger of the oaks in front of the church and fanned themselves in the shade. As Alfred stepped out onto the sidewalk, he felt a nudge at his back and stumbled forward a step before catching his balance.

"Oh, dear, I'm so sorry—"

He turned and locked eyes on the delicate features of a familiar face. "Miss Keller."

Her eyes narrowed as she smiled in the sun. "Why, Mr. Ridgeway! This is a surprise."

"A pleasant one, I hope."

A small laugh left her throat and she glanced at her gloved hands. "By all means."

Her face beamed beneath the brim of her straw hat. A thin white ribbon was tied at the side, a faint accent to her light blue dress. She lifted a gloved hand to hold it in place as a breeze carried the scent of honeysuckle around them and into the church.

"I had no idea you were a member of St. John's," she commented as she tilted her head to block the sun with her brim.

"Oh, I'm not. Not yet. This is my first service on the island."

"Ah, so you are not yet familiar with Reverend Bradfield's sermons, I presume."

"I'm afraid not. He is a little heavy-handed on the embellishments."

"Perhaps theatrical is a better description." He chuckled as he sidestepped to allow an elderly couple to pass toward the street, and her smile widened. "I'm so very happy to see you today, Mr. Ridgeway."

"Alfred, please."

She nodded as she glanced toward the street where covered coaches were gathering in a line to pick up their fares. He took a step closer as a rotund man laughed boisterously and attempted to skirt past them.

"Do you have a coach?"

"I do," she replied, tilting her head back further so that a strip of sunlight caught her chin and illuminated her neckline. "I've come with Evelyn and William today."

"Would you like me to fetch them for you?"

"Not in the least," she replied matter-of-factly. "They'll find me soon enough. Tell me, Alfred, what sort of work does a climatologist do?"

Despite his uncertainty of how to answer, he was relieved at her having asked any question at all, anything to keep her there in front of the church in what was quickly becoming a sweltering May morning. She arched an eyebrow at his hesitation, holding the brim of her hat between her thumb and index finger.

"That depends on the climatologist," he answered. "I do a great deal of assisting at the moment. I am still learning the way the bureau goes about things."

"And others? There are three of you, yes?"

"Yes, Dr. Cline and his brother, Joseph."

"I've heard of Dr. Cline, but what does his brother do a great deal of?"

He thought for a moment.

"Complaining."

She gave a hearty laugh that sent his mind floating as he drew in a deep breath, inhaling her voice with the warm air. With cheeks glowing a pale rose and eyes sparkling like beads of dew, she was the image of a perfect summer day. She let go of her hat as the breeze eased and held one hand in the other as if to cradle them.

"And what of you, Miss Keller—"

"I thought we were beyond formalities, Mr. Ridgeway."

Her smile carried on for a beat longer as he let out a chuckle.

"My sincere apologies," he joked, waiting for a nod of mock agreement. "And what of you, Florence? What is it that takes up your days here on the island?"

Her eyes lingered on his for a moment before searching beyond the crowd and into the street, her mouth holding the frame of a smile as she searched for words.

"I'm not certain how to answer that question."

"I apologize if I overstepped. I didn't mean to pry."

"No, of course not. It's simply that I've never had a gentleman ask about my interests."

Any chance he had to reply was cut off by the sound of her name carrying over the thinning crowd. He looked beyond her to see William Goodman standing by an open door of a coach, a top hat dangling from one hand. She waved before turning back to Alfred, her fingers going instinctively to her hat as she bent her head back slightly to look into his face.

"It was a pleasure seeing you again, Alfie."

She lifted the side of her dress as she turned to go and the word escaped before he could think better of it.

"Florence?"

She turned partially, keeping her hat so that it shaded her eyes and her dress lifted just above the tips of her boots.

"I was wondering if you—"

He had no idea how he intended to finish the sentence and knew asking her to any private affair would seem rather illicit. She knew little more about him than his name and post, but he had put faith in the universe to bring him some sort of inspiration, some sort of muse to whisper in his ear. None appeared. He forced air out of his lungs as she spoke for him.

"The ball?"

Her words were bright in the oppressive air, a mix of anticipation and a piqued intellect that he wanted to know more intimately. He took a step to close the small distance between them.

"The ball?"

"You were wondering if I'll be attending the ball next month?"

"Yes." He cleared his throat. "Yes, of course. The ball."

She squinted beneath her hat. "It is rather exclusive, and I admit that I wasn't sure if you would have made the invitation list so soon. Membership can be rather difficult to come by. Have you already joined?"

He had absolutely no idea what she was talking about. He raised his eyebrows as if he hadn't heard her questions to urge her on.

"At the Garten Verein?"

"Oh, yes," he lied. "I've found myself lucky to keep good company. You'll be attending then?"

Her eyes flitted toward the reverend, who was making rounds nearby.

"I will. Shall I save a dance?"

"Please do."

"Until then, Mr. Ridgeway," she remarked with a smirk and turned to go.

He watched her slender figure move through the remnants of the crowd. William helped her into the coach, giving Alfred a quick wave before disappearing behind her into the shade of the buggy. The horse's hooves clopped heavily as it pulled the carriage away. The sweat that had prickled at Alfred's neck and shoulders now clung to his shirt and he let out a moist sigh as the anticipation of the week melted into the realization that he needed more than new clothes for such an event.

The first thing he would need was an invitation, and he hadn't the faintest idea how he was going to pull that off.

———•●•———

The street was littered with coaches and carriages, buggies and the occasional trolley as church-goers made their way home. Mrs. Poplar's yellow ribbon fluttered in the wind as the open carriage rattled down Broadway. The more than twenty churches were scattered across the island, leaving the city singing with bells of all faiths as the services came to a close

"Yes, Reverend Bradfield can be as long-winded as he is strapping. I should have warned you."

Mrs. Poplar held her hat atop her gray bun as the carriage rocked on wooden wheels. The smell of the ocean air mingled with the horse and sweaty driver as the wind gusted from the southeast. Mrs. Poplar's offer of a ride had saved him the trouble of bicycling back in the mid-day heat, but he was growing weary of the open buggy.

"I quite enjoyed the service," Alfred lied. He wondered at the implications of lying so readily and so often before his noontime meal on a Sunday, but the guilt melted away in the sun as they turned down 14th Street.

"A very appropriate sermon given the recent climate. Him going on about man keeping his dominance and all that."

He pulled his bowler at an angle to block the arcing sun. "How's that?"

"There's a proposition to expand the channel to accommodate more ships. I read in this morning's edition that it would require a sizable addition to the depth as well as some expansion in girth, essentially merging our two smaller islands in the bay into one."

"Reverend Bradfield is not in favor?"

"Oh, I've no idea Reverend Bradfield's opinion on the matter. I should think he shouldn't have one in the end, what with him representing the church." She adjusted her hold on her hat. "But I would imagine there will be a good deal of disagreement within the city about it all."

Alfred let his eyes venture into the yards of the lots as they passed. The clop of the horse's hooves was steady with the rocking of the wagon, and it lulled him into relaxation as the heat of the day beat down on them. The reins shuddered and clinked where they met the horse's bit, and the mare snorted.

"I would imagine a larger channel would be good for the wharves," he observed.

She turned, giving a quick tilt of her head. "I didn't have you pegged as an industrialist." The challenge in her voice was clear and unexpected. "The Deep Water Committee no doubt has a similar opinion, given their function."

The wagon bumped against the trolley tracks, jolting them as she explained the island's history. The wharves that had built the city had been bought out one at a time, creating a monopoly that had made a handful of men wealthy in the process, and now the island exported the world's cotton like it was water being poured back into the ocean. The port's growth had been at the hands of the Deep Water Committee, comprised of the same wealthy exporters who garnered federal funds to deepen the channel for larger steam ships. It was a money-driven cycle that had played out well. The port expanded, the wharves gained business, the city boomed, and the men became wealthier, backing yet another expansion. It was a simple plan, and one that Mrs. Poplar wasn't hesitant to spell out in lackluster phrasing.

"The last expansion was in ninety-six and it kept us ahead of Houston, the fastest route to the Midwest. But this new one will make the same men all the wealthier as I see it."

"Who?"

A seagull cried overhead and dove at the foot of the horse, sending it into a sidestep to dodge the bird. Both passengers gripped the side of the wagon as the horse recovered.

"The usual suspects when it comes to Galveston, owners of more than half the city's businesses. Harris Kempner, Colonel Moody, George Sealy, John Sealy, Walter Gresham, Leon Blum. The names you see every day without noticing them. The ones with the greatest interest in our wharves."

"Double profit," Alfred ventured.

"They're intelligent men, exactly the sort needed to fund Galveston's rise to fame, but I suppose that's what makes them so dangerous. I'm not one to sell them short. They've all done their share to help this city become what it is, but it leaves you a little suspicious." She threw a glance his way as she lowered her voice. "About their motives."

The wagon slowed to a stop in front of the boardinghouse.

"Will you be coming in?" She set a boot on the first rung of the ladder and gave her hand to the driver.

Alfred stood to follow.

"No, I've the bicycle on the back of the coach. I need to return to the bureau office to finish the day's observations."

"Oh, no need to pedal back that far. The driver can take you back."

He shook his head as he made to follow her down the ladder. "I haven't brought enough for the fare. It's really alright. I don't mind the trek back."

She put up a hand to stop him on the first rung as the driver took his fare and returned to the horse.

"Too late. I've already paid."

"Really, Mrs. Poplar," he said with a blush, "I couldn't let you do that."

"Return the favor of good company?"

"I was going to say pay my fare," he asserted.

"It's all the same," she said with a shrug. "I prefer the company to pocket change."

He settled back onto the bench and furrowed his brow. "May I ask you a question?" She drew nearer the coach and looked up at him. "If the Deep Water Committee brings so much business to the island, wouldn't they know what's best for the city? I mean, I understand your concerns, but it sounds like they know what they're doing."

"They do. That's the problem. And they do it with everyone that they meet."

"Competition, you mean?"

She stole a glance toward the driver, causing Alfred to lean down a few inches to make out her eyes in the shade of her hat.

"The wharves deduct for in price when buying cotton what they charge for when selling it."

"What would that be?"

"The same thing that drives every business here, Mr. Ridgeway." Her eyebrows arched sharply. "Water."

The driver stepped up onto the wagon and settled onto his seat. Mrs. Poplar backed away and started toward the house as the reins whipped against the horse. He watched her make her way through the yard until his neck ached at the angle and he was forced to look forward again.

His head ached from the heat of the day and the conversation. Mrs. Poplar was not one to speak ill of others, but her concern over the nature of the proposed expansion had settled in Alfred's bones. He was fresh in her world and not entirely naïve enough to think that gave him more clarity that others. He watched a group of children play in the street ahead of the horse as his mind worked through her words. The island was becoming an enigma for him, a life-size puzzle he couldn't quite figure out as if he had yet to learn all of the rules. Every day they seemed to change slightly from the day before and wriggle around his perspective like a wet fish. If a city couldn't trust its most successful businessmen, who could it trust?

He chuckled as an answer came to his mind. With the darkening horizon, the Weather Bureau would be at the bottom of that list. A forecast for sunny skies with light winds was about to take a turn and offer another reason for John to smirk at the breakfast table. He leaned back as they continued down Church Street, the motion of the coach rocking him into a light sleep.

CHAPTER THIRTEEN

*N*eed a lift?"

The man leaning out of the open carriage door shielded his face with a naked hand.

Monday's sunrise had brought with it torrential rain that far surpassed the Weather Bureau's forecast of light precipitation and a southerly breeze. A small spit of rain that had originated over the Gulf of Mexico's June-heated waters had amassed into a thunderstorm that stretched more than seven miles out into the ocean. It had made landfall just after six o'clock, presenting Alfred with a view of the tides as they brought in the grays and blues just off the rising sun's shoulder. It had been pouring since.

Alfred had made his way down the stairs to head to the boarding-house for supper and been met with the deluge at the door. In the street toward the wharves a group of children played in the water, splashing each other with the trapped rainfall. The current moved steadily toward the harbor and carried floating debris along the street like willing passengers. Loosed pages of a newspaper, a piece of torn cloth, a child's ball—they all slid down the street and toward the ocean waters. He imagined them washing off the edge of the wharf and tumbling into the waters against the hulls of moored ships. His mind lingered near their keels where years of lost possessions, washed overboard in the rain and rough waters, had no doubt accumulated in the darker depths of the channel.

"Where are you heading?" Alfred leaned off the edge of the portico along the Levy Building, keeping behind the curtain of rain.

"Thirteenth and Market."

Alfred looked down the street toward Broadway, only seeing as far as the corner of Postoffice where a line of carriages crossed the flooded intersection in a slow train of tired horses. It would be madness to try to bicycle to the boardinghouse in such a downpour, and the added obstacles of slowed carriages and pedestrians huddled in crowds on the sidewalks would make the commute all the more treacherous.

"I'm close," he shouted over the roar. "On fourteenth and Postoffice!"

"Come on, then!"

Alfred nodded at the man and gestured for him to wait. Propping the door open with his foot, he deposited the bicycle against the wall of the first flight of stairs. Any concern he had at it being stolen washed away. It would surely be faster to try to outrun the rain than to navigate the rusty thing through the traffic.

He held his shoulder bag over his head as he jumped into the open door, rocking the buggy with his weight as the stranger slammed the door against the rain and knocked on the wall behind him. The carriage began to move, swaying heavily as the horse pulled the wheels through the water. The passenger's voice was deep and filled the cabin.

"I told the driver there would be someone else in need of a carriage if we waited long enough."

Alfred shook his sleeves loose of their water. The gentleman gave a smile that put him at ease, but it was his hat that set Alfred on edge. Silk and well cut with a thick black ribbon about the brim. It was much more than a simple day hat.

"I'm thankful you had the patience to wait," he replied as he offered a damp hand. "Alfred Ridgeway."

"Julius Runge."

The name caught in Alfred's ear, but he didn't ask questions, simply grateful to be under any sort of covering. Both men looked out onto the flooded street beyond the window.

"It is quite a storm, isn't it?" He didn't wait for Alfred to answer. "The boards on the Strand were floating away by eleven. That'll be another day of replacing planks and muddy boots."

"You mean the sidewalks?"

"Indeed. They make their escape with every flood, which seems to be nearly every rainy day this season."

"Are they not nailed down?"

The man snorted with a huff and turned a smile toward Alfred. "You'd think we would have learned to nail them down by now." He gave a curious knit of his brow. "You are not from Galveston, then?"

"I just arrived a few weeks ago."

"For business?"

"The Weather Bureau."

The man gave a raise of his eyebrows as he looked back out onto the street. Thunder rolled somewhere overhead and temporarily muted the splashing of horses' hooves in the water and the rumble of carts as they pushed their way through the streets.

"We have plenty to keep you busy, I would imagine. What do you think of it?"

"The bureau?"

"The island." He looked once more at Alfred with genuine interest. "I'm always fascinated to hear outsiders' views of our little world."

The carriage rocked violently to one side as a wheel caught a pothole beneath the water. The horse stuttered in his gait before pushing on to free the wheel from its watery trap.

"It is a fascinating place, to say the least."

"And to say the most?"

Alfred shared the man's smile as he slid his shoulder bag onto the floor and leaned back against the wall.

"I have never seen so much wealth concentrated so tightly. It entrances the mind when one thinks of how much power and prestige emanates from this island."

"That is one of our greatest prospects, to hold on to our grip of the export industry. Without it, we are nothing more than waterfront property." He chuckled. "Could you imagine anything worse than Galveston becoming a festering pool for tourists and thrill-seekers?"

Alfred kept quiet, certain the man was musing on his own discontentedness with the island's few but possible debts to providence. Another thunderclap bellowed over the island and rattled the door handles.

"What is it that you do, Mr. Ridgeway, at this Weather Bureau of ours?"

"I am an Assistant Observer."

"Interesting work, is it?"

"It is," he replied, surprised to find some honesty in the statement.

For most of the morning, Joseph had been in a less critical mood than of late, and Alfred found the two brothers conversing much more fluidly on subjects from wind patterns to Cuba's own attempts to forecast weather in the Atlantic, both of which he had listened to intently while responding to telegrams and assisting with maps. After only two weeks, much to his relief, a routine was beginning to take shape in the office.

The man nodded as he gazed back out the window.

"And what is it that you do, Mr. Runge?"

"Oh, a bit of everything, I'm afraid. Until recently I made my wealth with imports."

"Goods?"

"Mostly, yes." He smiled mischievously. "Kauffman and Runge, importers of the world's greatest luxuries. We offered the finest collection of South American coffee and European liquors on the island. In fact, I've come to judge a man on his drinks." His eyes narrowed. "Tell me, Alfred, how do you like your coffee?"

Alfred's mind made the connection as he spoke, and he heard Charles Bendrick's voice as he complained of Runge's importing practices. Alfred attempted to discern the best approach to the conversation before deciding on honesty.

"I can't say that I've had enough to have an opinion just yet."

"Ah, tried the wrong sort, have you?"

"Not enough, I'm afraid."

"It's a man's drink, that's for certain. But American coffee is like our tea: weakened for the masses and stripped of all dignity in the process. It is best enjoyed in its origin, much like liquor."

"You're a connoisseur of both, I take it."

"Neither. I'm simply a German who understands good coffee when I taste it."

Alfred's nod was lost in the rocking of the carriage as it slowed upon reaching Postoffice Street. The water seemed to have receded and the horse moved at a slightly faster pace, though the splash of hooves in the water returned as the carriage turned and started west.

Alfred ventured a question. "You've been on the island a while?"

The man nodded absently as he watched a driver work a horse whose carriage had broken a wheel. "Thirty years feels like a lifetime when you've seen as many generations disembark at our harbor as I have."

"How long does it take one to become accustomed to the weather?"

"I should think it will take you until October in shirts of that blend." Alfred blushed at the comment, but Runge took no notice. "Plenty of people find their way here from overseas and make do without much more than what they wear across their shoulders. They seem to adjust perfectly well, to be honest. I thank God every day I didn't have such a lot in my younger years."

"You're not German, then?"

"What makes you say that?"

"If you didn't come off a ship."

"I am German, I assure you." He kept his eyes on the rain-smeared glass. "My arrival, however, was by birth, much preferred to the months on deck over the Atlantic. My parents were immigrants, the same as those that dock practically every week in our harbor."

Alfred let his attention roll back out to the storm as another thunderclap threatened the island with more rain. In the heavy shadows, he strained to recognize landmarks or houses for a sense of their location but all were lost in the haze of the rain.

"You arrived at the start of our worst weather," the man commented to the window. "It will be sweltering afternoons and humid rain until autumn."

A thick splash rang against the door as another carriage drove closely by, slowing their own buggy.

"So I keep being told."

The carriage came to a halt, and Alfred caught himself on the door as Mr. Runge fell back against the wall.

"What the devil?"

Mr. Runge leaned over and looked out the window just as the door swung open. A slender man jumped onto the bottom rung of the short ladder and rocked the buggy toward him as he stepped into the carriage, rain trailing after him. Alfred reached out into the rain and pulled the door shut.

"A mighty big storm," the man exclaimed as he sat himself down next to Alfred. "You'd think these weathermen could get it right for once." Alfred knew the voice before the man's face appeared in what little light remained in the cabin, but it did little to squelch his disappointment at John's smirk as he smoothed his hair back. "Ah, Alfred. What a pity that bureau of yours missed another mark. Said it would be light showers today, didn't you?"

The door to the buggy lurched open, letting in the roar of the rain and another rush of muggy air scented with dirt and horse hair. The driver climbed onto the bottom rung and stuck his head into the cabin. Water dripped from the brim of his hat onto the floor with loud thuds, splashing onto Alfred's shoes.

"What is going on here?"

"No worries, cabbie," John replied. "Just needed a quick ride. My heading's the same as this fare's." He gestured to Alfred with a tilt of his head as he wiped water from his sleeves and onto the floor.

"John, this isn't my carriage."

"Do you know this man?" Mr. Runge demanded.

Alfred sighed with resignation as he shot John a sharp glance. "We board together. I had no idea he would be joining us."

"At least not in this manner," Mr. Runge remarked as he watched John slick his pant legs of water, adding to the puddle that had pooled at their feet. "I'm apt to believe you."

"Shall I get him out, sir?"

The driver's voice was gruff, and Alfred believed the man capable of anything he offered to do to John. For a brief second, he hoped Mr. Runge would be sufficiently insulted and take the cabbie up on his offer, if only for the amusement of seeing John thrown back into the rain.

"No, that's quite alright, Bert. But let's take these two straight home before Johanna minds my being late."

The door slammed shut as the handle locked into place. The buggy rocked as the driver settled in, and they began their way south once more.

"Your name, sir?" Mr. Runge was calm as he watched John's attempts to dry his suit at the expense of their shoes.

"John Briggs."

His casual tone struck Alfred sharply, and he turned to see more of John's appearance. His face was flushed, as if he had been running, which was quite possible given the weather, but his shirt hung oddly at his neck, the buttons misaligned. He smelled heavily of lavender oil.

"Pleased to make your acquaintance, Mr. Briggs." Mr. Runge's words carried flatly. "In desperate need of a cab, were you?"

"You know how it goes," he replied, finally settling onto the seat and looking across the carriage. "Caught in the storm with no rides on this side of Broadway."

"It appears you managed to find a free ride in the end."

John nodded at the sentiment with obvious misunderstanding, and the cab grew silent. The air between the men was hefty with sweat and rain and stuck at Alfred's lips as he breathed. By the time the carriage slowed at the corner of 14th Street, his muscles were stiff from the rocking and the tension of the company. Luckily, he found the rain had lightened for the first time in hours, making his stomach loosen at the thought of walking half a block to the boardinghouse. John leaned forward to look out the window toward the boardinghouse. He scoffed as he reached across Alfred and unlatched the door.

"Some sort of cabbie that doesn't open the door for you." The steady noise of rain seeped into the coach as he opened the door and started to descend onto the flooded street. John glanced back as he stepped off the ladder. "I wouldn't tip him if I were you."

With that, the door blew shut and John's figure jogged down the street in small splashes at his feet. Alfred let out a sigh as he looked to Mr. Runge.

"I sincerely apologize."

The man lifted his chin with a deep breath.

"I wouldn't make it a habit of apologizing for that man. You might very well be apologizing for more than you can afford."

"One would imagine a man studying medicine would be capable of a little more decorum." Alfred hoisted his wet bag over his shoulder. "Thank you for the coach nonetheless."

The warm air met his face as he stepped out onto the first rung and splashed down to the street. The water was surprisingly cool on his ankles, but a ripple of thunder from the east end of the island reminded him that the storm was far from over. He turned to look up into the cabin where Mr. Runge had leaned out.

"I would appreciate it if you would let me pay for your kindness, Mr. Runge."

"Nonsense. In this weather, the city should provide carriages for free if they can't provision streets that do not flood!"

"Or think to nail down the sidewalks?"

The man laughed before staring down the street after John. "I would watch that man closely, Mr. Ridgeway," he said with a scowl. "I've seen that look of desperation before."

"Desperation?"

"He wasn't running toward us. Rather, I think he was running away from something and my coach happened to be the quickest escape."

Alfred stole a glance behind him where John's figure had dwindled in the distance. "And given that he came from the opposite direction of the college," Mr. Runge continued, "I would presume it had little to do with his studies."

He gave a small nod as he pulled to door shut, and the driver gave a whip of the reins. The horse began her steady gait for a final time, steering the buggy through the sloshing water up to 13th Street before turning north back toward Market Street.

The rain pounded the earth around Alfred in a steady tropical beat that reminded him of summers in the prairie where the oak leaves played like drums, the wheat stalks like violins in the afternoon storms. Alfred made his way through the gray pall of the island rain to the covered steps of the boardinghouse, his pant legs dripping on the porch and his mind replaying the man's words to the sound of the rain.

CHAPTER FOURTEEN

*A*lfred hadn't seen Mathias since Saturday afternoon, when the man had been on his way to a nickelodeon. He had managed to keep himself absent during the subsequent dinners, leaving the evening meal to Alfred, a good-natured Mrs. Poplar, and a somewhat composed and slightly less-ruddy-cheeked John.

"Another plate of roast, Mr. Ridgeway?"

"No, thank you, Mrs. Poplar. I've had my fill." She acquiesced with a nod and settled for retrieving herself a roll from the basket. "How was your study group, Mr. Briggs?"

Alfred looked up from his plate and stared at John, who spoke without missing a beat.

"Quite enlightening."

Rain beat softly against the window behind Mathias's empty seat and made the meal seem all the more intimate. Alfred continued to stare.

"Study group?"

John lifted his eyes from the evening edition of the gazette. A moment passed without comment, and his eyes fall back to the newspaper.

"John was meeting with a few others to discuss cases," Mrs. Poplar explained. "Cholera was the topic, I believe."

"Indeed, it was." He folded the paper and unfurled it again in his hands to move to the next page of articles.

"I didn't take you for the sort to study with others," Alfred commented.

John's eyes flitted over the paper once more, and he loosened his jaw to show a relaxed smile.

"It's not a study group per say. I simplified its function for Mrs. Poplar's sake." She gave a polite smile that Alfred knew was unsentimental. He kept his eyes on John as the man spoke. "A few of us from the hospital met to discuss two case studies, cholera patients that the good Dr. Barton treated in Africa earlier this year. We have clinical meetings once or twice a week. It's nothing new."

Thunder rolled in the distance, closer to the mainland than it had been earlier in the evening. Alfred wiped at his mouth with his napkin.

"I had no idea clinical meetings were held outside of the hospital."

John's eyes darted to their proprietor as he lowered the newspaper again. The corner of his mouth moved upward with a chuckle.

"How's that?"

A noise came from the front of the house, ushering in the sounds of the night as the front door opened to the rain. The thud of footfalls followed the door closing, and a rugged-looking and slightly damp Mathias appeared at the entrance to the room.

"Beg my tardiness, Mrs. Poplar. I'm afraid I was caught by the rain and forced to keep my own company in town for the evening."

"Of course, dear. You were able to find a coach?"

"Yes, thankfully."

She began to stand with a small grimace. "Have you eaten?"

"All's well." He held up a hand to stop her. "Please, I didn't mean to intrude on the dinner."

"No harm done," she replied, making her way to the kitchen.

"Indeed, we were just finishing up," John added, setting the newspaper aside.

He kept his eyes on Alfred as he stood, and the two men let Mrs. Poplar carry the conversation into the kitchen, appealing to Mathias to take a roll to his room, before they broke the tension. John excused himself without further conversation as Mathias rejoined the dining room with two rolls and a slice of chocolate cake on a small plate. He glanced down the hall at John's form as he disappeared up the stairs.

"Entertaining dinner?"

"The same as always."

He took a bite of his roll with a nod and made toward the front of the house. Alfred turned after him. "May I speak with you for a moment?"

Mathias nodded as he chewed on the roll and lifted the plate of cake between them.

"Let me see to a few things and I'll join you in the parlor. John looks to be in for the night, so we should have it all to ourselves."

"Of course," Alfred said with a casual wave. "I've a mind to get myself a piece as well."

"Ten minutes," Mathias called out through a mouthful of masticated bread as he left the room.

Alfred gathered his plate and the bowl of green beans and carried them into the kitchen. Mrs. Poplar was busily cutting pieces of roast from the leftovers of their dinner. He set the plate and bowl on the counter nearest the door and watched her at work. She hummed quietly to herself, something familiar that he couldn't quite place. She turned to set some utensils in the sink and caught sight of him by the doorway.

"Oh, no need to help, dear. I'll see to the table after I finish cutting away the spare meat for breakfast."

"It's no trouble."

"And that's why I don't mind seeing to it myself," she retorted.

He watched her hands navigate the knife expertly, slipping the blade through the meat with minimal effort. He wondered how many meals she had cooked for boarders like him who always abided by her preference and left her to clean up their meals. She glanced up at him with down-turned lips.

"Unless there's something else?"

His eyes met hers, and a moment passed between them, timed by the steady beat of rain on the backdoor.

"John wasn't meeting with colleagues this evening."

She nodded with a tight smile that pushed up her cheeks. Her eyes returned to the meat as her fingers resumed their work. "I know."

His eyes watched her. "You do?"

She let out a gentle sigh as she cut the last strip of roast into a manageable size before wiping at her hands with a tea towel.

"I find it troublesome to gossip about my boarders. The less I know about them, the easier it is for me to avoid such situations. However, Mr. Briggs has never been the most honest of men. It didn't take me long to see that he keeps a different sort of life than I would have a young bachelor lead in my house."

"Then why don't you say something?"

She shrugged and pulled a small plate from the cupboard. "He doesn't bring it into my house, which is all I have any right to ask of him. What he does with his life out there is none of my business." She tilted her head down, peering at him over her glasses. "It's none of our business as it is."

He bit his lower lip and gave a nod.

"But that doesn't change the fact that he is the least trustworthy of my boarders," she continued. "And I can't see a change in boarders moving him any higher in my esteem either." She slid a piece of chocolate cake onto the plate and handed it to Alfred with a dessert fork and a smile. "Don't fret about the decisions of others, dear. You keep to your own choices. It'll all work out. You'll see."

He gave a tired nod, and her eyes brightened as she laid a gentle hand on his cheek before turning back to the roast. He turned to go but paused in the doorway, seeing that they were now the only two on the first floor.

"How did you know?"

"What's that, dear?"

"About John. How did you know he wasn't telling the truth?"

She continued to work the meat until it was packed tightly in a pot, her bun and the tie of her apron bobbing with her movements. Alfred hovered in the doorway, thinking she had decided to leave the question alone until she turned and held a pained expression. She rubbed at her chest in front of her shoulder.

"My husband told me many things about the business of being a doctor, and when he was alive, his schedule was the only one I tended to. It was much easier then, with only one man to feed. And they may have changed many things since his death, but clinical case studies are not one of them." Her arm dropped as she took on a serious face. "And they have never been held on Monday nights."

———•••———

Despite the rain trapping the warmth of the June evening, Mrs. Poplar had lit a small fire in the parlor with the excuse that men with wet pants and soaked shoes were likely to catch cold, even in the summer. While Alfred had changed clothes and dried his hair with a rub of his towel, his feet had never sufficiently warmed outside of their shoes. Given the weather, Mrs. Poplar had made an exception to the dress rules for dinner and informed the men that slippers would be acceptable if they did not have something more suitable. John, of course, had had a spare set of dress shoes to accompany his fresh shirt and trousers; Alfred had set his only pair by the heel over the stoker to dry them before morning. He sat in front of the now smoldering coals, his feet on top of the rug and his pants rolled up to the knee, his sleeves up to the elbow, and his collar open, a half-eaten piece of cake in a plate on his lap.

The rain had softened to a subtle tap at the front window of the parlor when Mathias came down the stairs. He had removed his tie and opened his collar to reveal a smooth neckline. He fell into the other armchair with a grunt and looked at the fireplace with a questioning glance.

"A fire in June? I'm starting to worry about our dear Mrs. Poplar."

"She insisted," Alfred replied.

"It's is a little extreme, even for worrying minds like hers. It was practically ninety degrees today."

"That's why I let it die. I'll need another shower after sitting here for ten minutes."

Mathias fanned his collar. "Did you and John go out together?"

"No, but we arrived home together."

"Coincidence?"

"Hijacked carriage." Mathias narrowed his eyes, and Alfred waved off his expression. "It's a long story. Look, I have a question and a favor to ask."

"Are they the same thing?"

"Are a question and a favor the same thing?"

"Is the question the favor, or are you really asking me two separate things: a question and a favor?"

His smile revealed a hint of entertainment at the attempted repartee, and Alfred returned it with a grin of his own. His head was beginning to ache, and he feared he wasn't on par with his housemate's witticisms.

"Both."

"Go on with it then," Mathias mused.

Alfred took the last bite of cake and set the plate down on the round, wooden table between them. He wiped at a piece of rogue chocolate that stuck to his bottom lip.

"Do you know the Garten Verein?"

"The German club?"

"It's a German club?"

Mathias stretched out in the chair so that his feet rested on his heels and the soles faced the glowing embers. "I've heard anyone can petition for membership, but it started as a social club for German immigrants."

"What about their ball?"

"The Sommerset?"

"Have you been?"

Mathias scoffed and grinned at the dying fire. "I'm not really the sort to get an invite to European-inspired evenings."

"That's the issue." Mathias shot his eyes at Alfred as he continued. "It's by invitation only."

"As most dances are." Mathias sat upright and leaned onto the arm of the chair. "Why would you want to attend The Sommerset anyhow?"

"I might have implied in conversation that I would be attending, and I would prefer to keep to my word."

"Who is she?"

Alfred tilted his head. "Is there a way to get an invitation or not?"

Mathias pursed his lips and let his eyes drift to the empty plate between them.

"I might be able to assist you, but you should know what you're getting yourself into. One, invitationals are a mix of culture and status, neither of which you've quite gotten down yet when it comes to Galveston." Alfred's nod was small but weighed heavily on his mind. "Two," Mathias continued, "whomever you are chasing might seem like fair game now, but that won't be the case if she's a lineage that keeps a membership at the Garten Verein. You and I might be good-hearted men who strive to keep to our word, but that isn't worth much in the courting game. And, unfortunately, that doesn't do very well for us in this city. Not to mention our lack of German heritage."

"I'm not after money, Mathias."

"Neither am I, but that doesn't change others' opinions of my having less of it. People make their opinion of you by how you talk, how you dress, and how you pay. This city was built on enterprise, and neither of us is in the market to capitalize on that."

"Meaning?"

"Neither of us will get rich doing what we do."

Alfred gave him a sharp look. "Can you get me in or not?"

"Yes, but you'll need to get a member to sponsor your application." Mathias leaned back in his chair, his voice softening to match the hum of the rain. "It'll take a little work. But there is something you can do to get the wheels moving."

"Anything."

"Buy our first bargaining piece." He swung his gaze back across the table between them. "It won't be cheap."

"What is it?"

"A bottle of the finest whiskey you can get on the island."

"I'm bribing a sponsor with whiskey?"

Mathias stood and stretched his arms skyward with a groan. When they settled back by his sides, his shirt had pulled loose of his pants and hung awkwardly at his waist. He gave Alfred a grin.

"No, I am."

CHAPTER FIFTEEN

*M*ud sucked at the soles of his shoes as Alfred stepped out of the carriage and onto the desolate street. The rain had continued into the early hours of the morning and left puddles of soiled water and a thick sludge of mud and sticks on the avenues. The carriage wheels had carved gummy trails in the road's surface, the horse's hooves smacking like taffy with each step. When he reached the hazy business district, the only anticipation of returning life was the orange orbs of the gas lamps along the street. The hollow thwap of hooves faded into the mist until the click of the door lock was the only sound in the pre-dawn of 23rd Street.

The gray outline of the bicycle rested against the side of the stairwell where he had left it the day before, and he let out a breath as he settled the frame in the crook of his elbow and began to climb the stairs to the fifth floor. Each step creaked with the weight, sounding ominous in the heavier shadows of the morning. Alfred had grown familiar to entering the building alone in the dark, but the mysticism of the city in the early hours after a storm unsettled his mind.

When he reached the fifth floor, the door to the office was open and a single strand of light lit the floorboards of the hall in a faint glow. A single gas lamp in the center of the room flickered, its flame swaying in the hurricane glass. He checked the wick; it had a full reservoir of oil, likely a remnant of a late night by one of the other two men.

He shed his jacket onto his chair and let his skin breathe in the cooler air. The day would soon begin, the sun burning up the haze until only a slight distortion remained on the horizon. So near to the ocean, the island was prone to an overly moist climate, one that Alfred had underestimated. The days following such heavy storms, Joseph had kindly pointed out, tended to be the most oppressive. He tugged at his collar and let his thoughts drift back to his need for fresh clothes, at least a thin suit for warmer days and a true gentleman's dress for the dance.

If he could get an invitation.

His fingers found only bare wood when he reached for the logbook. They instinctively ran along the bookshelf until they reached the back wall, nothing blocking their path. As he took a step back to search the titles on the shelf, the door opened behind him with a complaining creak. He whirled around, catching the edge of the table with his hand and sending fluttering shadows around the room. He cursed and flung his hands wildly to shake off the pain. His eyes strained to focus for a moment before he recognized the slender, upright figure of Dr. Cline.

"No need to worry," his superior assured him as he shut the door behind him. "It's just me."

Alfred let out a long breath. "Yes, good morning, sir."

Dr. Cline made his way across the room and set the logbook on the table between them.

"I hope the lamp gave you sufficient notice that I had come in early." Alfred nodded, embarrassed by his surprise at the man's entry and the tingling sensation in his hand. "I struggled to sleep last night with the storm so raucous as it was. I thought my time better served taking early readings as the storm passed."

"Oh, had I known you preferred intermittent readings during stormy weather, I would have arrived earlier."

Dr. Cline waved off his comment. "It wasn't a bother. I simply thought it more interesting to see the changes myself than sending a post for you to come in at an earlier hour."

"Shall I take the six o'clock readings?"

"Already done." He tapped the logbook with a pencil. "I thought you and I could use the spare time to discuss your work."

"My work?"

"Your research. What you would like to pursue with your time here."

Alfred's stomach grew heavy as he watched him return to his desk. He had been so involved in his day-to-day duties that he hadn't taken the time to consider what else he could contribute on his own. He felt somewhat ashamed at having missed the mark on Dr. Cline's expectations, despite the man having blocked his previous attempts at getting started, and pocketed his hands.

"To be frank, I haven't given it much more thought since our last conversation."

"I hadn't assumed you would," he replied, sorting through papers on his desk. "I was hoping you would be more distracted with things beyond the office. Ah, here it is."

He pulled a handwritten manuscript from the pile and tapped the edges of the pages against the desk to straighten them into a clean stack. He turned and held them out to Alfred.

"This is a revised manuscript that I wrote three years ago. It includes new data and a few more assertions regarding oceanic storms. It has been accepted for review by the Weather Bureau as an official publication, but I am waiting for approval."

Alfred read the cover page. "Oceanic Winds and Their Relationship to Storm Formation."

"You see why I wanted you to wait?" He lifted a single eyebrow. "It's not a matter of pride, I assure you. I am more than pleased to have someone working with me who shares the same interests and passions, but I take my work very seriously. If it is not done well, it should not be done at all."

He crossed his arms and leaned back so that he sat on the edge of his desk.

"You have a lot of potential, Alfred, but no amount of intelligence can substitute for the experiences that come with this sort of post. It will come with time. However, in the meantime I need you to understand that, if I hesitate or ask you to step down from your ambitions, it is only out of guidance."

The room was silent but for the distant sound of carriages pulling at the street below. He tilted his head.

"Are we on the same page?"

Alfred let his breath pass in and out of his lungs before he answered, feeling both buoyed and anchored by the man's reasoning.

"I believe so."

"Good. Then let's start with this, shall we?" He gestured at the manuscript in Alfred's hands. "I am interested to hear what you think of it. And if you have any suggestions."

"Shall I begin reading it today?"

"I should think immediately, at least before Joseph arrives. The only good silence we have is when he is asleep."

Dr. Cline grinned as he turned back to his table.

———•◦•———

It was half past ten when Joseph arrived at the office, a fresh shave on his face. The day's warmth had already crept onto the island, leaving a smoky scene along Market Street as cart vendors sold fresh breads and ointments and children made mud patties that they stacked along the raised sidewalks beneath the storefronts. Alfred was looking down onto the street when Joseph dropped a telegram on the table next to him.

"You had a note at the post office," Joseph commented as he sorted through the telegrams and letters. "A local delivery."

The envelope was simple, made of crisp cream paper, with two lines of scrollwork, bearing only his and the bureau's names. He flipped it over. It had no sender or address written anywhere on the envelope.

"Captain Montaigne is requesting a forecast for the end of the week," Joseph announced as he read a telegram aloud. "He's putting out tomorrow for Mexico City."

Dr. Cline glanced up over his bifocals. "It'll likely be rough seas. There's a patch of winds coming through the gulf this week."

"I'll tell him to keep to the coast," Joseph replied, jotting a note on the telegram.

Alfred's thumb popped the envelope flap to reveal an appointment card. He slid it out with care and held it up to the sunlight.

"Any news from the D.C. office?" Dr. Cline asked.

Joseph finished sorting the telegrams and held one in the air.

"Just one."

Dr. Cline's shoes clicked on the wooden floorboards as he crossed the office. Joseph kept his interest in the pile of telegrams as his brother took the envelope, the sound of Dr. Cline ripping the envelope echoing as all three men read their messages.

Alfred turned the appointment card over and back again. The card was embossed in forest green ink with a single line: Mr. Daniel Jeffries, Tailor. A time was scribbled in the middle of the card, nothing more. He flipped the card over once more before looking up in confusion. Joseph had sorted the telegrams into their usual piles, one for local farmers inquiring about the land's weather, one for ship merchants and captains asking about oceanic forecasts, and a final one for odds and ends, inquiries and messages of various topics dealing with their daily work; he busied himself with a response to Captain Montaigne. Dr. Cline had returned to his desk, his form bent over the telegram as the office was filled with the scratches of men furiously writing with their chosen instruments.

Alfred checked his pocket watch as he neared Dr. Cline's desk. The man's head moved back and forth as he compared information from the telegram with an old map spread across his desk.

"Sir, it appears I have an appointment at eleven o'clock."

"You forgot it?"

"Not quite, sir." He lifted his gaze, his thin eyebrows furrowed as his assistant continued. "But I am concerned I might be a bit delayed. Should I reschedule?"

Dr. Cline shook his head as he returned to the map.

"Not necessary. We're on schedule for today's work. But please take the map sketch with you. I need it printed by the morning."

Alfred swung his coat over his shoulder but left his shoulder bag on his desk. Whatever the day had in store, he was certain the less he was carrying with him, the better it would be. He scooped the map under his arm and made his way downstairs.

The day was well underway on the street level, where the mud had begun to dry in cracked angles and flake into pieces as horses pounded against the ground in their steady gaits. Alfred breathed in the steamy scent of coal and sweat and let out a small cough to clear his throat. Heavy after the storm, the air was a blanket on the city, keeping the odors and by-products of the wharves pressed tightly between the walls of the streets. He rubbed at his nose as he walked down the sidewalk toward Postoffice Street.

The door gave a quiet jingle as Alfred stepped into the printing shop. Buttons was bent over the large table behind the clerk's desk with a magnifying glass pressed against his orbital socket. Alfred waited a moment, and when the man didn't look up, he tapped the bell on the front desk. The older man jumped at the sharp metallic ring and gave him a stern look. His magnifying glass fell onto the table and he shuffled over to the desk, setting a hand on the bell to quiet the noise as his other hand slid his oversized glasses onto his face.

"Yes?"

"This is for the Weather Bureau."

"Hm." Buttons unrolled the map and looked it over. "Which size?"

"Pardon?"

Buttons looked up at him with his magnified pupils.

"Which size paper?"

"I, uh—standard," he fumbled, "map size?" Buttons didn't move, and the silence between them let Alfred's ears sort out the sounds of someone setting type in a machine in the back. "What size does the bureau normally print?"

"Thirty-six by forty-eight."

"Let's go with that then."

Buttons nodded and made a note at the top corner of the map.

"Paper type?"

Alfred glanced about the clerk's station helplessly, seeing the man's pencil poised over the map as he awaited the next note.

"I don't suppose there's a standard map paper?" Buttons met him with sympathetic eyes and shook his head. Alfred let out a loud breath. "What does Dr. Cline usually prefer?"

"Thick cotton blend."

"Alright, use that then."

He scribbled an abbreviation below the paper size in both corners. "Ink colors?"

"Whatever Dr. Cline prefers."

"Black and red?"

"Sure."

He had no idea what he had just agreed to, but he had no grounds to think any differently about what was needed. Caught in the moment, he couldn't recall the map he looked at nearly every day. If this one came out wrong, he'd either have it out with Buttons or be taken off map duty, and either sounded more pleasant than the knots twisting his stomach in that moment.

"They should be ready by four o'clock."

Alfred turned to go and stopped at the doorway, turning back toward Buttons, who was rolling the map gingerly.

"You didn't ask Dr. Cline these questions when he brought me in last week."

"I knew what he wanted."

Alfred took a step back into the shop with a small laugh.

"You do realize, of course, that these maps are being printed on his behalf."

The clerk nodded as he shuffled back to his table. He removed his glasses, lifted his magnifying glass back to his eye socket, and returned to his task without another word.

———•●•———

The tailor shop was in the center of the most expensive street in Galveston. Formally known as Avenue B, the Strand found its identity in elaborate facades of red brick and washed stone while exaggerated windows exuded the colors and scents of exotic lifestyles. This exuberance was magnified by the district's proximity to the wharves, the wood-on-wood moan of docking ships mingling with the wood-on-brass jingle of shop doors. Housed in the lower level of a red brick building just east of 21st Street, the shop had a simple sign that hung above the door with a flourishing scroll: Hand Tailor.

A small bell rang overhead as Alfred entered the shop to the smell of lemon oil. He looked about the shop as he made his way past cloth mannequins of partial torsos. Hats filled the front window and a table was pushed against a wall with deep sapphire silk rolled atop it; a straight edge sat with a chalk line slightly askew along the material. A set of mirrors stood in front of the opposite wall with a covered crate on the floor between them.

The shop, otherwise, was empty.

"Hello?"

A muffled voice came in reply from the back of the shop, beyond a closed door. Alfred waited a beat before calling out again, this time moving closer to the door. The voice came louder but still distant.

"Come in."

He was paused at the back door, his hand over the doorknob, when it opened outward and caught his shoulder. He stumbled backward, bumping into a partially covered mannequin. It wobbled on its wooden legs as he, too, searched for his balance. He caught it with his arm as Mr. Jeffries came around the door with a roll of emerald silk beneath his arm and an open mouth below his stern nose.

"Alright there?"

Alfred nodded as he checked first the mannequin and then himself to smooth his shirt.

"I didn't expect you at the door," Mr. Jeffries commented as he walked the roll of silk to the table.

"You said come in."

"I meant into the shop."

Mr. Jeffries turned, one hand in his pocket and the other against his chest, and looked Alfred up and down. Alfred cleared his throat as pulled the appointment card from his pocket.

"I received this appointment card in the post today. I think there's been a mistake."

"No mistake," Mr. Jeffries replied, checking his pocket watch. "You're right on time."

"But I didn't make an appointment with you."

Mr. Jeffries ignored the cream-colored card in Alfred's hand and walked to the back wall of the shop. He eyed a set of sewing tapes that hung on tacks and took down the longest of the three.

"I know you didn't, but Mrs. Poplar did."

"Mrs. Poplar?"

Mr. Jeffries gestured for him to stand on the covered crate between the mirrors and asked him to remove his jacket. Alfred did as he was asked, using the wall to keep his balance. The tailor began measuring his limbs, holding Alfred's arms out to his side and tucking the start of the tape beneath his client's armpits.

"Mr. Jeffries, at the risk of insulting your abilities, I feel there has been an error on your part. I assure you Mrs. Poplar and I have not discussed my having clothes tailored."

The tailor squatted at Alfred's knees, the hem of his suit jacket brushing the shop floor. He marked the measurement on the tape and stood to mark the number in a small notepad that he pulled from his jacket pocket.

"She expected you would say as much."

"Pardon?"

"We came to an arrangement before I had my assistant post your appointment card this morning." Alfred's lips pressed together, and Mr.

Jeffries looked up with a raised eyebrow. "She was very specific."

Alfred sighed at himself in the mirror. "I'm sure she was."

The tailor measured the girth of Alfred's thighs and then fingered his trousers at the knee and the ankle, getting a sense for how they fell on his leg. Alfred let his lips loosen as he spoke.

"She is a tenacious woman."

"Indeed. I assume that's the reason Dr. Poplar married her."

He looked down his body at the thick, gray curls atop the man's head. "You had the pleasure of knowing her late husband?"

"I did. I personally tailored his suits for thirteen years. Straighten up, please."

Mr. Jeffries's measurements were polite but precise. He stretched his measuring tape along Alfred's arms, along his side, and around his chest. The bell over the door rang as a pudgy man stepped into the shop. His young face was aged slightly by dark shades beneath his eyes. He flashed a warm smile at Alfred as he passed with three rolls of material in his arms.

"Did it arrive?" Mr. Jeffries asked without looking up.

"Yes, sir. All three."

"Just in time. We've had several orders the past few weeks for dark silks this season."

"Special orders for the Sommerset," his assistant explained.

"Anything at the Garten Verein becomes the fashion," Mr. Jeffries added. "Outside of debut season, it's the closest to goose season. The women flutter in like birds, excited and cackling. It turns their husbands into geese."

Alfred thought on it for a moment. "Why geese?"

"After they pay, their husbands are honking as they leave the shop," the chubby assistant said with a laugh.

Mr. Jeffries wrapped Alfred's torso in the tape as he made introductions.

"This is my assistant, Edwin MacIntosh."

The man gave another bright smile, and Alfred returned it with a quick wave of his hand, careful not to lower his arms.

"Fresh off the boat yourself, are you?"

"No, the train," Alfred answered.

"A mainlander? Whereabouts?'

Alfred found the man's energy somewhat exhausting, but he noted a friendliness that he admired.

"Indian Territory."

The man nodded as he unrolled a deep graphite material over the sapphire silk and began measuring it with the straight edge. Alfred was relieved at his lack of a reaction and turned his attention back to Mr. Jeffries, who was exacting a measurement of his chest. The burning in his shoulders was intensifying.

"Your arrangement," Alfred started, "with Mrs. Poplar?" The tailor's attention was very much in his notes, but Alfred continued in a voice just above a whisper. "You said she was specific."

"She is rarely anything else."

"Might I ask what she has already paid to have made?"

Mr. Jeffries turned his head a measure to keep from shouting into Alfred's face. "Edwin?" The man looked up from the table. "Will you pull Mrs. Poplar's ticket, please?"

The assistant moved through the shop on quick but short, stalky legs and returned with a handwritten ticket. Mr. Jeffries read the items without emotion.

"Three summer cotton-blend shirts, two day-trousers, two day-jackets, a full set of tails, two ties, and a hat."

"You can let your arms down," Mr. Jeffries replied as he measured Alfred's neck. "You can choose the hat of your liking. She already chose the rest for you. However, you'll need to see Maneshewitz's on 24th Street for your shoes." Mr. Jeffries finished his final measurement of Alfred's back and buttocks. "You may step down. For the two suits, is one black and one gray satisfactory?"

Alfred nodded, his voice lost in the thought of having clothing tailored to his measurements. It was something he'd thought only for the upper class, and somehow that expectation made the situation all the more embarrassing. He wasn't paying for his own first tailor fitting; Mrs. Poplar had taken the liberty of doing so. He rotated his shoulder to loosen the muscles, wondering if a gesture of thanks was in order.

The shopkeeper made his way to the back of the shop without another word, leaving Alfred to the sounds of Edwin measuring vibrant shades of silk. He compared his own dress with the man and found himself lacking more than he had expected. Where the assistant's hems were crisp, Alfred's were rough and dull. Despite having a larger frame, Edwin fit into his suit well, the vest cinching just right at the back to keep him contained where it worked best. Alfred was fidgeting with his loose tie when Mr. Jeffries returned, a fresh cigar in his hand.

"Take your pick," he instructed as he gestured to the hats on the shelf in front of the window.

"Any of them?"

The tailor nodded and returned to the table to evaluate the chalk outlines on the sapphire silk. A silk top hat in the center of the shelf caught Alfred's attention. He ran a finger along its smooth edge and imagined himself removing it as he helped Florence into a carriage in the same way he had seen other men do for women after the service on Sunday. He bunched the corner of his mouth, slipping out of the image the hat brought to mind, and let his hand drift across the edge of the shelves as he looked over the selection.

His eyes wandered from his hand and up to the top shelf where a smaller but striking hat of black matte silk sat askew on the crown of a mannequin head. He pulled it down and felt it between his fingers, a smooth cloth that gave a slight shimmer without boasting its presence. He glanced at the two men, both lost in quiet conversation over the material, before resting the top hat on his head. He stepped closer to the mirror until he caught his reflection. It was a wealthy man's headpiece, something Mr. Jeffries had likely designed with the likes of Mr. Runge in mind. He imagined the businessman tipping the hat at passing couples as he stepped into the Tremont House, the streets abuzz behind him.

His face gave away his discomfort, something akin to disappointment in his gaze as he took in his own reflection. He massaged the brim a moment more before reaching up to remove it. He wasn't good enough for that sort of dress. Florence would see right through it.

"It looks good on you."

Edwin hoisted a large roll of material into the crook of his arm, a smile fattening his face. Alfred glanced back at the mirror with a crooked grin, leaving the hat in place.

"Do you think so?"

"I do. You wear that new tie and the ladies'll be smitten with you at the Sommerset."

Alfred let the hat rest on his head a few moments longer, imagining himself beneath it as he entered the Garten Verein. Despite having no idea what the dance would require, what the ladies would wear, or even how he would manage to get himself invited to the event in the first place, he liked the imagery. And he liked the hat.

Mr. Jeffries boxed it up for him and gave him another card with a time to pick up his clothes. Alfred awkwardly held the box with his free arm as he pocketed the card and made his way to the door.

"Brazilian chocolates," Mr. Jeffries called out. Alfred looked back at him with a furrowed brow, his hand on the doorknob. Mr. Jeffries gave him a knowing smirk. "A treat for Mrs. Poplar. You can procure a box at Tentman's on 24th and Postoffice. She prefers the cream-filled sort."

CHAPTER SIXTEEN

*T*he rhythmic creak and chirp of insects held their symphony as an easterly breeze played the cordgrass and sang the bay to sleep. Overhead a full moon was rising as twilight twinkled above the water, the last colors of the day bleeding into night. The evening was cool on the water, and Alfred had found their row out onto the bay pleasant, with only the swoosh of the oars on the water's surface and the occasional seagull call at his ears. He hadn't been aware of what a din the city composed each day—the clapping of hooves, the rolling of wooden wheels, the roar of steamships putting into port as dockworkers called out to their seaward mates. It was the ever-present murmur of voices as life came and went along the streets below the bureau's windows. In the stern of the row boat, however, his ears took their freedom and found the creak of the wood as the boat rocked with the weight and the shushing of buffalo grass as the first of the night's breezes ruffled their stalks after skimming the water.

"This is far enough," Hilary instructed.

Alfred held the oars in the water to slow the boat before pulling them up and through the oar locks. Their wake kept its momentum and washed against the stern, rocking them unevenly as Hilary began to unpack his daypack. Alfred glanced back at the shore to see the faint haze of the city's electric glow; it was centered on land and left a large swath of black on both sides of the island. As his eyes drifted closer, he could make out the silver lining of the bank in the moonlight but little else. He slapped at a mosquito that buzzed around his ear.

"What do they sound like, the pelicans?"

"*Pelecanus occidentalis* does not have a call." He handed Alfred the binoculars. "Juveniles have distinct, high-pitched chirps, but they stop calling after eight or nine months."

"They make no noise at all?"

Hilary paused and looked out over the water in thought.

"They do clap their beaks when threatened. I had a male snap at me when I tried to steal a look at his nest, but it wasn't a vocalization per say. More of a behavior."

"Odd." Hilary hummed in agreement as Alfred scanned the dark shore. "They nest along the shore?"

"And in trees. As large as they are, it's a wonder they find branches wide enough." He removed two copper mugs that shimmered in the moonlight. "I observed one last season while she roosted, the largest one I've ever seen. Big Petunia, I named her. Half her fluff hung over the boughs when she sat on her nest."

Alfred let out a laugh that echoed across the water.

"Big Petunia?"

"After my late wife," Hilary mused as he balanced a bottle of scotch between them. Both men chuckled as he revealed a sketchbook and leather pouch from the bag. Opening the leather pouch, he unrolled it across his lap where several pencils were loosened of their camp and spread out on the leather.

"How is it you expect to see any birds at that this time of night?"

"By moonlight."

Alfred's eyes drifted up to the orb that shone from a few feet above the horizon. Its trajectory had led it over the edge of the mainland, just below a string of stretched clouds.

"But your field guide noted that most birds don't fly at night," Alfred challenged.

"Ah, so you did read it!"

"I did."

Having selected his pencil, Hilary rolled up the leather wrap and sat it back in the daypack. "And?"

"I had no idea a landmass this small could have so many species living together."

"As far as islands go, Galveston is well-suited for the plethora of life that has made its nest here. Before we white men came along and made our triumphant albeit disastrous settlement, it was likely a roost for many more species than we see today."

Alfred's mind was drawn back to evening drinks at the Tremont House and Charles Bendrick's comments.

"That seems like it would be too many creatures." He waved away a mosquito that attempted to land on his nose.

"For the island?"

"For the resources."

Hilary picked up the bottle of scotch and removed the cork with a pop.

"Nature has a phenomenal way of balancing herself on a delicate string. She often survives quite well on her own until someone decides she needs a hand in the matter."

He filled the first copper mug and handed the bottle to Alfred.

"We couldn't have disturbed it that much."

"Oh, dear boy, you have no idea."

Alfred listened quietly as he filled his own cup and returned the bottle to the bottom of the boat. A splash sounded near the shore, followed by a squeal as a small animal fought its catch on land. When Hilary looked up to see his assistant's eyes trained on him, he continued with an energy that Alfred felt was more boisterous than the hour called for.

"We've built houses, buildings, and docks. We've dredged the channel to make way for larger ships to put in. We literally deepened the ocean floor to accommodate our own stocks because the island was insufficient. Rather than finding a suitable landscape for our needs, we altered a natural land to make way for enterprise and industrialization."

"Isn't that what a species does when it makes a place its habitat?"

"Man does not have a habitat, save his vulnerability to the water. He lives wherever he is. We are the only animal that can do that, and yet we choose to explore and exploit, taking what is not ours. We are never content with what we find just beyond our doorstep."

He considered Hilary's words as he took a sip of the scotch. It was warm and smooth as it traced his mouth, stinging as its tail flicked against his throat. "I read once it was man's destiny to explore and expand," he commented. "It was what our intelligence led us to do."

Hilary gaffed.

"Whatever colonial determinism you've been ingesting is better left on the floor."

"I wouldn't argue that it is determinism per say." Alfred gave the scotch another taste. "More an insistence that man shouldn't simply take what is given to him. We all have a responsibility to make what we can of ourselves."

"Too true," Hilary replied with a mark of sincerity. "However, making something of oneself should never invite the eradication of life, animal or otherwise."

"But animals move on. They migrate. Your field guide said so. It seems to me that where they come to roost after they've left us seems a very little matter in the grand scheme of things."

"Did you read the book in its entirety?" He shot Alfred a glancing, looking back to his supplies when the younger man nodded. "Then you read of the Roseate Spoonbill."

The boat rocked gently as a disturbance in the water left its mark on the surface. In the quiet of the bay, the man's voice was both gentle and forceful.

"It's what I call a spectator's bird, the sort that one-time watchers look for when they set out in linen suits with binoculars, thinking they'll catch a rare sighting just by looking up into the sky like any man can do. They're large, pensive birds that roost along the bay's shore with terribly ugly beaks, but what draws attention is their plumage. Lush, pink plumage that stands out along the water and makes them perfect game for the local sportsman."

He reached for the bottle and topped off his mug, his voice sliding into a relaxed tone.

"The Karankawa lived on this island well before we all arrived, and we must've looked a sorted lot to them. Spanish explorers shipwrecked and starving. Galveston was nothing more than a dismal sand bar back then, with only a handful of trees and two bayous for hunting. But it was all well-stocked for the taking, mind you. More oysters than they could carry, from what I've read, and plenty of shoreline for fishing. And enough spoonbills to turn the water pink." He rubbed a knee with his palm as if dissolving the image. "That's the difference between the natives and the so-called civilized man, you see. A native hunts only for what he needs. It's survival. But we indulge. We make a sport of it all."

He flicked an eye at Alfred with a raised eyebrow.

"Do you have a lady?"

Alfred leaned back at the question before shaking his head. Hilary looked out over the water of the silver-tinged bay as the cordgrass sashayed in the breeze.

"I think at first it was the thrill of the hunt, to shoot down so colorful a bird and have it stuffed upon the shelf. But somewhere it gave way to fashion. The first hat I saw was in a window on Market Street. It had a wide brim and was light emerald like the wings of a ruby-throated hummingbird when it rests just after sunrise. That subtle shimmer of gold catching your eye." He focused on the horizon, and Alfred didn't dare move for fear of rocking the boat and emptying his thoughts into the water. A mosquito buzzed about his ear mercilessly. "In the thick of the hat's dressing was a bouquet of plumage, and there in the center was a spoonbill's pink feather."

Crickets broke the silence that followed, and Hilary took in a sharp breath as he looked back to Alfred.

"That was in the eighties. I've no idea how long they were hunted before fashion put a price on their heads, but I know they are dying off.

There are many fewer nests than there were ten and fifteen years ago when I first started tracking them. And fewer adults as well. Now the water is occasionally dotted pink, like an afterthought of nature. And all for the sake of a pink feather in their caps."

Alfred let the silence sit around them as he finished his mug of scotch and watched a large beetle crawl across the oar locks. Its feet marched at odd angles as its body crested the metal ring and disappeared from the moonlight.

"Perhaps they moved on. Migrated."

"A good hypothesis." Hillary held out the bottle and Alfred offered him his mug. The bubble of the liquid sounded deceptively cold in the night, and he reminded his tongue to expect warmth rather than refreshment. "But an incorrect one. Roseate spoonbills migrate in the same way most birds do. They head south in the winter."

"And north in the summer."

"Precisely, and I count their numbers in the peak summer months, not the winter. Their migrations have been consistent, but their population has not. And if we can lead a bird as plentiful as the Roseate Spoonbill to near extinction merely for sport or fashion with single-handed guns, imagine what we could do with the largest steamships in the world."

"You make the island's expansion sound so vulgar." Hilary made a noise of agreement as he drank his scotch, and Alfred gave a chuckle. "Would you have us stop progress for the sake of the birds? I can imagine the campaign as you explain to ladies that what time they've had to pamper themselves by electric light was the whole of it and they're to return to applying rouge by gas light."

A hearty laugh escaped Hilary's throat as his hand came down on his knee in a slap. "My God, the carnage! It'd be worse than the war!"

The breeze carried their laughter into the night as the boat steadied. Alfred quieted his voice as the sounds of the bay returned.

"What are you criticizing then, if not the industrialization?"

"It's the exploitation that scratches at the keel. What premeditation is had is poor, weak. It's irresponsible. Our industrialization at times seems unsteady despite what the newspapers prefer to print, and all at the expense of our land for the good of the economy, as the men would say."

Alfred looked up from his mug.

"Men like the Deep Water Committee?"

Hilary gave a slow nod.

"It was barely four years ago that we deepened the channel, bringing in the largest of the steamships at the time. There hasn't been sufficient time for me to adequately study the impact on the birds by such a large project, but it is there nonetheless. I can see it. Now they propose to widen the channel and excavate land to build more wharves and more docks. To bring in more ships. To combine the two islands to the north into one. At some time or another we will run out of land and push our civilization out into the water."

Alfred mulled over Hilary's words as they watched the shimmer of the bay, the patchwork of constellations a thick backdrop to his thoughts. He recognized that he was but a speck in the light, a float of dust in the moon's eye, but the world still buzzed around him with humankind at the center. Glancing at the dipped corners of Hilary's mouth as he searched skyward for birds, he felt an appreciation of the man's devotion to what was more than a simple hobby. It was a fascination and a purpose. As Alfred rocked with the gentle rise and dips of the boat, he finally settled on why the advertisement had been for an inexperienced notetaker rather than a knowledgeable assistant. It had never been notes Hilary had been seeking. It was companionship.

Alfred shifted on the seat and set his mug at his feet, pulling up his binoculars.

"You never addressed my confusion over our spotting the pelican."

"Which one was that?"

"You wrote that birds do not fly at night."

Hilary squinted over the horizon of the bay as if watching something move in the distance. Alfred tried to follow his gaze but saw nothing but ripples in the water. He let his eyes roll upward as he took in the night sky, each star a hole through which a hidden light shined from somewhere beyond. They were countless, too many to even name.

"The Eastern Brown Pelican is a rare exception," Hilary explained. "It has been known to hunt at night where there is sufficient light."

The surface glistened like untamed ice as the moon continued to rise and spread its aura on the water.

"Such as a full moon," Alfred replied with a nod.

Hilary began sketching their surroundings, dragging long strokes for grasses and shooting quick, short bursts for the rough outline of the water's edge. The rhythm of the water lapping against their boat and the nearby shoreline was a soothing bass line as the scratching of the pencil joined the midsummer chorus of insects and grasses. As Alfred brought his binoculars up to his eyes to scan the distance, the boat rocked as Hilary's stabbed at the sky with a bony finger.

"There," he whispered, his word a raspy utterance laced with excitement.

Alfred looked up to see the outline of a black figure flapping once, twice, and then soaring on the breeze. It floated as if buoyed by the moonlight with massive wings spread to either side. In a snap, the smooth line it had drawn in the moon broke, and the bird jerked its body downward, its wings pulling in slightly as it barreled toward the earth. Alfred grabbed the edge of the boat in horror as it neared the water. The bird spun a degree or two before thrusting it wings backward as it jutted its neck forward and opened an exaggerated bill in anticipation of a catch. It disappeared in the water of the bay with a shattering splash. Alfred's breath caught in his throat, and both men leaned toward the water, eyes transfixed on the bird as it surfaced and floated on the water. A pouch beneath its beak was swollen to a bulbous size, and the bird threw its head back and up, clapping its beak open and closed as it swallowed a fish. It floated for a moment more before spreading its wings and launching skyward from the bay.

Alfred sat back onto the seat with a burst of noise that caught him off guard, rocking the boat as he did. He looked to Hilary, who was still leaning against the edge of the wood, a smile overtaking his mouth as his eyes followed the bird's flightpath.

"How on earth did it do that?" Alfred blurted.

"Thousands of years of experience."

Hilary's last word was lost in his throat as he gestured toward the sky again. Alfred's eyes found another inky form that traced the stars and hovered just above the tree tops of the shoreline before flying over the water. Silently, its wings thrust backward in a sharp motion, it swooped down and burst into the water. It appeared behind a stand of grass seconds later only to take skyward, its catch already down its gullet.

Another splash came from behind them, and both men reeled to look toward the other side of the bay. They gripped the sides of the boat to steady themselves as they caught sight of a smaller pelican guzzling a pouch full of water before she seemed content to float on the rocking water between stands of cordgrass. The sound of wings flapping overhead drew their eyes upward as three more pelicans joined the hunt and cast shadows on the boat as they flew farther out into the bay.

The birds began to dive, one by one, plunging into the water and coming up from the brackish water with swollen pouches. The occasional splash became a bombing as the moon rose higher with fleets of pelicans arriving from the island, soaring in and out of the moonlight and tracking schools of fish in the water below. The night was filled with the din of the pelicans' attack as each bird executed the same maneuver—soar, dive, turn, and catch—rocketing toward the water in smooth lines, their wing tips traced in the silver of the moon. The boat rocked roughly in the water, waves pushing it from every direction as the bay was shattered by the precision of the diving birds.

The scene continued for nearly half an hour as hundreds of pelicans crisscrossed paths and left the moon a flashing light that made the waters sparkle with motion from above and below. As the cloud of birds began to thin, the last few latecomers took to the remaining fish on their own and came up as well-fed as their predecessors had been. With only the occasional splashing, the chirps and hum of the insects returned to the bay.

Hilary's sketchpad was at his feet, the pencil in the pocket of his shirt, and both men's mugs dry in the bottom of the row boat. They were laughing by the time the last pelican turned back toward the island, a humor only born partially of scotch and mostly of adrenaline. They relaxed onto their seats as the water was left to its nightly routine once more.

"I had forgotten how thrilling that was to see," Hilary intimated as he uncorked the bottle to refill his mug.

"You've seen this before?"

He nodded as he passed the bottle to Alfred.

"Only once, which seemed enough at the time. It was the year my wife died." He looked out onto the bay. "She was too sick to come with me, so I came alone. I remember it being miraculous, seeing so many birds diving like arrows into the water. I tried to sketch the scene for her, but I was too excited to focus, only watching the birds instead. I put it aside to sketch it for her later." He stared into the copper-rimmed scotch. "She died the next week."

A cricket joined the chorus, and Alfred spoke softly.

"I'm sorry." Hilary nodded and took a drink; Alfred gave him a few moments of silence. "Did your wife go out with you often?"

"No, I went with her." He glanced at Alfred and chuckled with wet eyes. "She was the naturalist. She's the reason I came to love this the way I do. I was nothing more than a banker with a few books when we met, and I thought I'd found the perfect woman for a man like me. Simple, quiet, and beautiful."

"Was she not?"

"She was beautiful, but that was about all I had gotten right. She put me in my place from the start, and I learned how to live through her. I was very little of myself before she came along. Some days I wonder how much of me is left now that she's gone."

The moon had settled high above them and lit up their faces as they drank the last of the scotch. While he was certain the scotch played a fair hand in it, Alfred knew his request came from somewhere deep within him, a place that was overrun with memories of bringing flowers to his grandmother's bedside and the smell of fresh baked bread in winter.

"Would you tell me more about your wife?" Hilary looked at him with a knitted brow and the first instance of skepticism Alfred had seen on the man's face. Alfred cleared his throat and looked down at his mug. "I've found the island quite different than I expected, and some veins seem to run much deeper than others. Some are even harder than others to judge. If it's all the same to you, tonight I would like to hear a good story. A real one."

Hilary leaned back to straighten his knees in the boat and lifted the mug to his lips, his knuckles popping out on the side. Alfred leaned back so that his elbows rested on the edge of the boat and he was looking out onto the shining sketch of Galveston Bay. The night, unlike the day, was steady in its mood, only cooling off slightly as the chorus lost members throughout the hours and the rustling of the trees gave way to a motionless air, as if the world had stopped turning. As Alfred let himself rock with the gentle sway of the bay, Hilary talked of falling in love with his wife, of learning how to paint on the edge of the water, and of the commonly unknown beauty of the Eastern Brown Pelican, his late wife's favorite bird.

Chapter Seventeen

The entrance to the stationery store was just off of 22nd Street between Market Street and Ship Mechanic Row, a simple red door between a boot repair shop and a pharmacy. A plain green sign hung overhead and read *Brighton Stationary* in gold letters. A brass bell jangled at the street door as Mathias led Alfred up the stairs and they slipped through a doorway at the top. Alfred stepped into a large store that filled the second floor above the pharmacy. It was lined with oak shelves displaying hand-sewn leather journals and examples of embossed paper products. A small table toward the windows at the front of the store held an assortment of pens and inkwells while a cabinet against the wall offered a variety of inks behind glass doors. Alfred stepped farther into the store and lost himself in the world of paper.

Thomas Brighton emerged from an open door at the back of the store and gave a cheery smile.

"Well, hello, you two." He set a stack of journals on the counter and leaned onto his palms. "Right on time."

"I'd hate for Alfred to miss your sale." Mathias leaned on the counter with his elbow and let his shoulder cock his arm so that his legs could stretch out. "Everything's thirty percent off after six o'clock."

Alfred furrowed his brow, a box of pencils in his hand. "Really?"

"For Mathias, yes, and so for you. But please do not spread that gossip around town. I'd be out of business in days."

Mathias turned his attention to the proprietor. "New shipment?"

"Just arrived. They're far better than those pulp ones you prefer."

"Old habits are hard to break."

Alfred made his way through the shop, collecting a new rubber stopper and admiring the fountain pens. He lifted one from its velvet-lined box. Its marbled blue and black casing was interwoven with gold. He felt a sting of recognition, one that reminded him of how little was in his pockets, and he replaced it gingerly. Mathias tapped Alfred's shoulder and gestured for him to look into the room behind the counter.

Mathias let Alfred pass before pausing at the doorway and leaning over the register, talking quietly to Thomas. The room's setup was simple, a few crates stacked against a wall and two shelves of unpriced merchandise. A large table in the center of the room was covered with scraps of leather and thick thread. Loose paper was stacked at one end beside two completed journals. The entire room smelled of freshly cured leather, and Alfred breathed it in deeply.

"He makes his own journals?"

Mathias nodded as he made his way around the table and toward a small cabinet against the back wall.

"All of them?"

"Oh, no." Mathias bent over and sorted through the cabinet before returning with a liquor bottle. "It takes him nearly a week to finish a journal what with him being the only one in the store. He orders from all over but reserves a small part of his shelves for his journals as well. More of a hobby."

Mathias found scotch glasses on a nearby shelf and pulled down three. Alfred watched him fill the glasses halfway and then picked up the bottle to inspect the label.

"Disaronno?"

"Amaretto." Mathias slid a glass across the table toward him. "It's a liquor made from almonds. A tad bitter, but it does wonders to your morning coffee."

Alfred sniffed the liquor and made a face.

"It smells like cherries."

Thomas joined them with two packages, each one wrapped in crisp brown paper and tied together with string. He sat them on the table between the men.

"You pay on a tab and drink my liquor." He took the third glass and leaned against the table. "You're the worst customer I've had all day."

"If you would start importing this, I wouldn't have to keep drinking yours."

Alfred took his first sip. A silky coating overtook his throat and he smacked his lips. The two men waited with interest. He nodded and swirled the liquor in his glass with approval.

"It's not easily imported?" Alfred asked.

Thomas shook his head and poured himself a fresh glass. "It doesn't seem to catch on for some reason. The new Victorian man is much more a whiskey drinker than his father claimed to be. Julius Runge used to import for me at a fair price. Now I have to pay Steinman two dollars a bottle."

Thomas held up the bottle to Alfred, who waved it off, before returning it to the cabinet.

"I met Mr. Runge the other day."

"Julius Runge?" Thomas inquired.

"He offered me a ride in his coach during the storm."

"He's an awfully nice fellow. A little strong-headed but kind just the same."

"He kept his cool when John barged in."

Mathias furrowed his brow. "Into the coach?"

"Pushed his way in without warning." Alfred's grin turned into a smile.

"That's a gentleman if I ever saw one," Thomas retorted. He finished off his amaretto and pulled his jacket down from a rack near the entrance. He faced the men as he slid his arms into the cotton.

"How did he know you were in the coach?" Mathias asked, taking a last drink as the other men moved into the store..

"He didn't," Alfred replied as he joined Thomas at the top of the stairs. "Just saw a coach pass by Twenty-Second Street and thought it appropriate to commandeer it."

"Lucky you," Thomas quipped.

He let Mathias and Alfred pass through and pulled a key from his pocket to lock the door at the street. Mathias stopped on the sidewalk and looked at Alfred with a curious expression.

"Twenty-Second?"

"He said the storm caught him on his way home from his study group."

"That can't be right."

The summer air had begun its ritual procession of weighing down the day and lifting gently in the evening, and Alfred felt a light breeze blow at the edge of his jacket as watched Mathias's expression intently.

"Why's that?" He knew the answer but realized in the seconds that passed that he wanted confirmation of his suspicions.

"Study groups are on Tuesdays and Thursdays."

"Mrs. Poplar said just as much," he replied. "But I can't figure out why he would lie about where he'd been."

"Your guess is as good as mine." Mathias shrugged with a grin. "And it might be better for us to know as little about John's activities as we can. I'd hate to think that sort of arrogance is contagious."

Thomas joined them with a quick step and gestured toward the harbor.

"Ready?"

———•●•———

The Union Jack was a small pub, smashed between a warehouse and a dry goods store at the west end of Water Street overlooking the harbor. The bent boards made up its front walkway below a sign over the door that refused service to confederate soldiers. The saloon's name, as Mathias had whispered as they neared, was more of a bitten thumb than nostalgia, but the owner had found more than enough drunks missing the pubs of their homelands to keep the doors open and decided to keep the name. The din of the evening's customers greeted Alfred's ears well before he smelled the heavy scent of beer and smoked meats, and a roar of laughter erupted from within as Thomas opened the door to lead them in.

What looked small from the street swelled to fit tables and a long bar with room to spare. Groups of men in smudged shirts with rolled up sleeves talked over tables while three men crowded a corner and a fourth threw darts at the wall. Several men held up the bar along the far wall where a barkeeper served beer from kegs. Alfred knew they were out of place before he caught their reflection in a mirror behind the bar. He leaned over Mathias's shoulder.

"I thought we were meeting someone about the club."

"We are."

Thomas gave a short wave across the room and began to cut his way through the tables toward the back of the pub. Mathias followed with Alfred closely behind. The voices fell to murmurs as they passed but quickly rose back to bouts of laughter as they reached the table nearest the dartboard. A stocky man rose from the table, and Thomas clasped his hand with a generous shake.

"Another round?" he asked with a gesture toward his glass.

"Only if you're buying."

The man's German accent was subtle but gave him away.

"Barkeep," Thomas called across the room.

The gaunt-looking man behind the bar looked their direction and nodded before disappearing beneath the wooden ledge. Thomas stepped around the table and motioned for everyone to sit.

"Bertrand Hartmann," he introduced, "this is Alfred Ridgeway, a friend of mine."

The man offered his hand, and Alfred watched his own disappear beneath thick calluses and scarred knuckles.

"Bertrand is in our sailing club," Thomas added.

Alfred sized up the man's frame and tried to imagine him perched precariously on the bow of a small sailboat. The image didn't fit, and he wondered if the man simply launched the ships across the waves rather than actually sailing boats that were practically designed to tip over.

Alfred took the seat between Mathias and Thomas as the barkeeper set four glasses on the table. Alfred slid his glass across the table and felt it catch on the sticky wood; it teetered for a second, sending beer over the lip and down his fingers. He sucked at the lost beer on his hand and then at the foam atop the glass.

"I heard you had a run in with a drunk man that thought he'd have his way without paying," Thomas commented.

Bertrand chuckled and his muscular frame bent over his glass. A grin cracked at his lips.

"More like he had a run in with me." His voice was silky and smooth, contrasting with his hands. Alfred eyed him again as the three talked, an intimacy they unknowingly gave up in conversation.

"I'm sure Madam Tellsen had her way with him in the end."

"That was the trouble," Bertrand remarked. "He tried to have his way with her."

"That's rather audacious," Mathias barked as his glass hit the table. "Trying to have your way with a madam."

The man waved it off with his free hand while the other dropped the glass from his lips. "There's two kinds in her world, and I'm meant to interfere with his kind so they don't make it up the stairs to the girls."

The men nodded in an unsaid agreement, and Alfred sipped at his beer. It was bitter and tasted of almonds as it mixed with the aftertaste of Thomas's liquor cabinet.

"Does she still split your wages?"

"Half in money, half in board. I think the girls like having someone like me in the house while they're sleeping. It lets them sleep a little more easily."

"And you have a softer pillow under your head," Mathias remarked.

Bertrand looked down at the table as he nodded, and Alfred felt the mood shift. His eyes wandered from one man to the other as they all played with their glasses. He was staring at Mathias when the German finally spoke.

"So, Alfred." He squinted his brown eyes across the table. "Thomas tells me you're in need of a way into the Garten Verein."

Alfred cleared his throat. "Yes, I'm hoping for a membership. And rather quickly."

"Is that so? Itching to get to the ball, are we?"

"I'm hoping to make an acquaintance at the ball." His faced warmed with his words. "But I hadn't realized it was for members only."

"More to the point," Mathias cut in, "he wishes to make her acquaintance again."

Bertrand's eyebrows danced. "A lady, then?"

Thomas let his glass hit the table with a thud, sloshing his beer.

"It isn't Evelyn Goodman, is it?"

Mathias fell back against his chair. "Good God, man!"

"What?" Thomas shrugged. "She's not all that bad, especially considering she comes from the same stock as William." He laid a hand on Alfred's arm. "You just have to look past the spitting veracity that is her social persona and imagine yourself living a cuckhold's life of regular tirades on fashion and perhaps the occasional bedding."

"Of a porcupine," Mathias quipped over his glass with a grin.

The table burst into laughter, and Bertrand's fist landed hard on the wood as his voice boomed over the din of the pub. The table next to them glanced their way before returning to their drinks. The men at the dartboard, their game ended, slid by their table toward the door. Bertrand leaned back in his chair and kept one hand on his nearly empty glass.

"Anyone can be a member," he explained, the remnants of the humorous moment at the creased corners of his mouth and eyes. "You just need a sponsor."

"He just arrived on the island barely two weeks ago," Mathias added. "He won't know anyone to sponsor his application."

"I see." He shook his head with a quick turn. "I wish I could help, but you know I can't sponsor him. I'm not a member anymore. You'll remember I was pushed out."

Thomas nodded with closed eyes as if absorbing Bertrand's frustration as his own. "But you do know quite a few people who are still members, and you're still on good terms with a few, aren't you? Perhaps one of them would be willing to sponsor him?"

Bertrand kept his eyes on Alfred as he thought aloud, turning his glass on the table with his fingertips.

"Perhaps. I have a few favors that need turning in." He raised an eyebrow. "It won't be an easy sell with him being fresh off the boat."

"Train," Mathias corrected.

"Where from? Carolinas?"

"Indian Territory," Alfred replied.

"Oh, sorry." He shrugged. "You have that look about you."

Alfred glanced down at himself and then back to the table as the men continued their conversation.

"I can think of a few names, but they'd need a reason for knowing him, something that didn't come through me."

"We've already settled that," Thomas replied with a broad smile. "He's our acquaintance."

Bertrand's eyes narrowed. "But you two aren't members."

"Precisely," Mathias said. "But we'd like to be."

Bertrand lifted his chin and made to speak but stopped, his eyes flicking between the two men as he pointed at one and then the other. "You two want to be sponsored as well?"

They nodded excitedly.

"All three of you? You want me to find sponsors for all three of you?"

"It'll make the process easier," Thomas started.

"It most certainly won't. One sponsor in time for the Somerset is difficult enough, let alone three. The ball is in what, a few weeks?"

"Six days," Thomas corrected.

"Not three sponsors." Mathias leaned over the table to close the distance between them. "One sponsor for three men."

"How on earth am I going to sell that? I don't even know anyone that knows all three of you."

Thomas gestured at the barkeeper for another round and rejoined the conversation.

"That's just it. We think it'll be an easier sell. Think of it this way." He let a hand rest on his chest. "As a shopkeeper, I'm well-known around town, even among the high lot." He let his hand fall to gesture across to Mathias. "And he is a medical student with an impeccable reputation. The two of us would be easy to justify as applicants."

"And how does he fit into it all?" Bertrand gestured roughly with his empty glass.

"Alfred works for Isaac Cline, the climatologist."

"So?"

Thomas let his head fall to the side as he kept his eyes on the man. "Let's not pretend we don't know each other well, Bertrand."

The German let out a sigh and fell back into his chair. "What are you getting at?"

"The Garden Verein is a German club, yes, but it's still a social club. And it would be a good connection to have someone in the Weather Bureau on the club's side of things."

"What are you implying?"

"I'm not implying anything. I'm simply stating the fact that, even though immigration serves this island well at the moment, that doesn't mean German sentiment will always play out like it has."

"German sentiment? You make it sound like we're on the verge of something."

"I only mean that Julius Runge keeps that pipe running smoothly," Thomas replied, lowering his voice. "His business was what sent the ships to Europe and brought back German immigrants, and he still works to employ them to keep the people fed. Can you imagine what it will look like when he's gone?"

Bertrand sat with his thoughts, chewing on his lower lip. After several moments, he cut his eyes at Thomas.

"That's a crackpot scheme you've thought up."

Thomas straightened with a smile. "But it's hard to deny. It would be a good connection for them to get to know Alfred. Government officials are always good to have on your side."

"Oh, I'm not an official—"

Thomas lifted a hand to quiet Alfred. Bertrand was nodding, but lines pulled at his mouth. The barkeeper set four more glasses on the table, and he was the only one who pulled a glass toward him. He let out a sigh and lifted his chin.

"Alright," he said to the glass. "I'll find you a sponsor." He pointed a finger at Thomas. "But I can't promise it'll come cheap. The man I'm thinking of might want a little something for his trouble." He nodded at the other two men. "And you'll all have to pay your dues before you join."

"Not to worry," Thomas replied cheerfully. "I've already got that covered."

Bertrand shook his head as a grin returned to his lips. "I'll never understand how you've managed to keep your name as clean as it is."

"Pompadour's Polish and Shine."

The table erupted in laughter again as they took the last three steins. Thomas lifted his glass in a toast, and beer sloshed from the rims as they clinked together overhead. The men kept pace with the pub for over an hour, Thomas sporting the tab in celebration of their soon-to-be social step, and Alfred felt himself become part of the atmosphere.

When the evening wore out, the men parted ways at the door, and Mathias and Alfred left Thomas on Postoffice Street, where he changed directions toward his apartment. The night air was cooler than it had been the previous week, and Alfred relished the tingling touch of the breeze on his face. Mathias meandered along the sidewalk as they made their way toward 14th Street, passing dark businesses and wooden houses with turrets and wrap-around porches. Their front windows glowed, some with the flickering warmth of gas lights and others with the whiter burn of electricity that seemed to spotlight their path along the sidewalk between the gas lamps.

"Bertrand seems like a nice fellow," Alfred mused.

"He is. He's had a few tough breaks, though."

"How so?"

Mathias was quiet as they crossed the intersection. His eyes looked down the street beyond the light.

"He used to work at the docks, but he had a run in with a few of the workers."

"They didn't get along?"

"You could say that. They beat him up and left him inside an empty barrel overnight. Another worker found him the next morning, barely breathing."

"Dear, God. That sounds rather crude. What had he done?"

Mathias fell quiet again, and Alfred sensed he had broached something that was hidden under the surface. Something he was uncertain he wanted to tug any further. When Mathias spoke again, his voice was sharp in the quiet street.

"Sometimes people simply don't understand one another. The world can be a dangerous place for a lot of people, and all it takes is a misunderstanding or lighting a prejudice you didn't know was there." He took in a deep breath. "People will judge you for the littlest things, even those that have nothing to do with them."

Alfred watched his feet as he walked, putting one foot directly in front of the other.

"You mean it was because he was German?"

Mathias chuckled. "No, if this island has one thing going for it, it's a good mix of cultures. Immigration is only a hot topic for the upper class, the ones who prefer to keep their docks mixed but their families pure."

"But Thomas alluded to there being some trouble."

Mathias waved him off.

"Thomas was playing the cards he had to get us all in the club. I mean, he's not wrong. If Julius Runge and his kind were to leave the island, there are many groups that wouldn't be able to afford to travel the ocean and come to Galveston. And that would be a shame. But there's no true concern behind that happening any time soon. Galveston is a wealthy city with a booming port. It'll take the hand of God to slow us down."

When they climbed the steps of the boardinghouse, Mathias pulled out his key and quietly unlocked the front door. It creaked on its hinges as he opened it to let Alfred in. Both men clumsily removed their shoes and took the stairs one at a time in their socks to muffle their late return.

"I guess it's good night, then," Mathias whispered. "I hope Bertrand wasn't too much of a rough sort for you."

"Not in the least."

As Mathias turned toward his room, Alfred took a step closer. "Why is he no longer a member of the club?" Mathias turned, his face hidden in the shadow of the lamp at his back. Alfred sensed a shift in the man's muscles. "I got the impression that he didn't leave the club on good terms."

Mathias's form was exaggerated by the shadows, and Alfred squinted to make out his expression. After an extended silence, Mathias's voice came quietly across the hall.

"Like I said, he's had a few tough breaks."

With that, he made his way into his room and shut the door, leaving Alfred in the hall with only the light of his gas lamp.

CHAPTER EIGHTEEN

The city's rooflines were a pale pink as Alfred recorded the morning's observations from atop the Levy Building. The sky was a deep purple over the water, letting hues of orange and yellow peek through a gathering of clouds as the sun rose to the east and a strong wind came off the ocean. He wiped at his upper lip with the back of his hand as he read the barometer, a hefty 26.4 millibars of atmospheric pressure. Fighting the flapping edges of the logbook's pages, he recorded the reading. His shirt tugged at the sleeves, their cuffs rolled up at his elbows, as he packed up the logbook, scooted the crate beneath the anemometer mount, and made his way to the staircase.

Joseph's form was bent over the table in the middle of the office when Alfred made it downstairs. His attention was lost in a set of telegrams, and Alfred slid the logbook onto its shelf and eyed the man's collection as he walked back to his desk.

"You're in early."

Joseph made a noise as he jotted down a line in his notebook, keeping one finger on the telegram at the top of the pile. He looked up as he slid it to the side. "We've received several wires that there's a storm closing in on the coast. I wanted to read them myself to see if we could better determine their path."

"Are they nearing Galveston?"

"I'm afraid so," he replied as he bent over the next telegram. "The winds have been rising steadily since four this morning."

Alfred glanced out the window that overlooked Market Street. The flag that hung from the market on the opposite corner whipped back and forth with the gusts that blew between the buildings.

"Should we release a new forecast?"

"We will need to update it, but we've missed the morning edition. It looks like they are not going to dissipate any time soon, so we might be able to make the evening post."

The office door opened with the drag of swollen wood, and Dr. Cline came through the door with a satchel over his shoulder and his hat in his hand. His hair was slicked back at the front but pushed against his part on the side, evidence of the wind's intensity. He nodded at Alfred as he passed.

"Apologies for my tardiness," he started. "My horse wasn't keen on the weather, and it took a little coaxing to get her on the road."

Joseph swiveled on his stool as his brother settled his items at his desk.

"We need to raise the storm flag."

"She's truly a remarkable horse, but she's egregious when she decides she'll not leave the stable."

Joseph lifted his chin to look at the ceiling. "Isaac, we've received wires from Louisiana, and reports from Cuba are that the storm is developing over the gulf. With winds like this, it'll be here by midday."

"Yesterday's observations showed that it would keep with the coastline and pass us by." Isaac kept his back to the office as he pulled his papers from his bag.

"That was yesterday. It looks like a front has moved in and changed the storm's course."

The climatologist looked out the window at the same flag before turning to face the two men.

"When were the sightings reported?"

"Yesterday evening and late in the night. Two steamers reported gale force winds a little over a hundred miles out from New Orleans."

"Any reports since daybreak?"

Joseph crossed his arms, his voice tinged with frustration. "No. But there hasn't been much time for them to come in." Dr. Cline nodded, but Joseph refused to wait for another question. "I know what you're thinking, but it's dangerous to wait."

"It's premature to raise an alarm now when we've yet to hear how ships are faring. The storm could have passed us by now."

"With these winds?"

Alfred crept to the instrument case and took down the box of cleaning paraphernalia and a field anemometer. If any of the instruments needed to be ready for the field today, it would be that one. He set them on his desk as the two men continued to argue.

"You're putting these ships in danger." Joseph gestured toward the harbor a few blocks beyond the office's northern wall, his voice booming in the small office.

"These steamers have captains to make such decisions," Dr. Cline replied in a stern tone. "And I am doing nothing of the sort. Those men are well aware of the dangers that weather can provide and understand what their ships are capable of sailing through. Raising a flag now could only compound their circumstances."

Alfred poured a dot of polish onto a rag and began to clean the cups that stuck out from the center ball on metal arms.

"Compound their circumstances? You'd rather have them push off into a storm?"

"They will have all received the forecast in the morning paper. It's not like they're going out blind."

"They shouldn't be going out at all!"

Dr. Cline turned back to his desk and began sorting his papers. "This discussion is over, Joseph. We will wait until midday to verify the reports."

"That's too late, Isaac. Even Alfred understands the severity of what sits offshore." He swung an arm toward Alfred's desk, raising his eyebrows as he spoke. "The winds are pushing inland off the water. If that storm has come any closer to the coast, those ships could—"

Dr. Cline's fist met the edge of his desk with a bang that reverberated between the walls. Alfred jumped at the noise and saw the balance of the anemometer falter between his fingers. Joseph fell silent, his arm still outstretched. Dr. Cline turned to face his brother, his jaw tight.

"The matter is decided. We will not elicit a criticism on the Weather Bureau of raising false alarms and stalling ships on shore unnecessarily. And I will not request permission to issue a storm warning."

Alfred rubbed at the metal cups of the anemometer without looking up, his ears piqued to catch any words that might escape. Joseph's stool creaked as he stood. With the stack of telegrams in his hand, he walked over to the desk where his brother was reading over hand-scrawled notes. He dropped the telegrams onto the desk and watched them splash over the man's papers.

"Cuba reports sustained winds of thirty-eight miles per hour before it entered the gulf."

Dr. Cline glanced down at the scattered telegrams as his brother made his way across the office, pulling down the logbook as he neared the shelf. Alfred opened his mouth to stop him but thought better of it. He dropped his chin as the wood scraped along the jamb, making an exaggerated exit. The wind gusted against the windows, rattling the panes, and he glanced out at the burgeoning morning, wondering which of the men would be proven right.

"My brother can be rather hot-tempered at times." Dr. Cline turned with the stack of telegrams in his hands. "Please forgive his habit of impatience. I've learned it comes from a good place, albeit an immature one."

Alfred offered the best smile he could find. Dr. Cline pulled down several books from the top shelf nearest Joseph's desk, and Alfred watched him glance at the titles and then reorganize them in his arms before returning them to the shelf. His stomach fluttered with nerves as tension seeped from the room and he finally found his voice.

"At the risk of sounding impertinent, sir—"

"You're wondering why I am not heeding the reports as strongly as my brother?"

He turned and looked at Alfred over his bifocals. Alfred dropped his eyes instinctively and feigned interest in the base of the anemometer, rubbing at it with his rag. When he found the courage to glance up, the man had returned to organizing the books.

"Joseph is an intelligent man, but he lacks the ability to evaluate what is a phenomenon and what is simply weather. To him, any change, anything outside of the expected, is cause for an alarm, and the bureau simply will not tolerate that sort of exhibitionism." He slid the last book back onto the shelf and removed his glasses as he faced Alfred. "It undermines the science behind it all. How can we be taken seriously if we give false alarms that stall ships and delay exports? The bureau faces enough scrutiny without adding to the gentleman's opinion of our work."

"It seems, then, that there must be a sort of inherent danger in treading such a fine line," Alfred replied, folding his rag.

"Indeed." He returned to his desk and replaced his glasses onto the bridge of his nose. "Our work is a constant balance of the beautiful and the deadly. No one is interested in the weather until it turns dark or cold. Then everyone is wanting to know what we know, most notably when it will go away."

He gave a grin that eased the tension, and Alfred continued.

"What I meant to say was that, with science still advancing as it is, we can't expect to know the answer all of the time, can we?"

"Of course not. Science is not a rule book."

"Then how do you know that Cuba's reports are unfounded?"

"I don't."

His words came clearly, but Alfred struggled to parse them. The man's temper, though it had been short-lived, had lighted Alfred's anxiety at upsetting the climatologist, keeping his tongue snugly against the roof of his mouth. After a long minute, Dr. Cline pulled a map from the collection on the shelf and rolled it open on the table, gesturing for Alfred to join him. A detail showed the gulf with the edge of Mexico moving up to the southern coast of Texas. Cuba was in the bottom corner. Red and black lines crisscrossed the water. Alfred followed Dr. Cline's index finger as he traced the thickest line that ran through the center of the gulf.

"A hurricane in 1875 came across Cuba and intensified over the water before making landfall along the western edge of the Texas coast. Records indicated that winds were as high as eighty-eight miles per hour." He pointed to another line that crossed the first, landing closer to Galveston. "The storm of 1886 ravaged Indianola. It was already a hurricane when it entered the gulf, but it strengthened as it traveled."

His finger slid along the paper until it found Cuba's outline at the bottom of the map.

"Look at how many of these storms have originated in the Atlantic. Some cross the Cuban borders but rarely. More often they turn north and head up the coastline toward Canada. It's a simple matter of how storms behave. If it runs north of Cuba, it goes north via Florida." He looked at Alfred with sharp eyes. "I won't deny that Cuba knows hurricanes better than we do, but it has recently become the bureau's policy to determine our own forecasts rather than taking others' guesses as our own. That's why our line to Cuba is closely monitored. What reports we do get come from unofficial channels. I don't doubt Cubans' fears when they have nothing between them and whatever the ocean sends their way, but that doesn't mean they always know what's happening."

Alfred scanned the map once more, taking in the crossing lines that seemed to pierce the coastlines at random.

"If they know hurricanes, then they know what to look for." He looked up to see Dr. Cline give a small nod. "Then why do you not trust them with today's reports?"

"Our relationship with the Cuban climatologists is a strained one." He stood and let the map roll up against Alfred's hand. "While they are often the first to know of anything coming off the Atlantic, their training is weak at best. And their instruments are old."

"Does that really dispute their ability to recognize a hurricane?"

"No, I would venture they can recognize one quite well when it is on top of them."

Alfred let go of the map and let it finish rolling itself into a tube. "You don't believe they can predict one?"

"No, I don't. Their observations are occasionally on par with our own, but their ability to understand the weather and what it means is limited. And while I do take some of their reports into consideration, I am required to keep the public opinion that their efforts are of little consequence to us."

"It just seems crass to ignore their reports when people's lives could be as stake."

"True, but I don't honestly feel that this instance warrants a storm warning. Cuba has likely exaggerated the situation. I'd like you to remember, Alfred, that a climatologist reads the weather, but a scientist reads the evidence."

"And you're reading the evidence?"

He tossed his gaze toward the bookshelf where maps jutted out unevenly from the shelves. "Joseph read the telegrams and last night's reports, but I requested a report from D.C. before returning home last night. My data is much more scientific and recent than his own."

He turned toward his desk and chose a telegram from the top of the stack.

"But, sir, even with old instruments, what makes them any less scientific?"

"Their climatologists are monks," he said with a casual tone. "And they keep their anemometer on top of a church observatory."

JUNE

CHAPTER NINETEEN

The rain had started midday and, combined with the gusting wind, made for a noisy night, but it was a note in the post, not the weather, that had kept Alfred awake into the early morning. Mrs. Poplar had greeted him at the door, holding it with a knowing grin. His tailored clothes would be ready on time and waiting at Mr. Jeffries's shop.

The table was already set for breakfast when he took his seat. John was hidden behind a newspaper and Mathias's chair was empty. Mrs. Poplar joined them with the last of the meal, setting down a plate of sliced melons and a bowl of leftover rolls from the previous night's dinner. Alfred slid two slices of melon onto his plate and passed the dish to John's side of the table.

"Is Mathias ill?" Alfred inquired.

Mrs. Poplar took her seat at the head of the table and began to pour coffee into their cups. "Had a late night, I believe." She slid a saucer and cup toward Alfred, steam rising from the rim. "No use in disturbing him."

"Yes, we should let the poor lad sleep," John said with a smirk, as he set the paper at the far end of the table. "What with being so busy with his sailing club and all."

He filled his plate with ham and melon and took a bite of a stale roll before letting his eyes drop to the page beside his plate. Mrs. Poplar cleared her throat.

"We shouldn't expect you tonight at dinner, I assume, Mr. Ridgeway?"

He cut into his egg and watched the yolk run along the curve of his plate. "No, I should think not." He glanced at John, who was preoccupied with the news, and then flashed a smile at Mrs. Poplar. While he didn't know John's opinions on social balls, he didn't care to find out at the breakfast table or to let the man know he planned to attend one.

"What of you, Mr. Briggs?"

He fumbled absently with his roll and kept his eyes on the print. "No, I'll be out this evening."

"Another study group," Alfred asked, working to keep his eyes on his plate.

He saw John's head rise at the question but kept his interest in his eggs and ham.

"Not quite," John replied flatly.

Mrs. Poplar scooped a small spoonful of oatmeal out of her bowl and looked between the two men. "I believe Mr. Ortiz will be absent this evening as well."

"He will," Alfred replied.

"Perhaps I could persuade one of you gentlemen to bring home a few items for me before you depart for the evening?"

Alfred wiped at his chin as he scooped a helping of ham from the dish and let it rest in the remnants of his egg yolk.

"I can do that for you."

"Oh, thank you, dear. It's only a few things, but my hip is quite sore today." She disappeared toward the front of the house, leaving the two men to eat in silence. When she returned, she handed Alfred two dollars and a handwritten list. "You can get them all at Steinman's."

"On Market Street?"

She nodded as she returned to her seat, and he pocketed the list and money.

"It says here," John interrupted, "that they're surveying the channel for expansion next month."

"Well, that was mighty fast, wasn't it," Mrs. Poplar mused.

"It says the survey will be published in October. No use in delaying progress, I suppose."

"Oh, I don't know about that," Alfred remarked.

He topped off his and Mrs. Poplar's coffee, and she nodded in appreciation. John let the paper fall a few inches in his hand. "And why's that?"

Alfred shook his head with a thoughtful expression as he lifted his cup and blew on the surface. "Another expansion? And within three years. It seems a few people feel that the island must realize its own limitations and slow its progress before it outgrows its own borders."

John let the paper fold onto itself atop his plate and gave a tight-lipped grin. "Are you suggesting that we shouldn't expand our most impressive industry?"

"Not at all. I'm simply saying that perhaps it would benefit the island as a whole if the committee would wait to see what impact the previous expansions have had."

"It's increased our exporting abilities threefold. That's the impact."

"No doubt, but at some point there will have to be consequences to altering the landscape so diligently."

"What do you mean, dear?" Mrs. Poplar asked as she mixed together the last of her oatmeal.

"Simply that dredging the channel can have unforeseeable consequences, and we've already deepened it, what, ten," he looked to Mrs. Poplar, "twelve feet? In such a short time, we haven't even begun to see how it will affect the ocean currents, the shoreline, the wildlife."

John scoffed. "The wildlife? What concern is that to us?"

"A great one, I should hope."

"I'll wager that the men who are investing in this expansion find little benefit in concerning themselves with the fish and birds."

"Then what of their ships?"

John's screwed his nose up with squinted eyes. "What?"

"Their money is in importing and exporting. Shouldn't they be concerned about their ships and cargo?"

"Perhaps you missed the point, but that's why they're expanding the channel."

"Which will open the harbor and make it more vulnerable to the weather."

John stared for a long moment before giving a small laugh. "It's protected by the island. It's literally the safest harbor in the country." He let the paper fall away once more. "I thought you called yourself a weatherman."

"Now, now," Mrs. Poplar interjected. "I'll not stand for impolite conversation at my table."

John let his eyes linger on Alfred as he pulled the newspaper back up. Alfred felt his ears burn and took another drink of coffee. What patience he'd had for the day had already begun to drain; his lack of sleep was quickly catching up with him. He wiped his mouth and scooted his chair away from the table.

"Thank you for breakfast, Mrs. Poplar."

"No need for all that," she replied with a wave. "You've got my list?"

"I'll run it all by at lunch."

———•••———

The tailor shop was closed for lunch when Alfred arrived, a bag of dry goods under one arm and a rolled map in the other. He cursed under his breath. Thankfully the weather had cooled after the storm and left midday ideal for running errands about town; at least he didn't have to worry about sweating through his shirt before the evening. He cupped his eyes with his free hand and peered into the store. Scissors and cloth were strewn across the measuring table and an incomplete garment was pinned to the mannequin in front of the mirrors. He knocked softly at first, though he soon realized that he would need to leave the office early for the day if no one answered the door. After several seconds of silence, he banged against the wood until it reverberated through the doorjamb.

A couple stared at him as they walked by, and he gave an embarrassed smile as he glanced back through the front windows. He slid the bag into the crook of his elbow and stared down the street in a hopeless state. With the ball only a day away, what confidence he had in setting foot inside the Garden Verein was evaporating, and the tug at his heart was going with it.

He jumped when the door opened at his back, his arms losing their grip. A small bag of flour dropped onto the sidewalk with a thud. His eyes shot up to the doorway as he scrambled to catch the other items before they followed suit. Edwin stood in the doorway with a half-eaten sandwich in his hand. He chewed slowly as he gazed down at the bag of flour.

"What are you dropping things for?"

Alfred bent down to pick up the bag and nearly lost his grip on the maps. He regained his balance and dropped the flour back into the sack.

"You took me by surprise."

"But you knocked, didn't you?"

"Yes. I didn't realize anyone was in."

Edwin took a bit of his sandwich as he leaned his back against the open door. "Then what were you knocking for?"

Alfred closed his eyes to search for his patience. "I received a note in the post that my clothes are ready."

"Aye!" Edwin's eyes brightened and he began chewing more quickly as recognition took hold. "You had the tails for the ball."

He waved for him to come into the store, and Alfred squeezed between the man's stomach and the doorjamb. Edwin sucked himself against the doorframe as a map poked him in the face.

"He said you would be coming 'round," Edwin explained as he locked the door. "He's left your tails in the backroom. You can try them on back there."

"Try them on?"

Edwin bobbed his head, taking another bite of what smelled like a spicy blend of sauerkraut and sausage.

"I'm in quite a hurry," Alfred replied, lifting the bag and maps by way of explanation.

"Don't matter. Mr. Jeffries won't let you leave without making certain

I cut the fit right."

Alfred glanced around the dark room. "Is Mr. Jeffries here?"

Edwin shook his head as his eyes roamed the room, and Alfred raised a daring eyebrow, hoping whatever communication they had going would keep its momentum. The man's eyes widened as he caught Alfred's intentions.

"Oh, no, sir," he insisted through bits of bread. "I'd be hung if I let you leave without trying 'em on."

"It can't be as bad as all that."

"Mr. Jeffries takes his clients very seriously, sir."

"I'm sure he does." He looked for a place to set his items. "Let's get on with it then if I'm to make it back by one."

"If you're rushed, sir, I've only eaten half my sandwich. The other half is in the back."

Alfred chuckled and felt his impatience slide away when he saw the man's earnest expression. "I'm quite alright," he protested, "but I appreciate the offer. And I sincerely apologize for interrupting your dinner break." He followed Edwin to the back of the store.

"Oh, it ain't no break, sir."

"You're eating while you work?"

Edwin nodded as he tucked the last bite of sandwich into his cheek and wiped his hands on his pants. He began sorting the clothing that hung on a rack on the left side of the room. Alfred glanced about the space. It was in disarray with rolls of material stacked on shelves and collections of ribbons and buckles in cubbies. The only organization seemed to be in the finished outfits—men's suits on the left and women's dresses on the right.

"When else would I eat?"

Edwin pulled several hangers down from the rack and inspected each one before walking them to a door on the right wall. Alfred had missed it among the blend of colors that washed over the tables and shelves around it.

"Don't you get breaks?" he asked as he followed the man into a small changing room.

"I ain't union."

"Union?"

Edwin brushed at the leg of the pants before hanging them on a hook on the wall. He turned to Alfred. "You know, union. The groups that get workers all that extra pay and such."

Alfred gave a slow nod as he stepped into the sowing room "You work here all day without a break?"

"It ain't so bad. I'm indoors and all. It's a lot better than when I worked at the docks."

"You worked the docks?"

Edwin nodded enthusiastically, his voice betraying his naivety. "It's good work when you're new on the island. Hard work but steady pay. And you ain't got to do much except move the crates off the ships."

"You didn't work with the steamers?"

"Oh, no!" He laughed so hard his belly shook beneath his waistcoat. "They wouldn't never let a worker like me near the fancy ships. They got some rich people coming off those ocean liners."

Alfred's voice dropped as he spoke. "Some poor ones as well, I understand."

"Ain't that right." Edwin pointed toward the shirt that hung behind Alfred. "Now be careful not to wrinkle the sleeves when you button it up. I'll put on your cufflinks for you so you can see how it looks on you all nice and proper."

"Cufflinks?"

His gut tightened. He hadn't thought beyond getting the clothes from the shop. He felt totally unprepared for this ball, and if he had to buy anything more to get himself in a proper state, he'd end up selling his socks to pay the tab.

"You ain't got no cufflinks?"

Alfred shook his head and looked back at the clothes.

"Well, I can show you how to do the collar and tie. You'll have to have someone help you with the cufflinks when you dress at home."

With that, Edwin shut the door and left Alfred staring at dress tails that were somehow made for his body. He ran his fingers over the material and breathed in the scent of the freshly hemmed pants. They were the fanciest pair he had ever touched, and he knew he would look awkward in them before he took them off the hanger. The pants fit perfectly, though they looked slightly long in his everyday shoes. The shirt was difficult to tuck in and button without wrinkling the sleeves, but he did his best. When he stepped out of the dressing room, Edwin gave a whistle.

"There's a gentleman if I ever saw one." He situated Alfred's collar and tied his ascot with ease before motioning for him to take his place in front of the mirrors.

The man who stared back was a stranger. He had Alfred's slight wave atop his head and his sharp chin; his arms even hung in the same loose manner, but the rest of him was painted in a style he had never worn. He lost his attention in the reflection and was startled when Edwin rested his new hat on the crown of his head. He watched as the assistant straightened it.

"Well?"

Alfred searched for the words, and his mouth gaped as he tried to find the word to describe how he felt. "I look—"

"Fancy," Edwin said with an emphatic smile.

"That's one way to put it."

Edwin tilted his head to look Alfred in the face. "Want me to show you how to do the tie?"

"Please."

Edwin removed the hat and Alfred's jacket before having him untie the sapphire blue material. He traded Alfred spots, stepping up onto the crate to gain height while Alfred stood flat-footed on the floor. He worked his hands slowly around Alfred's collar as he showed him once in the mirror and then walked him through it so he could learn the motions. After being shown three times, Alfred still struggled to do it himself. It wasn't until the fourth try that he finally mastered the steps.

"See? It's ain't so hard. All those fancy men do it every day."

"Or their valets do it for them."

"Aye," he said to Alfred's jacket as he brushed it off and took it back to the fitting room. "Can you imagine having your own valet, someone to dress you and call you sir all day?"

"No," Alfred replied honestly. "I think it would grow tiring after a while."

"Not me. No, sir!"

He held the door for Alfred, who spoke toward the ceiling as he undid the tie.

"Maybe you'll have your own valet someday, then."

"Maybe I'll have my own sewing shop. And they'll call me Mr. MacIntosh and I'll smoke cigars with them outside the Tremont."

The reference to the hotel struck Alfred like a blow to the head. He closed his eyes and turned to see himself in the small mirror of the dressing room. Edwin closed the door, and Alfred felt the room close in on him as the reflection took on a new color. In this suit he was a stranger to himself, but he looked no different than the rest of the ball-goers, at least to men like Edwin. Men who dreamed of having midday breaks and were thankful to have the sabbath to themselves. He swallowed as he stretched out his arms and then let his hands come to rest on the lapels of the jacket.

His mother would have cried if she had seen him standing there looking the part of a Galveston gentleman. The thought saddened him. Here he had the role handed to him, even if just for a night, and it was already soiled by everything around him: the man whose dreams were purer than his own, the shopkeeper who worked him six days a week, the city that was expanding yet again at the expense of the nature that harbored it. Everything around him pulled at his conscience but nothing as strongly as how he looked in the dress tails.

That, he knew, weighed him down the most.

When he came out of the dressing room, Edwin was pinning a ribbon around a hat. He looked up with bright eyes and tapped the top of a hat box.

"I got it boxed up for you. I put it in the sort with a handle because I know you gotta walk back with all of this."

"Thank you, Edwin," he said with a smile. "That is most helpful."

The man nodded as he carried the box to the front table and helped Alfred balance it all in his arms. They made their way toward the door, and Alfred's curiosity took hold. "If you don't take a break, why do you lock the door?"

"Mr. Jeffries likes me to work on the stuff in the back while he takes his noontime break. He doesn't like me to do any business without him here."

"Ah."

Alfred felt a tug at his stomach, and he considered with a soft stare Edwin until the man glanced down at his vest and wiped at it self-consciously.

"I got 'kraut on me again?"

Alfred shook his head with a laugh. "No, you look fine."

"Whew! My wife would fix me good if I ruined another waistcoat." He made his way past Alfred and toward the front of the store. Alfred followed.

"I'm sorry to pry earlier, Edwin," he remarked. "I was surprised was all. I had taken Mr. Jeffries to be a kind man."

"Oh, he is, sir." Alfred's head tilted as he watched the man's animated face. "He pays me extra when I finish the work early, and he lets my wife bring me supper so we can eat together most nights." He unlocked the door and opened it, letting in the sounds of the harbor just down the street. "And he lets me off on Sundays for mass."

"I see." Alfred walked out onto the sidewalk. "Well, I'm pleased you find your situation tenable."

The man straightened as the corner of his mouth rose into a grin. "What's that mean? Tenable?"

Alfred thought for a moment. "Happy. I'm glad you're happy."

The man gave a hard nod as if nailing the thought into the ground before sliding his gaze off to the passersby on the street. He wiped at the doorjamb with an open palm.

"I ain't never had any of Mr. Jeffries's clients talk to me like that before."

Alfred smiled as a silence crept between them. "Yes, well, thank you for assisting me. You've set me right for the ball." He worked to keep the hangar balanced over his shoulder, and Edwin's finger shot out toward the tails.

"Don't forget to tell Mr. Jeffries that I had you try them on before you left. He'll want to know."

Alfred closed his eyes as if sealing the reminder in his mind.

"It'll be the first thing I mention."

CHAPTER TWENTY

The aster tie was more difficult to knot on his own than Alfred had expected. His fingers fumbled with the silk as he kept his chin up and his eyes down, watching his hands make foreign motions while being mindful of the sharp collar. Edwin had pressed the shirt expertly, but Alfred wasn't use to wearing such stiff material. The formality of simply dressing in the suit made him feel awkward, as if he didn't belong in his own room each time he caught his reflection in the table-top mirror. He finally pulled together a passing knot on the third go and stood back, trying to fit more of himself in the mirror.

Satisfied, he stepped back to the bureau and pinned the tie in place with the golden orb that Edwin had tucked into a small box. It nearly matched the cufflinks he had borrowed from Mathias. Brushing his shirt one last time, he pulled on his jacket, ran his fingers along his hair to keep it in place, and snuffed his oil lamp.

John's end of the hallway was dark, but Mathias's lamp lit the floorboards through his open door. Alfred stepped into the room's glow to see Mathias pulling at his own tie, smoothing his shirt and buttoning his waistcoat before turning around. His eyes ran over Alfred and he whistled.

"Those cufflinks really made that suit, didn't they?" A laugh filled the room as the two took in their suits.

"Does it look alright?" Alfred asked. His hand went instinctively to the tie.

"Like a well-made man." Mathias slid into his jacket. "You'd never know it was your first set of dinner tails."

"I feel like a fish."

"Well, you look like a gentleman." He stepped in front of him and measured him up. "She'll never know the wiser."

"Until I open my mouth."

Mathias let his head tilt an inch. "I have a feeling that's when she likes you best, just like the rest of us."

Alfred's cheeks went warm, and he gave a nod before turning toward the stairs. Mrs. Poplar was sitting in the front room when he stepped onto the landing. She looked up from her embroidery and tugged as her glasses.

"Oh, my!" A broad smile spread over her face and she let her hands fall together in her lap. "Look at you two."

Mathias tugged at his jacket as he came down the stairs. "Think we can pass for gentlemen tonight?"

"I don't think either of you are passing for anything you're not. Now come let me see you properly in the light."

They stood in front of her, Alfred stepping back a bit to share the lamp light. He watched her cheeks push up so that her eyes squinted the way older women's faces did. He felt a yearning for his home, for his mother to see him dressed as he was, for his grandmother to kiss his forehead like she always did. The thought made him self-conscious. He stretched his neck and adjusted his tie.

"Oh, my dears! I know I'm not either of your mothers, but I am so proud of how you both look tonight. Like proper gentlemen."

"Well, if we've fooled you," Mathias said as he bent down and gave her a kiss on the cheek, "we've made it."

She slapped his arm as he stood up and beckoned Alfred to come closer. He leaned down, expecting to follow Mathias's example, but she caught his cheek with the warm palm of her hand. Her voice was soft and lilted as she kept his gaze.

"She'll have a hard time not falling for you, dear."

His breath caught, but he had no time to reply. She kissed his cheek and swatted his shoulder in the same way as before.

"You two have a key?" Mathias held the bronze piece in the air before pocketing it, and she gave a nod. "They'll be bread and sausage in the kitchen if you're hungry, but I won't expect either of you for breakfast in the morning."

"Smart woman," Mathias replied as he pulled the door closed behind them.

Mathias had ordered a coach, and Alfred was glad of it once they were on their way. His stomach lurched with every pothole, but he couldn't imagine having walked the nearly two and a half miles to the club. Coaches and carriages filled the streets as they drew closer, and the evening had grown warmer since the cooler remnants of the storm had passed. He felt as though he were sitting beneath a fox's fur as the coach joined the line on Avenue O, and he fanned his jacket by the lapels as he stepped onto the sidewalk.

The walkway along the street was a mass of people, but none of them rushed, strolling and weaving amongst each other instead. Men in tails and top hats escorted women in colorful, flowing dresses while children in cropped pants and pastel ties ran along the fence and coachmen assisted patrons as they stepped into the late evening air. Beyond the fence a building glowed in the fresh dark of the evening and the muted sound of strings carried through the trees. Alfred felt the world orbit around him like moons in his gravity, and it was intoxicating. He turned to Mathias.

"You've been to this dance before?"

Mathias gave a laugh as he shut the coach door. Looking around at the people as they walked through the front gate of the club, he shook his head and slapped Alfred on the back.

"Like I said, I know my way around all of this just as much as you do."

"Oh, right."

Alfred drew in a deep breath, feeling that Mathias meant more than just the layout of the club. They followed the line of couples along a wrought-iron fence that opened at a large gate and onto a wide walkway. The Garten Verein sat at the end, a pale green octagon that glowed in the night. It was in the center of the landscaped green with trees interspersed along the front yard and bushes lining the walk. Land stretched beyond the structure with groves of trees and a garden stretched off behind the dance hall on the left.

Light emanated from the building in every direction, through tall windows on every side of the lower floor and out of small circular windows higher up. Two bay windows flanked the sides, pouring an electric glow onto the park as the open front door spotlighted the steps leading up. It was like nothing Alfred had seen before, and he slowed his walk.

Mathias looked back at him.

"What?"

"It's magnificent."

Mathias glanced at the dance hall and back at Alfred. "It's a building."

"I've never seen so much light before."

"Oh." Mathias stuck his hands in his pockets as he up at the club. People walked past, lost in their own conversations, as the two men took in the sight. Mathias looked at Alfred and watched his eyes roam the scene before gesturing toward the steps.

"You know there's more inside." He smiled as Alfred nodded and nudged the man to follow.

They walked behind an elderly couple, taking the steps one a at time, until they came up to the porch and Mathias pulled him to the side. The porch stretched in both directions around the octagon building before leading back down into the gardens, and Alfred looked out into the park where young men mingled on the edge of the light, smoking cigars and talking. Mathias made his way back down to a walkway on the side of the building and lifted his hand in a wave. Alfred followed at a slower pace.

The side garden was a crisscross of paths made up of laid rocks and seashells that crunched beneath his shoes. The perfect squares of plats between them were planted with cropped bushes that flowered in pink and yellow buds. Their hues were slightly skewed in the light from the windows, but they colored the backdrop nonetheless. Mathias greeted one of the men with a hearty handshake, and Alfred recognized Thomas's voice as he drew nearer the group.

"Mathias Ortiz, an acquaintance of mine."

A thin-framed man with long limbs and thick-rimmed glasses nodded vigorously. "Yes, yes, we met at a lecture last month."

"Dr. Litton's talk on women's hysteria," Mathias replied with a nod.

"Fascinating work, isn't it?" The man drew on his cigar and let out a cloud of smoke overhead. "I had no idea caffeine could be so influential in bringing women back to snuff after childbirth."

"Well, it does have its uses, but I am weary of pushing such a strong stimulant on women during their recovery. Their minds are in such a fragile state during the first few months."

"When is a woman's mind not in a fragile state?"

All of the men but Mathias laughed, and Thomas let his hand come to rest on Mathias's shoulder. "Let's not get too lost in business talk," he commented with a gesture toward Alfred. "This is Alfred Ridgeway, another new member."

"Ah," the man noted as he stuck his cigar-free hand between them, "my third new recruit. Adolph Grier, and these are my colleagues, Freidrick Bach and Stanton Hendleman." Alfred shook each of their hands in turn, addressing them by name as he did. "Thomas says you are a climatologist," Adolph announced with another puff of his cigar. "What interesting work that must be on an island like this. Our weather is something of an anomaly, at least to me. It never seems to follow a pattern."

"Oh, there's a pattern alright," Freidrick corrected, his rotund body bouncing as he rolled onto his toes. "It's called irregularity." Alfred gave a smile at the men's laughter as Freidrick ushered the men toward the Garten Verein. "My wife is no doubt anxious to be rescued from her chattering mess of women."

"You've done it quite right, Thomas," Adolph commented with a slap on the man's shoulder as they made their way back toward the stairs.

"Keep to bachelorhood as long as God grants it. Marriage can be a bitter affair."

"That's why I pepper mine with business trips and whiskey," Stanton joked, sending the group into a roar.

"Younger beauties never hurt the flavor either," Adolph replied under his breath as he motioned for Alfred to join his friends at the front of the group.

Alfred held the man's gaze as he passed. Despite Adolph being kind enough to get him into the club, Alfred felt uneasy about their company and being associated with him. Before they made it to the door, he was wondering if they would be keeping to the man's side all evening. He drew his attention to the light beaming through the open doorway and decided that, whatever Thomas's plan for the evening, he would be a part of it for as short a time as possible.

His purpose for making his way into the Garten Verein had nothing to do with other men's marriages. Alfred was set on a different sort of love altogether.

———•●•———

The dancing hall smelled of honeysuckle and lavender, a blend of the gardens' blooms and ladies' perfumes that mingled just inside the doorway and set Alfred's senses on alert. Light radiated from the ceiling and sharp-angled walls and lit up the men and women that chatted in groups along the walls and the couples that danced in the center beneath the cupola. The room was alive with well-timed steps and twirling dresses moving to the lilting notes that were carried on the strings of a piano, two violins, and a cello. Alfred let his eyes wander across the scene without any thought to the people behind him waiting to enter.

Mathias nudged his arm. The dance floor centered the scene as dancers circled one another in perfect rhythm. A wooden railing separated the dancing arena from a walkway that encircled the building. People chatted, women laughed, and men negotiated along the walkway as some took their rendezvouses to the quieter spaces nearer the windows looking out onto the park. Others made their way through the crowd toward the side doors to partake in a cigar or evening stroll away from the bright lights of the hall.

A bay window pushed out from the walkway on the side of dance hall, creating a small alcove where a bar had been built into the space. Mathias pulled his wallet from his pocket and ordered two mint juleps. He handed one to Alfred and turned back toward the dance floor.

"When I was a boy," Mathias commented, "my mother insisted on teaching me how to dance. She said a gentleman never turns away from the opportunity to treat a lady."

Alfred sipped at the sharp drink. "Which dance?"

"All of them." Alfred raised his eyebrows while Mathias let out a sigh, letting his eyes wash over the dancing crowd. "The waltz, the cotillion, the quadrille, the cakewalk."

"You can dance to all of those?"

Mathias nodded, glancing down the row toward a group of men that were outlined by Adolph Grier and Thomas.

"She would be rolling in her grave if she knew how little I employed her hours of work."

"I'd trade you in a heartbeat." Alfred took another drink of the mint julep, letting the flavor of the herb linger on his tongue before swallowing. Mathias eyed him for a moment.

"You can't dance?"

"I can dance," he clarified. "I'm just not very good at it."

"Too little practice?"

"And the wrong dance partners. Dancing wasn't in my father's purview when it came to being a good farmer. I didn't learn how to dance until I entered the Signal Corps. It's a requirement of the Corps to be able to dance at balls while in service."

Mathias nodded as he took another drink and tapped his fingers against his glass as he spoke.

"Is this your first ball?"

"Of sorts."

"I see."

The song came to an end as the piano pounded out a final chord. The dancers slowed and a small applause filled the room as women thanked their dancing partners. As a few young men found their courage to ask women for the next dance, the cellist warming up his strings for the next tune, Mathias grabbed Alfred's upper arm and pulled him toward the side door. Alfred held out his glass, working to keep the drink within its walls as he followed his housemate out into the warm night air.

Mathias slowed his pace and stopped just beyond the edge of a window's light. Alfred pulled his jacket sleeve down where it had bunched at the elbow and straightened his jacket.

"What has gotten into you?"

"I'm helping you out." He looked around them and settled his drink on a small wooden bench before gesturing for Alfred to do the same. Alfred eyed him as he set down his glass and then glanced back at the pavilion where the side door opened momentarily, letting out a rush of music before closing again.

"What are we doing out here?"

"Stand here."

Mathias motioned for him to step closer, and Alfred shook his head as he closed the distance between them.

"I don't understand."

Mathias held up his arms, one to his side with his hand open and the other up and out as if to rest it on Alfred's shoulder. He waited. Alfred looked from one hand to the other and shook his head.

"What?"

Mathias outstretched his hands as if to emphasize their function. "Well, come on then."

Alfred's eyes grew as large as the moon. "You want to dance?"

"Yes. Unless you can teach yourself in the next ten minutes."

Alfred shot a glance toward the main entrance and then gave a small chuckle. "We can't dance together."

"Why not?"

He let out a noise as he thought of an answer. "Imagine what people will think if they see two men dancing together in the park. At night."

"They'll think one of us is a fantastic dancer while the other has two left feet. Besides that, there's barely enough light out here to see anything. Now come on. My arms are getting tired."

Alfred took a step back and shook his head. "No, I'm not dancing with you."

Mathias let his arms drop and his head tilt to the side. "How many men do you think Florence has danced with?" Mathias raised his eyebrows to emphasize his point.

Alfred stilled at his question and locked eyes with his friend.

"What is that supposed to mean?"

"I mean that she is a beautiful woman, and beautiful women tend to be the focus of attention at balls like these. You are not going to be the only man in that club looking to steal a dance with her tonight." Alfred's eyes dropped as he listened, and Mathias's tone softened as he continued. "They taught you to waltz, yes?"

Alfred nodded.

"Is that all?"

He sighed as he scratched at the back of his neck. "I might be able to do the quadrille if I had time to think about it."

"You don't." Alfred's head snapped to attention, and Mathias raised his eyebrows. "You're lucky if you have ten minutes before the rest of society walks through those front doors, and you have a poorly construct-ed waltz and broken pieces of the quadrille in your pocket. You went through all of this trouble to get here tonight to see her. Are you really going to let this opportunity slip by because you are afraid to dance with another man in the dark?"

Alfred's lips puckered as he considered his words.

"You're only going to have four minutes to make an impression, Alfred," Mathias observed, rearranging his arms in the air once again.

"And you've already told me every dance you've ever had has been with corpsmen."

A small grin spread across Mathias's face. Alfred took in a deep breath and closed the distance between them with slow steps. He looked from Mathias's arm to his face and raised an eyebrow.

"Not every dance. I danced with my sister at her wedding."

Mathias gave a grave head nod. "I am certain Florence will find that comforting. Now, take my hand and wrap your arm around my waist."

Alfred stole a last glance toward the glowing window behind him before doing as he was instructed. Mathias's palm was soft and his jacket caught on the callouses at the base of Alfred's fingers. He looked straight ahead, his eyes looking at the well-groomed top of Mathias's hair, and breathed in the man's pomade.

"Lower your left hand a bit." Mathias directed their hands so that they were closer to their waists. "Now, the waltz is danced to three beats, so remember to count to three as you move to keep time." Alfred gave a quick nod. "You will start with your left foot, and Florence will start with her right. And you will lead her with your hand."

"My left hand?"

"You're right hand. If you try to lead with your left hand, you'll get a lot of this."

He pulled at Alfred's right hand and swung their arms back and forth wildly. Alfred let out a small laugh. "Okay, okay. I got it. Lead with the left."

"And loosen your grip a bit. You're not saving her from a fall."

Alfred loosened his grip and stretched his fingers before letting them relax around Mathias's hand.

"There. How do you feel?"

"Awkward and uncomfortable."

"Excellent. You're ready to dance. Now take your left foot and step out at a forty-five-degree angle. Right here."

Mathias motioned for him to place his foot out and to the side, and Alfred did so, looking down at his feet.

"Good, now rotate as you follow through with your right foot."

Alfred stumbled as he turned, and Mathias tried to guide him with his hand, pushing against his shoulder. The music died to applause within the pavilion and they realigned their bodies as the violins struck a chord and a new song floated out into the garden.

"Right." Mathias took a deep breath and gave a tight-lipped smile. "Let's try a different tactic."

CHAPTER TWENTY-ONE

*A*lfred and Mathias returned to the dancing pavilion through the main entrance, mingling with the newly arrived couples and groups of women as they spread throughout the room. Mathias gravitated toward the bar and refilled his glass with a second mint julep before joining Thomas and Adolph Grier. Alfred walked the edge of the dance floor, letting his eyes float from face to face as he searched for anyone he recognized among the crowd. As he neared the bar, a familiar voice filled his ear.

"What a man like you must've had to do to get his name on this social calendar."

Alfred kept his eyes on the dance floor as John stepped up beside him, a fresh glass of brandy in his hand. He took a drink and flashed a smile at Alfred as he spoke, scenting the air with liquor.

"That's quite a feat. Fresh in the harbor and you're already making your way into the Garden Verein, though by what means is still up for grabs." He made a click with his tongue. "I had you pegged as more the type to be tipping bottles by the dock than counting steps on the dance floor."

Alfred drank the last of his mint julep and thanked God that John hadn't witnessed his struggle with his tie. "A pleasure to see you here, John."

"Oh, no need to mix pleasantries. We are housemates after all. And

I doubt we'll be seeing much of each other at these sorts of soirees in the future, what with your position at the newspaper and all."

Alfred cut his eyes at him as they both stepped out of the way of a group of men moving toward the bar.

"The Weather Bureau."

"Oh, it's all the same when you're doing little more than writing weather forecasts for the printing press, don't you think? And poor ones at that!"

John let out a laugh as he leaned into Alfred and nudged his arm with his elbow. The stench of brandy and musky cologne raked across Alfred's senses, sending him recoiling as John took a step to regain his balance. Alfred sized him up before returning to his search of the room.

"Go home, John. You're drunk."

"Far from it. I'm merely starting the night off right. Isn't that what Goodman always says? Something like that." He sniffled. "I heard you made quite an impression at the last gathering, making friends with the higher sort."

"What would you know of it?"

"Not much to be honest." He took a drink and bowed out his chest. "There's not much fun to be had with old Charles Bendrick there." Voices rose from the front of the pavilion as a group of women chatted and swooned over their dresses. John's voice broke Alfred's concentration as he whispered in his ear. "Besides, I'm saving the fun for later tonight."

Alfred grimaced and pulled his ear away from the man's face, but John took a step closer as he pointed toward the front of the dance hall.

"And I've got a certain woman in mind."

Alfred followed his gesture toward a group that poured through the entryway. A tall woman in an emerald dress laughed with an older woman in a simple peach outfit. All around them couples talked, men greeted one another with sturdy handshakes, and women leaned in to comment on their newest fashion. Alfred focused on the woman in the emerald dress. Something in her mannerisms felt familiar, but her face was obscured by a wide-brimmed hat that boasted a peacock feather. After a moment, he recognized her rehearsed manner as Evelyn Goodman. He sucked in a breath as she stepped aside and Florence appeared between the two women in a fitted sapphire dress. He watched her as she laughed, her casual nature putting the other women at ease, and followed her as she moved through the group.

John's voice was beside his ear within seconds.

"You didn't really think she would entertain the thought of someone like you, did you?" Alfred's jaw tightened as he watched her offer her hand to a young man as the two exchanged introductions. "A small-time weatherman who can barely afford his board." Alfred felt him tug at the hem of his jacket. "Who'd you steal these tails from anyway?"

He watched as Florence made her excuses and broke free of the young man's conversation, pulling her gloves from her hands and glancing about the dance hall as if searching for someone. In that moment, his heart racing and his breath short, he made his decision. John began to slur against his shoulder.

"You look like an absolute ass—"

"Excuse me."

He shoved his empty glass against John's chest as he stepped away, leaving the man grasping at it to keep from spilling his brandy. Alfred crossed the room quickly, taking purposeful steps around the mingling crowd, and came to rest behind Florence's figure, her attention caught by another group of young women. He drew in a deep breath as he leaned forward just behind her ear.

"If they had only known."

She turned in surprise, a smirk caught at her lips. He stepped back to give her room and felt his heart flutter as her face broke into a wide smile. Her hair was pulled up behind her head and fell in thick curls behind her neck.

"Why, Mr. Ridgeway, this is a pleasant introduction." She waited for him to return her smile. "But I'm afraid I didn't quite hear you."

"I said that if the other women had only known."

Her smile widened as she tilted her head to look up at him through veiled eyes.

"Known what, I wonder."

"How beautiful you would look tonight. I imagine they wouldn't have even troubled with their coaches."

Her laugh filled her cheeks and lit up her eyes. "I must say," she replied, "you look like quite the gentleman."

He glanced down at his shirt and back at her with a grin. "Am I playing the part well enough to fool the crowd?"

"I'm afraid that depends on your dancing."

A song ended and one crowd began to ebb away from the parquet floor as another flowed back onto it. Alfred stole a glance toward the band as the pianist announced a waltz.

"Perhaps you can be the judge of how I fare as a dancing partner."

He stepped closer to her and offered a hand. She took it without a word and followed him onto the dance floor, lifting the hem of her dress as she moved. The sapphire silk sashayed about her legs and stole the light from every direction. Couples gathered around them as they made their way to the center of the floor until they all stood like silent figurines atop a music box, waiting for the lid to be opened. He felt her hand rest gently in his and breathed in her perfume. The violinists' bows pulled at their strings with the first note of the music, and he took a deep breath.

Mathias had been right that the first two steps were the strangest, but their bodies fell into time with one another as they spun around the pavilion. The vibrant movements of the other dancers orbited them like planets in perfect rhythm so that the world moved about them as a single piece, tightening their space until Alfred felt as if everything else had melted away and all he could see was her soft hazel eyes.

After their third rotation, he found the rhythm naturally along with his confidence to do something other than count the beats. He cleared his throat.

"You dance beautifully, Ms. Keller."

"Oh, really, Alfred! I thought we were past formalities."

He smiled and she gave a coy glance toward the orchestra before letting her eyes settle back on him. "Do you dance often?"

He swallowed, deciding in the moment that the world around them could neither hear nor judge him as long as they kept to their spinning arc.

"No, I'm afraid this is my first formal ball outside of the Signal Corps."

"Well, a lady would never know by your dancing."

"I've passed, then?"

"Your secret is safe with me."

She beamed, her high cheek bones adding a dramatic depth to her eyes. He felt the weight of her hand grow as she slid it down farther on his chest and he realized how close they had become as they twirled around the pavilion.

"Would it be appropriate for me to ask a question in return?"

"I believe that would be fair."

He gave a curt nod as they neared the quartet. The strings intensified as the cello struck a set of eighth notes that sent them spinning toward the edge of the dance floor.

"You were called away before you could answer my question after Sunday's service."

"Which question was that?"

"How you prefer to spend your time."

She held his gaze for a long moment before her fingers tightened along the back of his hand. "I play piano."

"Piano?" His eyes drifted as he considered something. "I think my grandmother had a piano when I was younger. I recall sitting on a bench as a young boy and pounding on the keys in her parlor."

"A young Mozart?"

"Nothing of the sort. I wouldn't know my way around a piano any more than a steamer."

"It's not as complicated as all that, I assure you."

He held her gaze. "I think it might be more complex than you lead on."

She blushed and let her eyes drop as he led them around the start of another tour of the pavilion. "But playing Mozart and Bach can't take up all of your time."

"On the contrary, it takes up a great deal. I teach a few children in the mornings at the orphanage. They have an old piano there."

"That must require quite the reserve of patience."

"Perhaps," she replied with a small shrug, "but I find it rather rewarding to watch a child work at mastering something so difficult."

"And entertaining I would wager."

"Always," she chuckled.

"And in the afternoons?"

"I paint."

A grin spread across his face. "You are quite the creative woman."

"My father says my head has always been in the clouds, even as a child."

"Some of the most beautiful sunsets happen in the clouds." Her eyes twinkled as he dared to lean closer to whisper. "And I would know."

The cello faded to a deep note as the violins sang the last of the waltz. As the room quieted, they held their pose for a moment longer before joining the dancers' applause. The couples around them moved toward the edge of the dance floor, and Alfred offered his arm to lead her back to their origin. A boisterous laugh erupted from the group that had gathered around William and Evelyn, and Florence tightened her grip on Alfred's arm, slowing his pace.

"Would you fancy a walk in the gardens," she asked, looking up at him with raised eyebrows.

Alfred hesitated before catching her gaze and giving a small nod. Allowing the growing party to fill the space between them with Evelyn's over-rehearsed laugh, he let her guide him toward the door and down the front steps of the pavilion.

———•●•———

The park beyond the pavilion was a maze of walkways lined with tropical flowers glowing in the light of the dance hall. The grounds opened into acres of well-manicured lawns spotted with the sharp angles of palm trees, their fronds dusting moonlight over the grass. The strings of the band faded until they were only a whisper above the locusts.

"The sky made quite the showing tonight," Florence commented.

Alfred followed her gaze to see a mat of shining stars speckled across the night sky, a half-moon perched over the city. The scene overhead wrapped their world in a galaxy of light, and he let his head roll back as he became smaller beneath the ever-growing dome of stars above them. His eyes traced the sky around them until he looked back toward the pavilion. Florence followed his gaze toward the dancing hall, taking his arm.

"Let's walk."

"Away from the lights?"

"For now." She gestured toward a far corner of the park that glowed more brightly than the pavilion. "I thought you would like to see the fountain. Unless you prefer the stars?"

He preferred anywhere that let her arm stay in his. "Do we have time for both?"

She gave a small laugh and laid her other hand over his arm so that her hands rested together. Her body moved closer as they walked, and he breathed in the scent of lavender from her skin.

"The park is beautiful," he commented.

"You should see it during the day. In midsummer it's flush with fresh blooms and vibrant blossoms all along the walk. And the petals smell divine."

"Is that where you're often found, walking the island smelling flowers?"

"Daily," she replied with a grin, letting her eyes drift to his before looking back toward the fountain. "My doctor says that walking every day is good for my health, so I make a sport of it. Looking for flowers I've yet to discover, perhaps something new that someone has brought to the island from their travels."

"You walk the island alone?"

"My grandmother joins my outings when she visits from Oregon," she mused. "Otherwise, I prefer to keep my own company."

Their walkway met another as they made their way beyond the light of the dancing hall. The crisscrossing effect made the park look as if it stretched forever with crushed shell paths lined with rose bushes and tropical plants leading to all corners of the city. He slowed their pace and instinctively laid a hand atop hers where it rested on his bent arm.

"Perhaps we shouldn't venture too far," he announced as he looked about the darker sections of the park.

"And why is that, Alfred?"

His eyes locked on hers as a small grin pulled at the corner of her lips. He laughed nervously. A chorus of cicadas began their symphony in a nearby oak tree.

"We're unchaperoned, Florence."

Her grin spread into a smile that melted with the warmth of the night air. "Really, Alfie. You must try to remember not to let others tell you how to live." She turned back toward the lawn and led him toward the path, the fountain glowing in the distance as a cascade of yellow light. She paused at the mouth of the new path and let her hands fall from his arm. She bent down and cupped a blooming yellow rose with her fingers. The bud came up with a quick tug and broke the stem in half. She brought it to her nose and closed her eyes as she inhaled the scent.

"You're in Galveston now, where life is lived a little more extravagantly than in the rest of the world." She looked back up at him. "You need to open your eyes to see the island for what it is."

She held the flower up toward his nose. He kept his eyes locked on hers as he bent down and breathed in the bloom's essence. It was light but distinct and lingered in his senses as he straightened.

"What do you smell?" she asked.

"A rose." She rolled her eyes and a small laugh escaped her lips as she slapped his chest. He rolled onto his heels in mock surprise.

"Am I wrong?"

"No, you're not wrong." She took a step closer and tucked the stem of the rose into his breast pocket. "But you're still not thinking like a Galvestonian." She lifted the edge of her skirt to clear her boots and he offered his arm. She led them toward the fountain as the cicadas' song faded with the oak trees behind them.

"I believe you're mistaken, my lady. Some of the greatest literature has proved you wrong."

"Oh?"

"A rose by any other name would smell as sweet."

She tightened her grip on his arm. "I didn't realize you were a Shakespearian!"

Two men materialized on the path ahead of them and stepped aside to let them pass, a trail of cigar smoke lingering in the thick air around them. Alfred waited for the sounds of their shoes on crushed shell to succumb to the rustle of the trees in the breeze.

"Is that the problem then, that I'm thinking like a Shakespearian and not a Galvestonian?"

"Perhaps," she replied with a smirk.

"Alright. What does a rose smell like to a Galvestonian?"

"Like a rose."

He tilted his head to look down at her. Her dress shimmered with each step like the stars overhead. "If it smells like a rose—"

"You asked the wrong question."

He let out a long sigh. "I hadn't realized how incomplete my education was." He felt the weight of his suit grow as he began to sweat beneath his collar. "What is the right question?"

"Look at where we are, Alfie. Walking one of the most beautiful gardens on a June evening. You have to consider the world around you, what you are experiencing." She tugged at his arm, stopping them in the middle of the path. "Close your eyes."

He felt her hand on his arm and did as she said.

"Just listen."

The world around him was quiet at first, only the sound of his heartbeat in his ears. Then the summer evening began to unfold around them. Cicadas chirped in the trees, the breeze rustled oak leaves and palm fronds overhead, and a trio of bullfrogs bellowed from somewhere in the dark. The trickle of water carried from the fountain at the end of the path, and he imagined it glistening in its man-made moonlight. He was opening his mouth to speak when the scent of honeysuckle tickled at his nose. He breathed in the warm air and caught a whiff of freshly cut grass mingled with saltwater. It smelled like summer on the island.

A small smile crept along his lips as he spoke. "What does a rose smell like in June in Galveston?"

"Yes! You see? Not all roses are the same because not all flowers are the same. Even roses."

"And not all months and islands are the same."

He opened his eyes to see her smiling up at him. He nodded toward the fountain and she followed. It grew before them, a stone pelican lifting up from the center as if about to take flight. Lights illuminated the spouts of water that came from beneath the bird and lit up the circular pool of water that swirled with koi. He stopped as the path opened up to a wide circle that encased the fountain's base and let his eyes follow the light up to the tips of the outstretched wings.

"Worth the walk?" He nodded as he took in the artistic majesty of the bird's stance. She turned to face him and gestured behind them. "But the other view is just as breathtaking."

He turned to see the Garten Verein across the park, its octagonal shape radiating light through its windows where couples danced and toasted through the panes. The mighty oaks lining the path tossed their branches in the breeze, making the light from the dance hall sparkle like fireflies as their leaves bowed back and forth in the moonlight-crusted air. The music was silent to their ears, but the movement inside hinted at another waltz. Alfred looked over to Florence, her eyes focused on the scene.

"What is it about these gardens that you find so beautiful that you'd endanger your reputation to take an evening stroll with a man you barely know?"

"I like to think we know each other better than that." She grinned and loosened her arm from his, making her way toward the fountain. "There's something raw and untamed in the nature of the island. It's in the way the sun paints the sky an almost burnt red, like a fire just out of reach. And in the way the breeze tastes of the saltwater, as if the ocean could rush onshore at any minute." She looked over at him and held his gaze. "It's as if the island is telling us her story, one flower at a time. They're her love letters, from the island to the world."

"Who are they for?"

"To islanders. To lovers." She cut her eyes at him before looking up at the moon. "To us."

"I'm not certain how comfortable I am knowing you brought me into the garden at night to smell the island's love letters."

A smile cracked at his lips, and she dismissed him with a wave of her hand. Their laughter drowned in the fountain's splashing water.

"How many of its love letters have you read?"

"All of them."

"You're confident? You know them all by heart?"

"I am." She gave a strong nod. "I do."

"Alright. Which flower is best?"

"Best?"

"I haven't read many love letters, but I assume they're much like lovers. No two are the same." He glanced about at the flowering bushes and plants. "So which one is the best love letter?"

She considered his question as she looked about the fountain, her eyes searching for something. After a moment, she stood, taking his hand. He followed her around the stone rim until they were practically on the other side, the lights from the Garten Verein now washed away by the glow around them, the dance hall completely out of view.

Florence stopped a few feet into a new path that led farther into the park, a large bush at the edge of the crushed shells beneath her feet. He watched her fingers caress the small petals of the flowers that were nestled between thick green leaves that came to points like darts ready to be launched. Her hair glowed in the light of the fountain as she pulled him next to her. His heart pounded in his ears as he felt her smooth skin against his. She pulled at the blossom, careful not to detach it from the bush, and took a step back to let him get closer.

He leaned down and took in a deep breath. He had expected an overwhelming sweetness, something extraordinary that would give him a scent to remember the evening for months to come, but it was nothing of the sort. It was subtle and soft, almost earthy with a hint of nectar, like the scent of the summer as its moves on the wind.

"Well?"

He straightened, considering his words. Florence answered for him. "It's not floral."

"No, it's not. I thought it would smell sweeter."

"But you didn't ask for the sweetest flower. You asked for the most romantic of the island's love letters."

His head tilted as he tried to follow her words. Her lips turned up as she continued.

"I think this one smells like the island. It's not overly sweet, just enough to remind you of what it is, and sometimes it smells like the earth, like it's remembering the dirt that helped it grow. And on particularly windy days it catches the salt from the ocean breeze and has a hint of the sea on its petals. It reminds me of the warmth of the island."

"Like summer."

She nodded. "Like the summer winds off the water. And its colors. Its bushes can bloom in pink, peach, yellow, white. When several bushes are near each other, they remind me of the sunsets, the way the colors paint the sky over the rooflines."

She pulled the flower out an inch more, tugging on the spiky stem.

"Smell it again."

He bent down and closed his eyes, picturing her descriptions. As he breathed in the scent of the petals, a sensation washed over him. The ocean breeze and salty air. The fresh dirt of the bayou. The warmth of the sunset over the water. It was all there, wrapped neatly in the pink swirling star that brushed against his nose.

He felt warmth against his cheek and opened his eyes to see Florence bent down next to him, their hands still intertwined at their sides. Her eyes were closed as she drew in a breath. In the shaded light of the fountain, her eyes twinkled as she opened them to look at him, their faces only inches apart.

"Now do you understand?" she whispered.

He nodded, unable to find his voice among the warm breeze of the night.

"These are oleanders. They are my favorite flower." She closed her eyes and let her nose drop closer to the petals. "Oleanders in June are the island's love letter to people like us."

Chapter Twenty-Two

Joseph greeted Alfred at the doorstep to the Levy Building the following Wednesday with an apple in his hand and a sack at his feet. The street smelled of smokestacks and lumber, the start of the work day at the harbor.

"No need to go up." Joseph shouldered the sack, which clanked with the movement. "We're heading out." He gestured for Alfred to pick up another canvas sack that sat against the door.

"Where are we going?"

"To the west end to take observations."

"I don't have a horse."

Alfred sat the sack at their feet when Joseph stopped next to a mare and began securing his sack on the saddle.

"Isaac said you could ride Daisy." He pointed to the alley between the buildings where a chestnut mare chewed on the grass along the bricks. Joseph took a bite from an apple, crunching loudly. "I'd mind her on the roads, though. She's easily spooked by the trains."

Alfred watched Joseph loosen the rope and mount his horse, turning her in circles in the street. Daisy seemed less enthused about their journey and pulled at her rope as he secured the sack of instruments behind her saddle. As he took hold of the saddle, she side-stepped, pulling away from him, and he hopped with her before pulling himself up and onto the seat.

Dr. Cline appeared on the raised boards of the sidewalk, his sleeves rolled up to his elbows. Daisy moved toward him unbidden. She nuzzled his shoulder, and he patted her cheek, glancing up at Alfred in the saddle.

"Did he tell you she's spooked of trains?" He let a grin slip between his lips. "And snakes and turtles and birds."

Daisy shook her head with a shudder, causing the sack of instruments to clank on her back. Dr. Cline handed Alfred a brown panama hat with a wide brim.

"Take this."

Alfred recognized the style from his last outing with Hilary and tried to imagine the doctor wearing something so relaxed in public. "Your hat?"

"I'm surprised you haven't baked in the sun already, and this outing isn't the place to start. Now keep her reins tight near the beach," he instructed with a quick tug at the bridle, moving the horse to the side and starting her toward the road.

Alfred let her walk a few feet before tapping at her haunches with the stirrups. She huffed and started a trot, hooves echoing between the buildings. Joseph was already crossing Postoffice Street when Alfred caught up to him and slowed the mare to a brisk walk. They rode in silence, passing early risers and house staff on their way to the markets, until they reached the end of 23rd Street where it emptied onto the beach. Joseph gestured to the west where the first warmth of the day had begun to burn off the early morning haze.

"We have a platform a little over two and a half miles on the beach."

Alfred followed Joseph's canter as they cleared the empty beach. A wind rushed off the water with the scent of saltwater, and his mind drifted back to Florence in the gardens. He had given very little thought to the nature of the island before meeting Hilary, but Florence's ardor for the flora seemed to surpass the old man's passion. The contrast of the pair's fervor for nature with his riding companion's own appreciation of a different sort of nature held him in check as the lead mare slowed her gait where the boundaries of the road thinned, giving way to tall grasses that obscured the view of the beach.

The world around them had changed drastically within a matter of minutes, transforming a cleanly defined beach with bathhouses and piers into a wilderness of grasses that nestled their roots in sand dunes, melting into an untamed seascape. The smell of horse manure and black tar smoke was replaced with the sweet odor of something blooming on the wind and the water's salty mist as it clung to the air around them.

Alfred adjusted his hat as Joseph pointed toward a small house in the distance.

"That's Captain Gregory's house. That's our marker to turn. It's just across the way there, on the other side of the road."

He followed, keeping a tight grip on Daisy's reins as Joseph's mare navigated the trodden road to find a small path, overgrown but visible, that led away from the house and toward the beach. The horses traversed the change in terrain as if they knew it by heart, and Alfred was hesitant to try to correct Daisy's direction, certain she knew the way better than he did.

Just off the road and beyond the first of the sand dunes, a large wooden platform came into view. Daisy dutifully followed Joseph's mare toward the structure and stopped at the pole next to the stairs that led up from the sand.

"It's been windy," Joseph commented as he slid off the horse. He untied his sack, glancing about at the dunes. "There's quite a bit more build up than we usually see this time of year."

"What does that mean?" Alfred pulled his sacks loose of the saddle as Joseph began to climb the steps up onto the platform.

"That it's been windy."

Alfred licked the salt from his lips as he watched the observer make his way up the last step, his boots calling out along the beach against the hollow boards beneath him. Alfred rolled his eyes, slinging his pack over his shoulder as he made toward the stairs. The platform was just over six feet off the sand and lifted their figures above the tallest sand dunes on the beach. The wind whipped at their collars and the brim of their hats, rushing warm air off the water toward the road behind them. Alfred dropped the pack and removed his jacket.

"Is this the bureau's platform?"

He rolled his jacket into his shoulder bag as Joseph began to unpack his own sack. He set several pieces on the planks at his feet and rolled up the empty sack.

"We have several platforms around the island to let us take more accurate measurements. Three on the west end, two on the east end, and two on the bay side. You probably saw one when you came in on the train from the mainland." Alfred searched his mind for the memory but couldn't find it among the instruments he pulled from his sack. "We take field measurements at least twice a week," Joseph continued, "unless there is cause to take them more often."

He squatted over the instruments.

"We'll be taking more observations in the coming months when tropical storms are more likely to develop. Hand me the toolkit."

Alfred leaned down and handed him a canvas wrap that Joseph unrolled between them. He removed a small wrench and began working two poles together. Alfred waited dutifully by his side.

"I recall that hurricanes thrive in warmer waters."

"Storms." Alfred held a metal pole against his side as Joseph secured another piece to extend it farther, letting it reverberate against his ribs as the man ratcheted a bolt into place. Joseph kept his eyes on his work as he continued. "The bureau doesn't like for us to use words like hurricane or typhoon or tornado. They say it incites panic, even when talking hypothetically."

"We just call them storms then?"

"When we're talking outside of the office. Isaac believes that people should be aware of the dangers that surround them, but he still keeps to his duties. That's our job until the political climate calms down."

Alfred helped him position the pole over a plank. They slid it into the hole, and Joseph secured it to the platform. He picked up two smaller poles and handed one to Alfred.

"Headquarters operates on shifting sands." He twisted the pole into place and began tightening its bolts. "The Weather Bureau is understaffed most of the time with growing demands for more resources and more accurate forecasts. We're expected to develop the science behind our forecasts while keeping up with administrative work." He tested the bolts' grip before passing the wrench to Alfred. "But there's not much they can do about it. They have unprecedented political pressures to see disasters before they occur, like the nation's mind readers, but the science simply isn't there yet."

He waited for Alfred to finish tightening his arm of the pole and checked it with a tug before picking up a flat metal arrow. He set it into the arm and screwed it into place. He tapped it with his palm and watched it spin circles before the wind caught its tail and slowed its pace. It settled with its tip pointing northeast.

Joseph looked out over the ocean and let the breeze blow his hair loose of its pomade at the temples.

"We're scientists trying to catch lightning in a bottle on the edge of the world."

The wind rushed against their bodies and for a moment they were equals, two men standing above the water. The untamed heat of the oceanfront rolled in with the water, the only true instrument in the thick of it. They shared the experience of wanting to tame the waltz that nature played every day with rising tides and swirling clouds, but the moment passed and Joseph was at work again, setting up the portable barometer. And the distance between them returned.

It took nearly twenty minutes for them to arrange the instruments to Joseph's specifications, but the platform had transformed into a field office when all was said and done. The weather vane fidgeted with the gusting wind, the barometer's needle dropped, and the thermometer's mercury rose like a slug on a warm day. It was growing hotter.

"We'll let these adjust while we speak with Captain Gregory," Joseph announced as he rolled up his sleeves and started down the stairs.

Alfred followed as he attempted to navigate the shifting sand with less grace than the mares, his shoes sliding with the loose soil. The road was exposed as they emerged from the grasses and the change in climate was immediate. The wind was blocked by the grasses, now a breeze that lingered about rather than cooling the air, and his skin longed for its sensation. He loosened his tie at the knot and felt his body heat vent along his neck as they crossed the road toward the house in the distance.

It was a small farm house, not at all what he would have expected for a sea captain. Its windows were open to the ocean air and curtains swelled with the breeze beneath the simple overhang of the front porch. Two rocking chairs filled one side of the porch, welcoming them as wooden steps announced their arrival. Joseph knocked on the jamb of the open door, taking in Alfred's appearance before loosening his own tie.

The clack of boot heels came from within and the figure of a slender woman came into view. Her skirt billowed as she approached but her arms went out to her sides when she reached the doorway.

"Joseph!" Her voice was like butter on a summer table. Alfred breathed a soft sigh at the thought of better company. "Do come in."

Joseph stepped into the cool shade of the house and gestured behind him.

"This is Alfred Ridgeway, our new assistant."

"How wonderful!"

Her exuberance was contagious, or perhaps it was simply the relief of the house's cool interior. Whatever the root, Alfred welcomed her invitation and prayed she was the sort to have tea ready for unexpected guests.

"Yes, let's sit in the parlor where it's cooler." She motioned for them to move through to the next room. "And I'll make you each a glass of sun tea."

Alfred felt his shoulders relax.

When Mrs. Gregory returned with two glasses of oak-colored tea, each with a slice of lime floating at the top, Alfred rose to assist her with the tray, but Joseph remained seated.

"I do hope we are not interrupting your day," Joseph commented. "We had not planned on taking observations today, but the forecast calls for storms off the west shore."

Alfred glanced at his colleague and wondered which sort of storms he meant.

"Not at all! You know Terrance so enjoys your company. And Lord knows I am not one to discuss these sorts of things with him." She beamed as she took a seat across from them. "He'll be down shortly. He was quite tired after breakfast."

Joseph nodded and took a drink of his tea. "Are these limes from your trees?"

"Yes, we've had glorious luck with it all this summer." She beamed. "Two lime trees in the back and oleanders all along the side."

Alfred felt his lip pull up into a smile at her words. "I wouldn't have thought much would grow out here, what with the sand and all."

"Neither did my husband and he was right for the first two years. But the third time was the charm, as they say!"

He nodded and drank greedily from his glass, savoring the fresh aroma of the citrus and the cool sensation on his tongue. A creak of floorboards came from the hallway and she rose.

"We're in the parlor, darling."

The clack of a cane beat with every other step until a man appeared in the doorway. He was tall and his shoulders argued that he had once been a stout fellow. But his shirt hung more loosely at his shoulders than it once had and his stature had fallen so that he hunched slightly as he walked.

"Here, darling." She cleared a pillow from the sofa beside Joseph. "I'll make you a glass of tea. Sugar?"

The man nodded as he sat with a sigh, and the air around him seemed to clear of dust with the movement. His wife's boots mapped her steps through the house and into the kitchen.

"I see you finally got your assistant," the man commented. His eyes connected with Alfred's. For all the years in his skin, his eyes were steely and blue like a clear morning at sea.

"This is Alfred Ridgeway, our newest recruit." Joseph's voice was softer than usual. "This is Captain Terrence Gregory."

"Retired," the man corrected in a gruff voice that hinted at a reserve of energy. "For a while now it seems. It takes a keen intellect for a man to steer his crew across the depths of the Atlantic without knowing what lurks just over the next wave."

Mrs. Gregory returned, a smile on her face and a glass of tea with two limes. She handed it gingerly to her husband as he spoke again.

"I seem to have lost a bit of that foresight before retiring," he continued.

"What's that dear?"

"The ability to keep myself in one piece."

She hummed in response and returned to her seat. The captain took a long drink of the tea before glancing up at the group. His wife picked up a towel that was locked into an embroidery loop, and Joseph spoke softly.

"We're expecting storms off the west shore later this week. Moving up from Mexico."

"A Mexican rebel?"

"Something like that. They're predicting heavy winds and a lot of rain. Alfred and I finished setting up the instruments about half an hour ago."

"What of the winds?"

"Steady at six with gusts around thirteen from the southwest. Pressure was dropping from twenty-nine point nine-four."

"It'll be a strong one, then," the captain commented. "The season has already started. I heard reports of Cuba being sidestepped by a strong one that built up over the Atlantic."

Alfred leaned in to rest his elbows on his knee. "The season?"

Captain Gregory took a long drink of tea and then looked casually toward Alfred, as if his words were meant as much for his wife as the newest member of their group.

"Hurricane season. The storms wait for the summer months when the water is at its hottest. They build from below, churning with the current. I've seen them form over the water as if from nothing." He gave a cough and took another drink of tea.

"Have you ever seen a storm change course?" Joseph asked, rubbing his palm along the arm of the sofa.

"It's hard to say for certain. If we hadn't gotten a report at our last port, it was hard to know which direction the storms were meant to be heading." His voice lost the rough edge that had defined his words up to that point, and he let his eyes wander to the window across the room that looked toward the city in the distance. "But I recall a trip when I was young, just a sailor pulling lines on an old fishing vessel. It was mid-summer when the winds tended to turn and the waves grew stronger away from the shores. A storm was reported in the open waters to our port side, just south of our intended crossing. We turned the sails and pushed northward, but the storm had changed course. When the sun set, we heard the storm off our starboard and found ourselves heading into the southern tip of the hurricane."

"When was this?"

The man's face scrunched in thought. "Eighteen fifty-two. The year before I joined the navy. We heard reports once we made landfall that the storm had been bound for the Yucatan and turned at the last minute. They didn't know why."

"The currents?"

"Or the winds. There's no way to know for certain. The ocean does as it chooses." He straightened a bit as he drew a breath that wheezed in his lungs. "Why do you ask?"

"There was a storm that moved along Cuba, catching it on the southern tip, and it was tracking for the coast. All reports said it was heading inland, but the official stance is that it stalled in the ocean. But I believe it turned and missed the coast."

"It's not unusual for them to stall over the waters." He coughed and pulled a handkerchief from his pocket to wipe his mouth. "I've seen hundreds die out before reaching the shore."

Joseph nodded and sipped his tea before continuing.

"We think the summer will be a hot one. We have had an unusual spike in heat waves all across the country. It's a bit disarming to think that the weather patterns are changing before we can even understand what they are doing."

"Perhaps it's all of the industrialization."

Both men looked at Alfred, their faces blank. He cleared his throat.

"It just seems like the growth of industries, what with factories abounding and smokestacks being pushed out to sea with steamers, that there might be a correlation of some kind."

The men were silent, and Joseph took a drink of tea to break the tension.

"Or perhaps not," Alfred conceded.

"You sound like those lobbyists who oppose the channel expansion, going on about the birds and the habitats." Captain Gregory raised an eyebrow. "Do you support the expansion?"

Alfred stole a glance toward Joseph, who had diverted his eyes. "No, sir. I'm afraid I do not."

"Neither do I," the captain remarked with a cough. "I think we've done enough to this island. A man can't walk down the Strand without breathing in the steam of the ships. When I first arrived, nature had done the landscaping, and done it quite well enough before we all stepped in and started dredging a channel for more ships."

"That's a touch ironic, don't you think, dear?" His wife grinned from her chair. "That a naval captain opposes more ships coming into dock?"

He shrugged his shoulders. "I suppose it is. But it doesn't make it any less relevant." He turned back to Joseph. "I spoke with Isaac a few weeks ago. He was doing some observations of the tide and stopped to say hello on his way back into town. He said Cora is doing well."

"Yes," Joseph replied, "she's about five months along now. Her sickness comes and goes, but it seems to be easing some."

"Poor dear," Mrs. Gregory lamented, dropping her embroidery into her lap. "Pregnancy can be such a bother when it comes to the summer. The heat can be so unrelenting for us."

A cough erupted from her husband's chest, and he leaned forward, his glass hitting the table with a thud. Mrs. Gregory was at his side with a fresh handkerchief and eased him back onto the sofa as the coughs subsided. She patted his shoulder and swapped handkerchiefs, putting the clean one in his lap as he settled against the sofa. Alfred watched her fold the bloody square of cotton as she made her way out of the room.

"We've taken up enough of your morning," Joseph commented quietly.

The captain nodded as Joseph set down his tea and rose to his feet. Alfred followed his example and took a last drink of his tea before standing. Captain Gregory cleared his throat and dabbed at his mouth.

"It was kind of you to stop by," he wheezed. He swallowed with a hum of discomfort and glanced at the doorway. "I'm afraid my wife is rather optimistic about my condition. She has come to believe that fresh air and rest is all a man my age needs to find his health. She'll soon learn it takes much more than that."

The sound of her boots carried through the house, and his eyes settled on Joseph.

"She'll have no one left."

"Would anyone like more tea," Mrs. Gregory called from the hallway as she approached.

She entered the room with a bright tone, her eyes darting desperately from one man to the next as her lips pulled into a tight smile.

"No, ma'am," Joseph replied. "We really must be heading back."

She nodded and fumbled with her cuffs as she made her way back into the hallway. Joseph led them out of the room and thanked Mrs. Gregory for the tea. Back in the warmth of the June day, they walked across the street and climbed the platform in silence. He handed Alfred a logbook and began instructing him on how to record the observations, including noting the tide and the behavior of the waves. When another silence settled between them, Alfred spoke softly.

"They have no children?"

Joseph, his hands in his pockets and the wind blowing at his collar, kept his eyes on the waves as they rushed the sand.

"They had a son."

Joseph watched the water for another moment before returning to the observations, letting the rush of the wind carry his words across the sand. Alfred stood at the edge of the platform, noting the water's movements and the size of the white caps as the wind pushed the ocean toward the shore. His mind drifted to the image of the captain as he had slumped back on the couch, and he wondered how much it took for such a man to become too beaten to chase the water that had once buoyed his life. He didn't, however, wonder at how overwhelming it was to watch someone wither away; that sensation he knew all too well.

"Come on," Joseph called from the sand. "No use wasting the day here."

"What about the midday observations?"

But the man was already on the back of his mare and turning her toward the path to the road. Alfred watched him walk the horse through the dunes, the man's figure growing smaller with each hoof that hit the sand, his shoulders slumped as his head bobbed with the horse's gait. By the time Alfred had cleared the sand and made it to the path, Joseph was awaiting for him well beyond where the grasses cleared and the road returned, his eyes on the surf and his back to the house on the edge of town.

CHAPTER TWENTY-THREE

*S*poonbills are the brightest birds on the island."

Alfred followed Hilary through the tall grasses, a sack on his back and a walking stick in his hand. Despite Hilary's knobby knees and permanently bent spine, he moved along the shore of Offat's Bayou with ease. Alfred chocked it up to a hardy memory of where to step and when to shift his weight because, no matter how hard he tried, he couldn't quite keep pace and kept slipping into muddy puddles that Hilary managed to avoid.

"This should work."

Alfred pulled out a thin blanket from his sack and fluffed it in the air to spread it out before settling it along a section of shorter grass. Hilary pulled out a compact piece of wood that he began unfolding, popping corners against each other until three legs came together and a single piece of wood slid into place on the top. Hilary smiled at the stool and settled it onto the blanket as his eyes scrutinized the horizon.

"Yellow-crowned night heron."

A slender grey bird strutted through the shallow water, spiky yellow feathers poking out along the crown of its head. In the distance a small rowboat slid along the water's edge, cracking the smooth surface of the bayou.

"They'll be more common as the summer wears on," he commented as he pulled a copper mug from his pack. "They like the warmer weather."

"Do they migrate?"

"They go rather far north in the summer, well north of Mudville."

Alfred held up a scotch bottle, and Hilary held out his mug. The sound of the bubbling liquid mingled with the noises of bayou. Frogs bellowed from the grasses as a fish broke the surface of the water before splashing back down. A warm breeze whispered through the grasses as another mosquito buzzed through their meal. Alfred swatted, landing hard on the back of his neck.

"The bugs here are ridiculous. I don't know how you put up with them."

"Time and patience."

"That makes me wonder if you've never lived somewhere where the insects are less persistent."

"Of course, I have. Georgia and Mississippi before I met my wife. But once we settled here, she wouldn't let me leave. At least not with her."

"What made her stay?"

His skin pulled tightly against his cheek as he thought about the question. "The sunsets, I think. She used to paint them. Creative women are a different breed, you know. They see the world differently than the rest of us." He looked back at him with narrowed eyes. "Remember that. They see things in the world that most of us miss. They sense beauty where most of us only see commonality. It makes them smarter and braver. It makes them better than people like you and me."

Alfred chewed on Hilary's words before taking a drink. The scotch burned but warmed his chest. He breathed in the earthy scent of the bayou.

"I met one."

"Hm?"

"A creative woman. She's a painter. And a pianist." A smile took over his cheeks. "And a very good dancer."

"She sounds dangerous." His eye twinkled as he glanced over. "That's good."

Hilary set his mug down on the blanket, bending over to pull his sketchbook and pencil tin from the sack. Alfred peered out across the water where the row boat had stopped several hundred feet off the edge of the grasses, its hull bobbing from side to side as the two men inside it adjusted their positions. He wondered if the men could see them, hidden behind the curtain of grasses with only the raising of their copper mugs to catch the setting sun and offer a momentary glint of light.

"My wife liked to dance." Hilary sharpened a thick pencil and let the shards of graphite fall to the blanket at his feet. "I was never very good at it."

A flock of pelicans beat at the air overhead as they moved out across the bayou. Alfred watched their flight and the two men in the boat as they pointed toward the birds with excitement. He leaned back on his hands and stretched his legs forward until his shoes rustled the grass. Hilary's voice came softly.

"Who is she?" His hands jerked in long strokes as he outlined the grasses and edge of the bayou water that connected to the bay. Alfred kept his eyes turned upward.

"Who?"

"This painter you've met."

He looked at his feet and then over toward the old man. His stomach tightened at the thought of sharing the intimacies of his thoughts, as if saying her name gave the world permission to judge him for thinking so longingly of her.

"Florence Keller."

Hilary nodded. "She would be a good fit for you. She's spunky like my wife."

"You know her?"

"I've lived here for thirty-two years. I know everyone."

A movement over the water caught his attention, and Hilary straightened to bring the binoculars to the bridge of his nose as he looked down the edge of the bayou shore.

"Ah," he whispered, "there she is."

Alfred pushed himself onto his haunches and looked over the old man's shoulders. A set of dead trees stuck up from the water about two hundred yards to their west. Stiffened branches jutted up from the silky water just inside the cordgrasses that lined the quiet shore. In the crook of the tree where a lower branch wandered from the trunk, a mature Roseate Spoonbill perched just within sight, a bright pink against the grey and green of the bayou's landscape. Hilary handed him the binoculars but kept his eyes on the bird.

"She's got a nest," he announced, his voice blending with the breeze. The grasses shushed his words as their stalks brushed together. "There should be more nests. They usually colonize together."

"I see one." Alfred pointed higher up into the tree's twisted form. "Two branches up. A mass of sticks and twigs. It dips down like a bowl?"

Hilary nodded as another pink bird, larger than the first, approached the tree and flapped its wings forward to land near the middle of the tree.

"Yes, that'll be one. They push them in to cushion and protect the eggs. Can you see anything in the nest? Any eggs or hatchlings?"

Alfred squinted into the binoculars, adjusting the lenses and making the scene come into sharper focus. "Not that I can see. But there are several nests. At least five in that tree alone."

The smaller bird extended its wings and took flight, lifting gracefully into the air. The larger one cocked its head to watch it fly and then turned back toward the water as if listening. Hilary hummed in thought.

"She must've heard something."

Alfred scanned the water with the binoculars, trying to find anything that would have scared the bird away. As he lost sight of the water's edge, he caught sight of the two men in the rowboat again. Their craft now buoyed silently no more than a hundred feet from the shoreline, their bodies rocking slowly with the current and the muzzle of a rifle extending over the edge of the keel.

Alfred's breath caught in his throat and he shot to his feet, dropping the binoculars. He knew he had made to shout, feeling his muscles tense as his jaw opened wide and his throat burned with words. But it was too late, the strain of his body useless, as the roar of the rifle boomed across the water and echoed down the bayou. He turned away from the scene, instinct taking over as he looked down to see Hilary's face beside him. It was loose and sullen, his eyes opened wide.

When he looked back toward the tree, the sound of the gunshot still rang in his ears, blotting out the whoosh of wings and the echo of calls that rose up from the nearby grasses as birds took to the sky in fear. Flocks rose by the dozens around them until the sky was a parade of feathered forms that scattered in all directions. The two men in the rowboat pointed toward the sky in amusement before storing their weapon and rowing toward their target.

Alfred and Hilary watched silently as the men searched in the grass, taking what felt like days before they claimed their prize and rowed back out into the water. His eyes still on the tree, Hilary began walking through the cordgrass, pushing tall stalks out of his way. Alfred started after him.

"Where are you going?"

"To retrieve the bird."

"They already took it."

Alfred's voice betrayed his emotion, and he swallowed it down into the pit of his stomach where it roiled and fumed. He tried to keep up, stumbling on the uneven ground and losing distance between them.

"Hilary!"

"They weren't after its body."

When he caught up with the old man, Hilary's small form was hunched over the ground. A patch of grass near the tree was disturbed, the stalks bent, and Alfred followed the trail back toward the water. The hunters' path had destroyed everything it had touched. He took two cautious steps until he stood beside Hilary and looked down at his feet. The twisted body of the Roseate Spoonbill was a mix of pink and red. What had once been a beautiful contrast now sickened Alfred and made him gasp for breath as he looked back out toward the water and spied the men rowing their way farther down the shore toward the dock.

Hilary lifted the bird's head and slid his fingertips over her eyes before examining her beak and feet. He laid her out on her side and stretched out her wing. His hand held the tip of her wing up to Alfred's thigh. The man drew in a loud breath.

"She was mature. Perhaps seven or eight years old."

Alfred didn't know what to say or how to help the situation. He had only ever been the student, dutifully asking questions to learn all that he could. He did the only thing he knew how to do in the bayou. "How long do they live?"

"About ten years, maybe twelve. It's hard to say for certain."

Hilary sniffled as he let the wing come to rest at her side and began examining her beak. Alfred let his eyes trace the bird's body before squatting next to her.

"Do you think they couldn't find her?"

"No, they found her."

"I don't understand."

Hilary's hand paused at the tip of the bird's beak and then gently rocked the bird onto her feet before laying her down so that her other side was visible. Her pale grey skin was exposed where a patch of feathers had been plucked from her wing. The brightest feathers that blended into the deepest hue were now missing from her body. Alfred felt a lump swell in his throat as he lost his breath. Hilary turned to him with soft eyes that made his form look even smaller as Alfred found a shaky voice.

"Her feathers? They shot her for her feathers?"

He nodded and led their eyes back to the bird. Alfred shook his head as anger boiled up into his chest.

"This isn't right. This is—"

"Perfectly legal." Alfred clenched his jaw as Hilary's words pierced the air. "It is perfectly legal for any man to hunt anything he stumbles upon in the wild." Hilary's voice soft but firm. "He is not required to give it any mercy, any consideration of its life, of its feelings. Any consideration of its children."

The breeze gusted into a wind and rushed through the grasses that concealed them from the water. From somewhere above them, a small feather, grey and fluffy like the down of Alfred's pillow, floated on the breeze. It paused between them before drifting down toward the bird and landing on her bare wing. Hilary lifted his gaze up toward the tree, following the path the feather had traveled and rose to his feet slowly. Alfred watched him, remaining crouched next to the bird.

The old man took cautious steps, trying to dampen their sound as he approached the tree. After a moment of listening, he beckoned Alfred to join him and pointed toward the middle branch where the bird had been roosting. Alfred looked at Hilary without a word, begging with his eyes, but the man gestured toward the nest.

"Go look."

Alfred braced himself against the trunk and hoisted himself into the tree with a quick but quiet motion. His boots threatened to slip, and he kept a firm grasp on the trunk as he took another step onto the large branch, pulling himself higher. There, at the base of a middle branch, was a nest the size of his dinner plate. It was deep, made of twisted sticks and twigs with mud caked along the sides like brick and mortar. Grasses poked up from the inside, their tips waving in the breeze. He paused, straining his ears to hear a sound, anything that would give away the little bird that he prayed was hiding within. When the silence continued unbroken, he braced himself against the trunk and leaned toward the nest, careful not to rock the branch.

When his eyes breached the edge of the nest, his heart sank and his throat tightened. The anger that had been born on the ground melted into a sob that quivered at his lip and escaped as a huff that sent a shiver through the tiny feathers. He looked away, his eyes blurry as he focused on the city in the distance. Large plumes of smoke billowed from the electricity company's stack, and the train glistened as the last car left the city, taking its final fare of the day to the mainland. Standing in the tree, blinking away the tears, the contrast struck him hard in the chest. The birds watched them from their nests, content to keep to themselves, the world erupting around them in gunshots.

Hilary's voice was gentle.

"Come down, Alfred."

He obeyed, moving much more quickly than before, and stumbled onto the grassy floor with a hard breath. Hilary had already wrapped the bird in a small blanket, and Alfred looked at him with hard eyes. The old man had known what they would find and had had the presence of mind to bring the blanket with them. The sound of his heartbeat pulsed in his ears.

Hilary seemed to recognize his thoughts and gave a small smile as he held the clothed bundle in his arms, turning to go back toward their plot.

"What about the other one?" His tone was stronger than he'd expected.

Hilary kept walking, taking his steps more slowly than before as if his body were as exasperated as his emotions.

"Hilary!"

The old man turned, his jaw set and his eyes red.

"The mature ones can teach us about their species. They are specimens that I can study." He took a deep breath as if the words were painful to let out. "The fledglings are not specimens. They're victims. I'll not do them any less justice."

He turned without another word and made his way toward their camp. Alfred looked down the shore, the rowboat nothing more than a dot on the horizon, and began to trudge back through the grassy landscape, leaving the tree behind him.

They packed in silence, returning everything as it was. When he had closed the packs and put them beside the basket, Alfred stood a few feet behind Hilary while the man looked out into the bayou. He gestured toward the opening where it fed into the bay.

"The Karankawa used to hunt on the island. They would cross the bay in canoes and men would hunt the birds while women collected oysters along the shore. They say the oysters were so thick that they could wade just a few feet into the water and come up with arms full of large shells." Alfred looked past his shoulder to the orange glow that gave a halo to the bay waters. "Now we search for them, the oysters. They're fading away, leaving or dying. We've stripped the oysters of their water." He looked up toward the sky. "And the birds of their sky."

Alfred shoved his hands in his pockets. "Isn't there something we can do?"

"We are a cruel species, Alfred. We could do many things, but we have chosen not to."

"I meant you and me."

Hilary glanced back at him with a tired grin. "Yes, there is a great deal we will do. We will finish our field guide and soon I'll introduce you to a society that works quite arduously to put a stop to this very problem." The breeze blew across them, cooling Alfred's face and neck as Hilary looked back to the water. "We are a cruel species indeed. We are so entitled, so ready to take whatever is here. We think we can live in another's habitat without consequences, but nature doesn't work that way. It must always find a balance."

Alfred's voice relayed his disgust. "What's a balance to this?"

Hilary turned back to him. His eyes were hard but glistened in the warm light of the setting sun.

"The only difference between us and this bird is that nothing hunts us with a rifle. But we are not infallible. We are a species that must learn to share the island before it is too late."

"Too late?"

Hilary made his way back toward their packs and lifted one over his shoulder. "This isn't hallowed ground. It can't survive everything that comes its way."

Alfred considered the words as he lifted the other pack and took hold of the basket.

"What could possibly destroy an entire island?"

"I wasn't talking about the island." Hilary cradled the swaddled bundle in his arms, his silhouette against the smoke stacks a stark contrast to their surroundings. "I was talking about the city."

CHAPTER TWENTY-FOUR

*M*rs. Poplar called the weather a wash-out, a storm that moved onto shore during the hours before sunrise and left Sunday services empty. The day broke with a pall over the island as Alfred made his way across town. Grey clouds tinted the air a steely shade that blurred in the rain while deep navy clouds rested on the shoulder of the horizon.

The steeple of St. Joseph's peaked over the rooftops as the carriage slowed along 23rd Street, the rain becoming a drizzle. Florence's house was a light blue façade with oleander bushes along the fence, exactly as he had pictured it would be. He adjusted his tie and gave the door a hearty knock before nervously adjusting the bouquet in his hands. The door opened with energy.

A fair-skinned woman stood in the doorway, the house open behind her, and a carefully-cut collar of lace at the middle of her neck. She clasped her hands and tilted her head as she scrutinized him.

"Hello?"

"Good afternoon. Mrs. Keller, I presume?"

"Heavens, no!" She gave a small chuckle and flashed a bright smile, her cheeks lightening with the humor. "What a world that would be! No, Elaine and Robert are on holiday in Vienna. I'm Katherine Goldman, Elaine's sister."

Florence's aunt. He let out a small sigh that he hid with a smile. "I hear Austria is beautiful in the summer," he commented.

"I've heard the same."

Her eyes softened as she raised her eyebrows, and he faltered with his realization.

"Oh, yes. Please forgive me. I'm Alfred Ridgeway, an acquaintance of Ms. Keller's."

Her eyes traveled down his suit and up to the flowers. "I see."

"I was hoping to call on her. That is, if she's feeling well. I heard she's been ill and was hoping to make a visit."

"Naturally," she replied, her tone covert. "I'm certain Florence could manage a visit. Please come in."

She stepped aside as he stepped into the shade of the parlor. The front sitting room was bedecked in blue and lace from the upholstery to the Chinese vase that adorned the mantle. A photo of a young man in uniform, a rifle swung casually over his shoulder, caught Alfred's eye. He swallowed and turned back to Ms. Goldman.

"This is a lovely home."

"Yes, it is. Elaine has exquisite taste and Robert the money to afford it." She motioned for him to follow her. "Please have a seat in conservatory. It is much cooler this time of day."

He followed her through the house, past a dining room, and into a room at the back of the house. Despite the large windows that looked out onto a garden, the room was in the shade of a giant oak tree, cast in immediate relief from the sultry day that was pressing on the island. She held out a hand for his umbrella and gave a knowing smile.

"Water?"

"Oh, no. That's quite alright."

She had disappeared before he could finish his answer, but he knew that it wouldn't matter. Ms. Goldman seemed the sort to do as she pleased, whether that was fetching men glasses of water or beating after geese with his umbrella. Either way, he hoped Florence would be well enough to join them. And soon.

A grand piano took up the farthest corner of the room, its lacquer shining in the dancing light that played with his eyes as it moved in and out of the room through the branches of the oak tree. Two wicker chairs and a matching love seat filled the other end of the room. Sheets of music were spread across a small table between the furniture. He bent over them, reading their German titles.

The tap of boots on the floor brought his eyes up the doorway. Florence wore a simple cream-colored dress with lace at the cuffs and a pleated front that narrowed at the waist. Her hair was swept up in a loose bun that looked as if she had just come in from a walk, but her eyes said otherwise. A bright smile crossed her tired face.

"What a pleasant surprise this is!"

His chest grew light at her words. "I hope my coming without invitation isn't too much of a disturbance for you." He lifted his chin as he tacked on a final thought. "Or your aunt."

"Of course not."

Her movements were slow and cautious as she crossed the small room toward him. He held up the flowers.

"I brought these for you. I heard that you haven't been well and thought they might brighten a gloomy day if you haven't been able to walk any gardens lately."

"How lovely." She motioned toward a small vase on the corner table between the chairs. "You can put them there while we talk. Day lilies? They are so vibrant. Wherever did you find them?"

"Mrs. Poplar's garden," he replied as he slid them into the vase.

She motioned for him to sit in one of the chairs, a smile at her cheeks. She sat on the love seat, one hand supporting her on the armrest at the ball of her palm while she worked her way onto the seat. Her smile faded for a moment as she settled in and then returned as a small pull at her lips.

"It's been quite rainy the past day," she commented.

"It'll continue through tomorrow. Dr. Cline tells me it's not unusual for it to be stormy like this well through September."

She raised a knowing eyebrow. "We have beautiful summers, but the rain can be quite the obstacle when it comes to enjoying the weather here."

"How long have you lived here?"

"My entire life much to my mother's insistence."

Her voice was soft and frail, and he saw her chest rise in deep breaths beneath her dress each time before she spoke. He was about to ask if she should be out of bed when her aunt returned with two glasses of water and a plate of cookies on a tray. She set the tray down on the low table with a small clink as she glanced at Florence.

"Not too long of a visit. You've been up too much today already."

"Of course." She tossed a mischievous glance at Alfred. "Mr. Ridgeway has just come to check on me after my absence in church this morning."

The woman made her way out of the room, calling behind her. "Shall I heat up some water bags for you?"

"Yes, thank you," Florence replied, her voice trailing with her aunt's footsteps. Her eyes flitted to Alfred as she motioned to the tray. "Please help yourself. Aunt Katherine is a renowned baker in Chicago. At least that's what she tells us, but her cookies seem to agree."

Alfred snapped a cookie in half and sent a spray of sugar and cinnamon into the air, eliciting an amused hum from Florence. The dough was soft and reminded him of Mrs. Poplar's baked cinnamon bread.

"What are these called?"

"Schnecke Knödel."

He looked at her blankly as he chewed the cookie, and she gave a bright smile that made his face warm.

"It's German." She paused to think. "It means something like snail dumpling." He looked down at the cookie with big eyes. "There's no snail in the recipe," she assured him with a laugh. "They are meant to be shaped like snails when they're baked."

"What a relief," he announced, reaching for a glass of water.

"She said they have an American name. Snickerdoodle or some funny word, but I prefer the German name."

"But not the cookie?"

Her smile faltered as her eyes dropped to the tray, a sprig of mint floating in her untouched water. She let out a small breath.

"I'm afraid I'm rather weak today."

"Then please allow me," he replied, reaching for the tray as he stood.

"That's quite alright."

She tried to argue, but he was already at the table, her water in one hand and a cookie in the other. She looked from his hands to his face without taking his offer. He watched her cheeks push up into a tight smile.

"Why don't you sit beside me, Alfred."

He felt his breath hitch in his throat as he sat the glass and cookie back down on the table. His heart kicked in his chest as he sat on the sofa, careful not to become too comfortable and keeping a distance between them in case her aunt returned. Her expression told him that whatever explaining Florence had to do wouldn't be lighthearted, and his mind began to race with all the things he had said since he had arrived. All the things he could have done differently. When her eyes stayed on her hands, he dared to lean in an inch.

"Are you alright, Florence?"

"I hate these conversations."

He became more aware of his breathing and rubbed his palms on his thighs. "I can leave if you would prefer."

"No." She turned to him with wide eyes, surprise in her expression. "No, that's not what I meant. I assume Mrs. Poplar told you I hadn't been well?"

He nodded, his mouth parched despite the water. She gave a small, understanding nod and looked down at her hands where they rested in her lap. They were still, he noticed, very unlike her usual expressive way of talking, and he heard John's words in his ear, the man's drunken breath scratching at his conscious.

"She's right. I haven't been well," she continued. "I haven't been feeling well for some time now, and the doctor says it is not an easily curable illness." She looked up from her hands and across the room. "He says it's not curable at all really, only something I can try to manage."

"What sort of illness?"

She looked at him with a forced smile. "I have arthritis of the joints.

Rheumatoid arthritis, he calls it."

"Arthritis?"

She nodded patiently. "To hear my doctor describe it, my body has trouble with my joints. They became swollen and inflamed, but he's not certain what causes it. And there's nothing to be done about it really. Just some heated water bags when it bothers me, a salve for my knees and hands, and an herbal tonic that my aunt brings me from Chicago. That's all they know to do."

"Does it hurt?" he asked softly.

She nodded as she looked back down at her hands. "At times it can be quite difficult to do simple things like walk or grip a glass."

He looked toward their glasses of water on the table. "I see."

She looked across the room again and wiped absently at her eye, returning to him with a smile on her face and an attempt at a lighthearted voice. "I understand it's quite the revelation. And you wouldn't be the first to find himself wondering at the implications. Please do not feel obligated to stay."

"Obligated?" She held his gaze as he let out a chuckle. "Florence, perhaps I should take this opportunity to say that I would consider myself a very lucky man indeed if I were to have any reason to be obligated to you. Though, I can't imagine how that could be considered an obligation in the true sense of the word." He glanced at her hands and back up to her face. "Would you mind terribly if we were to continue the conversation?"

Her eyes brimmed with tears, and she blinked them away before giving a small nod. "What would you like to know?"

He thought for a moment. "I only have two questions. First, does it interfere with your playing piano?"

She looked longingly toward the shining grand piano in the corner. "It does when my fingers are stiff and my hands go weak. If it is bad enough, I have to cancel my lessons, but that seems to happen more in the summer when the children prefer to be outside. So they don't seem to mind as much."

He nodded as her voice came more brightly.

"And the second question?"

"Is there something I can do to help?"

Her cheeks pulled up into a smile. "No. I don't think there is. The salves help, as do the warm water bags when my knuckles swell. More than anything I need help doing things. Cooking, dressing, heating the bags. The little things that require more strength than I have on days like this."

"Hence your aunt's visit."

"My parents always travel in the summer, and I went with them when I was younger. But traveling so much, days on trains and weeks on ships, puts quite a strain on my body. I haven't felt up to it the past few years. My mother insisted on staying home the first two years I wasn't well, but Papa said it wasn't good for her to stay at home so much during the summer months. So they sent for Aunt Katherine to come stay with me while they are gone."

"That's very kind of her to do so."

"It is. And she is wonderful at it." She chuckled. "I keep telling her they accept women at the nursing college now, but she won't hear of it."

He looked at his own hands. They were tanned and rough along the palm from his work in the field and his outings with Hilary, but they were strong. Looking up at her tired face, he slid down the love seat and closed the distance between them. She glanced up with attentive eyes as he reached out and gently lifted one of her hands and rested it in his own. They were warm to the touch, and she didn't attempt to pull away, letting them fall over his palms.

"How long do you usually feel this way?"

"It depends. I haven't felt well for days, but it is easing up a bit. My hands are only sore today but last week was swelling and painful fits. And I grow tired quite quickly during it all. It will take me a few more days to be feeling right again."

"We shall have to wait until later in the week then."

She tilted her head. "For what?"

"For you to play the piano for me."

Her smile spread, and he noted how her eyes twinkled once more despite their exhaustion. She turned her face down as she had the night when they danced.

"You asked three, you know?"

"Three?"

"Three questions. You said you were only going to ask two."

He gave a look of mock apology. "In that case, I must make it up to you. But first we must have more of these cookies." He cut his eyes at her. "These schnooka noodle?"

She gave a hearty laugh that filled the room and left the air light and warm, and he let her take her hand back as he reached for a cookie.

"Schnecke knödel."

She enunciated the words for him, but he only gave her a smile, breaking the cookie into smaller pieces on the tray before handing her one. She held it gingerly between her finger and her thumb and slowly moved it to her mouth.

"My German is a little rusty," he admitted, holding her glass of water out for her. Watching her take it with both hands, one beneath it to support the weight and the other steadying the glass, he noted how much smaller the glass was than his own. Her aunt had been more thoughtful than he had given her credit for.

"You speak German?"

"Not a lick. That's why it's rusty." He pulled the tray of broken cookies closer, handing her another piece. "Now," he continued, licking a bit of cinnamon from his fingertips, "when do you think you'll be feeling up for one of these infamous walks?"

CHAPTER TWENTY-FIVE

*T*he next day was steamy. Heat radiated from the streets and the mules walked slowly, pulling the drays with grunts as their heads hung low in the baking air of early evening. Alfred had chosen to take the trolley over his bicycle after Dr. Cline had warned of a heat wave making its way across the gulf. Men held their jackets over their arms with rolled up sleeves and women fanned themselves desperately, longing for the occasional breeze. Something that continued to amaze Alfred was how vulnerable the island was to sudden changes. If the waters stalled the winds, it became little more than a loaf of bread stuck in the oven. It swelled until it was bloated and could do little more than bake.

It was a sweltering eighty-six degrees. Joseph had explained how the island's constant moisture affected how hot the air felt, tricking their bodies into believing it was even hotter than it was. A heat index, he had called it. He loosened his tie and took a deep breath that seemed to stick in his throat, never fully filling his lungs.

Mrs. Poplar was at work in the kitchen, the sound of pans knocking against the stove and cutlery being moved about carrying through the house. He had neither the energy nor the care to inquire about her day. Even the interior of the house was sultry and hot compared to most days, and he firmly believed that anyone who had been alive at sunrise and had survived through the afternoon would have the same opinion of the day's events.

When he reached his doorway, his tie already in his hand and his collar open at the neck, he saw Mathias's door was open. The man looked up from his desk as Alfred gave a small wave and stepped into his room. He threw his jacket over his chair and began unbuttoning his shirt. The cooler air of the dark room felt like water against his skin and he closed his eyes, bargaining with God about what he would give to find time for a swim.

"Your office had this one right."

Alfred glanced at the doorway to take in Mathias's form. "Dr. Cline said it's nearing a record for the island."

"No doubt." Mathias leaned his shoulder against the doorway. "Thirteen people were admitted today for heat sickness alone. Two died before noon."

"That's awful." Alfred thought back through the day to find the same hour in his routine. He'd been eating a sandwich from the deli on Market Street. His stomach growled at the thought.

"Not terribly uncommon, though. The humidity down here is so overwhelming. Tourists are unprepared."

"Were they all tourists?"

"Most of them. One was a friend of Mrs. Poplar's." His voice quieted. "She passed."

Alfred slid off a shoe and let his shoulders slump. "Is she alright?"

"No," he replied with knitted eyebrows. "She died."

"I meant Mrs. Poplar."

"Oh, yeah." Mathias shifted to the other shoulder. "She was understandably upset, but she had calmed down by the time I came up to dress for dinner. I couldn't stay in my work clothes. They were drenched."

"Mine as well," Alfred commented as he slid off the other shoe. He fell into his desk chair with a huff. Mathias watched him for a moment, his face sliding into a smile.

"So how did you get along yesterday?"

"Yesterday?"

Alfred moved his shoes to the foot of his bed and rolled his wet socks down his ankles, where they stuck to his skin and pulled at his leg hair.

"A little birdie might have let it slip that you paid Florence a visit."

"Was this bird by chance grey-headed with a fashionable skirt and a mean bone for cooking?"

Mathias raised an eyebrow as he waited, and Alfred fell back against his chair.

"She was ill so I paid her a visit after services." Alfred tilted his head. "Which I noticed you did not attend."

"As did Mrs. Poplar," he replied with a glance toward the stairs. "Thomas had an opportunity to sail and needed a mate."

"It was horrible weather to sail, wasn't it?"

Mathias shrugged. "We didn't make it too far before the winds picked up, but we got a few hours in before it turned into rough seas."

"It looked rather rough to begin with. Joseph said there were swells reported a few miles out that were tilting steamers."

Alfred opened his bureau and pulled out a clean shirt. The lighter cotton shirts he had ordered from Mr. Jeffries made his commute much more tolerable, but the linen shirts were by far the coolest. He saved them for his outings with Hilary when shade was a luxury and for his planned outing with Florence later in the week. He could make do with a heavier shirt for the hour they would eat together, but he hoped Mrs. Poplar would overlook his lack of a tie.

"It wasn't as bad as all that," Mathias explained. "Besides, the danger of the open sea is half the fun."

"Thank you, but I'll stick with my reading."

Mathias left him to dress and was already seated at the table when Alfred came down with a fresh shirt, a washed face, and combed hair. Mrs. Poplar was setting the table as he took his seat.

"I'm afraid it's much too hot to be cooking. It's a simple meal tonight, gentlemen. Cold pea soup and leftover rolls." She set a plate of magenta beets between the men. "Sliced beets, fresh tomatoes, and an onion from my garden." She put her hands on her hips and looked down at the meal. "It's meager but it'll keep you until morning."

"It's perfectly fine, Mrs. Poplar." Mathias took up the saucer of beets and began spooning some onto his plate. "Much better than anything we could have put together."

She nodded as if satisfied and took her seat at the head of the table. Alfred handed her the basket of rolls and caught a pained expression at her eyes. Fearing a revisit of the day's bad news, he treaded lightly.

"Are you alright, Mrs. Poplar?"

"Oh, fine, dear." She let her hand go up to her shoulder. "Just a little tightness is all. It seems my shoulders aren't much better off than my hip nowadays."

Mathias passed the beets to Alfred and began spooning the green soup into his bowl. It splattered on the sides and he wiped at the loose specks with a torn roll. The moment passed and her face calmed.

"Mr. Briggs will not be joining us tonight," she commented.

"And where might he be?"

Mathias's tone was sharp, and she shot him a look before returning to her soup. "I'm sure I don't know. He returned after lunch to change into more casual dress and said he would not be home for dinner."

"Seems fitting for such a gentleman to dismiss his landlady so casually. Perhaps John had an appointment. A transplant of sorts. I hear our surgeons are quite skilled, especially with the more sensitive types. Why, it would be quite feasible for a good doctor to have found a freshly acquired cadaver, preserve an organ, and replace John's selfish insistence with a grown man's—"

"That is quite enough!" Mrs. Poplar's voice was shrill. She closed her eyes and brought her hand up to her chest as she breathed deeply. She opened her eyes to glare at him with a tight jaw. "Really, Mathias. What has gotten in to you?"

He let his spoon fall into his bowl with a clank and wiped his mouth.

"I'm sorry, Mrs. Poplar, but John has exhibited quite ungentlemanly behavior on more than one occasion in this house."

"Alerting me in advance of his absence from dinner when he has no obligation to eat at my table is by no stretch considered inappropriate behavior." Her brow creased and her tone softened. "What has brought this out in you?"

He picked up his spoon, fingering it before scooping up a spoonful of soup.

"My lecture notes and one of my reference books have gone missing from my room."

The table fell silent and only the rise and fall of their chests seemed to move in the house. After a moment, Mrs. Poplar rubbed the fingers of her left hand together, her right still gripping her spoon.

"Surely Mr. Briggs is above stealing."

"Surely."

Mathias resumed his meal but kept his eyes on his bowl of soup. Alfred speared a beet with his fork and chewed quietly.

"Mathias, you know I have expectations of my boarders. If you believe Mr. Briggs had something to do with this, I would prefer to know."

He gave an apologetic smile and took another roll from the basket. "I'm sure I am overreacting. Perhaps I've misplaced them is all."

She watched him with keen eyes, and Alfred felt the tension melt with the heat. After several moments of only the clinking of spoons on bowls, the conversation turned to the heat and Mrs. Poplar's hip pain. Mathias instructed her to use a rosemary and witch hazel salve for her inflammation, which she took with a smile as she insisted on putting away the dishes without them.

Alfred followed Mathias up the stairs in silence. Once they reached the second floor where he was certain their proprietor was out of earshot, he touched Mathias's arm.

"Not that I don't believe you," he remarked. Mathias turned with tired eyes. "But I'll help you look for your notes if you'd like."

"There's no need. I've already torn my room to bits looking through it all. They were on my desk Sunday morning and they were gone when I returned from sailing. And I can't imagine you'd have a use for them."

He gave a shrug, his figure shrinking with the motion as he stuck his hands in his pocket. He turned and made his way into his room, closing the door softly. Alfred sighed as he turned to his own room. He knew John was capable of stealing anything he set his eyes on, but somehow he found himself not wanting to believe it. He sat down on the end of his bed and looked out the south-facing window at the glowing rooftops. The terra cotta tiles of the larger houses had turned a deep orange with the light from the setting sun, and he felt a sudden pull at his memories, at evenings on the farm where the wheat danced in the wind with the hues of the sunset. Things were so simple there, very unlike Galveston where a man had to work his way into everything, from charge accounts to restaurant reservations. It had turned out to be so much more difficult than he had expected.

His eyes drifted to the top of his desk where the old cigar box sat in the corner against the wall. It was on the shelf, just above his pen and ink bottles, and it hung over the edge, casting a small shadow along the shelves below.

A shadow it had never cast before.

His stomach tightened as he stood. He slid the box off the desk. It opened with a creak to reveal a collection of coins and a roll of bills. He knew it had been disturbed before he touched the paper. The roll he had made before, held neatly together by a string of jute, had been hastily retied. He pulled the loose bills free of their string and counted them. He was missing three dollars and twenty cents, nearly a week's pay. His face grew hot as he closed the box and looked out the window on the darkening horizon of Galveston, a city he had yet to figure out and worried he would never understand.

CHAPTER TWENTY-SIX

*M*oving the instruments will take too much time. We'll need to take measurements for platforms and stands, recalibrate them, test them before reporting observations. The entire process could take weeks." Joseph stood facing Dr. Cline's desk with his arms crossed, shaking his head. "The best solution is to have new instruments ready before the channel expansion is completed."

"That takes money," the older brother replied. "And frankly I've grown tired of asking the bureau for more funds. It was difficult enough to have Alfred's position approved. Do you honestly think the bureau will agree to spend more money on instruments? We're an island, Joseph. I've heard their arguments too many times to count. We've only got so much land to cover, and they think our weather is quite predictable."

Dr. Cline returned his glasses to his face and turned back to his desk as Joseph scoffed.

"And only so many men to work it."

"You are being dramatic."

"No, I'm being realistic. And it's about time you were as well."

Joseph glanced back toward Alfred, who removed his hat and smoothed back his hair with his palm. A stack of telegrams fresh sat on his desk. Joseph motioned with a head tilt.

"Alfred has enough smarts and muscle. He can assist me in installing them."

Alfred looked at each man and then tilted his chin slightly to the side. Whatever Joseph had just volunteered him to do had sounded like a compliment and made him suspicious. "What's this now?"

Joseph turned back toward his brother. "This channel expansion has the potential to affect some of our instrument locations, but it also gives us an opportunity to install new instruments in more strategic locations. However, Isaac believes the gain is not worth the effort and refuses to request funds to relocate the current instruments or purchase new ones to move farther out in the channel."

"You are wasting your words, Joseph." Isaac kept his eyes on his papers. "They would be better spent on the day's reports."

His brother stared him down, and Alfred took the first telegram from his desk, watching the men in his periphery. Joseph finally conceded, albeit stiffly, and walked back to his desk, dragging his chair legs across the wooden floor before sitting at the desk. The envelope paper was crisp as Alfred unpacked the first telegram. He ran his finger across the flap, felt a sting, and pulled back with a hiss, immediately bringing his skin to his lips. He let his tongue warm it before taking a look. A small slit of blood formed along the edge of his index finger. He cursed under his breath before pulling the telegram free. He skimmed the print and stilled.

"Dr. Cline?"

"Hm?"

Alfred glanced up to see the climatologist bent over a manuscript. He walked the telegram to the man's desk and held out the telegram.

"It's a report about Cuba."

The climatologist looked up at the slip of paper and glanced at Joseph, who was watching them over his shoulder. His mentor took the message as he moved his attention to his finger, pinching his thumb tightly against the cut as Mathias had taught him to do. The silence that followed was punctuated by the creak of Joseph's chair and the throb in Alfred's fingertip.

"Cuba's reporting sustained winds at forty-two miles per hour and flooding along the southern shore," Isaac announced.

"Let me see." Joseph took the telegram. Alfred watched his expression change from interest to contemplation as he looked up at the weather map on the wall. "If the winds were gale force when they passed south of Cuba, the storm could be a fully developed hurricane by now."

"What was the last report we had from New Orleans?" Isaac asked.

"A front moving in from the east and rain predicted for the coming week."

He turned to Alfred. "Any maritime reports from the eastern gulf?"

"I'm not certain. This was the first telegram I opened."

"Pull any messages from the southern offices or ships." He rose from his desk and made his way toward the stack of telegrams. "Was there one from D.C.?"

Alfred sorted through the telegrams quickly. "Nothing. Is that a concern?"

"No, it's expected. But it complicates matters. We'll need to dispatch a request to the main office for more information on forecasts for the gulf." He motioned toward the telegrams. "Finish sorting these, will you? I'm going to send a wire asking for an update."

Alfred took his seat as Dr. Cline grabbed his bowler from the coat rack and left the office. His footsteps were still in earshot when Alfred turned to Joseph.

"Will the D.C. office know anything?"

"I doubt it." He let the telegram fall back onto the pile. "There used to only be a crevice between the U.S. and Cuba when it came to all of this, but lately it has widened into a canyon. I think Cuba could stand on their heads and wave flags as a hurricane barreled over them, and the D.C. Office would proclaim it a money-making circus before believing that any of their reports could potentially provide us advanced warning."

Alfred leaned back in his chair. "That sounds pompous."

"Extremely so."

"Well, we can't very well ignore it."

A small grin formed at the corner of Joseph's mouth, and Alfred had a sense that he had struck a chord. "Precisely."

"What are we to do then with all of this information?"

"You are going to finish sorting through the telegrams while I arrange for an outing."

He took quick steps toward his desk, grabbed a fresh piece of paper, and began writing in furious strokes of his pen. Alfred glanced toward the door, certain Dr. Cline would return any minute.

"An outing?"

Joseph finished his message and folded the paper before turning with an energetic expression.

"Yes, an outing. Isaac is likely to return before I do, so I need to you explain I've gone to fetch supplies if he inquires where I am."

Silence settled with the humidity, and Alfred breathed it in slowly. The thought of lying to Dr. Cline made his stomach tighten, but his curiosity got the best of him. He decided on a question instead of a protest.

"Where will you be?"

"Arranging for us to make the best of the situation. Can you slip away for the afternoon?"

"From the office?"

"Yes. Bring your logbook and meet me at Water Street and Twenty-Seventh at one-o'clock. But wait until Isaac has left for his dinner."

He searched his shelves before removing a wooden box the size of a shoebox, sliding it into a sack along with several other small instruments. Alfred turned to watch him go.

"And what should I tell Dr. Cline if he asks why I'm out all afternoon?"

Joseph opened the door and grinned. "Tell him I was too righteous to go take measurements off the east end myself and sent you to do my work for me. He'll believe that in a heartbeat."

The door slammed shut, and Alfred sat in the quiet office, the morning sun streaming through the windows, with only specks of dust floating in the sunlight to comfort him. He had just conspired to lie to the Chief

Climatologist of Galveston Island and follow one of the most impulsive men he had ever met into a plot that would likely go against the Weather Bureau's every expectation of his post. He swallowed and prayed he had misunderstood entirely, but he doubted that was the case.

When Dr. Cline returned, he asked only of the remaining telegrams and nothing of Joseph. Alfred had sorted through them and found only a single telegram from Panama City reporting increased winds and higher tides. It provided nothing of certainty, though the climatologist seemed bothered by it. Alfred offered the suggestion that it meant the storm had turned north and was heading toward Alabama. Dr. Cline agreed but remained quiet the remainder of the morning.

When it grew nearer to one o'clock, the man did his usual ritual of putting away his maps, marking his books for when he returned, and neatly stacking his manuscripts at the corner of his desk. Alfred's heart raced.

"I'll return around two-thirty," he commented, letting his hat fall atop his slicked-back hair. A small tuft poked out behind each ear at the brim of the hat. "Will you be taking your break soon?"

"Yes, sir, before heading into the field."

He slid into his jacket and adjusted the sleeves. "Are you going out today?"

"Joseph said measurements need to be taken on the east end."

"Wasn't he supposed to do that?"

Alfred nodded and forced a tight smile that he knew appeared uncomfortable but for a very different reason. "He was, but he sounded as if he had no intentions of doing it when we last spoke. I took the impression that he expected me to say I would do it."

"I see," he replied dryly. "And did he say why?"

"No, but it isn't a bother. I'm all too happy to assist him if I can."

It wasn't a lie. He had spent the last three and a half hours crafting the words that would keep him from technically lying to the man. In the end, he didn't think semantics would matter much to the Weather Bureau or his mentor. The implications were what mattered, and in those he had been very deceiving, but in his mind he was able to tell himself that he had simply relayed exactly what Joseph had asked him to do. He hoped in the end he wouldn't be letting either man down.

"I'm sure you are, but don't let yourself be taken in by him, Alfred. Joseph is a very intelligent man, but he is hot-tempered and emotional. From now on, I want you to stick to your duties only. And let's discuss any changes in responsibility beforehand?"

"Yes, sir."

Alfred gave an earnest smile that felt like his cheeks were too tight to cooperate.

"I'll hurry back," he remarked, opening the door with a glance at Alfred. "The office should only be unattended for a bit."

When the door finally shut, Alfred let himself fall back into his chair and gasped for breath. He shared his secret only with the walls, and he liked to think that the ferocity of the sunlight pouring through the windows and the humid air that had crept into the office told him the island understood his predicament more than anyone else.

———•●•———

A stone fountain sat at the corner of Strand and 25th Street and was a common locale for businessmen meeting on their way to lunches, women greeting one another as they walked on to activist groups or club luncheons, and the occasional homeless man or dockworker down on his luck asking for spare change. It was a bustling crossroads, and Alfred understood immediately why Joseph had asked him to rendezvous beyond the fountain. Water Street lined the harbor and was possibly the busiest street on the island. But the crowd that gathered there wasn't interested in others' business, only its own. Dockworkers loaded cotton bales and oversized sacks of flour and unloaded shipments of South American coffee and European liquor. Wealthy patrons lined up with porters to board steamships bound for the east coast or the rainy England countryside while tired immigrants poured onto the platforms and were ushered into customs lines for documentation and potential quarantine. Drunks walked the boards, weaving in and out of businessmen who left the bank or headed to the Cotton Exchange for their newest investment. It was easy to get lost along Water Street and even easier to blend in.

When Alfred saw him, Joseph was on his horse, holding another mare by the reins. A steamship bellowed down the way and the clink of black-smithing carried from nearby. The smell of woodsmoke and coal filled his lungs as he took the reins from his colleague. Alfred gave him a stern look, his mind racing with the worst imaginable possibilities.

"Where are we going?" he asked, prepared for the man to ignore him altogether or at best give him an unclear answer.

"Pelican Spit."

Alfred rolled the name around in his mind. "Off the north side?"

Joseph nodded, and Alfred's throat tightened. Pelican Island was a small isle just north of Galveston that blocked part of the passageway from the channel-side into the bay. To its east was an even smaller island, Pelican Spit, which was used for practically nothing according to Hilary. It was excellent for birdwatching, fishing, and, lately, hunting, and it wasn't a short trek. They would have to ride east until they reached Ferry Road, practically the last road on the edge of the city, and then head north to the shore before taking a ferry across the water to the smallest island. It would take half an hour just to reach the ferry and nearly another hour to navigate the channel and get them to the island. And how were they going to explain their voyage? The ferry logged official Weather Bureau trips to charge for their fare.

"This seems rather impractical. What's the meat of all of this?"

"We need to be prepared to capture this storm if it keeps its heading."

"We don't even know it's heading, Joseph." His horse reared its head and stepped sideways, anxious to get going. "Dr. Cline is still waiting to hear back from D.C. All we have is a minor report from Panama City. It could have shifted north and be dousing Florida in rain by now."

"Or it could be heading straight for us."

Alfred narrowed his eyes at the man. He couldn't make out Joseph's expression in the shadows, but his stiff upper body and straight neck said enough. And Alfred was tired of sitting in the dark.

"Why are you so convinced that a disaster is going to hit?"

The sound of a trolley turning on 25th Street caught his ears, partnered with the mare's hooves as she danced impatiently. He usually appreciated the sounds of the city, but now he was well aware of the silence between them. Joseph looked down at him, his face shaded by his wide-brimmed hat.

"Why are you not?"

Perhaps it was his tone, serious and urgent like Reverend Bradshaw at the height of his sermons, or it might have been the simple phrasing, no argument or evidence to the contrary, no attempt to convince him otherwise. Just a simple question that begged a hundred more with their shared knowledge of what could happen when the sea broiled and the winds changed direction. Whatever it was, it was heartfelt, and Alfred was unable to protest. For a moment, he was terrified that there was nothing he could say that could disprove the theory that had already formed in Joseph's mind.

"Now, are you going to waste time scrutinizing every little detail or are you going to come with me?"

Alfred looked at his boots, their toes dirty from his walk, and the horse's hooves, trimmed and scarred. He wanted to know what Joseph knew. It was an urge he couldn't dismiss.

He pulled himself up onto the saddle and situated his pack. Joseph was already trotting down Water Street, his hat pulled low on his face, and Alfred followed, keeping a small distance. The irony of their appearance struck him as they turned onto Ferry Road: two men working for a government office off to disobey orders entirely with their faces hidden beneath their hats. It sounded like one of the penny novels his brother had brought back from New York City, the kind his mother disapproved of and his father secretly read when she was visiting her sister.

The ride to the ferry went by quickly—though that might have been his anxiety passing the time—and the sun was already starting its arc in the sky when they walked their horses onto the boat. Alfred dismounted and tied the mare to a post before stepping under the shaded awning. Joseph had gone ahead of him and was talking to a gentleman in one of the few seats. Alfred removed his hat as he approached and gave a start when he saw the man's face.

"Captain Gregory?"

"Ah, Alfred! I had hoped you would be joining us for our outing." The man smiled, full of more vigor than during their previous visit, and Alfred returned the greeting.

"You look well."

"That I am, son. That I am. My age betrays me, but my lungs occasionally have their days. Usually when the wind is low and the air is cooler, but today is a good day indeed." He gestured to the empty wicker chair beside him, and Joseph stepped out of the way to let Alfred take the seat. "Of course, any day is a good day at my age, I suppose. That's what my grandmother always said. She was eighty, mind you." He leaned a little closer. "I obviously did not inherit her spunk."

"Perhaps you spent it all at sea," Joseph conjectured with a warm smile.

Alfred watched Joseph's face. He was a handsome man, no doubt, but his expression was often darkened by worry and constant frustration. Here, outside the office and in the captain's presence, he was relaxed as he had been with their previous visit, and Alfred wondered if this was simply his personality when away from the watchful eye of his brother. Perhaps he had misjudged the man. The thought, however, did little to erase the nature of their rendezvous with the captain.

The ferry was moving slowly, and the boat only rocked on occasion as larger waves moved against them. Despite the bit of wind from the southeast, the waters were calm on the north side of the island, especially between Galveston and Pelican Island, where the strip of water was so narrow that only pelicans searching for fish and the occasional dolphin made appearances.

"You're joining us on the island today?" Alfred asked.

"Joseph had a keen sense I would find the outing of interest, and he was right." The man hummed in thought. "This island is not the safe haven his brother seems to think it to be, and I agree that we've got to make the most of our time to help those around us." He looked back to Alfred. "And I fear I don't have much of it left."

The three men guided their horses off of the ferry and onto Pelican Spit in the mid-afternoon sun after Joseph paid for their travels in cash. The air was stale, having lost some of the ocean breeze to the larger island, and what wind did carry was tinged with the scent of soot and steam. Even across the water the odor of industrialization carried on the breeze. Joseph led the group inland to where a small path had been carved along the shoreline. They stopped along the eastern shore where the cordgrasses and overgrown trees gave way to small sand dunes and a narrow beach line.

The view was enviable. The spit was situated between Galveston Island and Bolivar Peninsula, a strategic location to catch the waters as they entered Galveston Bay from the east. The channel curved south of the spit and directed ships along the northern edge of Galveston while another channel bound for Houston took ships north between the spit and Bolivar. With an unobstructed view of the ocean, Alfred stared out into the waters that glistened from the waves of incoming ships. Captain Gregory stood next to him, leaning on his cane.

"I reckon it's a more profound view than that of the Galveston's beaches."

Alfred squinted his eyes in the sun. "How so?"

"On Galveston, you see the ocean as it once was with only a hint of our progress. The ships are specks on the horizon, only whispers of our presence. Here, you see the ships, bulky and black, smoke filling the air, and the ocean is now the whisper. It's our way, Alfred. It's what we do best."

"Disrupt nature?"

"Oh, don't be fooled." He shook his head as he turned to follow Joseph.

"She's never down for long. She has an eye-for-an-eye mentality, the likes of which most men have never seen."

He watched the two men head toward the sand, two souls separated by years and experience but with the same convictions. Alfred wondered where he fit in.

"This will do," Joseph announced. He set down his pack and looked to Captain Gregory. "Your man packed the wood?"

"On my horse."

Joseph pointed toward the horses. "Alfred, go and get the packs off of his horse. They'll be heavy."

He did as he was told and broke a new sweat in the process. When he set the long wrap down at their feet, he bent over and breathed heavily. Somehow the air felt heavier on the spit without the wind coming off the water. He rolled up his sleeves while Joseph unwrapped several cut and planed boards. He pulled a box of nails and a hammer from his pack and began marking the boards with a pencil. Alfred helped him in the work, holding boards together and assessing angles. At the end of two hours, Joseph and Alfred had three stands with brackets for instruments and Captain Gregory had fallen asleep beneath an umbrella against a sand dune.

"Should he be out in this heat?" Alfred asked, keeping his voice low as they unpacked the instruments.

"I think it does him good." Joseph glanced at the man. "He spent his entire life sailing, being on the water without constraints. Now he's reduced to afternoon walks, gardening with his wife, and visits to town for the doctor." He caught Alfred's eye. "Would you want that life?"

Alfred watched the man sleep as he waited for Joseph to finish assembling a barometer casing.

"Is it fluid in his lungs? Is that why he coughs?"

Joseph nodded and screwed on a cap to seal the metal casing.

"He suffered from a severe bout of tuberculosis several years back and never quite overcame it. He's had a bad cough since then. His wife said the doctor doesn't expect he'll recover." He handed the barometer to

Alfred. "It seems a horrible way to go if you ask me."

"It is." He locked eyes with Joseph before testing the barometer casing. "My grandmother died of lung disease."

Joseph looked up at him, a bracket in his hands. Alfred was embarrassed, unsure why he had spoken the words. Their cut was still fresh, and he wondered if his father felt the same sting when he said them aloud. There was something genuinely cruel about a prolonged death, more so, he thought, when you were fully aware that you were dying. When you knew there was nothing you could do but wait for your body to give out. In that, he was certain: no matter who sat around you, you were alone at the end.

Joseph looked into his pack. "I'm sorry. That must have been painful to watch."

Alfred nodded, a knot in his throat, and took the bracket from Joseph. The two men shifted to the last stand and began screwing the bracket in place. Captain Gregory woke soon after and the three men stood around the stands, assessing their fortitude and balance as they secured them to the ground. The sand on Pelican Spit was different than on the main island. It was rougher, more like heavy dirt, and spotted with thousands of little shells, so many that they crunched beneath Alfred's feet as he walked. Joseph had been right about one thing, though. It held the stands in place perfectly.

"The instruments should catch anything coming out of the southeast off the gulf. It's the perfect location, and it'll help us better understand how a storm evolves if we have readings here and on Pelican Island in addition to the main locations on Galveston."

"When will we check them?"

"During the storm is the best time."

He began repacking his tools. Alfred felt a groan grow in his throat. "And who will be doing that?"

Joseph stood with a smile. "That sounds like a job for an Assistant Observer."

Alfred looked sideways at Captain Gregory as the older man laughed.

"I'll volunteer to help you, son! There's nothing like the fight of a man against a storm when she's blowing saltwater in your face and putting hair on your chest."

The man slapped him on the back with a cough. Even if he managed to keep Dr. Cline from finding out about their excursion, the time it would take to check the instruments during poor weather on Pelican Spit would be a hassle he preferred not to contend with. But the smile on Joseph's face told him he had signed up for it the moment he'd saddled up on Water Street.

CHAPTER TWENTY-SEVEN

The storm had bypassed the coast, staying out over the water, and the week had been long, a humid blend of hot mornings and overcast afternoons. As Thursday drew to a close, the city began to breathe a little lighter in the lessening heat. But the evening was already wearing thin as Alfred leaned against a palm tree outside of Big Red, a monumental structure of red stone where the medical lectures were held. Dozens of men poured down the stone staircase and spread across the manicured lawn, leaving the day's lecture behind. He watched the crowd, Mathias leaning on the other side of the palm tree, until a familiar face appeared on the stairs. They pushed themselves off the trunk without a word and blended into the crowd as they began following the man across campus.

Their theory had developed quickly, and they'd bet their time that it would be proven correct. Stealing a textbook and notes for his own use wasn't John's game, but selling them to another student for extra money fit him like a tailored suit. When Alfred's room was disturbed for a second time, they'd formed a simple plan to figure out what John was up to, and Alfred thanked God he'd had the forethought to hide the rest of his money in his spare pair of socks.

Now, as John moved in and out of the crowd, seeming gregarious with his classmates, Alfred began to wonder if they had it all wrong. Maybe it wasn't simply that John wanted more money, as Mathias had thought. What if he needed the money? He seemed likable enough to his classmates that surely he wouldn't fall low enough to stealing. Would he? Maybe he simply didn't get on with living in a boardinghouse. Stealing was a far fall, no doubt, but Alfred knew it didn't take much to make a man lose his ethics altogether. And he had to admit that John had as much potential to get into trouble as anyone else, probably more so.

When the rest of his group headed east on Market Street, more than likely toward a bar, John separated and steered west. Mathias and Alfred dropped back, creating a little more distance between him, and continued to follow him onto Twenty-Sixth Street where he slowed on the corner of Postoffice and slipped into a shop. The two crossed the street and walked up onto the sidewalk of a market. Alfred leaned over Mathias's shoulder.

"Do you think he'll see us waiting?"

"I don't think he's smart enough to know to watch for anyone."

Mathias leaned against a porch column, and Alfred nodded, letting himself fall against the window, their figures hidden by the shade of the awning. Mathias jingled coins in his pocket, making a metallic symphony as they waited, and Alfred checked the time. It was nearly a quarter to seven, but John seemed on a path away from the restaurants and boardinghouse. His curiosity piqued, he watched the shop across the street, and when John emerged, both men squinted to see what he carried: a small paper bundle tied with a ribbon that he cradled in the crook of his arm. The two men exchanged a look and watched as their housemate made his way west on Postoffice. Mathias waited a beat to let John make progress down the street before crossing toward him and peering around the last building on the block.

"Where do you think he's going?" Alfred asked.

"I've an idea, but it's not a very exciting one."

They watched John walk purposefully down the street before Mathias motioned for Alfred to follow. Alfred was certain they were too far away for John to recognize them, but he worried that their stark contrast in height would give them away nonetheless. But again, Mathias had had a point when he'd tagged John as not being the observant sort. Would he even be paying attention to the people around him? Alfred kept an eye on their surroundings for a place to duck into or a gate to inspect should John take a long look behind him, but he doubted very earnestly that they would need it.

"Don't worry," Mathias commented, keeping his eyes on John. "He won't be watching the other men around him. Trust me."

As they neared Thirty-First Street, the neighborhood took on a different look altogether. While the houses were well-maintained, the yards were bare. Few lots boasted landscaping, and the porches were simple with only a few chairs. The intimate touches that he had come to expect of the residential neighborhoods were missing as they continued west. They passed a two-story house with heavy curtains at each window. Music came from within while two men sat on the front porch, one on each side of the door. Their upper bodies were hidden by thick netting that hung from the porch. Alfred could tell they were keeping their distance, sharing the space but not speaking. They were waiting.

He shoved his hands in his pockets and leaned closer to Mathias. "Where are we?"

"Postoffice Street."

"Right, but the houses." He glanced at a smaller house across the street where a young woman in a revealing dress fanned herself in a upper-floor window. "What's going on?"

A small grin spread across Mathias's face as he let his eyes cut to Alfred and then across the street to the woman. She tilted her head and watched them walk, making no effort to cover her bare arms as the evening light began to filter through the trees.

"I guess you haven't traveled the entire island, eh?"

"What do you mean?"

"This is the red light district."

Alfred's pace slowed as he took in the scene with a new lens. Men sat in chairs, waiting to be called in, the netting blocking their identities from passersby. Only their shoes could give them away. Most of the windows were heavily curtained despite being open to the weather, and the smell of perfume and cigar smoke carried on the air as they passed Thirty-Second Street. Alfred took several wide steps to catch up with Mathias.

"We should take another route."

"We can't. We're following John."

"We'll follow him from a block over. He'll be less likely to see us."

"Where exactly do you think he's going?" He let the question sink in before continuing, shaking his head. "No one walks through here unless they are looking for a place to go. The Dirty Thirties aren't exactly where upstanding gentlemen take their evening strolls."

"Exactly."

"Look, no one is going to think the worse of us if we just keep our eyes straight ahead."

They slowed at the next intersection to let a carriage move down the street before continuing after John's bouncing figure in the distance.

"I can't believe you brought me here."

"I didn't. John did. And it would do you well to give a little more thought to the world around you before you go snubbing your nose at it."

"I'm not snubbing my nose." Alfred tightened his jaw. "It's just, this is an unseemly place for us to be seen, Mathias. We can't be thought to be falling in with these women."

"These women? Look, most of these women fell onto hard times, Alfred. And society hasn't exactly made it easy for a widowed woman to feed her children. Trust me. I see plenty of them in the hospital, and they have enough hardship without adding our judgment into the mix."

Alfred grew quiet as the sunlight dimmed with clouds that moved overhead.

"I didn't mean to be so condemning," he said after a long minute. "I haven't met anyone in that circumstance before."

Mathias stopped on the corner and looked at him. "Yes, you have."

"Who?"

"Bertrand Hartmann, for one."

"Bertrand?" Alfred couldn't keep from smirking at the thought.

"Don't tell me he's selling himself beside the ladies."

"Who do you think Madam Tellsen pays him to protect?" He waited for recognition to pass in Alfred's eyes before looking back toward the street. "Damn."

The street was empty. They jogged to the next intersection, and Alfred pointed down Thirty-Seventh Street, where John's figure headed south. The men crossed the street and kept their distance, walking in silence until he turned back east onto Sealy Avenue. The two paused as they reached the corner and spied on him from a set of bushes. John had slowed as he reached the middle of the street. When he stopped at a decorative gate and glanced about the street, Mathias pulled Alfred down to squat behind a fence.

John fumbled with the paper bundle and pulled out a single rose bud with a few inches of stem still attached. Pushing his chin down to this chest, he found the edge of his jacket pocket and slipped the stem into the pocket so that the bud rested above his breast. He adjusted it for a few moments before pulling back the rest of the paper to reveal a bouquet of flowers. The two men waited as they watched their housemate close the gate behind him and walk up to the front door. He gave a small knock, and the door opened a second later, letting him inside. He was gone with a single step.

They kept their position for several minutes, letting the clouds darken the street and hoping John would have moved away from the front windows. As the wind picked up and began to throw small gusts up the street, Mathias glanced about the street and motioned for Alfred to follow. The two walked slowly down the street, their hands in their pockets and eyes taking in the neighborhood. They didn't stop as they passed the house; Mathias didn't need to.

"That's Charles Bendrick's house," he announced as they passed.

Alfred snapped his head toward his friend. "The opinionated grocer from The Tremont House?" Mathias nodded, his face shadowed by the gathering clouds. The air cooled with the wind, and both men buttoned their jackets to keep them from flying behind them like women's robes.

"What on earth would he be doing there?"

"Probably Mr. Bendrick's wife."

"Oh, come off it!"

Mathias looked surprised at Alfred's insistence. "What else could it be? The man stopped for flowers and put a rose bud in his pocket before walking up the stoop."

Alfred shook his head. "That's a low blow, even for John."

Mathias shrugged. "I think you're giving him a little too much credit."

"It does add up with his route, though," Alfred mused.

"How's that?"

"You said so yourself that no one shares names when visiting the district. Think about it. If he wanted to make it to Mr. Bendrick's house without anyone owning up to having seen him, walking the Dirty Thirties would be the best route to take."

Mathias nodded as he put it together. "And if anyone saw him walking this way, they'd assume he was going to a house in the thirties."

"Better to be visiting a prostitute than a married woman," Alfred observed.

"I suppose so in John's case. But that makes the entire situation all the worse."

"That he's seeing a married woman?"

Mathias shook his head fiercely. "No, that he's buying her flowers with stolen money."

Alfred was quiet as they made their way back toward the main business district. Mathias was right of course. It wasn't simply that John had stolen his money and Mathias's textbook or that they now knew he was likely sleeping with Mr. Bendrick's wife—but that it was all connected. It all brought John into a new light in Alfred's mind, and he was disgusted at the image. Mathias's insistence that he follow the social protocol of keeping other men's secrets bothered him, but this was more than he had ever expected to know about another man's private dealings, especially one with whom he ate breakfast every morning. As they neared Twenty-First Street and the smell of fresh bread and beer wafted from the harbor pubs,

Alfred brought his thoughts into the street light.

"What do we do now?"

"With what?"

"With this." Alfred gestured back the way they had come. "Knowing what we do about John."

"Nothing."

"You just want to sit on it?"

Mathias let out a breath. "There's not really much we can do, Alfred. If we tell Mr. Bendrick, John will be lucky if he doesn't get boxed down the street. If it gets out, he'll likely be expelled from the medical program for unethical behavior. And we'll be the two who ruined the man's life." He gave him a small shrug. "I mean, the man's an insolent pain in the side, but I don't think he deserves it all as bad as that. Do you?"

"No," Alfred said with a sigh.

Alfred meant it. He didn't care to see the man's life ruined, his career stripped away, and his nose broken, but he had a burning sensation in his stomach that it wasn't at all right to just leave it be. Something had to be done. Something about John's brazen attitude, his constant need to show them up, had left a wound, and Mathias's righteous comments about men like him on their walk earlier had lit a spark inside of it. He wanted John to know his secret wasn't safe. He wanted John to worry.

"What if we didn't tell anyone per say?"

Mathias let his head drop back and his chin come up. "Go on."

"Do you think Thomas would loan us a piece of parchment and a pen?"

"I'm sure he could come up with something with all that inventory."

"Good." Alfred let a smile take over his face. "Make certain it's not anything like what's in our desks at the boardinghouse. And have Thomas practice his script. I have a note for him to write."

Chapter Twenty-Eight

*T*he weekend arrived as promised with clear skies and the scent of saltwater and seaweed on the breeze. Alfred had spent the time between rooftop observations reading a book on migration patterns of coastal birds, and, while the occasional concept or scientific name would stick, a good deal of it did not. He was constantly pulling at threads to piece together the full tapestry of the island's ecosystem, but it was a complicated pattern that he feared he would never fully understand. His frustrations flamed in the breeze in much the same way they did in the weather office.

His attention distracted by the rising temperature and sketches of birds in flight, he was running late by the time he realized the hour. Hilary had told him the day's outing was unusual, giving him an address off of Broadway, but he'd had little time to consider what it could be. But as he squeezed the brake of the bicycle and slid off of it at a jog on the corner of the thoroughfare, he knew he never would have guessed the location.

A mansion towered over the intersection. Three-stories of red brick stretched skyward, topped by a flat roof with white buttresses between each window. Every window was open with shutters carefully latched against the house to let in the day's breeze. The house was a perfect square and seemingly simple, but a wrought-iron porch brought flare to the front and elevated the facade with a second-floor balcony. Alfred stood on the sidewalk of 24th Street, a narrow gate in the wrought-iron fence between him and the gardens. A large oak tree skirted the path into the yard and shaded the walk up to the house while palm trees of all sizes filled the interior of the fence. Oleander bushes bordered the house and ivy grew up the side of the house, reaching the third-story windows before winding its way up onto the edge of the brick where it met the roof. Somehow, though he was certain it was an illusion that only the wealthy could afford, a palm tree in the front yard reached toward the sky and exploded with fronds above the roofline like fireworks.

A voice carried from high above, and Alfred gazed up. He saw a figure moving through the oak branches and walked his bicycle through the open gate, keeping in the shade of the tree as sweat began to slide down his back. It was a summer day to be sure, but the lack of humidity did little to cool his skin. He silently thanked Mrs. Poplar for the cotton shirts.

Hilary's linen shirt hung loosely about his arms as he stood on the balcony and gave a wave. His outing boots were laced up to his calves, his pants tucked in tightly, and would have looked out of place anywhere else in the city. But here, motioning excitedly from the balcony of a confidently exotic house on Broadway, he seemed to fit the scene, and Alfred had a twinkling of curiosity as he rested his bicycle against the porch, careful not to disturb the oleander bushes.

A maid met him at the door and showed him to the second floor. The house felt tremendously cool given the day outside, and Alfred was relieved to find that it became even more so as he climbed. Soft sunlight poured through open windows at the end of the second-floor hall, lighting a group of wicker chaises.

"Ah, Alfred, my boy!" Hilary had stepped back into the house and was motioning for him to come closer. "Thank you, Matilda. Alfred, come in. Come in."

Alfred's face felt sticky in the cool air, and it became apparent why the space before him was likely the best seat in the house. A view of the city's rooftops stretched out until the haze of the ocean filled the horizon.

The breeze that carried over the city and into the house was refreshing. Hilary let a hand fall onto Alfred's back as he motioned to a chaise where a pair of cotton-clad legs lounged toward the balcony. A short man bent over to look up at him, and Alfred did a double-take.

"Buttons?"

"Ah." The man's spectacles magnified his eyes as he scrutinized Alfred's figure. "I remember you. You're Isaac Cline's boy. Can't keep your printing papers and typesets straight."

Hilary gave him a sympathetic pat as if he were privy to the printer's reasoning. "Yes, yes. Alfred has quite a bit on his plate at the moment, what with me dragging him out into the wilds. I'm sure you can forgive him a little forgetfulness with weather maps."

"It takes quite a man to tame the wild," came a sultry voice from behind them. "An even braver one to harness the weather."

Alfred turned to see a pair of legs slide from another chaise, the pale skin only partially hidden by the tresses of cream skirt. The woman's boots hit the floor and sent a cascade of material toward the floor as she sat up. Leaning her left shoulder against the wicker back as cotton and lace pushed up her bosom, she held the racy pose as her large brown eyes moved up Alfred's form. They stopped on his face as a wide smile took over her cheeks.

"This is Miss Bettie Brown," Hilary said with a gesture toward the woman. "And this young man is Alfred Ridgeway."

"My pleasure," she replied, her voice smooth like gin.

She let her head roll back as she glanced out the open windows toward the city, and a hairpiece of turquoise and gold shimmered in the late morning light. Hilary motioned for Alfred to take the chaise between him and Miss Bettie, and Alfred removed his jacket before settling into the wicker chair. Miss Bettie lifted her legs back onto her chair.

"Tell me, Alfred," she started, her eyes moving down his frame once more, "what it's like chasing this old man through the bayous?"

Alfred drew in a breath. "Exhausting."

The room lit up with laughter, and he relaxed.

"The joy of Ashton Villa," Hilary commented as the maid returned with a fresh pitcher of water, "is that one can find the most capitalized view of the island if he just allows himself the time to breath it all in."

"You're such a romantic, Hilary," Miss Bettie commented.

Her voice carried an air of natural refinement tinged with a hint of purposeful provocativeness, and Alfred felt out of place beside her. She leaned toward him so she could be heard by all three men.

"But my daddy built it right. He knew what he was doing facing Ashton Villa to the south. There are few views this grand in the city."

Matilda handed Alfred a glass of ice water. He shook the glass and grinned at the knocking of the ice cubes against the sides, something he had rarely experienced before. He took a sip and fussed with the slice of lemon as it bumped his upper lip.

"It's better to just take it out," Miss Bettie whispered. "Matilda insists on plopping them in the glasses, but I prefer to toss them to the birds."

He looked down into his glass before darting his gaze back to her. Miss Bettie gave a nod. Water ran down his thumb as he pulled the slice from the glass. She made a mock gesture of tossing something through the balcony doors and cackled when he hurled the fruit through the opening and beyond the wrought-iron lace that bordered the balcony.

"Hilary tells me you are his right-hand man when it comes to drafting his new field guide," Miss Bettie noted, her head falling back against the chaise.

"I suppose I am."

"Likely his eyes and knees as well, I suspect." She shot him a sideways glance. "Do you paint, too?"

"Not at the moment."

"That's a shame," Buttons announced.

Alfred turned to see the two men staring at him, the man's scrunched nose beneath his magnifying spectacles. Buttons let his face fall as he looked back out toward the balcony, talking to the trees.

"My mother was a painter and taught me all of that. I never much cared for it until I found my father's maps. Ones of Africa and Asia and cities like Seville, Rome, Buenos Aires. That's where the detail comes in. It's the maps that make a steady hand."

"You've traveled enough to know the details of every city, Buttons. I should imagine you could draw them from memory by now," Miss Bettie commented.

Buttons nodded as he took a drink of water, and Miss Bettie turned her attention back to Alfred, a smirk taking over her smooth mouth.

"Do you travel much, Alfred?"

"Only to Virginia for training and then to Galveston for my post."

"From whereabouts?"

"Indian Territory."

Miss Bettie's glass jingled as ice hit the crystal. "How extraordinary," she roared with a laugh. "I believe you've won, Hilary. You've managed to bring the rarest of breeds to tea this summer after all."

"Ha!" The old man slapped his leg. "Kudos to me!"

"And a glass of Daddy's whiskey if I remember correctly."

The maid set a tray of round cookies dusted in sugar on both tables, and Alfred examined one before taking a small bite. A sweet crystalized texture crunched against his teeth. He took a swig of water, washing the dough down his throat as the woman spoke again.

"It all just seems a bit overdone, don't you think?"

"What's that?" Hilary inquired.

"The expansion. And the port. It's a fine one and all that, but it seems so unnecessary. A waste of time in the end." The older men hummed in agreement as she slung open a fan and began cooling her face. "I suppose it all comes down to business."

"Your father would have agreed," Hilary commented.

"With the lamentation but not with the city's plan. There comes a time when the strings to others pockets must be cut loose."

"Now, now," Buttons interrupted. "Let's not talk about others' pockets unless we are filling our own."

Miss Bettie crowed with a broad grin before letting her attention fall back on Alfred. "Tell me," she started, "how a man from the Indian

Territory finds himself in Galveston?"

"I work for the Weather Bureau."

"Oh, I know all that." She waved off his answer. "I mean to pull at your personal strings, the ones that make you hesitate at garden gates."

He fidgeted at her comment, uncertain how to respond to her intense attention. "I'm not sure I know what you're getting at."

"At my age, Alfred, you've learned a few things about people. I might be an old maid to some, but believe me when I say my life of unmarried luxury rivals that of many of the married millionaires in this town." The warm air circulated around him as she fanned her bosom. "I like to get to know the people I meet. It's one of my indulgences as a free woman."

"One of many," Hilary commented.

"You seem to be a gentleman," she continued, ignoring the other guests as they began to talk amongst themselves. "No doubt you find our little interlude informal—and, dare I say, a bit risqué. Or is that something you prefer?"

Alfred coughed as he swallowed a drink of water and coughed, his voice coming back gruff. "Miss Bettie, I'm afraid you've misread my intentions."

"On the contrary, Alfred, I'm quite aware of my own intentions." Setting her glass down on a table beside her, she waved him up with her hand. "Join me on the balcony so we can let these two grackles chatter amongst themselves." She stood quickly, her figure showing hips and a tight waist that accented her height from heel to hairpin. He set down his glass and stood, watching her walk. She glanced back at the doorway. "Come on. I'm not going to bite on your first visit."

This woman was confident and straightforward, a personality that intimidated him, but he followed her onto the balcony where the city hummed like a rooftop portrait of a Dicken's play.

Broadway ran below them just across the lawn. The median was lined with expertly spaced palm trees that swayed with the breeze like curtains of green swishing in the ocean tide. Beyond the thoroughfare, the roofline of houses led toward the beach. Hundreds of homes peeked over one another with the occasional widow's walks taking top sail. The air smelled of lilacs, and Alfred understood what Hilary had meant about the joy of the house. Its view was spectacular, though he knew the Levy Building's rooftop would give it a run for its money.

"They erected it just this April," Miss Bettie announced, interrupting his thoughts. She nodded west along the street. A block beyond the house at the intersection of 25th Street and Broadway stood a marvel of a statue. It was fresh stone and glowed a polished grey in the sunlight. "Lady Liberty pointing toward the battlegrounds."

"Which?"

"San Jacinto." She hummed to herself as she skimmed the street and looked east. "It was quite the celebration. A parade and a crowd of thousands settled onto the street and along the fence to see its dedication."

"This house must have seen many celebrations in its time."

"Oh, glory be. Yes." Her voice was tender now. "When my father had it built, this was the outskirts of town. His business partner joked that he was making his move to start his own New Galveston where the proper ladies could let loose of their corsets." She chuckled. "It was the first house of its sort on Broadway. The town has grown around us, and we're all still fighting to keep ourselves at the forefront of it all, I suppose."

"Why Ashton Villa?"

"For my mother's heritage."

He felt a surge of bravery and chanced a step in the mud. "The well for your adventurous spirit?"

A hard laugh escaped her throat, and she let her head tilt back with the force of it. Her eyes twinkled as she looked back out to the city. A bird called from a nearby tree and joined her in song. "Yes, she's a forthright woman."

"The best women are." He kept his eyes on the horizon but saw her look at him with a tilted head.

"You're a surprising one. And to hear Hilary speak of you, I've come to think perhaps you are like-minded for our little group."

"Saturday talk on the balcony?"

"Oh, no." She waved his comment into the trees. "We usually walk the gardens. Hilary likes to tell me about the flowers and the birds, and Buttons tries to remember their Latin names. It was simply too hot to be out and about today, though. Wouldn't you agree?"

He nodded, though he knew from her tone and how her eyes moved languidly back toward the street that she was not waiting on his agreement. She needed no confirmation. Her thoughts spoke for themselves, and she was used to company that felt similarly.

"Our gardens are quite lovely. It's a shame it was too warm to walk them today."

"Perhaps I can see them another time?"

"It is already planned." She smiled and then let her eyes drift back to the gardens. "I'm told you have a habit of finding more than prized blooms in the gardens."

Her tone cut an edge in the air, and she locked eyes with him. He felt small in that moment. The woman's strong nose and supple chin gave stark contrast to the light that caressed her face, and he struggled to put together the pieces that would complete the scene before him.

"I'm afraid I don't follow."

"Miss Keller is a fine woman, Alfred." Her voice was sharp and clipped her words neatly, a rapid change from her words only seconds earlier. "I've yet to find a better student when it comes to painting my orchids, but I hate to think of her giving her life away for the sake of decorum and expectation. I'll not have her stunted for the sake of a marriage."

She watched him, measuring his confidence. That much he could tell, but the thought of what else roiled beneath her luxurious exterior worried him. Her sentimentality had already been made apparent, and he was not about to discount her power. He spoke cautiously.

"I had no idea you were an acquaintance of Miss Keller."

"Nor I of you until this week. Imagine my astonishment to learn that Hilary's very own protégé was the young man who has been courting my Florence's heart." He kept his eyes on hers, unwilling to be the first to break the tension. He was all in. "Hilary might not have prefaced your little visit today with the company you would be keeping, but let me be quite clear, Mr. Ridgeway. I do not take kindly to men who seek only wives. Our city would be better off if the lot of marriages were named for what they are. But be that as it may, I have no qualms crushing one spirit for the sake of another."

"I assure you my intentions are quite sincere," he replied quickly, his tone solid.

Consideration lighted her expression as she watched him, a silence passing as her eyes softened, and her languid tone returned. "As they should be." A grin pulled at the corner of her mouth as she let her eyes drift dreamily back toward the house. "And I find myself believing you, Alfred. You are a kindred spirit. That's hard to find in this town." She held out her arm and waited for him to offer his own. "Let's break up this party before the men argue themselves into a tirade. Last week it was a matter of properly budding rain lilies."

The men were discussing the mating habits of a bird when Alfred stepped aside to let Miss Bettie enter the room. Hilary looked up, a broad smile on his face.

"When am I to get my winnings? I've been waiting for a good whiskey for years."

"If you weren't so tight on the purse strings," she replied, "you'd have had your fill by now. The bar is downstairs." She started toward the staircase. "And you've only an hour left to drink it. Then I'm off to race the chariot down Broadway tonight. It's been a dreary day stuck indoors since breakfast."

Her footsteps carried down the stairs as Buttons started a slow shuffle after her. Hilary flashed a smile at Alfred as he stood.

"Really something, isn't she?"

"To say the least." He followed the man toward the stairs, letting the breeze have its last breath on his skin. "What does she mean by race the chariot down Broadway?"

Hilary looked at him blankly. "Exactly that."

And with that, he started down the stairs and left Alfred standing in the hall of Ashton Villa, fanning himself with the breeze and eccentrics of Galveston proper.

CHAPTER TWENTY-NINE

*O*leanders," Florence commented brightly, leaning carefully against the door.

Alfred grinned at her reaction. He had bought the roses but cut the oleanders from Mrs. Poplar's garden. He would be owing his proprietor several dozen bushes by the end of the summer.

"It's the last day of June, so I thought it appropriate to send it off with a love story."

She blushed and stepped aside to let him into the house. Aunt Katherine entered from the kitchen with a warm expression, wiping her hands on a dirty apron that was wrapped about her waist. "Good afternoon, Mr. Ridgeway. A pleasure to see you again."

"You as well, Ms. Goldman.

"I'll be tending to the garden," she informed Florence.

Florence nodded and watched her aunt move through the house toward the backdoor. When she turned back to Alfred, her eyes were a shade darker and the faint line of circles pulled beneath her eyelids.

"Shall I put these in water for you?"

"Aunt Katherine took the liberty of preparing a vase for you." She motioned to a crystal vase on a table in front of the sofa. "Her expectation. Not mine."

He grinned and removed the paper from the stems. The oleanders drooped from their thin vine-like stems while the roses remained stiff. He slid the bouquet into the vase, tidying the oleanders at the side, and creased the paper in his hands. He looked at her expectantly.

"Aunt Katherine prepared some sun tea this morning."

"An island special it seems."

"We make the most of the weather," she replied with a shrug. "Would you mind terribly if I asked you to carry the glasses?"

"Not at all."

They made their way into the kitchen, Florence walking at a slow pace, taking care with her footing. The heels of her boots hit hard against the wooden floor, but they had lost the energetic clack of his previous visit. Instead, each step sounded heavy and dull. She stopped near the doorway and directed him to the tray her aunt had left on the counter. He collected the glasses, a pitcher of tea, and a silver sugar bowl onto the tray and followed her into the conservatory.

The day was bright and steamy, the blooms outside the window drooping and the trees standing motionless in the yard. He filled their glasses and offered her sugar. She mixed in a spoonful and sipped gracefully.

"I apologize for altering our plans. I hope you aren't too upset about staying indoors today."

"I don't know how anyone could be upset about staying away from this heat today."

She nodded. "It's turning into a sweltering summer. I recall summers being slightly cooler as a child. Or perhaps that was before I understood the luxury of iced water."

"The summers are dreadfully hot in Indian Territory," Alfred said with a jerk of his eyebrows. "But not this humid."

"I would imagine it's more comfortable there."

"On the contrary, it's quite disgusting."

She laughed at his expression, and he kept her gaze, wanting to prolong the intimacy she drew out of him. Her energy was intoxicating.

"We islanders are rather staunch when it comes to boasting our hardships. It would not be difficult to find a handful who would wager our summers are far worse."

"No doubt." A grin pulled at one corner of his mouth. "But can you beat our winters?"

She swallowed a gulp of tea as she leaned forward. "Unlikely. But I've no idea what a true winter feels like. Father believes cold weather is bad for a woman's health. We've only ever traveled to warmer climates."

The sun moved in the trees beyond the windows, light slanting across her face, but Alfred sensed something else in her expression, a lightness that made her appear youthful. He drank it in.

"Winter up north is a beautiful time of year," he admitted. "The weather is treacherous, but when it freezes, the ice makes the grass and trees shimmer."

She watched his face. "Shimmering trees?"

"Like fallen stars." She smiled, and his breath caught. He looked down into his tea. "But I don't think Galveston has winters quite like that. So it appears I've out-done you."

"I wouldn't be so sure." Her grin turned mischievous. "We have floods from the rains."

"And ours from the rivers." He matched her grin as he leaned a little closer.

She narrowed her eyes. "Winds from the Atlantic."

"Tornadoes from the prairies."

"Hurricanes from the gulf."

His silence was unexpected, and she raised an eyebrow at him. He finally nodded in acquiescence. "You win. We've nothing to compete with the storms that push off the gulf."

She laughed and let her chin float up in pride. "Not that it counts much for Galveston. We don't have hurricanes like the east coast. Father says we're protected as a barrier island, so it's nothing much to carry on about. The ones we do have are minor and do little more than squirrel us away for a day."

He let his eyes wander about the room as he took a drink of sweet tea.

His hesitation to correct her came from somewhere deep within, more than what he felt when speaking to Mrs. Poplar or Mathias. He had tried to argue with them, right their views, but the thought of stealing away her comfort at a false notion of security made him hesitate. The truth was there was nothing to protect them from a hurricane of any magnitude. There was nothing between them and the ocean. All it took was the right temperatures and a little wind.

He forced a smile and gestured toward the piano. "Did you have any lessons today?"

She shook her head. "I teach privately throughout the week and visit St. Mary's Orphanage on Thursday. I keep the weekends to myself."

"To play what you like?"

She nodded, and he let his request slip out quietly. "Would you play for me?"

Her eyes drifted up to his and steadied. A bird sang a quick riff from a tree outside with lilting notes that reminded him of spring mornings.

"What sort of composition do you prefer?"

He hesitated, unsure. He knew little beyond the names of instruments and had always thought of most music as linear, simple. Not something to be preferred. He thought of those compositions he could remember and how they made him feel.

"A love story."

Florence smiled and stood unsteadily, using the arm of the sofa for support. He stayed seated but took the liberty of speaking before she made it to the piano bench.

"Your arthritis affects your knees as well?"

She let herself down onto the bench, putting her weight on her arms and the piano as she slid onto the bench. She kept her back to him as she played a few higher notes.

"Some days. Thankfully today my fingers are limber and so is the piano."

A melody of notes came from the grand piano and they carried through the room. The windows magnified the volume, but the furniture around him and the plants that lined the window panes seemed to dampen the higher notes. The music flowed around him in swirls that filled his eardrums and vibrated the floor beneath his feet. He had never heard someone play the piano so intimately before. His heart raced with the excitement of just the first few notes, and he struggled to discern if it was the experience of the music or the company.

She paused. A few silent beats passed and then she played a chord. It was deep and reverberated through the room. Another followed, slightly higher but pulling at his emotions all the same, and then the room took on a dreamy quality as she played a melody of flats. The day slowed and the sunlight softened as her voice, smooth and pure, poured on the air like silk.

"Alas, my love, you do me wrong." A pause was filled with sweet music that tempted his ears. "To cast me off discourtesouly."

Her voice rose as her fingers played a brighter chord. The notes seemed to swirl about the room, reaching his ears from every corner, as the floor vibrated up into his legs, the bass of the piano merging with her voice somewhere in his body. Her left hand stretched into arches, playing the deeper notes, while her right hand danced a waltz with the higher melody. Her head tilted back an inch as her eyes, he imagined, closed to the sunlight. The notes soothed his ears as her presence calmed his mind. He felt certain his time on Earth had been meant for that moment, the warmth in his chest that burned in his mind, the breath he fought to keep steady as she played, her mind somewhere on a plane that he wasn't privy to knowing.

He felt certain that this was what he had been looking for without knowing it was what he needed.

He felt certain that this was love.

JULY

*A*lfred hummed the melody for days, his mind transported to Florence's conservatory, the image of her shoulders moving with the chords like the sapphire material of her dress when they danced. He had never had the occasion to hear a pianist perform, let alone such a powerful piece, but he was hard-pressed to believe that all musicians met compositions with such conviction. He dreamed of Florence when he slept and found himself daydreaming of her as he worked. And Joseph, to both men's chagrin, had noticed.

She was always on his mind as of late. He drew in a deep breath, trying to focus. She wouldn't want a second-rate climatologist who couldn't keep his attention on the simple task of taking measurements. His pen paused over the telegram as a doubt took hold. Why did she want him in the first place? He had very little money, no place in their society as of yet, and was picking her flowers from his proprietor's garden. His thoughts tumbled back to John whispering in his ear at the Garden Verein.

"You didn't really think she would entertain the thought of someone like you, did you?"

He clenched his jaw at the thought and felt his grip tighten on the pen.

"Alfred?"

His ears burned as he replayed that night.

"Alfred?"

His eyes shot up in surprise. Dr. Cline was standing beside him, his glasses at the bridge of his nose and a manuscript in his hand. His eyes were intent and studied him. Alfred felt his gaze as he shifted in his seat and let his pen fall to the desk. He straightened and rolled his shoulders back as he forced a smile.

"Sorry," he said dryly. "My mind must have been elsewhere."

His mentor was silent for a moment. "Somewhere uncomfortable, I gather."

Alfred swallowed and gestured to the manuscript. "How can I help?"

Dr. Cline let his eyes drop to the manuscript and then brought them back up to Alfred's face. He was a stern-looking man who could command a room with a twitch of his brow, but his expression in that moment was unnerving. It was earnest and thoughtful, as if he were breaking down Alfred's exterior, pulling away the curtains and opening doors to see what lay at the center of his mind. Alfred wondered what the man was thinking but hoped he wouldn't verbalize his thoughts. After some time, Dr. Cline drew a quick breath and set the manuscript down on the desk.

"I am giving a lecture in two weeks on subtropical climate and its relationship to certain medical phenomena, particularly humidity. It will be based on a manuscript I've been writing, and I would like you to read through it to see if you have any questions." Alfred slid the manuscript closer as Dr. Cline continued. "It's not finished necessarily. I have several notes in the margins on additions, further research, but it's in fine enough shape for a review. In fact, there's one item I need compiled that I won't have time to complete before the lecture. A report on the historical path of hurricanes in the gulf."

"That sounds extensive."

"It is." He grinned. "I thought you might be willing to take it on."

A chuckled escaped Alfred's throat. He conducted a mental tally of the upcoming week's activities: daily observations, Pelican Island—still unknown to Dr. Cline, sketches for Hilary's field guide, an outing with Florence, the letter with Thomas. He wondered when his life had become so busy. He'd simply closed his eyes and breathed, and there it all was. He looked up at Dr. Cline and nodded.

"I'd appreciate the opportunity, sir."

Dr. Cline removed his glasses, concern returning to his face. "Do you like it here, Alfred" He let his head tilt to the side.

"With the bureau?"

"With the bureau. With us. In Galveston."

"Yes, I suppose I do," he answered honestly. "What led you to think otherwise?"

"You seem quiet as of late, more so than usual. You seem preoccupied."

Alfred swallowed and looked out the window beyond Joseph's desk. "I think I am still growing accustomed to it all. The work, I mean."

"It's too difficult?"

"No, not all." He shifted in his chair and turned it to face his mentor. "It's more a matter of knowing my place. Here. Most everywhere I suppose." He looked down at his hands, picking at a hangnail. Dr. Cline turned and sat on Alfred's desk, letting one leg dangle while the other grounded him to the floorboard. He drew in a loud breath.

"Joseph makes it clear to me often that I do not offer the praise that is due to others. He says it is my greatest flaw, though my wife would disagree." Both men chuckled. "I am sorry if I do not reward your work as you'd like. I hope you know it doesn't mean I don't recognize it."

"Oh, no, sir." He straightened and slid back in his chair. "It's not that at all. My pay is enough recognition for a job well done." Dr. Cline nodded with a thoughtful expression, and a pause settled between them. "It's the whole of it all, I suppose."

"The whole of it?"

"Well." He glanced around before letting out a sigh. "To be honest, sir, what am I but an assistant to an assistant? You and Joseph do groundbreaking work in our field, and I am not convinced that I'll be reaching your ranks anytime soon. I imagine your work will carry on here for decades, which the city no doubt prefers. But where does that leave me?"

"I should think quite set for an adventure."

Alfred met his gaze with hesitant eyes. "How do you mean?"

He leaned back and looked out the nearest window.

"When I left the Signal Corps, I was posted first in Little Rock and then in Abilene. I traveled parts of the country few men had ever seen before landing here. I witnessed hail storms with ice the size of horseshoes. I saw a flash flood take over a dry gulch so quickly that trees toppled with the water." He rolled the earpiece of his glasses between his fingers and looked up at the ceiling in thought. "What we do, Alfred, it is a simple thing to most: we forecast the weather. Rain, snow, sleet—it's just a fact of life to most people, something about which they can complain when making small talk while in line for the grocer. But for us it is something grander, something magical. We understand the science of how God works his fingers in the clouds. How the flap of a butterfly's wings in the Sahara can bring about a monstrous storm on the shores of Texas."

He looked back down at Alfred.

"What you are doing and learning every day as you sit in this office might seem mundane at the start, but you are a smart man. I recognized that in your application. Few recruits have such high recommendations straight out of training, and you've proven your worth. You are starting a path into climatology that will take you to the ends of the Earth if you let it. But you must have patience and open your mind to the possibilities. You are right that there might not be much for you here when you are ready for more, but that only means you must redirect your sails. The wind can take you places far better than here."

Alfred's eyes dropped as he fidgeted with his nail. He was unsure how to respond. The man's words tossed him into a whirl of unease, not only for their unusual display of affection but for giving life to the potential that Alfred was not making his home as he'd thought he was. If he was right and Alfred's abilities took him to a position like his own, everything he was building in Galveston would eventually be scattered in the wind. Despite his hesitance in allowing himself to become fully immersed in the island, in that moment Alfred was taken aback by his own sadness at imagining a future beyond its shores. He looked up at Dr. Cline's soft expression.

"Thank you, sir."

The man nodded as he stood. "And I think it's time you called me Isaac." Alfred grinned as the man made his way back to his desk. "From now on I'll assume that any distractions are the work of whatever hobby you've found in your spare time."

"Birdwatching."

"Never cared much for it myself, but it's a fine hobby nonetheless. As is love. But I believe it is a private matter when it comes to affairs of the heart. So I make it a habit to never ask about it."

Alfred nodded to himself as he slid the manuscript in front of him. He felt more awake, if anything, and tried to focus on the papers in front of him. After several minutes of working in silence, Alfred let his pen drop onto a telegram.

"Do you really believe that a butterfly in Africa can affect the weather here?"

"I do." He kept his eyes on his papers as he scrawled across their margins, comparing the text to an open book. "I believe our lives are impacted in more ways than we comprehend."

"But a butterfly's wings are so insignificant."

"As are the winds." He glanced back at his assistant. "Until they aren't."

Alfred rolled the words over in his mind and returned to the telegrams. He thought about the insignificant parts of his life, the decisions he had made that had led him to where he was, the little things that crept up in memories and had stuck with him through his years. In the hours that followed, the thoughts that stayed were the smell of freshly baked bread from his grandmother's kitchen, his father's advice to never let a fire die unless the wind beat you to it, and the final notes of Florence's music as she serenaded him in the sunlight of that perfect Sunday afternoon.

CHAPTER THIRTY-ONE

*W*hen he had been paid for his week's duties, Alfred had only one purchase on his mind, and Vondell Pianos had offered the most promise. It had taken nearly an hour for the clerk to find a piece that Alfred felt was appropriate, most of which was spent with the clerk performing the compositions for Alfred's untrained ear until a particular piece stood out. It was a special translation, the clerk had said, originally composed for strings but rewritten to include a piano, and when he heard the piano sing Albinoni's *Adagio in G*, Alfred had known it was perfect. He paid nearly a day's wages for the sheet music.

He had it sent through the post with a simple note, hoping the surprise would brighten Florence's day if her knees were still keeping her from her daily walks. When he arrived home that evening, Mrs. Poplar had already cleared the table and was washing the last of the dishes. He poked his head into the kitchen and scrunched his face in preparation for a lecture.

"I've missed supper entirely, haven't I?"

"Oh, goodness, no!" She turned at the sink, wiping a pot down with a rag. "I couldn't have eaten it all myself if I'd preferred it. There's leftover ham in the box and biscuits and pickles in the pantry."

He stepped into the kitchen. "I'm afraid I lost track of time."

"Working late?"

"Shopping."

She narrowed her eyes at him with a grin. "Might I ask for whom?"

"An acquaintance."

She opened her mouth with a nod and turned back to the sink. He stifled a smile and thought back to the sheet music. His chest felt light as he thought of Florence opening the package and sitting at her piano to play the piece, one he hoped she was discovering for the first time. A noise came from the front of the house and he moved toward the doorway.

"That'll be Mathias," Mrs. Poplar announced. "He was dining out this evening."

Alfred looked toward the door where Mathias struggled to remove his jacket as he approached the stairs. His movements were exaggerated, and Alfred bid Mrs. Poplar goodnight before excusing himself. Mathias's shadow fumbled up the stairs. Alfred was only a few seconds behind him as the man stumbled into his bedroom, letting the door fall open, and plopped down onto his bed. Alfred stopped in the doorway.

"Are you alright?"

Mathias's eyes circled Alfred's face before focusing. "Just dandy."

"Did you walk home?" He stepped into the room, eyeing the man's discarded jacket on the floor.

"Of course not. It's scorching outside. What is it with this damned island?"

"Why are you so sweaty then?"

"I had an evening out," he replied with a sharpened tone. The smell of his breath hit Alfred's nose full on and he pulled back a step.

"Are you drunk?"

Mathias fumbled with the laces of his boot but only managed to tie the knot tighter. In a fit of frustration, he gripped the toe and heel with his hands and began pulling at the boot, a rasp escaping his throat. When he had finally managed it, his sweaty palms lost their grip, and the shoe flung from his grip and hit the wall. Alfred turned and pushed the door partially closed.

"You've got to keep quiet."

Mathias eyed him as he started on the other shoe. After several seconds, Alfred dropped his shoulder pack onto the desk chair and squatted down in front of him. "Let me." Mathias leaned back, teetering slightly on the edge of the mattress, as Alfred untied his boot. "You look a mess. Where were you?"

"Out," he clipped, his voice threatening.

"That's quite obvious." Mathias narrowed his eyes but didn't reply as Alfred removed his boot. "Did you at least take a coach home? I'd hate to imagine you making a fool of yourself carrying on like this through the streets."

"I'm not a child to be looked after."

Alfred balked at the statement, feeling his mouth draw up in defense. Mathias's face was tight with anger.

"Are you sure? Because you're acting rather petulant at the moment."

"Don't lecture me on responsibility. You've no idea what I'm going through."

Alfred rubbed his fingers together in irritation before taking a deep breath. "You're right. I don't. I'm sure your training is very stressful, but this isn't a proper way to handle it. Especially coming home to Mrs. Poplar in this condition."

Mathias barked a laugh. "My studies are the least of my problems."

"What is that supposed to mean?"

He waved Alfred off with a loose gesture and reached for a nearly empty glass of water on his side table. His skin glistened as rubber fingers gripped at the glass. Alfred's stomach tightened at the image.

"Perhaps you should get some sleep," Alfred suggested, hoping the man would succumb to sleep before Mrs. Poplar heard their raised voices.

"Sleep won't cure what's wrong with me. Nothing will." He let out a heavy breath. "I'm a lost cause in the great scheme of it all, just like you. We're nothing to anyone. And that's all we'll ever be." Alfred's gut tightened. This wasn't his friend, the man he'd come to respect. Mathias looked up before giving him a tired-eyed shake of his head and letting himself fall onto his side in the bed. "Just leave me alone."

Alfred hesitated only a moment before grabbing his sack and opening the door. He stopped in the doorway, his muscles tense. John stood in the middle of the hall, his jacket neatly folded over one arm and his bowler in his hand. He stared at Alfred as a small grin took over his face in the dim light of Mathias's oil lamp. The two men were quiet until John clicked his tongue and walked to his room, shutting the door softly behind him.

Alfred pulled his own door up to the jamb, careful not to let it close all the way, before dropping his jacket and pack onto his bed. How quickly his world had turned on its end. Mathias pulling his deepest fears into the open light, giving John something else to thieve. His work faltering with his wandering mind. Everything around him was on the verge of unraveling more quickly than he could thread it back together. Anger rushed his senses, and he palmed what few coins he had in his pocket and threw them across the room. They hit the wall like buckshot and fell onto the bed and floorboards, an odd sequence of metallic noises. A nickel followed his feet, rolling after him as he made his way back into the hall.

He brought a fresh glass of water to Mathias's room, where his housemate breathed heavily, his mouth ajar against his pillow, his shirt partially unbuttoned and hanging loosely. The smell returned to his senses, reminiscent of a night out, but he couldn't quite place the memory brought on by Mathias's drunken stupor. He leaned back against the man's wall as the wind assaulted the front of the house, pushing broken limbs and loose dirt against the window pane in a symphony of ticks and scratches. He welcomed the dark that was settling about them and let himself sink into the thoughts that had been pulling at him for weeks, the fear that Mathias had so easily latched onto in his ramblings.

He wasn't kidding anyone except himself. John had been right, and Mathias had finally put it into words. He was nothing but a small-time weatherman who could barely afford his rent. And thinking he would amount to anything more was becoming a smaller dream with each passing day until it was only a speck on the darkening horizon.

CHAPTER THIRTY-TWO

*A*lfred's head ached as he pulled out a tin of watercolors. Very little was going the way he'd hoped. Mathias hadn't appeared at breakfast for over a week, making excuses to Mrs. Poplar that he wasn't well and that he'd needed to study in the evenings. Alfred had been in a dreadful mood and made for poor conversation at nearly every meal, while John had seemed to make an effort to be at the table every morning in the happiest mood he could conjure. But Alfred had awoken too irritable to sit through another meal with the man and had taken off to Hilary's as soon as the sun had risen.

He pulled a copper mug off the shelf and started down the hall. Hilary's house was enormous by anyone's standards, and, despite having spent more hours in the study than he could count, Alfred had rarely explored the rest of the home. He needed a faucet but had no idea where the nearest one was. He made his way through the foyer, his steps echoing up the staircase, and started down a hall to his right. The silence let his mind wander. He and Mathias were still on edge and had taken to missing each other expertly in the hallway. Isaac was giving him a little more responsibility, but Joseph had returned to the same tack of a man that Alfred preferred to keep at arm's length.

Then there was Florence. His gift had surely arrived, by the next day he imagined, but he hadn't heard from her. No letter. No invitation to tea.

Nothing. He had prefaced the note with the hope that he could hear her play the composition soon, perhaps after a walk in the gardens or on the beach where Hilary had shown him a flock of nesting sandpipers. They were the smallest of the island's birds, and their fledglings promised to be the size of chocolates, just large enough to fit in the palm of her hand. He'd thought the idea of taking her to see something novel would tug at her sense of adventure, but he wondered now if he'd misread her intentions. Could her interests have changed so quickly? He nearly walked by the open door of the sitting room before the deep voice caught in his ears.

"And you would have us do what then? Shore up our business and let it sail to Houston?"

"Dredging up the channel cannot be your solution for every opportunity to gain more business. We are an island. There are only so many resources. If you keep pulling up the ocean and tearing down the island, we'll be left with nothing."

"Pulling up the island?" The man's laugh was small but earnest, as if humored by a child. "It's the ocean, Hilary. It's never-ending. And the channel has to grow in order for us to compete with New Orleans and Houston."

"They have no competition with us."

Alfred recognized Hilary's dismissive tone and imagined him waving off the man's comments with a knuckled hand.

"Houston is a very real threat, I assure you," the man replied. "And not one I intend to take lightly. It would only take a small setback in the grand scheme of it all to give them the time and opportunity to overtake Galveston as the primary port of Texas. And people like you who dismiss the reality of our situation do no credit to the island."

"I beg your pardon." Hilary's tone was agitated. "We do a great service to this island, preserving its nature, recording its history. You are the ones who are shortchanging our future. What do you intend to leave behind if not an overly industrialized, smoke-stained harbor where the fish float up to the surface when they head into the waters below the bathhouses?"

Alfred was listening too intently, not keeping his mind on his surroundings or his body. He recognized the mistake as soon his fingers loosened their grip, a trick of the brain to reroute his attention from his hands to his ears. But it was a second too late. The cup fell from his hand and hit the floorboards with a clank that reverberated down the hall. His ears ached from the sudden noise, attuned to the quiet voices in the other room, and he fumbled to recover the cup as it spun a noisy circle at his feet.

"Alfred?"

Hilary's weather-worn face looked out from the doorway. Alfred's fingers clamped the cup tightly as he straightened with a grimace.

"I'm so sorry, Hilary. I was looking for the washroom to fill the cup for the paintbrushes."

"That's quite alright," he said in a small voice, letting his eyes drift to the cup. "Why don't you join us? This will be good for you to hear."

Hilary disappeared into the room, and Alfred let his head roll back in frustration. All he had wanted to do was busy his mind with painting and sketching, take himself away from the world, and now he was being pulled into a heated argument that he knew practically nothing about. He smoothed out his shirt before stepping into the sunlight of the doorway. The room was a parlor of sorts with four upholstered chairs in a circle and a wooden table in the center. The walls were adorned with Hilary's artwork, oil paintings and watercolors of birds in flight and a grouse looking out from a stand of grasses. The windows were opened onto the garden beyond and the scent of the ocean lightened the atmosphere. Alfred's eyes settled on the guest and he stiffened.

Julius Runge, the man who had so kindly given him a carriage ride in the storm barely two months earlier, sat in an armchair. His legs were crossed so that the toes of his shoes shined with polish in the morning light and his broad shoulders filled the chair from one seam to the other. The man opened his mouth in recognition and let it spread into a smile as he brought his drink closer, his elbow bent on the arm rest.

"Ah! Mr. Ridgeway. What a pleasure to see you again."

Hilary motioned for him to sit in the chair across from the man, and

Alfred did so uncomfortably. "Mr. Runge."

"I understand you are assisting Hilary in his quest to document the island's great birds."

Alfred fingered the metal cup as he nodded. "I am."

"That's quite the undertaking." He grinned. "And I see you've got yourself some proper summer clothing. Grown more accustomed to the weather, I trust?"

"I have."

Hilary poured Alfred a drink from the wet bar along the wall and handed him a scotch glass. "Might I ask how you two have become acquainted?"

"I gave Mr. Ridgeway a ride not too long ago. A storm had moved in and coaches were quite difficult to find."

"Mr. Runge was very generous," Alfred added. "He had his cabbie drop me off near the boardinghouse to save me the trouble of bicycling home."

"It was a good chat, I thought. Until that rude fellow jumped into the coach."

"Let's not stray too far from the topic of conversation," Hilary interjected.

"Come now, Hilary," Mr. Runge remarked. "This has grown tiresome. Your pamphlets are wasted. They do nothing more than litter the streets and stick to coach wheels when the rains move out. It's time you understand what makes this island the industrial complex that it has become. Your outbursts at our meetings are becoming ludicrous. You're starting to sound like a raving madman when you accuse us of downgrading the integrity of this island."

"That is exactly what you are doing."

"According to you." He pointed a large finger at Hilary and let a silence fall on the room before continuing. "Not according to the rest of the city. Not according to the Deep Water Committee—"

"Who will have their pockets lined after the expansion of the channel."

Mr. Runge let out a loud breath. "That's an unfair accusation, Hilary. I thought you better than that."

"You know as well as I do how these things come to pass. More business for the members means more money for their coffers."

"Need I remind you who helped build Galveston into the city is it? These businessmen have given their life's work to making the island the success that it has become. They've helped build the hospitals, the banks, the wharves, and they take every aspect of the island's securities into consideration when they make plans for future business."

Hilary's voice grew quiet. "Not every aspect."

Mr. Runge let out a sigh that settled on the room. Alfred's eyes danced between the men as he sipped on his drink.

"You are a well-liked man, Hilary. And we loved your wife dearly. She did a great service to the community in her lectures and classes, but the future cannot be held back simply because a few birds will be misplaced. I am sorry that it has come to this, but that is simply the way it is." He stood, buttoning the bottom of his waistcoat and dwarfing Hilary in the chair beside him. His eyes were warm despite his words. "I came to you as a friend, not to argue or place blame. I came to warn you."

The clink of silver came from the hall as Ernst carried a tray into the room. "Tea, sirs?"

Hilary was silent as the butler set the table with cups and a kettle. Mr. Runge gave a final nod before starting toward the door.

"I'll see myself out."

His footfalls carried down the hallway until only the clink of tea cups filled the house. Ernst placed two fresh cups of steaming tea on the table between them and left the room. Hilary stood in place, his face turned toward the window that looked out onto the side garden.

"What a horrible mess."

"What was all of that?"

"A threat," he replied as he sat back into his chair. "And not a very well veiled one at that."

Alfred sipped at his scotch, preferring its sharpness to the heat of tea. Hilary blew on his cup before risking a test of its temperature.

"Have you really been doing all of that? The pamphlets and editorials?

Interrupting their meetings?"

"I have a right to my opinion, the same as everyone else."

"Yes, but they are very powerful men, Hilary. Even I know that."

Hilary locked eyes with him, his expression unreadable. "You mean even you, who knows so little of the politics of the situation?"

Alfred closed his eyes to reassess his words. "You know what I mean, Hilary. This is dangerous territory."

"Oh, come off it! They're not going to have me shot in an alleyway."

"What are they going to do then?"

Hilary looked up into the air of the parlor with pursed lips. He let his free hand float as if writing the answer between them. "Blanch my name and strip me of any future business holdings."

"You mean bring you to financial ruin?"

"More or less."

Alfred let out a laugh. "How can you be so calm about this?"

"There are much worse things than losing your future for something you believe in."

"Such as?"

"Losing your future for something you don't believe in."

A bird sang beyond the window, its voice frail and tired in the growing heat of the morning. Hilary set down his tea and rested his palms on his knees. He was right, Alfred realized. Mr. Runge had asked him to be someone other than what he was. It was an untenable situation to be in, but Alfred knew what the old man would do. And he took a deep breath.

"Alright then. What do we do?"

Hilary looked back toward him. "What?"

"What do we do?" Alfred repeated. "To make a difference. To let them know this is not the answer."

The old man's eyes were stern and wrinkles pulled the corner of his mouth into a frown. He shook his head slowly. "This is not a small ordeal, Alfred. Your reputation could be ruined before you've even had the occasion to make one."

Alfred nodded in agreement, well aware of what he was suggesting, but Dr. Cline's words sounded in his head like an old actor's lines being rehearsed for the eightieth time. His future might not be on the island. He knew nothing of where he would end up and, in the end, he only wanted to respect himself, something he was finally realizing was at the forefront of his journey.

"Perhaps that's the best time to do something so brazen."

Hilary's mouth drew up into a grin, but his eyes remained tired and fixed. He bent down and took his tea cup into both hands. "First, we finish our tea."

"And then?"

"And then we finish that damned field guide."

CHAPTER THIRTY-THREE

The following week was a flurry of rooftop observations, manuscript notations, historical storm data, and watercolors as several deadlines seemed to loom on the horizon along with another line of storms. The Deep Water Committee had called another meeting for the end of August, and Alfred was preparing by reading Hilary's notes and studying his pamphlets and editorials. His mind was a whirl of bird facts and storm headings when he came through the door the following Thursday evening. Mrs. Poplar was stretched out on the sofa in the front sitting room with Mathias on his knees at her feet. Both looked at him as he hung his hat on the rack and shed his jacket by the door.

"Everything alright?"

"Oh, yes, dear. You know how Mathias is, always overanalyzing every little thing."

Mathias stood and bent over her leg, taking it by the ankle and moving it at the hip. "Say what you like. Your limp has gotten worse this week and I'm no longer convinced the weather is to blame."

"My mother had the same problem," she argued. "It healed up just fine each fall and stiffened in the winter with the cold."

"And what about the summer?" Alfred asked, leaning against the fireplace.

"Well, what with the rain and all. It only ever let her walk in the in-between seasons, you know."

"So practically never," Mathias remarked, pulling her leg up a few inches and away from her body. "Alright." He let it rest on the sofa. "I'm not sure of the cause, but I'm quite convinced that you have severe inflammation in your hip."

"Oh, I can tell you the cause," she said with a laugh. "It's because I'm old!"

Alfred chuckled, relieved to find himself in familiar company as the day's work drained away and a new wave of fatigue began to set in. Mathias stood.

"You've got to help it heal or it'll only get worse."

She glanced at him and let out a huff. "No need to be so serious, dear. It's just a little hip trouble."

"I mean it. You either start resting it and doing as I say or I'm bringing Dr. Collins around to see you this week."

She lifted her hands in the air and let them fall to her sides against the cushions. "Fine, fine. I'll rest it."

"And I'm getting you a salve from the pharmacy. I want you to start rubbing that into your hip three times a day."

"Fine. Shall I take to my bed as well?"

He rolled his eyes as he removed his stethoscope from around his neck. "Your sarcasm is unnecessary, Mrs. Poplar."

She glanced at Mathias. "Will his majesty let me back into the kitchen to finish packing up the meat?"

Mathias stepped to the side and helped her up. She made a small noise as she pushed up onto her feet, finding her balance. She nodded with a smile and started toward the kitchen, her steps slow and stiff. Mathias let out a sigh once she was in the dining room.

"What a stubborn woman." He glanced at Alfred with a tight smile and reached for a medical bag at the foot of the sofa. "You've been working a lot this week."

"Dr. Cline has me assisting with research."

"In the evenings?"

"No, thankfully. Hilary wants to send his field guide off for publication next month, so I've been spending my evenings sketching spoonbills and painting pelicans." He let out a soft laugh and closed his eyes. "God, listen to me."

Mathias turned to face him fully. His eyes were warm but he kept his distance.

"I was afraid you were avoiding me."

"Why would I do that?"

His eyes dropped as he set the bag on the sofa, slipping his stethoscope between the leather sides. "Judging from John's well-timed comments to me over breakfast, I assume I didn't repay your kindness." He snapped the bag shut.

Alfred rubbed his fingers together and gazed into the parlor. "Not really."

A silence fell, punctuated by the sound of Mrs. Poplar in the kitchen. Alfred wished for rain, for something to hit at the panes or roar against the roof and alleviate the weight of the moment, but nothing came. After an uncomfortable shift, Mathias let out a deep breath.

"My mother always said drinking was only good for ruining boots and ruining brothers."

"You're starting to sound like Mrs. Poplar." Alfred have a tired chuckle and felt the mood diffuse an inch. He nodded toward the dining room. "What's going on with her?"

"More than she'll let on. I think she's got the start of severe arthritis in her hip. It's not going to heal itself and overworking it will only make it worse."

"You can't very well keep her on the sofa. She'll go mad." Mathias nodded and looked through the house toward the kitchen. Alfred scrutinized his face. "What is it?"

Mathias turned, his brow heavy as he tried to shake his head, but it was too late. Alfred had seen the concern on his face. He let his elbow slide off the mantle and took four slow steps toward him until he stood behind Mathias and looked through the house to the kitchen. Mrs. Poplar bounced and bobbed on a stiff hip between the rooms, setting plates back into the hutch as she hummed to herself. Alfred towered over Mathias as both men watched the woman work.

"What is it?" he asked again, his voice low.

They listened to her hum as she busied herself with the arranging the dishes in the hutch. Mathias found his voice and swallowed thickly.

"Her heart." Alfred glanced down at the man and watched his head move as he spoke between breaths. "It doesn't sound right. It was a little off at first when she complained of it being jumpy. That was last year. Now it flutters and skips beats, she says. When I listen to it, it fades in and out, like a child falling asleep."

Alfred drew his eyes back to the scene of the old woman, her grey skirt swishing with her steps while an apron hung in front of her shins. His throat tightened as he began to understand Mathias's words. He feared the answer but asked the question anyway.

"What does that mean?"

The tune she hummed reminded him of a hymn his grandmother used to sing on Sunday mornings while she baked bread for the day.

"I can't be certain."

"Your best guess then."

He trusted the man's knowledge and knew whatever came next would be the defining frame of how he saw the woman from then on.

"A broken heart," Mathias said softly. "But it's doing its job, and I can't stop it."

Mrs. Poplar's words came sweetly to Alfred's ears as the song rang through his memory, and in the quiet of the evening, the two men watched the woman put the last of the china into the hutch and return to the kitchen, her voice singing into the night.

CHAPTER THIRTY-FOUR

*T*he following day's breakfast was the first meal Alfred had eaten in the boardinghouse in nearly a week, and he was famished. Hilary was generous with feeding him, offering him anything his old cook could bake, roast, or boil and even taking him to dine one evening at The Tremont House after the last set of sketches had been finished. But his cook's meats were bland and the potatoes dry. Alfred missed Mrs. Poplar's cooking, and as he sat down in his seat, allowing himself a moment to dwell in the space before picking up his fork, he realized how much he had missed her company as well.

"Eggs and sausage, dear," she announced as she set a plate in front of him. "And toast with fresh preserves."

"Smells wonderful," Mathias added as he circled the table to take his seat.

He put a hand on Mrs. Poplar's shoulder as she passed and kissed her on the cheek. She swatted his shoulder as she headed for the kitchen. Mathias sat down with a bright expression and widened his eyes.

"I have it," he whispered.

Alfred was already cutting into his eggs. "Have what?"

"The letter for John."

He paused, his mouth full of yolk, and raised his eyebrows. Mathias smiled and nodded as he poured himself a cup of coffee. Alfred swallowed his bite of egg and glanced back at the kitchen as Mathias continued.

"It took Thomas a while and then you and I were—" He shrugged. "Well. Anyway, it's sealed and ready to go. Should I drop it in the post today?"

Alfred felt the same tension in his shoulders that had been making its appearance throughout the day as he sat hunched over his desk reading Dr. Cline's manuscript. It always seemed to make itself known when certain thoughts crept into his mind. Doubt had a funny way with things.

"I'm not so sure."

Mathias frowned as he chewed his toast. "Why not? I thought you were on board."

"What if it's a mistake?" He leaned over the table and lowered his voice. "I mean, this could get him into some real trouble. Or backfire on us."

Mathias mimicked his posture and volume. "Are you forgetting that this was your idea?"

"I know."

Both men straightened as Mrs. Poplar came back into the room, a basket of day-old rolls in one hand and a plate of freshly cut strawberries in the other.

"Coffee, dear?"

She looked at Alfred, who put up a hand in apology as he chewed a bite of toast. She scanned the table and gave a small hop.

"Pickles!"

Her skirt swished and left a breeze of soap as she disappeared into the kitchen. Alfred scrunched his face, one cheek full of bread and preserves.

"Who eats pickles with breakfast?"

"Don't change the subject," Mathias whispered, his finger pointed across the table.

"Look, I know it sounded like a good idea at the time, but we haven't any reason to keep at it. Nothing else has been disturbed in my room. Has anything in yours?"

Mathias leaned back and eyed him as he stabbed a piece of sausage. "No."

"See? And it's been almost three weeks. He would never know it was us so the entire scheme is somewhat lackluster. In the end all it will do is potentially ruin a marriage and give him a black eye."

"I'd happily pay for both if I could watch them unfold together," he remarked with a dark brow.

Alfred let his head fall to the side in disapproval as Mrs. Poplar returned with the pickle jar. As if on cue, John appeared in the dining room with his hair sharply combed to the side, smelling of aftershave.

"My, Mr. Briggs," she cooed. "Don't we look dapper this morning!"

"Thank you, Mrs. Poplar. I have a very important meeting with the dean of the college today and I'm keen on making an impression that will seal the deal for my career." He sat in his seat and settle his eyes on Alfred. "Which is obviously not the case for the rest of the crew."

"Classy," Mathias commented.

Mrs. Poplar cleared her throat and looked down at Mathias, who stabbed another piece of sausage and stared at Alfred as he chewed.

"Anything else, gentlemen? Before I make my oatmeal."

"Nothing else," John replied absently, filling his plate with strawberries.

"Thank you, Mrs. Poplar," Alfred added. Her figure had only just cleared the door when John's voice carried over the table.

"Fancy another late night out?"

Alfred flicked his eyes to Mathias and then back to John.

"And who would you be asking?"

"Mr. Ortiz, here. He seems to be developing a penchant for evening sails beyond the surf."

Mathias's color drained momentarily before it returned and deepened to a silky red. Alfred knew the path Mathias's words would take before he opened his mouth.

"That's better than strolling down thirty—"

"What is it, John?"

Both men looked at Alfred in surprise, one flushed and tight-jawed, the other oblivious, chewing loudly. Alfred raised his eyebrows.

"What is it that makes you think we would prefer to have our meal ruined by such impertinence as your commentary on island gossip?"

John sneered. "Struck a nerve, did I?"

Alfred speared a bite of sausage as Mathias topped off his coffee with a shaky hand. John watched the two men, waiting for them to return to their meals before taking a final bite of sausage and letting his fork fall to the plate. He stood noisily and dusted his hands over his plate.

"Not that it matters. Neither of you will be riding off to court a lady any time soon. So what's your reputation to do with any of it?"

"Who I court is none of your business," Alfred remarked, looking up at him with hooded eyes.

"But isn't it? When I see your Miss Keller on the arm of a fellow scholar attending an opera with Miss Goodman and her beau, you'd best believe I take a great deal of interest in your love life. Or at least what there is left of it." Alfred felt his face grow hot and tensed his jaw. John saw the restraint and chuckled. "You want some advice? Stop spending your time going to the fair with a pansy and you might have a shot at winning someone a little higher than your own station."

He slid out from behind the table and made his way through to the front sitting room, his bootheels clacking with each step. Alfred felt his hand start to shake, and he let go of his fork. It tumbled to the plate with a clink. He wiped at his mouth to give his hands something to do other than slam against the table. He looked up at Mathias to see the man was staring at his plate, his lips slightly parted and his eyes out of focus. Alfred took a deep breath and leaned forward.

"He's an ass, Mathias." He looked up, his expression blank. Alfred waited for the man's eyes to focus on his own. "He's just trying to stir up trouble."

Mathias slowly nodded but Alfred was uncomfortable with his demeanor, suddenly cowed and vulnerable. Mathias swallowed dryly, his eyes dropping as Mrs. Poplar returned with her oatmeal. Her voice rang through the house.

"Well, now, has Mr. Briggs already gone?"

Alfred stood. "He had business to attend to, and I'm afraid so do I."

"Oh, just us then, Mr. Ortiz." She glanced at Mathias, and her smile faded. "Are you quite well?"

Alfred cleared his throat, pushing his eyebrows together as best he could.

"Feeling ill again?" Mathias looked up with a furrowed brow that loosened into understanding as he nodded slowly. Alfred lifted his chin as he continued. "Something he ate, we think. For supper. Your stomach is still sensitive, I'd wager."

"Likely so," he replied with a weak smile, taking a small bite of a strawberry.

Mrs. Poplar frowned. "Oh, poor dear. At least it's not another stomach flu."

"Quite right," Alfred agreed, stepping away from the table. "I must be off. Mrs. Poplar, thank you for breakfast."

"Of course, dear!"

"And Mathias?" He looked up with more color in his cheeks, and Alfred held his gaze. "You can handle the post then?"

Their eyes locked as Alfred watched the resolve return to Mathias's expression, and the man gave a weak but determined nod. Alfred winked at Mrs. Poplar and made his way out the door. It was going to be a hot day, but whatever the day brought for him, he was going to make certain it would bring even worse for John Briggs.

———•●•———

The clouds that had gathered over the water midday had made their way inland, towering over the wharf like dark ship masts sailing in front of the sun. The daylight dimmed and the office slipped into an early night that even the electric sconces could not chase away. Alfred lit his lamp, casting a yellow hue across the map in front of him, as Isaac stepped up to the table.

"I was reading through your notes on my manuscript this morning."

Isaac removed his glasses, his nose appearing beak-like with a long shadow along one cheek, his mustache the lowered wings in flight. "They are insightful, but they make me wonder what has you so convinced that our island is in such a vulnerable state."

"All coasts are vulnerable in some fashion. It seems prudent to be abreast of all possibilities when in a state such as this, don't you think?"

Alfred saw Joseph's head rise from his desk but kept his eyes on his mentor. Isaac lifted his chin.

"And what sort of state would that be?"

"We have warmer waters and higher temperatures. We're butted against the gulf. My research on historical storm data shows that storms do tend to track on both sides of us. My apologies, sir, but it appears that our position is excessively vulnerable when it comes to hurricanes."

Isaac was silent, and Alfred looked toward Joseph, who had turned in his chair and now watched his brother. The clock on the wall counted the climatologist's thoughts with each swing of its pendulum. He met Alfred's eyes with a slow gaze that Alfred felt had been intentional, softened from his usual sharp nature, but he had little time to appreciate the gesture before the man continued.

"This fear is unfounded. There is no doubt that hurricanes will make landfall in Galveston. That is a simple fact of nature. It has happened many times before, more than we know, and will continue well after we are gone." He cleared his throat as another thunderclap shook the window panes. "Your miscalculation, however, is in the severity of the storm, not its path." Joseph leaned back in his chair, and Alfred bit his lip as the man glanced at Joseph. "The low pressure that is integral to a cyclone's development is likely to be found over the water, our warm waters. True, a cyclone could enter or develop in the gulf, but God has put an obstacle in the way of any storm that tries to enter the gulf."

"And what obstacle would that be, dear brother?" Joseph's tone was laden with sarcasm. Alfred felt the room seize once more, and Isaac's pupils sharpened. The windows darkened as rain began to splatter on the panes like coins being tossed by schoolboys at carnival sideshows.

"Cuba, gentlemen. Cuba is our protection. Any track that a storm followed toward Galveston would slow it down. Going over Cuba would cause it to lose momentum," Isaac explained. "Going north or south of Cuba would likely put it on a path to either side of us."

"Crossing Cuba would not be enough to keep it from reaching us. How can that protect us from a storm?"

"I never said we were protected from a hurricane. I said Cuba's location spares us from the degree of storms you and Joseph have convinced yourselves we are due. A storm that crossed Cuba would lose so much strength in the land crossing that it would be too weak to do more than cause a little flooding were it to reach Galveston. We saw that in 1886, so there is no denying that potential. But the possibility of a storm crossing Cuba and making headway for Galveston at such a devastating force? It simply won't happen."

Joseph stood with a shake of his head. "Where are the warmest waters in the gulf, Isaac? At the center. What could possibly possess you to think that a storm couldn't continue to build after crossing Cuba?"

"It wouldn't have enough strength to do so. It would blow itself out before reaching the open gulf. A more likely scenario is that it would follow what we know of storm behavior and turn north altogether, heading up the eastern coast."

"Storms behave irrationally," Joseph remarked, dropping a pencil onto his desk.

"Irrationally?" Isaac chuckled. "We study science, Joseph, not magic."

"And even science can't explain everything that occurs on Alfred's map. They crisscross from one direction to the next and at different points in the gulf. No two storms behave the same way. It is impossible for you to say for certain that you can predict the behavior of something so dependent on variables that we don't entirely understand."

Isaac gestured toward Alfred's desk with a rise in his tone.

"They aren't floating about the tides like a piece of driftwood. There must have been a thousand storms that have crossed Cuba since the beginning of time, and none of them have submerged this island yet. So you will do well to remember that sometimes history is exactly as it looks and waiting for a pattern to change is as good a waste of time as watching your mare eat the grass."

The wind blew rain against the window and rattled the pane behind Isaac. Joseph sat back down and shook his head in frustration. Isaac waited a beat and then spoke more softly to Alfred.

"Keep in mind that we are also a barrier island. Our presence disrupts the flow of water as it enters the bay. Even if a storm of such magnitude could reach our shore, the break in land would break up the storm much faster and any water would continue across the island and into the gulf. That is, of course, after they cross the jetties that create the channel to slow down the tides." He lifted his chin. "Do you see my frustration with your concern? This island is a refuge. A massive hurricane striking our beach is such a low possibility that, even if it were to occur, the city is a survivor by design." He watched Alfred in the lamp light as rain roared against the window. "It's not so difficult to believe once you understand how these things work."

"I understand how they work," Alfred replied, careful to control his tone. "But I don't understand how you can put so much faith in something we can't control."

The corners of Isaac's mouth rose into the beginnings of a smile, and he gave a small nod. Slipping his glasses into his shirt pocket, he picked up the manuscript with Alfred's handwritten notes in the margin.

"How is this any different from having faith in God?" He stared at Alfred, waiting. Alfred searched the question for a handhold but came up short, unsure how to go about it. After a long moment, Isaac tapped the manuscript. "Your thoughts were well-formed. I'll prepare a revised draft for the lecture."

With that, he crossed the office, slipped on his jacket and hat, and left with little more than the click of the door. Alfred heard Joseph's chair squeak but kept his eyes shut against the pale glow of the oil lamps.

"Please," Alfred begged, "don't comment."

Another squeak came from across the room and left him with the tick of the clock against the low hum of the storm as rain drenched the streets below. Alfred only knew what he knew, which was little compared to the chief meteorologist, but that didn't make it any less intangible. He opened his eyes and let his head roll toward the window. The world looked as if it had been painted in oils. He imagined the view as the interior of a snow globe where the ocean turned upside down and flooded the scene with a torrential rain at the flick of a wrist.

He knew the world, like all things, could be turned on its head and that even the simplest things he wanted in the world could slip away without a word, falling into the surf as rain turned into the tide. While Isaac had been right that there was little difference in having faith in God and faith in the weather, Alfred's experience told him that the weather had little invested in the survival of man, and his heart told him that that was all the difference that was needed to know that the climatologist was wrong.

Chapter Thirty-Five

*M*athias stood on the platform that overlooked the shoreline, his sleeves rolled up and a pair of binoculars against his eye sockets. His skin wrinkled at the corner of the metal rims as he scanned the beach. Thin red circles about his eyes gave him the look of a bird stalking surprised prey when he lowered the binoculars and pointed along the shore.

"There!" His voice rose in excitement. "On the edge of the tall grasses."

Alfred took the binoculars and adjusted the lenses. Two large birds walked the sandy dunes in the morning sunlight, their necks pulled back in sharp curves and their oversized beaks pointed toward the sand. One flapped its wings, sending the other into a small dance as the grasses bent with their weight.

"Brown pelicans," Alfred announced as he handed the binoculars back to Mathias. "Probably mates with a nest nearby."

"Are they common?"

He squinted into the binoculars as Alfred chuckled. "That's why they call it Pelican Spit."

A small breeze carried off the water as a steamer's stack churned smoke out in the channel. Despite the cooler temperatures, both men had open collars and rolled sleeves. Alfred motioned for Mathias to follow him back onto the beach where Hilary stood over the edge of the surf, his pants wet at the hem. Alfred slipped his logbook into his pack and hung it on his saddle horn. He looked across the beach at his mentor, squinting at his small figure. Mathias shaded his face with an open palm.

"What's he doing?"

"No idea."

"Is this how every outing goes, you doing work and him walking off?"

"No," he replied, starting toward the beach. "Sometimes we drink."

Hilary was talking to the water when Alfred approached. He observed the man, who had one hand on his knee and the other holding his glasses on the bridge of his nose.

"What are you doing?"

"Learning." The man reached down and traced a line in the wet sand. "A hermit crab. The surf keeps pulling him closer to the water, but he hasn't given up yet."

"If he's wanting to go into the water, why doesn't he just let it carry him?"

The water rushed in and flooded the toes of their boots with saltwater. Alfred lifted his feet instinctively, trying to keep the water out of the top of his boots. As the waves pulled back out toward the ocean, the shell was lifted away from the sand and tumbled out with the water. It was deposited several feet away, disappearing into the mix of silt and sand that clouded the water. Hilary looked up at Alfred with raised eyebrows.

"Wasn't ready until now."

A small splash came from behind them and Alfred turned to see Mathias wading into the water, his pants rolled up and his boots left on the sand. He peered around them into the water.

"Are we going in?"

"No, but you've got the right idea," he said with a nod toward his rolled pant legs. "Help me get the trowels."

They unpacked two small hand trowels, a metal bucket, and a small stool. Hilary took the stool and sat down in the middle of the beach with the sun at his back. With his pant legs rolled up his calves and his socks and boots drying on the platform, Alfred handed Mathias a trowel and watched as the surf washed the sand clean and then receded, leaving an oiled chestnut finish on the beach. He waited a moment, then stuck his trowel deep into the sand, wrenching the handle down and popping the blade up to bring a chunk of wet sand out of the earth. Mathias watched him dump the sand at his feet and chop at it with the blade. It fell apart, the drier grains separating as they were tossed aside, and a small crab, no bigger than a coin, scurried from the pile. Alfred jammed the blade of his trowel into the dirt in front of the crab to stop its escape, but it darted to the side and hurried around the obstacle.

"Have to catch it," Hilary exclaimed. "Use your hands!"

Alfred blocked its path once more, pushing it into the pile of loose sand, and grabbed at it with timid fingers. He wrenched his hand back when the crab tried to dart around the blade.

"Grab him by the back legs!"

Mathias bent down next to him as he paused over the crustacean, poised for the catch, and Alfred shot his hand down in a blur. He picked up the crab by a hind leg and held it up to his housemate.

"That's the smallest crab I've ever seen," Mathias announced. "That wouldn't feed any man."

"We're not feeding men." Alfred dropped the crab into the metal bucket with a thud. "We're feeding sandpipers."

"Sandpipers?"

"To draw them in. Here, look." He pointed at the sand. "Watch what the sand does when the water washes back out."

The two men stood barefoot on the beach, the old man squatting on the stool with his knees splayed as he drank from his copper cup. As the water receded, small holes in the sand became more visible as tiny bubbles rushed out of the tunnels. The sand boiled with hundreds of minuscule bubbles at their feet.

"Those are crab dens."

"All of them?" Alfred nodded. Mathias scanned the scene of brewing sand as the corner of his mouth lifted into a grin. He shot Alfred a look. "Ten-minute race?"

Alfred matched his grin and gave a nod. Mathis counted down and shouted.

"Go!"

The two men began digging up the wet sand, their forearms flexing as they buried their blades into the beach, pulled up the earth, and dumped their work at their feet. They sifted through the contents, separating inhabitants from their homes, and tossed their treasures into the pail. The sound of the crabs' bodies hitting against the lead sides echoed as the minutes ticked by. Hilary watched with amusement and called out the final seconds as both men ran to the bucket with their final tokens. Out of breath and sweating, they let their trowels fall into the sand. Alfred bent over to catch his breath as Mathias fell onto his back. They looked up at the old man.

"Well?"

Hilary lifted his sketchpad in the air, and the men squinted at the writing.

"Mathias by two."

Alfred threw his hands in the air as his friend gave a hoot from the sand. He shook his head. "Beginner's luck!"

"I didn't have you pictured as a sore loser," Mathias quipped. "Or is it just with crab digging?"

"Don't forget who taught you how to do this in the first place."

Mathias stood to collect the trowels while Alfred brought the pale to the edge of the platform.

"Right," Mathias replied as he beat the blades against a wooden post to free them of the sand. "And what a significant life lesson it has been. If I ever suffer for food, I'll know I can dig up fourteen crabs the size of beetles to feed myself for an hour."

Alfred shoved his shoulder playfully as he passed and hauled the bucket up the stairs and onto the platform. Hilary stayed where he was, his mind already lost in the motion of his pencil as it sketched the water's edge along the shoreline of broken crab dens. Mathias joined Alfred on the platform, and they sat on the edge, letting their bare feet dangle over the edge and dry in the sun beside their boots. Alfred poured them each a glass of whiskey and they drank in silence for several minutes, with only the sound of the waves and the occasional crab leg scratching at the inside of the pail to disrupt their thoughts.

Mathias set his empty copper mug beside him. "What is it?"

Alfred looked at him with innocent eyes. His hair blew about his ears and reminded him to visit the barber in the coming days.

"What?"

"Whatever's had you down lately."

He looked back out at the water and watched it lap at the sand, washing away the evidence of their hard work. "Have I been down?"

"That's the first I've seen you laugh in nearly a week."

"I could say the same about you."

Mathias shook off the comment and leaned back on the palms of his hands. "That's not the same."

"Isn't it?"

The two men locked eyes. Mathias sniffed the air and looked down at his feet as if inspecting them for sand.

"Is it the bureau?"

Alfred hesitated, considering how to best answer. He knew the one answer that would address everything inside him, everything that had been going on, but he kept it to himself. Mathias was the closest thing he had to a friend; the man asked very little of him. But he still struggled to give an honest answer.

"It's been a little difficult lately, what with the additional observations and assisting Isaac with his research."

"You said helping with the manuscript was the most interesting thing you'd done yet."

"It is. But it's difficult to be under scrutiny all the time. If it's not him questioning my comments or my research, it's Joseph asking me about field work or sending me here for observations."

"Cline still doesn't know?" Alfred shook his head, and Mathias glanced at the old man. "Hilary seems like an interesting bloke."

Alfred chuckled. "In every sense of the word." He took a drink of whiskey and let it slide down his gullet. "I'm authoring a pamphlet with him to hand out at the next town hall meeting about the channel expansion."

The air was little more than seagull calls and the rush of the waves for several minutes. When Mathias spoke again, his voice was soft. "That sounds dangerous."

"Perhaps. But it's better than sitting idly by and letting others tell me how it will be. I can't imagine letting others dictate how I live my life or who I'm expected to be. Not when I can make a difference." He watched Mathias in his peripheral vision. After a beat, he continued, glancing down at his mug. "Besides, I'm not likely here to stay. Even Isaac thinks I'll be bound for someplace else before it's over. So what's the harm in speaking my mind when there are people to listen?"

"The Deep Water Committee is a serious group, Alfred. They aren't men who take lightly to being trifled with. And they're wealthy, which means an awful lot in this city."

"More than it should."

Mathias nodded as Alfred took the last drink of his whiskey and set the mug to the side. They shared the silence as a flock of pelicans flew overhead, casting shadows on their forms, and headed farther out into the bay toward Galveston. The group spread out as they reached the water, each bird taking off onto its own and beginning the ritual of dive-bombing the water for food. Alfred envied their sharp focus, their ability to hone in on their target and plunge with all of their strength headfirst into the waters. What a terrifying feeling that must be the first time but how exhilarating every time after. Mathias's voice interrupted his thoughts.

"There's something else, isn't there? Something I haven't caught on to."

Alfred kept his eyes on the birds as they dove into the ocean one at a time, evenly spaced like a battalion in sequence. Mathias tilted his head as he looked at Alfred in the sunlight. "It's Florence, isn't it?"

Alfred was motionless, wanting to keep the words inside, as if saying them aloud gave them more power than he could muster. He simply nodded as another pelican threw itself waterward and spun like a corkscrew into the surf.

"What happened?"

Alfred let out his breath and swallowed, knowing his voice was somewhere in his throat but unable to find it fully. "I don't know."

"Have you spoken to her?"

"Not since my last visit nearly three weeks ago."

"I thought you made plans?"

"We did." He felt his voice rise with his emotions. "We had planned on a walk when she was feeling better. I bought her a gift and sent a note with it proposing a stroll in the Garten Verein one evening when she could show me the flowers by daylight."

"And?"

"She didn't reply."

Mathias thought on it for a moment. "Perhaps her reply was lost."

Alfred shook his head. "I'd thought the same, but she never came. I waited in the garden, thinking maybe she hadn't had the time to reply or had been too weak in her hands to write." He sniffed at the air. "She never came."

Mathias was silent, a gesture Alfred appreciated. But his heart raced as he thought back to the evening he spent alone in the garden, his new tie cutting in at his neck. His tone caught him by surprise when he spoke again.

"I must have looked like such a fool sitting there all evening waiting for her."

"I'm sure there's some sort of misunderstanding."

Alfred shook his head. "She's moved on to someone else."

"Says who?"

"John."

Mathias let out a large huff and looked out across the grass beyond their horses.

"John's as reliable as a pregnant mule."

Alfred shook his head. "Mules can't produce offspring."

"Precisely," he said gruffly. "And he's still the son of an ass."

Alfred laughed lightly and shook his head. "If he only knew how often he was the butt of our jokes."

"He'll know soon enough. He should be receiving a certain letter in the mail any day now."

"And I'll wager we'll have a good ribbing coming our way when he figures it out."

Hilary called out to Alfred, and the two men stood, their knees protesting as they straightened.

"It'll be well worth it," Mathias argued, a smile taking over his lips.

He reached out as Alfred passed, touching his arm lightly. Alfred looked back, sweat gathering on his lips despite the cool breeze. He was wearied but the talk had lightened his mood.

"Give it a little more time. That's all I'm saying." He gave his arm a small squeeze. "Don't give up on her yet."

Alfred nodded and picked up the pail, leading them down the stairs. The tide had washed away their piles of loosened sand and left smooth mounds of wet beach. The holes had collapsed onto themselves and were now shallow puddles of saltwater, leaving a smooth beach once again, ripe for the picking.

"Remember," Hilary said from his stool, "you want them to scatter and be seen, but don't throw them all the way into the water. The pipers will only take them from the beach."

Alfred reached in and took a crab by the hind leg. It wriggled in his grip, and for a moment he felt a sting of remorse for sending the small, shelled animal to its fate. But the thought was thrust out of his mind as the crustacean maneuvered its way around his finger and snatched onto the fold of skin between his index finger and thumb.

He let out a startled cry and swung his hand wildly in an attempt to free himself of the crab's pinchers, but it held tight. It stung like a deep cut, and he struggled to keep his arm still as Hilary took hold of his wrist to calm him. The old man walked him to the water and submerged his stinging hand, crab and all, into the saltwater up to his forearm. The crab released its grip, and Alfred let out an uncontrolled noise as the sting turned into a hot burn.

"So much for having dominion over the animals," Mathias remarked when they returned.

Alfred rubbed his hand where a bright red mark began to bruise. Mathias looked at it and waved it off, his medical expertise determining the pail of crabs to be more interesting.

"The circle of life is not so clear cut, gentlemen," Hilary noted, returning to his stool as the two men stood next to him with the pail of crabs between them. "Even the smallest of us can bring down giants if we know when to strike."

Mathias cocked his head. "I thought the circle of life referred to everything being connected, not one animal killing another."

"It is," Hilary replied, looking out at the water. "But it is rather simpleminded of us to assume that a circle like that doesn't include us."

Alfred heard their words but focused on the ebb and flow of the water, and for the first time in weeks he thought of home. Of the wind moving over the plains and through the wheat. He pictured his mother in her apron, fresh bread in the oven, and his grandmother embroidering at the table, feeling the pattern by her fingertips with her eyes glazed over and hooded. And he wondered if he had been right to leave it behind for something as simple as an island at the edge of the world—or if he'd been foolish to think he could do better than a farmer's life tucked away between wheat fields. Maybe it was selfish of him to want more.

Mathias's voice brought him back to the beach and his eyes flicked to the sand where a tiny crab landed on the glistening stage. It landed with a bounce and rolled onto its back, its legs flitting in the air as it tried to find purchase to flip over. A sandpiper, its small but plump white form darted across the sand from the grass toward the crabs, was on the crustacean within seconds. Its narrow beak crushed the shell with tremendous force. Alfred felt a sadness in his chest as he threw the last crab to the birds, knowing how relative the experience truly was, understanding that in the grand scheme of things the three men were nothing but tiny crabs on the edge of the ocean's surf, waiting to be freed or pulled out to sea.

CHAPTER THIRTY-SIX

*M*rs. Poplar had a habit of singing hymns while she cooked, something she said she had picked up from her mother. Alfred recognized very few of them. Old southerners, she called them, the sort her father sang with them on their way to church every Sunday after her mother had died. Alfred imagined they reminded her of a better time, and he wondered how far back she had to dream to find a happier place. He was certain it was before her husband became ill, before her hip had started stiffening up and her heart had started fluttering. He stood in the doorway of the kitchen, imagining what she might have been like when she had moved a little more easily and had a husband to keep in check. She turned with a towel in each hand.

"Oh, Alfred!" She flashed a smile and opened the oven. "Goodness, dear, I didn't hear you come in."

"I snuck in. No need to wake the entire house."

She pulled a pie pan from the oven and let it drop onto the stovetop with a bang. "If it wasn't you waking them, it'd be me."

He glanced at his pocket watch. "It's rather late to be baking, isn't it?"

"It is, but I signed myself up to bring a pie to the women's luncheon tomorrow," she replied with a sigh. "And this beats getting up at four to chop apples and work up a meringue."

She leaned against the counter, easing her weight off her right hip as one arm bent against her waist like a teapot handle.

"We've missed having you at supper."

"I'm sorry I've been so absent."

"No need to apologize, dear. Work is work, as my husband always said."

He nodded and felt her eyes on him. The warm smell of the pie reached his nose, and his mouth watered. He wondered if there would be an extra pie at the end of the line for the next day's supper. If he could make it home in time.

She began fanning herself with her kitchen towel and set a hand on her hip. "Now then, how have you been, dear?"

"Quite well," he assured her. "I'm just rather tired tonight. It's been an exhausting week."

"It's only Tuesday, dear."

"I know, but it feels like it should be next month already."

She shook her head in amusement and gestured at a covered plate on the counter. "I put some fruit and a roll aside for you. There's chicken in the ice box if you'd like me to heat it on the skillet for you."

"No need. Fruit and bread is plenty."

She scooted him into the dining room and took her seat at the head of the table. He watched her walk stiff-legged and lean against the table as she sat in the chair. He pulled his chair out and loosened his tie, certain her propriety would only go as far as formal dinners but left it about his neck for good measure. He lifted the napkin to see a fresh roll, a few slices of apple, and two sugar cookies.

"Henry's favorite."

He looked up to see her smiling at the cookies. A cloud passed over her eyes as her lips began to fall into a line. The twinkle was gone, replaced with something that made Alfred's heart ache, and the exhaustion that he had been keeping at bay threatened to rush out of him in a torrent of emotion. Without thinking, he reached out and took her hand. Her eyes focused sharply on his face and the smile returned, weaker but well-intentioned. Unsure of what to say and realizing that no decorum could better the situation, he said the only thing that came to mind.

"I can't imagine."

Her lip quivered, threatening her smile, but she held back the sob with a deep breath. "Neither could I until I could."

She squeezed his hand and withdrew hers. A small silence overtook the house as he bit into a slice of apple and listened to the sound of rain beginning to tick at the window panes.

"Life is a ridiculous thing when you think about it," she replied. "We spend so much of it trying and planning, always looking ahead, but never quite getting to the mark on time." She scanned the room around them, first glancing back at the hutch and then up at the ceiling as if collecting memories in the dust that had been left behind. "Henry planned for our old age. He said those were the years that were meant to be enjoyed." Her eyes shimmered in the electric light that hummed on the wall. "But he didn't even make it here. To where I am. It's a terrible thing, you know, to be the one that's left behind. We had made our life together, built this home. The china was his mother's, the hutch from Louisiana. He made this table."

She ran her hands across its smooth texture.

"But none of that matters now. It's nothing but ceramic and wood, and all I have left of him is a study full of dusty books and a painting of me as a young woman. It's the only way I can imagine I see the world through his eyes anymore."

She closed her eyes and sent tears down her cheeks. Alfred watched them streak her plump pink skin as they made their way to the edge of her jaw. His throat tightened but he stayed his muscles.

"I know now he was wrong," she said in a shaky voice. "Life isn't as kind as all that. These are the years that we must plan to spend alone. We made the mistake of spending the good years planning for the ones he wouldn't even see."

The wind picked up, brushing a crepe myrtle branch against the windows. In the yard, the evening was giving way to night and the colors of July were starting to fade to the purple hue of a late summer's storm.

Alfred stared at his plate of fruit. There was nothing to say. He could do nothing to ease either of their sorrows, hers for a life lost and his for a life yet lived. She drew in another breath, dabbing at her eyes with a napkin.

"I'm very sorry, dear. This was improper of me."

"Not at all." She returned his gaze with large eyes as he spoke. "Grief is a dangerous thing and not easily battled alone."

She nodded in slow agreement and stretched out a hand across the table. He took it and felt her warm fingers grasp his with a strength that surprised him. How familiar she felt, a soft assurance as the world seemed to fall apart around them. He wanted to ask if he could stay there, keep her beside him, as the rain moved through, but the moment passed. She wiped at her eyes once more, careful not to pull at her rouge.

"You know I care dearly about my boarders, dear." His throat had tightened again, and he realized he'd forgotten to get a glass of water. "And I'll not see you waste your time like Henry and I did." Her skin was streaked and her cheeks flushed, but her eyes glowed with severity. "I'll not see you or Mathias milling around life as others expect you to do when there is more out there for you, when there is happiness to make your own."

The noise that came from his throat was a remnant of a chuckle but shook like his nerves. He felt it unravel him as he feared what she might say next, that she might confirm what Mathias had admitted in his drunken stupor.

"There's no point in planning a future," he replied at last, "if you don't make a name to fall back on."

"A name isn't all that great of a thing to have when you're too dead to speak it." She held his gaze until her expression was burrowed into his mind. "There are much greater things than money and a reputation to spend your time on."

She stood and took two stiff-legged steps forward to cup his cheeks in her hands, pulling his chin up until their faces were no more than a foot apart.

"I want you to be happy, Alfred. Truly happy. Whoever you were before you came here, that's the man I want you to be, the one you keep buried inside."

He felt a sob in his chest and chose not to fight the tear that escaped as he closed his eyes against her face. Her lips were warm on his forehead, and the room felt cool after she let go of his cheeks. He knew the answer would only settle the night, setting in stone the emotions that he was afraid to release, but he asked before he could think better of it.

"Mrs. Poplar?" Her boots drug on the wooden floorboards as she turned at the kitchen doorway. "Has anything come for me in the post, by chance?"

"No, dear. Not today." He nodded and wiped at his cheek. "You've not gotten anything since your letter last week."

He turned to face her, his eyes stinging from exhaustion and what Mathias insisted was an allergy to the flowers that budded all about the city.

"My letter?"

"Yes. The letter you received last week."

He leaned against the table as he stood. "What letter?"

"A letter came addressed to you in the post," she thought aloud. "It was a week ago last Tuesday. I remember because it was the same evening that my hip began acting up again. You weren't home yet, but I couldn't take the stairs. I asked John to slip it under your door for you."

He felt a match ignite in the pit of his stomach, and he took in a breath to control his words.

"John took it up for you?"

"Yes. Did you not find it when you came home?"

"No." He shook his head slightly, working to control his breaths. "I didn't find it."

"Perhaps he forgot," she offered, her voice betraying her. "I'm sure it was a mistake on his part. He probably still has it mixed in with his things. Shall I go see?"

"No." His words snapped, and he closed his eyes as the word escaped his lips. He had no right to be angry with her. If anything, he could only be angry with himself at this point. He had let John play his role far too long without handling the problem directly. He forced a smile and apologized. "I'm sure you're right, an honest mistake. I'll ask him about it when I go up. Thank you."

"Of course, dear."

She returned to the kitchen. Alfred waited a moment, letting her settle into her routine and taking deep breaths to calm the heat that had spread into his face. He covered his plate with the napkin and slid his chair up to the table, leaving the room tidy before taking the stairs methodically.

All of the upstairs doors were closed. Lamp light crept from beneath Mathias's door, where he was likely studying at his desk; John's light was dimmer but still visible along the floor. Alfred hesitated only a moment at his own door, never letting his eyes leave John's doorknob. Before he knew what he was doing, he was across the hallway and pushing the door open with a single thrust.

A wash of light came from across the room next to John's bed where the man was stretched out, his back against the wall and only an undershirt covering his upper body. He jumped at the sudden commotion and was on his feet within seconds.

"What the hell?"

"Where's the letter?"

Alfred tried to control his voice, but he shouted the question. His ears burned and he knew his face was red, much to John's delight, though he honestly doubted the man had had any time to register what was happening.

"What letter?"

"The letter, John. The letter that Mrs. Poplar asked you to slip under my door."

"I don't know. Probably somewhere in your room, mixed up in that threadbare suitcase of belongings you dragged in off the train."

Alfred took two long steps toward him, letting go of the doorknob with a push that sent the door swinging against the wall. John took a step back, and his legs hit the mattress, causing him to stumble to keep his balance.

"Don't play games with me, John." He raised his hand, his pointer finger filling the few inches between them. "Where is the letter?"

The roar of rain came from above and locked the two men into a silence that only infuriated Alfred more. Slowly, a sneer spread across John's face. It pulled up one side of his mouth as his eyes narrowed on his housemate. Whether he didn't feel the need to raise his voice or had hoped anyone listening would be too far away to hear him, Alfred was unsure, but John's reply was a simple question.

"Do you want me to tell you what she wrote?"

A huff of air escaping John's nose was the last sound Alfred registered before his muscles reacted. He heard the crack of his knuckles connecting with John's jaw before he felt a burst of pain shoot through his hand and up his arm. But neither sensation compared with the look of recognition that John gave him a second too late. The man crashed into his side table, knocking the oil lamp against the wall and a glass of water onto the floor. Alfred shook his hand, willing the pain to leave before John regained his footing, and was standing over him when Mathias burst through the door.

"What the devil is going on?"

"He punched me," John shouted, holding his jaw with one hand while he shuffled to his feet. "He's lost his mind!"

Mathias looked from one man to the other, keeping his position at the door. John leaned against the bed to find his footing as Alfred took a step back, both hands in tight fists at his sides. Mathias's voice was quiet when he finally broke the silence.

"Alfred?"

He ignored Mathias. "The letter, John. I'll not ask again."

John seemed to study him before glancing at Mathias and then back to Alfred. He let his hand drop from his face to reveal a bright red mark on his lower jaw. The roar of the rain mingled with the man's quick breaths. Alfred felt a bead of sweat trickle down his temple as John took a step forward.

"Move."

Alfred stepped to the side, letting their shoulders brush, and watched as the man pulled a journal from his desk shelf. He flipped to the back cover and pulled out an envelope with a tattered edge. It slid across the foot of the bed, and Alfred snatched it up with his left hand. His right ached and was difficult to move, but he kept his attention on his housemate. Mathias's voice sounded far off as he tried to diffuse the room.

"Settled?"

Alfred held John's gaze until the man let his eyes drop, and he was out of the room in two long strides, leaving Mathias to shut the door behind him. He stopped at the top of the stairs and pulled the letter out of the torn envelope. A waft of honeysuckle met his senses as he unfolded the paper and began reading the words as quickly as his eyes could manage. Mathias was at his side, glancing downstairs as Mrs. Poplar called from the lower level.

"Everything's fine," he called down. "John just lost his footing."

He spun around to face Alfred. "What the hell was all of that?" His voice rose as he took a step closer. "Alfred? Hello?"

A smile overtook Alfred's face, and he looked up to see Mathias's bewildered expression. He glanced at John's door and back to his friend with wide eyes.

"Oh, right. Sorry about that."

"Sorry about that? That's all you have to say?" He examined Alfred's hand and shook his head at the bruises that were spreading across his knuckles. "What the hell has gotten into you?"

"I'll explain later," he replied, folding up the letter and tucking it into his pocket. "But right now I have to go."

"Go?"

Alfred pushed past him and took the stairs two at a time.

"Go where?" Mathias's voiced trailed down the stairs behind him. Alfred hit the bottom step with a thud, nearly barreling over Mrs. Poplar as he headed toward the door.

"Oh! Alfred! What on earth is going on?"

"I'm sorry, Mrs. Poplar," he called as he took his jacket and hat from the coat rack. "Mathias will explain."

With that he was out the door, leaving Mrs. Poplar's and Mathias to figure out their own explanations. He ran out into the rain and down Postoffice Street. The storm was obnoxiously loud with thunderclaps that echoed between the houses as the rain blew in sheets from the south. He jogged for blocks before he found an empty coach, his suit thoroughly soaked through. When they finally made their way, he tipped the cabbie to wait for him and ran up to the Keller residence without so much as a second thought.

He shook his sleeves and bowler, but it did little good. He knocked at the door and waited. The rain intensified and he knocked again, hoping to be heard over the downpour. When the door finally opened, Aunt Katherine looked out onto him with an open mouth and knitted brow.

"Good evening," he said with a wide smile. "I've come to call on Florence."

She gave a hearty laugh. "You can't be serious."

"Quite. If I could have a moment to speak with her." He glanced about him and chuckled. "Perhaps out here to save your rugs the trouble."

She gave a slow nod and let the door shut behind her. He smoothed his hair and waited for several minutes, pacing the edge of the porch and not caring when the wind blew the hem of the rain under the eaves and against his face. He was about to knock again when the door opened with a squeak and Florence took a tentative step onto the threshold. She stayed in the cover of the doorway and eyed him.

"Alfred? What are you doing here?" She raised her eyebrows and motioned toward the yard. "And in this?"

He stepped as close as he dared and let out a long breath that he had been holding for over three weeks. He knew he looked the part of a mad man, having run nearly half the way to her house in a torrential rain and with a smile that he couldn't keep from spreading across his lips, but he didn't care. He couldn't care about anything other than the fact that he was standing on her porch, her eyes focused on him.

"I got your letter."

She paused as her face relaxed. "My letter? But I posted that weeks ago. I thought you had—"

"I know." He nodded and swallowed his breath to calm himself. "I know. And I'll explain it in as much detail as you want me to. But it was important to me that you know that I do."

"That you do?" She shook her head. "That you do what?"

"Want to hear you play. I do want to hear you play Albonini. And Beethoven. And Mozart. I want to hear you play all of them."

She tightened her grip on her skirt and let out a small noise that turned into a smile, her eyes wide at the scene.

"You came here in this to tell me that?"

"No." She pulled back in surprise as he took a step closer. "I came to tell you that I'm sorry for missing our walk and for letting you think I had chosen to stay away. And if you'll let me, I'd very much like to make it up to you." He nodded toward the street. "But perhaps on a different night."

Her face brightened in the soft glow of the electric fixtures on the wall behind her, and he returned her smile, feeling the tension leave his body, the only ache remaining in his right hand. It pulled tightly at the knuckles, but he ignored it as he leaned closer to hear her reply. It came softly with the roar of the rain.

"On one condition."

"Anything."

She leaned in and looked up at him, breathing in the smell of the rain and the island.

"You promise to never let me go so long without your company again."

Alfred let out a soft laugh that seemed to set the world right again. He whispered so that only the rain shared their moment and spoke the simplest truth he had ever known.

"I promise to never leave you."

CHAPTER THIRTY-SEVEN

I don't understand."

Mathias's walked at a slower pace, but Alfred had yet to determine if it was solely because of his shorter legs or simply an aspect of the man's personality. Either way, it had proved to be a stick in his spoke, and now they were late. He jogged across the intersection without waiting on his housemate.

"What is there to understand?" Alfred asked. "There isn't a law but eventually there will be."

"To protect birds? That seems rather far-fetched when you think about it, to assume that politicians will care enough about birds to fine or imprison hunters for shooting the wrong species."

"They're not shooting the wrong species, Mathias. They're hunting all of them."

Mathias picked up his pace to keep up with Alfred as they moved on to the last block, taking a bite of his turkey sandwich as he trotted along. He spoke louder as they passed in front of two coaches.

"But you can't be suggesting that we outlaw hunting? That would never pass."

"No, we're not suggesting that."

Alfred stopped short in front of the printing shop. He lowered his voice as he bent down to talk nearer the man's face, their hats keeping their words more intimate.

"It's a simple matter of mathematics. There are only so many birds in a given species and they can only produce so many offspring a year. If more birds of a species are shot each year than offspring survive into the next year, the species will disappear."

"So we bring them back?" He chewed loudly as he spoke. "Make a few more."

Alfred squinted at him. "And how would we do that if they've all died off?"

Mathias thought for a moment, but Alfred was tired of waiting on the man. He grabbed the doorknob and opened the door with a clang of the bell. Buttons was assisting his apprentice at the back of the shop and gave a small wave before shuffling toward the counter.

"One-hundred pamphlets with standard margins on medium stock," Buttons said with magnified eyes.

The old printer gave him a knowing look, and Alfred's eyes drifted to the man at the back of the shop. His arms worked the press in quick motions that were accentuated by sculpted muscles. He paused his movements to look past the printer, sending an uncomfortable wave through Alfred. Saying his thanks, Alfred cradled the package and headed back outside, sending a last glance into the shop as he stepped back onto the sidewalk. Mathias was leaning against the brick building with one foot on the wall and one knee bent toward the street.

"It sounds like a stupid thing to do if you ask me. Risking your reputation for birds?"

"Says the doctor."

"I risk my safety for human beings. And please don't insult me by comparing my exposure to yellow fever to what I'm sure will be little more than a heated debate with the city's well-to-do."

Alfred nodded. He had a point that Alfred wasn't keen on arguing. Hilary was set on making a presence at the next city meeting to discuss the channel expansion, and neither man would leave in good standing with the Deep Water Committee. Given that the panel was made up of the city's wealthiest businessmen, Alfred was certain he would make some powerful enemies that were sure to outlive Hilary.

A thought crossed his mind.

"Would you want to attend a lecture with me?"

"To argue for the preservation of birds over industrialization? No, thank you. I've got quite enough to contend with being a man who lies to women about being a weaker sex."

"No, not that one." He shifted the package in his arms. "A lecture at the YMCA that Isaac is giving."

They slowed to let the trolley continue south along the road and crossed 23rd Street.

"The one you've been helping him draft?"

"Yeah, that one. Florence was going to attend, but she will be stuck entertaining some woman who's visiting her aunt."

"So you need a date then?"

Alfred chuckled with a nod. "I suppose you could phrase it that way, but I'm not buying you dinner beforehand."

Mathias tossed his hands in the air and the took the last bite of his sandwich. "It's like you don't even want to romance me anymore."

They stopped at the corner of 24th Street, where Mathias smoothed his hair back into place in the reflection of a boot store window. Alfred was minding the traffic and stepping out into the street as he called back. "I'm late for my observations."

Mathias gave him a wave and said something inaudible, but Alfred didn't have the time to ask him to repeat himself. He had had to run several errands on his hour break, the last of which was picking up Hilary's pamphlets arguing not only against the channel expansion but in favor of new laws to protect migrating birds. While Alfred had thought putting together a paper sack of chocolates for Florence had been the most signif-icant errand of the day, Hilary had set him straight, informing him that Buttons wouldn't hold on to the pamphlets for long. Apparently even printers were worried about losing business if they were on the wrong side of progress.

Alfred climbed the steps to the fifth floor of the Levy Building two at a time and stepped into the office at six minutes after two o'clock. Joseph was bent over his desk and Isaac was gathering papers into his leather bag. He looked up with a tight face.

"Ah, Alfred. I was hoping I would catch you."

"My apologies, sir." He set his package on his desk and stripped himself of his jacket. "I'm afraid I packed more into my break than was prudent."

Isaac seemed to have to digest the information before shaking his head with a wave.

"Not an issue. Listen, my wife has been taken ill, and I need to return home to care for her. Will you be able to finish my pamphlet for the lecture?"

"Your pamphlet?"

"Yes." He gestured to two pieces of paper on his desk, one with handwritten notes and the other little more than the start of a cleanly typed letter. "I've written it all down, but Buttons needs it typed and spaced before he can print it."

The mention of the printer's name made Alfred glance toward the package of pamphlets on his desk, and he gave a quick nod.

"Of course, sir."

He let Isaac pass by before retrieving the items from his desk. As soon as the climatologist was out the door, Alfred settled himself down on a stool at the center table where the bureau's typewriter sat like a giant metal paperweight. He skimmed the handwritten outline and notated the margins to indicate where the paragraphs should begin and where emphasis belonged in the text. Sliding the typed letter into the typewriter, he adjusted the roll to align the paper with the punch strokes. He clicked a key and held it halfway down so that the stamp was stalled in midair to ensure the previous typing lined up with the new letters. He placed his fingers on the keys, preparing to type the next word when Joseph cleared his throat.

He glanced up to see the man had turned in his chair and now faced him. A pencil stuck out from behind his ear.

"He's wrong about the island. You know that as well as I do."

Alfred let a small breath escape. "I'm not in a place to argue."

"You most certainly are." Joseph stood. "You're a climatologist, Alfred. Your duty to this island and its people is just as solid as Isaac's responsibility, even more so if you know him to be wrong."

"But I don't." Joseph stiffened, and Alfred melted back into the stool, letting his head fall against his palms as he closed his eyes to find his words. "All I mean is that neither of us knows as well as he does."

"You think he's right?"

Alfred looked at the man with tired eyes. The day had been so bright when had awoken, Florence on his mind and a pamphlet of his own writing waiting to be picked up fresh off the press, but the weight of the bureau had pulled at his shoulders as soon as he'd entered the office. Joseph stared at him with the same intensity he had seen the man have when guessing the windspeed before reading the anemometer. He was sizing Alfred up, and like with the wind, Alfred didn't think he would come away too far off his mark.

"I didn't say that."

"Do you honestly think this island is safe from something as unpredictable as a hurricane?" Joseph pushed.

"No," Alfred protested, his voice rising a pitch. "No, I don't, but it isn't very well my place to go about telling the Chief Climatologist that he's wrong, now is it? No, it's not." He let his words drop on the floor between them before turning back to the typewriter. "If you think it's such a grave misjudgment, then why don't you tell him off?"

"I have, but he doesn't listen to me."

Joseph's voice was softer, a touch delicate in its pausing. Alfred resisted the urge to turn, instead staring at the motionless stamps of the typewriter as the man continued.

"I was hoping you would be different."

AUGUST

CHAPTER THIRTY-EIGHT

utumn was a foreigner on the island. The winds had changed direction and the tides had become more agitated, but even what fronts moved in from the north did little more than cool the morning breezes. Nothing was permanent. The northern winds, especially at the head of the dying storms coming in from Oklahoma Territory or over from Louisiana, blew the waters back with low tides until sections of the bayous and marshes were entirely devoid of standing water. Only thick mud spotted with stands of grass remained, plagued by birds digging for buried crustaceans that were free for the taking without the water to protect them. The shores of Kennedy's Bayou had created such a spectacle when Alfred had taken Florence for a walk the day before that she had been fascinated to the point of canceling the remainder of the walk to watch the birds as he discussed the various species and their nesting habits.

Hilary's outings were less romantic, though they held a certain intellectual romanticism that Alfred struggled to find elsewhere. The man was full of sharp energy, but he was short-sighted at times and left Alfred wondering how he managed to dress himself properly in the morning with such a failed attention span. But Alfred could understand the issue now, as he sat at the table in the middle of Hilary's study, and worked on typing up the manuscript that would soon become a field guide.

Two stacks of typed pages were on the table, one neatly organized with fresh ink, to which he added a new page every few minutes, and another haphazardly put together with Hilary's scrawl along the tops and down the sides. Hilary had reviewed the manuscript; Alfred was translating his edits. When it was all reunited into a single document, it would be ready to send to the publisher. A new field guide would be printed, and they would have better footing when they attended the Deep Water Committee meetings, the next of which was coming sooner than the was prepared for.

"See here?" Hilary unrolled a map and pointed to a small inlet off the east end of the island. "This little cove. There was a small structure there, a fortress of sorts leftover from the war, that the colony of spoonbills had claimed a few years back."

"Are they still there?"

"No doubt run off by hunters. A few might have managed to roost this year, but there are far fewer than there were a decade ago." He let the map roll across the table into a tube. "I have a record of their numbers here somewhere. Petunia had recorded them up until a few years ago."

Hilary began searching his shelves, a comfort Alfred had learned to respect. Whatever the fact he struggled to recall—the exact location of an old colony, the year Roseate Spoonbill fledgling populations began declining, his wife's words to describe the fluff of a sandpiper's downy feathers—it was simpler to let him peruse his memory for a few minutes until he remembered. With the manuscript drafted and the paintings finished, all that was left were the notes and corrections and a proper bundling to have it dropped in the post by the end of the week. Alfred finished reading a page and added it to the pile before glancing up at Hilary. The man's eyes were squinted as he scanned a journal that he had pulled off the shelf.

"Tell me about this society you mentioned."

Hilary looked up with large eyes and snapped the journal shut. "The Audubon Society. It's a fairly new organization started up north by two women."

"And its sole intention is to watch birds?"

"Well, that sounds dreadfully boring when you say it like that." He hobbled over to his chair in front of the fireplace and maneuvered himself gingerly onto the cushion. "Conservation is its objective. The birdwatching and meeting fellow intellectuals are simply benefits of the work."

"Do they do the sorts of things we do?"

"Precisely that and a bit more. They're lobbying for hunting laws that would protect migrating birds and doing research on species to aid in protecting them where they can."

"How are they doing that? Lobbying, I mean."

Hilary poured himself a glass of water from a pitcher on the table and took a drink, smacking his lips.

"Like us. Showing up. Talking, sometimes loudly. Educating others. It's all rather simple when you look at it from the outside."

"I can't imagine more people listen elsewhere than they do here."

"They don't."

"Don't you find that infuriating?"

Hilary shrugged, and Alfred swiveled on his stool.

"It's just that we do all this work, documenting populations, observing habits and locations, identifying food sources, sketching, painting—everything we can to make them understand what they're doing to these animals. And it does so little."

"Does it?" He spoke softly, and Alfred knew there was more behind the question.

"I'm simply worried that you'll have a book that no one will want to read."

"And a pamphlet that will get me arrested?" Hilary nodded at the lack of a reply. "I already have a record for speaking my mind. I don't see a reason to stop now just because I've gotten old. That aside, if I don't do it, who will?"

Alfred's eyes drifted to the window where sunshine poured through the slatted shutters and spilled onto the papers strewn across the table. It all sounded so simple when he phrased it that way. Hilary rose from the armchair and stepped into his line of sight, letting a book fall onto the table.

"You must remember that time feels different to me. You're young and have time to do something meaningful yet, but you must understand how it feels to live in my bones. They ache to feel useful, to have left some kind of legacy beyond stories of the war and what will one day be an empty house." A sadness crept into his words that throttled Alfred's throat. "My wife is gone and I busy myself with birds. I'm well aware of how I look to those men when I show up with pamphlets and interrupt their meetings. But they have tomorrow. I only have today. And I want today to make a difference, however small. Do you understand that?"

Alfred nodded, and Hilary gestured toward the manuscript.

"Have you finished with my notes yet? I want to get it in the post tomorrow. I hope to have a few bound copies to take with me on my bird count."

"What's a bird count?"

Hilary opened the copy of an old field guide and began skimming the pages.

"It's tradition in many circles to go on a Christmas hunt. They all say it's to feed the women, but it's nothing more than a pissing match to see who can shoot the most birds. In protest, the Audubon Society is having a Christmas bird count to record populations, and I'm assisting with the count on the island."

Alfred slid another translated page into the stack and kept scribbling in the margins as he spoke. "And where do you plan on finding others who want to spend their Christmas morning counting birds along the shore instead of at home with their families?"

"In the jail when I'm arrested for disrupting the meeting next week."

Alfred shot him a look of disapproval that melted into a smirk. "Can I help with the bird hunt?"

"I've already volunteered your name."

Somewhere beyond the window, a grackle cackled in the August heat.

Chapter Thirty-Nine

*T*hat sounds too simple," Alfred argued with a shake of his head. "You're saying that you believe a man with lung disease can cure himself by learning to breathe more deeply?"

"It's not as preposterous as you make it sound."

Alfred let the book fall onto his lap as he leaned over the arm of his chair. "Mathias, if disease were that simple to cure, we wouldn't be paying men like you to do what you do." Mathias shrugged as he took a drink of whiskey. "Besides," Alfred continued, returning to his book, "a man can't force himself to breathe any deeper than he does."

"You're so certain?"

"I am."

Mathias scooted to the edge of the chair and motioned for him to do the same. He tossed his book onto the table and mimicked Mathias's posture.

"Back straight. Head forward. Good. Now take a slow deep breath. As deep as you can until you feel resistance."

Alfred did as he was told. The breath lasted a full three seconds before he let it out with a huff.

"Now slower." Alfred nodded and tried again, keeping his inhale continuous for nearly six seconds. "Good. Slower this time."

"Slower? I'm practically bursting at my chest."

"You're nowhere near full capacity. Trust me."

Alfred shot him a glance and closed his eyes, concentrating on his breaths. He tried three in a row before finding a pace, and on the fourth breath, breathing in continuously and as slowly as he could, he filled his lungs until it felt like his chest had risen into his throat and his sides ached from the pressure. As the last second ticked by, his diaphragm vibrated, and he let out a panicked rush of air. He gasped for another breath and looked wildly at Mathias, who wore a wide grin.

"Ten seconds. That's quite a breath."

Alfred drew in another breath and smelled the oily scent of the lamp on the table between them. He chuckled with a nod.

"Alright. Point proven. If it's that easy, why don't you have patients doing breathing exercises at home."

"It's not quite that simple. You see, the lungs are shaped a bit oblong like a potato."

The front door slammed open, and a rumble of noise followed after, intensified by the crescendo of rain against the front of the house. Both men vaulted out of their chairs and faced the doorway as the flame between them tossed within its hurricane slip at the sudden change in the air. Another thud sounded before the door shut and John's frame appeared in the entrance to the parlor. He was soaked through, with his tie undone and hanging loosely from his neck. His waistcoat was unbuttoned at its nape, and his jacket was draped over his arm, dripping little droplets on the floor. As he turned away from the door and shook the water from his sleeves, a dark bruise appeared on his cheekbone below where his wet hair had gathered near his left temple. Alfred shot a glance at Mathias, who stared with big eyes.

It took only a moment for John to notice them in the light of the parlor. His eyes darkened.

"Go ahead. Get a good laugh at your little trick."

Alfred swallowed, trying to think of something to say, but his attention could only focus on the dried blood at John's nose and his blackening eye. Mathias finally broke the silence.

"You should put something cold on that shiner."

John lifted his palm to his face and touched the swollen skin. Alfred winced in sympathy, but found himself holding his breath as he waited for the man to reply. John was short-tempered, to say the least, even when he had no reason to be. Watching the man's brow furrow in anger, Alfred realized they might as well have handed him their death sentences for him to carry out.

"I know one of you did this," he spat as he crossed the threshold of the parlor. Neither man moved as he neared, but Alfred straightened in anticipation of another brawl. His added height over the man didn't hurt matters.

"Maybe if you told us a little about what happened," Mathias commented, "we could understand what we've supposedly done."

John looked from Mathias to Alfred, his hand still on his face.

"I got a letter from a friend inviting me to supper."

"She must've been some friend for you to dress up like that."

John snapped his head toward Mathias, and Alfred stifled a grin that threatened to take over his lips.

"Imagine my surprise," John continued, letting his hand fall to his side, "when I arrived and found her eating with someone else."

"You mean her husband." Mathias faltered with a smirk. "I'm assuming."

The rain at the window lightened and the room fell quiet with Mathias's comment. John stared at the man, his breaths growing more rapid as the subtle static of the rain returned to the pane.

"You had no right to butt yourselves into my affairs." His voice grew quieter as his tone turned stern. "And you'll do well to keep your noses out of my business from now on."

"Your affairs?" Alfred had had enough. He took two steps around his chair so that nothing stood between him and John, his ears growing hot as he spoke. "You'd damn well better watch the accusations you throw around, John. They're likely to stick to you in the process."

"Still sick over your late love letter, I see. What's the matter now? Did she come to her senses and decide a pauper's life wasn't for her?"

"Watch your mouth, John," Mathias demanded.

"Why?" He raised his eyebrows in a dare. "Do you honestly think a man like you is going to stop me? If you're going to go about stepping in and disrupting my affairs, perhaps I should do the same to you. Perhaps I should tell your lower-class colleague here what sort of sailing you really do."

Mathias's frame was small but fast. It took him less than two steps to clear the chair, and his hands were on John's shoulders before Alfred could understand what had happened. The two men pitched toward the entryway before tumbling back toward the chairs. Mathias swung wide and caught John's chin with his knuckles. Alfred stepped forward to restrain John, but the man's jacket had come loose and slipped away in Alfred's grip. As Alfred recovered his balance, he looked up to see John clip the side of Mathias's jaw, sending him into the bookshelf at the back of the parlor. He hit the shelves with a crash that knocked them into the wall. Books spilled onto the floor as the shelf rocked back to center.

John approached with a finger pointed toward him, his voice as stiff as his gait.

"Don't you think for a moment that I won't destroy everything you've worked at, Mathias. I'm not above reporting you to the college. Or the authorities for that matter. I'll watch them send you home on the back of a vegetable cart with chains around your feet." The silence that followed felt heavy and intensified by the sudden change in volume, and only John moved. He straightened while he and Mathias caught their breath in short gasps. "You should think again before sticking anything of yours in my business." He turned and looked at Alfred with a smirk. "That includes you, weatherman."

Mrs. Poplar's boots clacked in quick succession on the floorboards, and all three men took a step back from one another, straightening their shirts and sleeves. Her form appeared in the doorway, huffy and slightly off-center as her weight shifted to one leg. She braced herself on the wall with a hand over her chest as she looked from one man to the next.

"What in God's name is going on in here?"

When John and Mathias refused to answer, Alfred made an effort to steady his voice.

"Just a misunderstanding, Mrs. Poplar."

"A misunderstanding?"

She looked about the room at John's wet jacket on the floor behind the chairs and the books on the floor. Her eyes traveled up Mathias's untucked shirt and over to John's bloodied face and wet hair. She shot her glance back to Alfred. He cringed as her voice rose an octave.

"And what sort of misunderstanding warrants a brawl in my parlor? You are three grown men. You can't have a civilized conversation to sort out your differences?"

Only the rain beat at the window in reply, and Alfred let his eyes drop to John's jacket on the floor. A piece of folded parchment had fallen out of his jacket pocket and now stuck out from beneath one of the chairs. He eyed Mrs. Poplar but didn't dare move to retrieve it.

"This is unacceptable, gentlemen." Her manner calmed, but her tone remained. "I will not tolerate this sort of behavior in my house."

"Mrs. Poplar," John started, turning to face the woman with his best attempt at charm. "I do apologize. I simply tried to talk to Mathias and he lost his temper."

"I don't want to hear another word from any of you," she retorted, sending John a step back. "Now if you would be so kind as to return my husband's things to their rightful place, I'll ask you all to retire to your rooms for the night."

John rocked on his feet with unspent energy as he looked from her to the shelves. Mathias bent down to pick up an armful of books, and John grabbed a few smaller ones that had scattered across the floor. As Mathias began to slide the books back onto the shelf, John leaned forward to set the two journals on the shelf in front of Mathias. Alfred saw his lips move as he lingered near Mathias's ear. His friend stiffened, and John walked across the room to pick up his jacket off the floor. Alfred watched him flap the material to loosen any dirt from the jacket and eyed the paper the he had overlooked beneath the chair. His eyes shot back to Mathias, who had left the books stacked on the shelf and looked down at the floor between them.

"Good night, Mrs. Poplar," John commented as he stepped past.

She ignored his remark, and the three of them stood silently as they listened to his footsteps carry up the stairs. When he had reached the second story, she turned and looked at Alfred.

"John came in—"

She silenced him with a raised hand and looked at Mathias, who refused to meet their eyes. He looked small and frail despite his jaw being set to a tight angle. Mrs. Poplar's voice was soft.

"Are you alright, Mathias?"

His eyes searched the floor before his body moved as if a wave of energy had passed through it. "I'm fine. Thank you."

He walked between them and started up the stairs. The sound of his bedroom door shutting followed soon after, and Mrs. Poplar let out a long breath as she looked toward the bookshelves.

"Will you be a gentleman, Alfred?"

He took several books into his arms and scanned their titles before slipping them back into their proper places. A minute passed with only the rhythm of the rain against the house before she spoke again.

"I'll not ask what set Mr. Briggs off the way it did." Alfred looked back at her, taking in her fragile shape in the entryway. Her gray skirt was illuminated in an orange glow by the lamp, and her hair was tossed about her face, her bun falling loose at the back. She had aged in the few months he had been residing in the house. "John is an angry man," she continued, "but I think he has some good down in him somewhere."

"I disagree."

She hummed a noise that resembled agreement as he slipped the last books onto the shelf. She took a few steps toward him and put her hands on her hips.

"Henry can rest easy now. Having the books all out of order would have had him turning in his grave."

Alfred set the last book on the shelf. "Well, what would we have done if we had went looking for a book on heart disease and found a volume on intestinal surgeries instead?"

A click beyond the room made them turn just as the door opened fully. Alfred saw Mathias slide out into the rain, his hat on his head and a heavy jacket covering his shirt. He stepped forward to follow, but Mrs. Poplar grabbed his arm with a sturdy grip.

"No." She watched the door shut quietly. "Let him go."

"He's obviously upset."

"That he is, but he won't talk if he isn't in the mood."

Alfred fell back a step and shook his head. "They were unfair, the things John said to him."

"I don't doubt it." She made her way to the front of the parlor and glanced up the stairs at the dark platform. "John is only one of his heavy burdens in life. A man of Mathias's empathy suffers more than others. The world is a difficult place, and I've learned that sometimes it's best to let him sort it out for himself."

"If he would only talk about it."

"It does no good telling someone they're different. He already knows that." She shrugged. "Sometimes people have to figure out for themselves where they belong without the world constantly telling them."

"I don't think he's that different than the rest of us. A little more intellectual perhaps."

She looked at him for a long moment before a genuine smile overtook her face.

"You are such a kind man, Alfred. Don't lose that part of you. No matter how life plays out and who disappoints you, don't lose that part of who you are."

She turned and started back toward the kitchen. He watched her walk, her footsteps singing quick couplets separated by a longer pause. Her limp was worsening by the day. He turned back to the parlor and let his eyes rest on the empty chairs, their books tossed haphazardly onto the table and their pages lost. The shadows created by the oil lamp laced the wall and mantle above the silent fireplace. As his eyes drifted over the back of the chair, they stopped beneath the rightmost chair where John's jacket had fallen. The floor was bare. The paper was gone.

CHAPTER FORTY

*A*ugust had grown heavy and weighed on the horizon like a hazy film. From their position beyond the dunes, Alfred could make out the edge of the Earth where the sherbet clouds blended into the darkness that was the center of the ocean. Large waves tumbled toward the shore with a roar that subsided into a hush of water spreading along the sand toward their feet. Florence's hand grasped at his arm, and he turned to face her.

"Doing alright?"

"My boots weren't made for the sand," she commented, watching her footing as they cleared a tiny inlet where the water had made its way farther inland during the day's high tide. "I'll have to buy more adventurous shoes if we're to walk the beach regularly."

She looked up and gave him a smile from beneath her parasol. He slowed his pace as a thick breeze came off the water, sending her dress ballooning like curtains. He drew in a breath of the sea air and was reminded of how foreign it all had been when he arrived not four months prior; now it felt comforting, like a familiar pen when one sits to write a letter home.

"You didn't finish."

He glanced down at his feet and watched the tips of their shoes move in rhythm through the sand.

"What's that?"

"About Mathias."

"Oh." He looked back out toward the ocean. "Right."

The sky was interspersed with seagulls that swooped overhead before landing on the sand. They scattered after crabs that scurried along the shore and shrimp that were caught in flotsam that had washed up onto the beach. A gust sent her dress higher in the air and she loosened her grip to calm it before returning to his side.

"I can't understand what's gotten at him."

"The altercation with John sounds rather insulting."

"Oh, no doubt. John's priggish and a ripe ass in all accounts." He closed his eyes. "Sorry."

She gave a small shake of her head as she watched a pair of seagulls swoop overhead. "You think Mathias's reaction was unwarranted?"

"Not at all, but I do think something more is going on. Something he isn't telling me."

"Something with the hospital?"

"Perhaps."

A loose dune stretched toward the water and blocked their path. He guided her around it and drew them nearer the water. The sound of the water lapping at the sand was soothing, and the heat of the day was having its way with his skin. He longed to shed his suit and dive into the warm salty bath, but his mind was immediately drawn back to Mathias. He had yet to explore the bath houses, something the two said they would do soon after he arrived.

"But I think it's something more serious," he added.

He caught her glance and looked out in front of them where green tendrils wound their way along the top of the sand. Vibrant purple flowers dotted the vines with paper-thin petals. He gestured toward the plants with his chin. "What are these?"

"Tie vine."

She let her parasol lean back farther on her shoulder as she bent down and snapped a flower loose from the vine. She held it up to his face.

An aroma that reminded him of sweet tea rushed through his senses.

"Adventurers. Pirates perhaps?"

She reached across him and tucked the stem into his jacket pocket. The purple of the petals was prominent against the black of his suit.

"No." She shook her head. "Pirates are notoriously romantic. That's why they spend so much time at sea. Love on land is too constricting, but making a mistress of the sea is liberating."

"I hadn't any idea." He repositioned the stem so that the flower hung from the corner of his pocket. "What is their flower then?"

"Bromeliads."

"Fitting," he mused, imagining the thick green plant with a wide orange blossom. "Not pirates then. What about sailors?"

"They are more prone to flings rather than romance. I could see a sailor having a remembered love on an island in the tropics."

"A tangled love?"

She nodded confidently. "I think you've matched it, Alfie. They are the island's love letters to sailors, giving them a last farewell from the shoreline."

He laid his hand across hers instinctively as they continued along the beach, her grip tightening on his arm. The city was well behind them, nearly a two-hour walk but barely a half-hour ride. The coach was waiting on the road, the driver tipped for his bored state, as they walked the beach in private. It had been a daring expedition, but Alfred's knowledge of the wildlife and Florence's insistence at seeing what he described beyond the city where the instrument platform had been installed across from Captain Gregory's house had been enough to inspire them. Their conversation had flowed easily on the rough drive out, and he had found himself talking freely with her about the argument the night before. Their arrival at the beach had ceased the topic altogether as he had helped her over the dunes and onto the platform to show her the instruments, but the subject continued to resurrect itself after each spread of silence.

"What has Mrs. Poplar said about it all?"

"Very little aside from her advice to leave him be."

"Then that's likely the best approach. Surely she knows his temperament after having him board with her for nearly two years."

He winced as another gust rushed against them, and he leaned closer to her to protect her from the brunt of the hot air.

"I know it is, but it makes me feel helpless."

"There's nothing helpless about patience, Alfie."

A burst of cries came from overhead as a flock of seagulls swooped down onto the beach and hopped in place. Their beaks pecked at the ground until a small crab, its shell caught in the beak of the largest gull, came up from the sand. It writhed blindly, and the bird took flight with the crustacean still in its grasp.

"What do you mean?"

Alfred let his chin fall as he looked down at her. The round outline of her jaw was shadowed by the parasol, and a few wisps of hair floated about her neck beneath her hat. He watched her as she spoke, keeping the moment to himself as he admired her.

"Do you know the Golden Silk Orb-Weaver?" she asked.

"It's a spider, I believe."

"Yes, a terrifyingly large spider with long legs and a black and yellow body."

"It sounds hideous."

"Quite the contrary when you better understand their motives. Orb-weavers are named such because of their webs, which are oversized circles that they suspend between trees. They're usually high up off the ground and span several feet between anchors."

He frowned. "You know, I much prefer to talk about birds nowadays."

"I've heard enough about birds today."

He suppressed a smile as he nodded and looked back down to watch the rhythm of their boots.

"Golden Silk Orb-Weavers are unique," she continued, "because their silk changes color when the sunlight hits their webs. It gives the silk a glow and the look of golden thread."

"Really?"

She nodded, her eyes now on their feet as well. "The golden web is ir-resistible for bees, but the spider must be very quick to capture something of that size in its web. To increase its chances, it stays in its web all the time. It never leaves. It spins a monstrous, beautiful web and then waits patiently until the sun is just right and a bee or whatever insect makes its way into the web."

He shook his head. "I'm not following."

She let out a small sigh and squeezed his arm.

"The point I'm making is that an outsider would likely see the spider and wonder at how something so helpless, sitting in its web all day up high where no other spiders spin, could survive. What they do not see is that the web is a beautiful creation that is designed to do exactly what the Golden Weaver needs. It is patient. It waits until the food comes to its web."

He slowed his pace, coming to a stop. She looked up at him from beneath her parasol with bright eyes.

"You think I should wait until Mathias seeks me out to talk?"

"See," she replied coyly, "I always knew you were a smart man." He laughed, and she scrunched her nose at the sunlight that peeked around the edge of the parasol. "Shall we stop here?"

"Whatever the lady prefers."

He slid his sack off his shoulder and pulled out a thick cotton blanket. Letting it unravel, he held it up over the sand, where it popped in the breeze. He pulled it down and set his sack on it as an anchor. After helping her down onto the blanket, he pulled at the corners and took a seat beside her. She curled her legs beneath her and bunched her dress at her knees to keep it from blowing up in the wind. He tilted the brim of his hat down to better shade his face. Her voice was smooth like the water.

"What a beautiful scene."

"Have you painted anything like this?"

She shook her head. "I've never been this far down on the island."

"Never?" He contemplated the fact. "You've lived here your entire life."

"Quite sad, isn't it? To live someplace for so long and never fully experience it as others do. I would reckon you've come to know parts of the island more intimately than I do."

Removing his jacket to cool his body, he leaned back on one arm and looked out at the water. A large steamer slid across the horizon with a cloud of smoke belching from its chimney.

"I would imagine some but not all," he replied. "There are some parts I fear I'll never come to know as well as I'd like."

"Such as?"

He looked over at her to find her eyes already on him. Her gaze was intense, and he debated how best to answer her question. "Certain experiences," he finally answered. "Certain people I'll never know. Perhaps glimpses of its nature I'll never see."

"That's life, though, the worst of it, I mean. To know there are things you'll never know."

"Surely there are worse things."

Her parasol tilted once more, but he kept his eyes on the ocean. The beat of the waves was enchanting. Its music blended with the warmth of the day, and he felt the urge to swim return. Perhaps Florence was right. Giving Mathias time might be the best thing to do; he certainly felt he had few other options. Unlike when the two men had disagreed when Mathias had gotten drunk, Alfred now found himself with company of another sort. He looked to Florence and gave her an earnest smile.

"That was a poor idea to put to words. I'm sorry."

"Don't be. I happen to enjoy when you think aloud. It makes me feel as though I am part of the conversation."

"You are."

It was her turn to smile, and he leaned forward so that they sat shoulder to shoulder, watching the waves collide with the sand and draw slowly back out to sea. Seagulls cried above them as the tide inched slowly away with each undulation. As the afternoon began to sink into what felt like early evening, Alfred became aware of the time. His body had cooled with the breeze, but his shirt stuck to him beneath the sleeves and at his sides. His fingers fidgeted at the edge of the blanket, and he pulled the flower from his jacket pocket beside him.

"Florence."

"Hm?"

She was watching a sailboat as it followed the shoreline. He spun the flower between his fingers as he thought of his next words. While he knew this was better said in a more formal setting with less sweat and a touch more class, he disregarded his inclination to think through the action and said what he had been thinking for weeks.

"I'm not a wealthy man."

The words were heavy and hung in the humidity of the beach. She turned and gave him a curious look.

"Was I to think you were?"

He shook his head and sat up, letting one leg go straight while the other bent at the knee. The flower petals spun as he twisted the stem back and forth.

"No, that's not what I meant. What I mean to say is that I will never be made wealthy at what I do. I am compensated well for my work, but it's a scientist's work. I'm not a businessman or anything kin to a banker or barrister. I'll never have a good deal to my name." She stared at him for a long moment, her eyes shaded by the parasol. He looked over at her but failed to read her expression. "Do you understand what I'm saying?"

"That we'll not be living like the Greshams in a palace built on Broadway." His head tilted instinctively as he opened his mouth to speak, but she cut him off. "Do you remember the painting I showed you of the Ashton Villa? The one from the garden looking up toward the terrace."

His mind faltered with the sudden change in topic.

"Yes."

"I used a deep orange, tangerine I think it was called, to paint the tulips in the foreground. I wonder if that would be sufficient to capture the color of the sky just now if I were to try to recall it well enough to paint."

He looked back out over the water, his mind clearing like a fall from the sky and his heart racing as he collected his courage once more. He saw a strip of vibrancy forming just above the clouds to the west and imagined her brushing the color across a canvas. He felt a surge of calm at the thought.

"I think it would. Very much, in fact."

"Good. I'll order another tube for the painting. I'll add a sailboat on the water."

"And oleanders in the foreground?"

She flashed a smile. "And perhaps a blanket on the sand from a long day's walk."

"Perfect," he said as he rose.

He dusted off his pants and slid his jacket back on before helping her to her feet. He packed the blanket back into his sack, struggling to close it with his sweaty palms, and began their walk back to the coach. It was well after eight o'clock by the time they returned to her house, and her energy had begun to fade. He walked her to the door and gave a polite excuse for missing tea, knowing the offer was more out of formality than intentioned conversation. And as he settled himself back into the coach, the jolt of the horse's first steps set in motion a flurry of sensations that filled his chest with emotion. He recounted her words, parsing their every meaning, until he was deposited at the curb of the boardinghouse. He paid the cabbie for his evening's troubles and started up the walk, making a mental note as he took the steps in quick hops that if there were to be any plans made, he would be in need of a loan. And a big one.

CHAPTER FORTY-ONE

*N*ews from the mainland!"

A rotund man sweating through his shirt stood on the edge of Market Street, yelling toward passing coaches and soliciting to businessmen as they strolled beneath the covered sections of the sidewalk.

"News from Houston! News from New Orleans!"

Alfred sidestepped the man as he worked his way through the crowd, pandering to every passerby and offering tidbits of news from beyond the island. The month had worn on into a sweltering mess that had women fanning vigorously and men taking liberties with their collars and ties. A dead man's summer, Mrs. Poplar had called it. He couldn't be sure if she meant it as a warning, given the tremendous number of cases of heat sickness that had come out of it, or as more of an insult to the young men who frolicked into the waters despite the heat warnings. Either way, Alfred heeded the advice and was content to keep out of the sun as much as possible.

The office was humid but cooler than the street, and he relished the air that moved around the space thanks to the room's height and the air flow created by the open windows. But the tension was already thick as he set his stuff on his desk and hung his jacket.

"We can't ignore something this significant," Joseph announced.

He leaned back against his desk with his arms crossed and the window at his back. Isaac was bent over the table in the center of the room, a large map unrolled at his fingers.

"I'm not ignoring it, Joseph. You know as well as I do that these are delicate matters. They must be handled carefully. A storm warning would send the island into a panic."

Alfred approached cautiously and stole a glimpse of the map on the table. It was of the lower United States with the Gulf of Mexico filling the majority of the lower half.

"An advanced warning would do locals good," Joseph argued. "Give them time to prepare. The sick and elderly could make arrangements to leave."

"While we could make arrangements to find other jobs."

Joseph threw his arms up in exasperation as Isaac looked over to Alfred. "You've come just in time."

"What's happening?"

"A telegram was intercepted from Cuba." He gestured toward his brother. "Joseph, will you?"

Joseph handed Alfred a telegram dated 2:53 AM that morning. The message was brief but clear: *Storm forming S-SE. NW track. Wind gusts 44. BP 28.21.* Alfred handed the telegram back to Joseph.

"It's heading our way then?"

"No," Isaac answered quickly. "We don't know that for certain."

"But it could very well be," Joseph corrected. "For all we know, it could enter the gulf and head straight for Galveston."

"Or turn entirely to the north or the west," Isaac countered. "Or keep on its track and land in New Orleans."

All three men looked down at the map where Isaac rested his index finger on an opening between Cuba and a peninsula that jutted out of Mexico, blocking what would have been a wide mouth to the gulf and creating instead a channel of no more than one hundred and forty miles between the two shores.

"If it is too far south," Isaac explained, "the likelihood of it turning enough to clear the channel is low. It has a greater potential of keeping to the west and landing in Mexico or turning wide and pulling across the Yucatan Peninsula. Either of which would weaken it enough to keep it from our shores."

"And if it's farther north?"

Both men glanced at Alfred. Isaac turned back to the map while Joseph gave a small grin. "If it crossed Cuba or stayed to its north, it will likely pull northward and hit Florida before heading up the eastern shore."

"It can't move into the gulf?"

Isaac chewed on his lips. "Not according to how previous storms have tracked." He slid his finger across Cuba. "However, if it were over the island, it could theoretically make a tight enough turn to clear the peninsula and Cuba. In which case, it would pass through the channel."

"And intensify over the waters," Joseph added.

"But we still have no way of knowing its trajectory," Isaac commented. "Not for certain. Not unless we have reports from ships who encounter it."

Alfred rolled up the cuffs of his sleeve, the warmth finally making its way through his shirt despite the cooler air on the fifth floor. "Why don't you request reports?"

"He's afraid of spooking the captains."

Joseph's arms were crossed again, and his chin was tilted upward in a defiant pose. Alfred admired him for a moment, very aware of the man's prerogative as Isaac's brother and assistant, but something about his tone put Alfred in a defensive frame of mind.

"Can we not veil it under some other pretense," he suggested. "A request for reports or trending?"

Isaac considered his idea and removed his glasses. "We must be mindful that certain people are very aware of not only our jobs but our methods. There isn't a single captain on the water that isn't in tune enough with nature to understand that conditions are ripe for hurricanes or typhoons or whatever they prefer to call them. We can't very well hide what we're doing."

Joseph huffed. "Your dramatics are becoming boring, Isaac."

Isaac's mood took a turn as he leaned his palms against the table and set his eyes on his brother.

"The one thing we can count on with a preemptive warning is panic, Joseph. We'll be center stage when absolutely nothing happens. No wind. No rain. Nothing but high tides that leave the beaches muddy. That's when the editorials will start along with dissension and calls for replacement because three grown climatologists couldn't tell the difference between a hurricane and high tide." Isaac rolled up the map and handed it to Alfred. "If you both feel that sending out a few requests for information is a warranted act, I will agree to that. But I'll not risk this office over a Cuban telegram with incomplete data."

He returned to his desk and retrieved a journal. Holding it out toward Alfred, he snapped his glasses shut and slid them into his shirt pocket.

"These are field measurements from my outing yesterday. I'd like you to enter them into the logbook for our records." He tossed a glance toward Joseph. "And I'd like the two of you to take measurements over the next two days along the southern beaches. Just to be sure."

"I can do them," Joseph announced. "There's no use wasting Alfred's time with one platform."

"Aren't you forgetting your new construction on Pelican Spit?"

Alfred snapped to attention. The man was peering down at his papers, ignoring their reactions. When Alfred looked to Joseph, the man was watching him with narrow eyes. Alfred shook his head quickly, and Joseph returned his gaze to his brother. After a while, Isaac turned and looked at his brother.

"Perhaps you'll prove your theory after all."

"And perhaps I'll earn the right to talk with headquarters."

"The D.C. office isn't going to care what your measurements say, Joseph. They are more concerned about money and reputation, neither of which is easily gotten at the moment."

"Then why keep the platform?"

"Because it's already there, isn't it?" The words came out as more of a statement than a question, a disguised lecture for having disobeyed a superior. "If you're right and this storm clears the channel and heads for our beaches, then I would rather know what's coming than be altogether wrong at the cost of unforeseen flooding. An additional platform at the mouth of the channel would be a benefit."

Isaac didn't wait for a response, pulling out his chair and returning to his papers. Alfred was unsure if a truce had been called and the tension was receding or if a pause had been placed on the disagreement for the sake of posterity. Whatever the case, a decision had been made, and Alfred prayed it would prove to be the right one.

CHAPTER FORTY-TWO

For one of the first evenings Alfred could remember, the sky was completely clear. No clouds were overhead and the coloring of sunset was present the whole town over. The rooflines ran a deep red as the terra cotta tiles caught the light, and the tree tops glowed yellow with the rays stretching across the island. He stood outside the Lyceum, a tall wooden building attached to the Episcopal Church on 20th Street, and admired the flaming fronds as they danced in the breeze. The love letters for sand dwellers, Florence had called them.

Hilary was late arriving, and Alfred was already on edge when the old man finally walked up, his goggles still wrapped around his forehead.

"You look like a horse jockey."

He stared at him quizzically before reaching up and sliding the goggles off his head. "I was in a hurry."

"What kept you?"

Alfred followed him around the corner of the building to a small green space between the structure and the church. He slipped Hilary's goggles into his sack.

"My Motorwagen."

He glanced around them as two men walked toward the entrance, their attention lost as they stepped aside for a young woman to pass. Alfred watched the men walk by and kept his eye on the larger of the two. Something about the man's broad shape was familiar, the way he carried himself and the darkness of his brow. Alfred watched him enter the building as Hilary continued.

"I think someone tampered with it."

Alfred looked down at him and bent over slightly to keep his voice low. "Why do you think that?"

"The engine had been disconnected."

Alfred shook his head. "What does that mean?"

"It means they tried to shoot my horse and keep me from making it to the meeting."

"Who would know how to do that? That's the only one I've seen on the island. No one even knows how it works."

"Exactly. It had to be someone who has some know-how."

Alfred glanced back toward the sidewalk as another group of men walked by. "And a lot of guts to try something like that."

"I doubt that's the case." Hilary took the stack of pamphlets from Alfred and handed half of them back. "With this crowd, it's more likely they just have a lot of money."

He wiped his brow and let out a huff to calm his nerves before giving Alfred a nod.

"Come on. Let's get inside before it starts."

Alfred followed him to the front of the building where several other men had gathered. They fell in line and moved through the large wooden doors. The interior opened like a cathedral with extravagant height and ran at least three hundred yards before reaching what had been set up to resemble a pulpit. Bright stained-glass windows depicted Biblical stories in reds, yellows, and greens on either side of the attendees taking their seats throughout the room. The building echoed with murmured voices, and Alfred stepped closer to Hilary.

"Why are they having the meeting in a church?"

"It's not a church," Hilary whispered. "It's a lyceum. The church owns it, but it's available for public affairs and the like."

Alfred peered up at a window depicting Jesus speaking on a small hill and began to second-guess their plan. A cathedral or not, the building added an air of approval to the entire ordeal, and he wondered if trying to derail the meeting's progress was such a smart idea after all. Men continued to trickle in from the street as the room filled with expensive waistcoats and ascots. Hilary's elbow nuzzled his side.

"I'll start here. You go to the front and start with the first row."

"What do I say?"

Hilary separated a pamphlet from the pile and gestured to the print. "Talk to them as a group, not one at a time. Don't get caught up in arguing. The point is to make an impression. Let the pamphlet do the work."

Hilary took a few crooked steps toward the back row of attendees and leaned over the shoulders of two men, talking in their ears. Alfred watched him move down the line before building up the courage to work his way to the front of the hall. Taking the side aisle, he passed row after row of businessmen and a few of their wives or female counterparts, all in good dress and fanning themselves against the warmth of the room. When he reached the front row, he turned back to see more men coming through the doors behind nearly fifty full seats. He gave a dry swallow and pulled the first pamphlet from the stack.

Two older men sat at the end of the row, one in a full suit with a golden chain dangling from his waistcoat and the other in a linen leisure suit with a straw hat. They both ceased their conversation and looked up at him with expectant eyes.

"Gentlemen."

His eyes flicked to Hilary, who had already cleared the first half of the back row and was now serenading a young woman with bird calls. When he looked back down at the men, the more well-dressed of the two was preoccupied with his pocket watch while the other held out his hand in anticipation. Alfred shoved the pamphlet into his hand.

"Reading to consider." He flashed a quick smile as he searched for better words. "For the expansion. And the island."

"Oh, how kind," the man replied, giving his thin mustache a quick jump as he nodded. "Thrilling stuff, isn't it, this expansion?"

The murmur of voices grew in volume as more seats were taken, and Alfred had to lean down slightly to be heard.

"Indeed. But it's not as clear cut as it all seems." The man furrowed his brow with a tilt of his head. "Give it a read," Alfred instructed with a quick nod.

He stepped down the aisle and handed another pamphlet to the next group of men.

"Gentlemen, a quick read on the channel expansion."

A man in a simple black suit read the few first lines and shot him a sharp look. "A danger to local birdlife? And a substantial decrease in the population of bay oysters?" He shook his head and looked at the men beside him. "What kind of meeting is this? I thought we were here to discuss the expansion, not vote against it."

Alfred continued down the line as the men grumbled to themselves. He handed a pamphlet to a young woman in a pink dress as he neared the end of the line, but her husband snatched it and shoved it back into Alfred's pile. The front row was now a growing hum of conversation as the topic of the pamphlets began to spread, and Alfred began to sweat beneath his jacket. He shot Hilary a glance as he started down the second row, but the old man was moving more quickly than he had ever seen him—and flattering the group as he went. After a few dismissals, Alfred took to simply passing out the pamphlets without explanation, letting them fall into partially raised hands.

"Pamphlet?" He rounded the end of the second row and started in on the third. He and Hilary were only a few rows apart now and would meet in the middle within a few minutes. The anxiety building inside him would soon be over, but a hand on his shoulder cut that thought from his mind as it whirled him around on his heels. He spun to find himself face to face with the same man that had warned him of losing his reputation only a few weeks before. He was staring straight into the hard eyes of Julius Runge.

"Mr. Ridgeway." His eyes dropped to the pamphlets before flicking back up to Alfred's face. "What a pleasure to see you at our meeting."

Alfred's mouth was dry, but he managed to find his words after a few seconds. "A pleasure to be here."

"And what is this fine piece of literature you've been handing out to our guests?"

He took a pamphlet from a man sitting between them and read it silently to himself. "A little harsh on the accusations, don't you think? I had you pictured as having more of a mind for business than this tittle-tattle over birds and fish."

"It's not tittle-tattle," he argued, surprising himself with the veracity in his tone. "Hilary has been researching this for decades. Your expansion—"

"Is going to make this island realize its own potential. It's a necessary step to guarantee our survival as a port."

He held out the pamphlet and let it fall against Alfred's chest. His head tilted to the side as if he were sympathetic to Alfred's cause, but the slight rise at the corner of his mouth said otherwise.

"Now, Mr. Ridgeway, I'll kindly ask that you stop disturbing our guests and let our meeting get underway." He turned and made his way toward the side aisle, and Alfred followed closely behind.

"This isn't right, Mr. Runge. The committee needs to find an alternative to digging and dredging before we start to see irreversible damage to the island."

"And what alternative would that be?"

He turned in the aisle and waited. Alfred was taken aback and quickly sorted his thoughts, unsure of the sincerity in the man's question.

"Perhaps work out a partnership with Houston."

The space around him erupted in deep laughter that echoed off the walls. Mr. Runge's frame leaned back as his eyes brightened while the men seated nearby bounced in their seats. The man looked back at him with a smile.

"A partnership with Houston? My dear boy, perhaps you are less prepared in this subject than I thought. A partnership is the precise opposite of our intent. Galveston is the port of the south. We surpass Houston,

New Orleans, and every other port in the gulf, and we mean to build on our accolades, not share them." He ran his fingers along the brim of his hat and took a step closer as Alfred straightened at his proximity. "You see, Alfred, Galveston is a prominent name. It's a status. And we're not going to let something as minuscule as a flock of birds keep us from maintaining our place in this business. As for Houston, those men can't keep their feet out of the mud and hands off their beer. I'd rather see this town fold than consider our port on par with theirs."

His breath smelled of fine liquor, and Alfred wondered how much damage he had already done to his fresh reputation with this man. He ignored the continued chuckles from the crowd and took a step closer to reply but was cut short as another man's voice boomed inside the hall.

"Julius."

Mr. Runge turned and Alfred looked beyond him to see a slender man with a balding head, thick white mustache, and sharp nose.

"Ah, Colonel, yes." He gave a curt nod to Alfred. "Time for the show. If you'll not leave altogether, Mr. Ridgeway, as least be wise enough to sit quietly in the back, won't you?"

Alfred bristled as the man made his way up the aisle toward the front. He watched Mr. Runge speak with the gentleman before both turned and gave him a once-over. Afterward, the man looked beyond Alfred and gave a small nod. When Alfred turned around, he understood why. In the aisle stood the man he had seen walking in, the one with the heavy brow and barrel chest. Now, as the man approached, his muscles taut and his chin set in that familiar way, recognition dawned on Alfred, and he let his lungs deflate. It was the apprentice from the print shop, the one who worked the machines for Buttons. He had looked smaller bent over a press in the back of the print shop, but in the Lyceum he looked larger than life, towering over everyone, even Alfred. And Alfred wondered how much the man had shared about the pamphlets before they were even bound up for the meeting. It seemed the Deep Water Committee had ears in all corners of the city.

Alfred nodded and made his way toward the back of the hall, gesturing to Hilary as he reached the last row. The apprentice followed them to the back until they took two empty seats near the door. When the man had taken a seat of his own on the other side of the hall, Alfred finally let out a breath and leaned over toward Hilary.

"Who is the man in the front? The one talking to Julius Runge."

Hilary stretched his neck to see over the crowd. "Moody."

"Colonel Moody?"

Hilary nodded as the room began to quiet down. Alfred closed his eyes and let his head fall back against the wall. Julius Runge had been right: he'd only just started his part in all of this and he'd already dragged his name through the mud with the owner of the largest bank in Galveston. His mind flashed to his ride with Mrs. Poplar after church services a few months before—she had warned him then to be careful of the men on the committee. They were powerful and good at what they did. Now he was sitting at the back of their meeting as the voice of opposition, and his future bounced between the stained-glass windows. He needed a loan to make a proposal, and the man who ran the island's wealth had just marked him as a disturbance.

The meeting started with a quick reminder of New Orleans's plans to continue expanding their port and a brief speech by a man Alfred didn't recognize. He was slender with a long face and hair that was thinning at the front. He held himself well, something Alfred recognized had been trained in him, with one hand always in motion as he spoke.

"Good evening, gentlemen," he started with a smile. "And ladies. I want to thank you all for coming out this evening in support of our island's future. We believe that Galveston is on the heels of something even bigger than we dreamed. But, as with all endeavors, this one is not without opposition and obstacles." Alfred flattered himself to think the committee had taken note of their efforts and leaned forward to hear the man's next words. "We are here tonight to discuss our plans to petition for federal funds to support this expansion and usher the Port of Galveston into the twentieth century."

Alfred pursed his lips and fell back in his chair. He crossed his arms and leaned over again toward Hilary.

"Who is that?"

"Ike Kempner. A leading name in the city. His father left him a line of credit all the way back to Paris and a portfolio of companies including the island's cotton exchange."

"Cotton exchange?"

"Cotton exporters work directly with the farmers to cut out the middle man. It all comes and goes out of our port."

A memory slipped into the light of his mind. "Isn't Colonel Moody in the cotton business?"

Hilary stifled a laugh. "They're all in the cotton business. That's the point." He gave Alfred a quizzical look. "What do you think this is all about?"

Ike Kempner continued to speak, drawing nods among the flapping fans throughout the hall. A charismatic speaker, he held the crowd's attention as he explained how the committee was lobbying in Washington, D.C. to fund the project. The Army Corps of Engineers were scheduled to survey the channel in a few weeks, and then approval would only be a few months away. Alfred felt the fight slipping out of his grasp.

"We would like to have an open discussion." Mr. Kempner continued. "An informal talk of sorts. This project will create an economic boom for the city and guarantee our place as the dominating cotton exporter. But we recognize that the people are part of this plan. That is why we are not only being transparent but offering opportunities for others to join this investment opportunity as we move forward in the coming year."

"Smart," Hilary commented to the open doorway beside him.

Alfred glanced at him and back to the front.

"What?"

"He's making them feel as if they are a part of it."

"Aren't they? If they're able to invest in it."

Hilary shook his head. "In a sense, yes, but not in the same way. They could combine the wealth of this entire room, and it wouldn't rival any of their own investments or the federal funds needed to make it a success.

This isn't an opportunity for these people. It's an opportunity for the committee to buy the city's support."

"But why?" Alfred watched the men at the front talk amongst themselves for a moment as he tried to follow Hilary's thoughts. "If they are so powerful, why not just do it? Get it over with and make their money."

"The political climate is a little sensitive at the moment. If the election turns and they're found supporting the wrong administration, funds will be more difficult to secure, and having half the city questioning their tactics is a poor place to be in. If they can get people to buy into the expansion now, those people are more likely to support their continued efforts, no matter how long the project drags on."

Mr. Kempner began speaking again and opened the floor for discussion.

"I don't know," Alfred replied quietly. "This seems like quite a lot to go through just to appease the locals. Surely businessmen like them are capable of pulling off even ventures of this size in private."

"Oh, I'm certain they are and have. And that is precisely why you should question why they're being as transparent as they say they are being."

A man in the center of the crowd stood and Mr. Kempner greeted him by name as the two shared a familiar nod.

"How deep are we anticipating the new channel to be?"

"Impressively deep," Mr. Kempner replied. "A massive depth of thirty-two feet. It will accommodate the largest steam ships known to man. It is our hope to welcome the *Kaiser Wilhelm* steamship as our first guest in our new harbor sometime in the next two years."

The group became excited, murmurs spreading through the crowd. A woman near the back commented loudly on the extravagance of the ship, and Alfred tried to imagine a steamship that would warrant a channel of that depth to port at the harbor. Another man stood from the crowd and spoke loudly over the group.

"What of the businesses already on the harbor? Some of us have investments in the warehouses and companies that line the wharf. Asking us to afford the time and business lost for dredging and lining is a hefty request to make."

Mr. Kempner shook his head with an amenable smile. "I understand and believe me that we will do everything in our power to minimize disruption to the channel's access to the wharves. The expansion looks to expand outward, away from the island, so direct impact to the harbor itself will be negligible. Dredging and digging will occur as we expand the channel away from Galveston Island toward Pelican Island to accommodate the new depth."

"And what will be done with the dredged soil then?"

"That is up for debate, but there has been a suggestion that the soil be used to fill in the natural channel between Pelican Island and Pelican Spit to form a single sister island to Galveston."

The man lifted his chin. "To what end?"

"That is unclear at this time. Some land on Pelican Island is privately owned and used for hunting and such. But expanding the shoreline to connect the two would offer potential space for further expansion if the city desired to do so. It would also allow us opportunities to offer extended wharves if the soil was hospitable to the construction."

"I think you'd expand us into the ocean if you could," the gentleman replied with a laugh.

"Let's save that for when we run out of shore, Charlie."

Another man rose before the first could take his seat, and his voice gave away a hint of anxiety.

"What about storms, Colonel?"

Colonel Moody raised his eyebrows at the man and took a few steps toward him. "What about them?"

"Indianola was wiped out less than fifteen years ago. The entire city was destroyed. Doesn't it seem a bit imprudent to be expanding our most lucrative industry along the water. We are putting our credit lines in the path of whatever the ocean throws at us."

The Colonel lifted a hand in the air with an open palm.

"I have it on good authority that these fears are unfounded. Even the

U.S. Weather Bureau believes many factors assist the island in defense against storms and they are of little consequence to us."

Alfred's mouth went dry. He turned to see Hilary staring at him with wide eyes and shook his head vigorously. He looked back to the man as his speech continued.

"Dr. Isaac Cline, the Chief Climatologist of the Galveston Office, will be giving a lecture next week on the local weather systems and phenomena of Galveston Island. He will be discussing the benefits of our little island's placement as well as putting to rest fears of monstrous hurricanes and the like."

His voice grew animated as he said the last few words, and the crowd responded warmly. He gave a nod that seemed to close the subject altogether.

"And if the Chief Climatologist of Galveston is so convinced of our safety that he has put to bed the suggestion that we need any sort of engineering to protect us from the ocean, then who are we to say otherwise?"

When the meeting had ended, Hilary was quick to leave the building, taking the stone steps in an awkward hobble. Alfred caught up in a matter of steps. When they had reached the end of the block, Hilary slowed and came to a stop in front of the Episcopal cathedral. He looked up at Alfred.

"Is it true that Cline will be saying these things in his lecture next week?"

"No." Alfred closed his eyes and shook his head to clear it. "I mean, yes, he is making statements to that point, but I think they were misrepresented. I've never heard him discuss the expansion, let alone give an opinion in support of it."

"That doesn't mean much, does it? Most everyone has an opinion on it."

"But I can't imagine him supporting something of that magnitude regardless of how he sees it. It has nothing to do with the bureau."

Hilary eyed him a moment before nodding. "I agree, but that doesn't change the matter at hand. If his statements at the lecture can be taken as being in support of the expansion, he'll need to make it clear if that's not the case." Hilary pursed his lips and lowered an eyebrow. "Can you speak with him?"

Alfred nodded, and Hilary forced a smile at a couple as they walked by toward their coach.

"Good. That will help, especially given his position on the sea wall. That had everyone convinced of our safety before the most recent storms started heating up again."

"The sea wall?"

A group of men walked together from the Lyceum, their laughter carrying into the evening sky with the smoke of their cigarettes, and Hilary took Alfred's arm and pulled him around the corner onto 24th Street. They walked slowly, with the older man wobbling more than usual on one knee. Alfred offered to help him sit on the stairs of the cathedral, but he waved him off as he leaned closer.

"A few storms have hit Galveston in the past thirty years that have more than scared the locals into reconsidering their residency," Hilary explained. "It's usually nothing more than severe flooding. You know, water up to your knees. The Strand boards floating into the harbor. We literally sit at the ocean's door, for God's sake. I'm not sure what people expect of living on an island."

"And this sea wall was supposed to stop the flooding?"

"Not the flooding. You can't very well keep the rain out, but it was designed to hinder any rising water. To keep the tide out."

"How?"

Hilary mimed with his hands. "Build a wall along the beach and raise the island. What once was flooded with two feet of ocean water now requires ten feet to breach the structure."

"And Dr. Cline disagreed with this idea?"

Hilary nodded. "He said flooding was part of living so near the coast and that storm surges that breach other parts of the southern shore are unlikely to occur here. Something about how the island sits and the shallow water."

"And the jetties."

Hilary looked at him and nodded. "Yes, and the jetties. He's spoken of this with you?"

Alfred nodded as he looked down the street at the throng of men and women filling their coaches or making their way toward their homes.

"And he's making similar statements in his lecture next week."

"About the jetties?"

"About everything."

Hilary let out a loud breath, watching the crowd move along the street like bobbing planks in floodwater.

"Damn."

CHAPTER FORTY-THREE

*A*nother telegram had arrived overnight telling of cyclonic winds pushing south of Cuba and into the gulf, but it was the report from a ship that had traveled somewhere between Galveston and the Yucatan Peninsula that had Isaac so talkative when Alfred arrived at the office the following morning.

"Coordinates?"

Joseph eyed the telegram as he read the numbers. "Latitude twenty-one degrees, fifty-seven minutes, and thirty-three seconds north." Isaac followed the latitudinal lines on a map that was unfurled on the table and marked the spot with his finger. "Longitude eighty-nine degrees, one minute, and twenty-six seconds west."

Joseph leaned into Isaac's space as the climatologist worked his right hand until it met up with his left at the bottom left of the map. Alfred chewed on the last bite of leftover biscuit as he stepped up to the table. Joseph pulled a pencil from behind his ear and set it down on the map, scooting it so that the eraser held the coordinates and the graphite tip pointed toward Texas.

"North by northwest," Isaac announced.

"At eighty-three miles per hour," Joseph added.

"Hurricane speed," Alfred commented flatly.

"Well above it by that point," Joseph continued as Isaac returned to his desk. "But the true concern here is if God has other intentions."

Alfred looked at him blankly. He didn't take Joseph for a religious man. Nearly every man who had any position in the city attended church, mostly out of obligation, Alfred assumed, but Joseph had rarely made comments about faith in anything outside of science. Not that Alfred could blame him. The more time Alfred spent studying the winds, watching the waves, and reading books on what they did and did not fully understand about the world around them, the more he'd begun to wonder where the universe stopped and God began.

"Not all storms turn," he continued.

Alfred glanced down at the pencil and noted its path. It pointed less than an inch to the left of Galveston. Joseph's concern had proved warranted, and now they had no idea what the storm was doing. It was somewhere out in the gulf, churning over warm waters. He looked to Isaac, who had turned his chair and sat facing the two men, watching their discussion as if he had no part in the plot. Alfred felt his heart give a forceful beat in his chest as he spoke.

"What do we do?"

Joseph looked to his brother and slowly crossed his arms as he sat back on the edge of his desk. His lanky form was exaggerated in the morning light that streamed through the window behind him, a stark contrast with Isaac's small frame as he sat in the chair, a pensive expression at his lips.

"Nothing." Alfred's head tilted a centimeter, and Isaac gave him an exasperated expression. "What is there to do? It's in the gulf. We can't see it."

"With a path heading straight for the island and wind speeds above seventy-four," Joseph argued. "All that's left is landfall."

"You think it's going to turn?" Alfred asked.

He surprised himself with the words, and judging by their reaction, he had surprised both men as well. It was an odd thing to be excited when a potentially deadly storm was barreling toward the coast, but the intimacy with which he was watching it all unfold weighed on his mind. And he felt a shift in the room. He was tuning into their senses. This was what he had studied for so many months in the Signal Corps, what he had been educating himself on for nearly four months as he read on the rooftop with the instruments. Isaac's reply flattened the sensation immediately.

"I am certain it won't land here."

Joseph's voice toed the tension. "And if it does?"

"Then we will be getting many, many more reports before the evening is out."

A knock at the door surprised them all. The pressure in the room eased as Alfred cleared his throat, Isaac leaned against the table, and Joseph moved toward the door. A small boy of no more than seven stood on the other side. He peered up at Joseph with a slack jaw before leaning into the room and eyeing Isaac. The climatologist waved him in before squatting to his level. They shared a quiet conversation before he handed the boy a handful of change. He tussled the boy's mop of curls and gave him a pat on his shoulder. Isaac unfolded a piece of paper with a sigh.

"My wife has been taken ill. Looks like I'm homebound. Alfred, I'll need you to do the field measurements I had planned for the afternoon on the west end."

"Of course."

"I don't have a preference for who keeps to the office through the evening, but I would prefer someone be here until at least nine o'clock in the event that more telegrams come through. The last thing we need is a storm tracking toward us and the three climatologists reading their papers over brandy in their parlors."

Both men nodded as he gathered his things and made his way to the door. When he'd gone, Alfred felt a craving for fresh air and stood to take a walk down Market Street to the deli. The morning rush would be nearly cleared and a nickel for a fresh croissant and salted meat sounded more satisfying than the day-old biscuit that had been his only option after waking late. Joseph ignored him, keeping his attention on the map on his desk, and for once, Alfred was relieved to be the center of no one's universe where he could slip away into the street below and mingle with the pedestrians as if he had no idea that the island's safety rested on a single storm's decision to bear eastwardly or stay on its path toward their shores.

Chapter Forty-Four

Alfred had kept to the office most of the day while Joseph returned telegrams and visited captains at the harbor to catch wind of any potential news before it made it inland. When the afternoon rolled around, Joseph relieved him, and he spent the warmer part of the day in the dunes collecting measurements, noting wave formations along the southern shores, and stopping by the telegraph office on his way back to the office. As afternoon grew into evening, the fourth envelope of the day arrived by messenger—the New Orleans office had received numerous telegrams of a potential storm in the gulf that was now tracking for the harbor. It had turned east. Galveston was safe.

When Alfred slid his bicycle behind the house, he adjusted his pack on his shoulder and made his way back toward the front. Despite Mr. Poplar's insistence that he use the back entrance, he preferred to keep to the front door where he was less likely to take her by surprise. One spilled jar of sun tea had been all he needed to make up his mind, and he'd kept to the routine rain or shine. He heard a noise on the porch as he rounded the house and looked up to see Thomas standing by the door.

"Oh, hello," Alfred called up over the railing.

Thomas turned quickly and looked back toward the street. He gave an unsure smile when Alfred appeared at the bottom of the steps and removed his hat.

"Scared me half to death," he laughed as he held out his hand. "Good to see you again."

Alfred shook his hand and removed his hat, letting the breeze cool the hair that had matted against his forehead. He motioned toward the door.

"Here to see Mathias, I presume?"

"Oh, yes." He fumbled with his hat. "I rang but no one appears to be home."

Alfred recalled the morning's conversation as he hurried out of the kitchen, a biscuit in his teeth. He nodded as he fanned himself. "I think Mrs. Poplar had a meeting at the church this evening. But I can let you in. She wouldn't want me to keep you out here in this heat."

"Perhaps I'd better not."

Alfred stared, unsure of what turn the conversation had taken. He motioned toward the door. "No, really. Mrs. Poplar would put me out with the wash water if she thought I hadn't invited you in. I can make some coffee if you'd like. She has this fancy press from Paris that she raves about every morning."

"I think it's best."

Alfred pulled his head back to straighten his shoulders and let out a small breath. "Alright. Shall I tell Mathias you came?"

"Yes," Thomas replied. "If it wouldn't be too much trouble."

The hesitation in Thomas's voice left him uncomfortable, but he couldn't explain why. Something in the man's expression tugged at Alfred in a way that made him want to force the man to have a cup of coffee and a piece of Mrs. Poplar's pecan pie, and he realized he finally understood the woman's inability to just let things go when someone insisted all was well. It was that look, the same one that held Thomas's face in unease, that Alfred tried to suppress when he wanted nothing more than to crawl into bed and leave the world behind.

"Of course not."

"Will you give him this?" He produced a long package wrapped in thick brown paper with thin twine holding it together. Alfred hadn't noticed the package before, so taken with Thomas's odd behavior, and felt like a child surprised at a magician's sudden manifestation of a rabbit. He took the package and shifted it against his body, surprised at the weight. The two stood in silence for a moment.

"Is everything alright, Thomas?"

The man gave a soft smile as he took a step back toward the street. "Let's hope so. In the end."

He turned a quarter of a rotation, jumping slightly at the sound of a coach as its wheel hitched in a pothole in the street, and Alfred saw the left half of his face. It had been hidden by shadow until then, and the golden rays of the evening sun lit up his face as he turned, showing a freshly mottled bruise on his cheekbone. Alfred couldn't take his eyes off the man as he watched him finger the brim of his straw hat and settle it back on his head. He looked back, only half turning, and gave him a quick nod.

"If Mathias won't have it," he whispered, "perhaps you can find some use for it."

With that, he took the steps in quick succession and was making his way down the street before Alfred could think of anything to say. He looked down at the package and back at the street, but Thomas was gone, his figure replaced with the sweet scent of a summer evening. The house was quiet when Alfred stepped inside. He shut the door quietly and visited every room downstairs to ensure he hadn't misunderstood Mrs. Poplar's schedule. A cooked ham was being kept warm in the oven and a fresh basket of rolls was on the stove, covered with a kitchen towel. Alfred considered eating before heading upstairs, but the package reminded him of his errand. He took the stairs slowly, letting the wood creak beneath each step as if to announce his arrival home.

He deposited his sack on his bed, shed his jacket onto the back of his chair, pulled his tie loose and unbuttoned his collar. A slit of light came from beneath Mathias's door across the hall, and Alfred stared at it for a long moment. Mathias had been so level-headed when Alfred had first arrived, but he had seemed reactive in the past few weeks. John had been an ass. There was no way around that, but Mathias had sunk into his own world since their fight with John. Alfred had barely seen him, and what he had seen had been in passing. He stood just outside his friend's door and listened, taking in the silence before knocking softly.

There was a rustle inside and a creak that sounded like weight on a mattress. When another silence followed, Alfred knocked again. Mathias's voice came from the other side as a murmur of exhaustion.

"I'm not hungry, Mrs. Poplar." His voice quieted. "I'll be down for breakfast."

Alfred took hold of the doorknob and gave it a small twist. He opened it just enough to peer through the crack. "It's me." When the mattress gave another squeak, he opened the door a few inches and looked in. "Mrs. Poplar is out this evening."

The room was dark but for the open window beyond Mathias, casting him in silhouette. He sat on the edge of the bed, his feet on the floor and his weight on stiffened arms that pushed his shoulders up to his ears. He was looking out his window at the evening that had settled on the roof tiles of the neighboring house, painting them a purplish red. Alfred stepped into the room and glanced about the room, waiting for Mathias to turn around. When he didn't, Alfred set the package on the desk against the wall.

"Thomas dropped off a package for you."

Mathias turned and looked up at the wall in front of him, letting the sun silhouette his profile. "Thomas was here?"

"I ran into him on the porch." He waited a beat. "He said he couldn't stay."

Mathias turned back toward the window, and Alfred caught sight of the man's shoes at the foot of the bed. They were coated in dried mud with patches of scuffed leather peering through the sides. His eyes slid over to where Mathias sat. The hems of his pants were stained the color of maple honey and the material over his left knee was torn. His eyes scrutinized the man's body. A patch was torn loose at his elbow and he had dirt in the back of his hair. Alfred took a step closer, unable to quell the fear that was rising in his chest.

"Mathias?" The man didn't respond. "Are you alright?"

Mathias swallowed, the motion exaggerated by his turned neck, and looked down at his feet. Alfred leaned down a little to better see his friend's face. There, just below his right eye, an inch or so off from Thomas's similar bruise, was a darkening mark that had erupted across his skin. Alfred felt his breath give way as he tried to find any words that would suit the situation. He finally did as he always did and said the simplest ones he could manage.

"What happened?"

"It's not what you think, Alfred." His voice was small and quivered, and Alfred fought a compulsion to kneel in front of the man, to comfort him like a child. Instead, he kept his distance, afraid of scaring him like a wounded bird.

"What is it that I am supposed to think?"

"Me. I'm not what you think."

Alfred shook his head. It ached from the constant drama and tension that seemed to encircle the island. If it wasn't Isaac and Joseph, it was John and Mathias or Hilary and nearly every businessman on the island. If it wasn't someone he knew, it was a storm threatening the shore. More than anything, he wanted a day when everyone else had their lives together and he could finally be the one to fall apart.

"I don't understand what you're getting at."

"I don't belong here, Alfred." A small sob escaped his throat, and he took a deep breath to calm it

Alfred grabbed the back of the desk chair and dragged it to the end of the bed, sitting himself only a few feet away from Mathias. "What are you talking about? You're one of the most successful residents at the hospital. You sail with the sailing club. I know for a fact you're the most practiced dancer at the Garden Verein."

Alfred had hoped for at least a chuckle, but the only sound was the fast intake of air as Mathias steadied his breathing. When Mathias finally opened his eyes and looked toward Alfred, he saw the full force of what had happened. A bruise was forming on his cheek and a cut had been cleaned just above his eyebrow. Another bruise was darkening along his jaw and a scab had begun to form along his chin. He held Alfred's gaze.

"Not everyone sees me like you do."

"Good God."

"Tonight he wasn't," Mathias quipped.

He reached out to his side table where a bowl of water and bunched rag sat beneath the window. He dabbed at his lip where a small cut had bitten into the skin. The rag was spotted with dried blood, and the sight made Alfred's face grow warm.

"Who did this to you?"

"Four drunk men looking for a brawl."

"They picked you out in a pub?"

"Something like that." When Alfred didn't reply, Mathias closed his eyes and twisted the rag in his hands. "Thomas and I were leaving his shop. We'd had a few drinks before deciding to eat around the corner. Perhaps we were too loud and drew attention to ourselves, but we hadn't made it past Market Street when they surrounded us. They had a hold of Thomas before we knew they were on us and dragged us into the alley."

He dabbed at his lip again, inspecting the blood that transferred to the rag before holding it to the side of his mouth again.

"Thomas went down with the first hit. I pulled one of the men off of him, but that turned them all on me. One of the smaller men held Thomas back when he managed to get his footing, but it was too late. The other three took to me. When they finally let up, one of them punched Thomas again before they made off toward the street."

"Did you find an officer and report them?"

Mathias shook his head. "There was no point. We couldn't have caught up to them. And a nightstick wouldn't have done anything about it."

"I'd like to think differently," Alfred argued. "Two men jumped for the hell of it?"

"It wasn't for the hell of it, Alfred."

The sound of children yelling along the street came in through the open window, and Alfred felt dizzied.

"They knew you?"

A chuckle escaped Mathias's throat, and he let the rag fall away from his face. "You really do think the best of people, don't you?"

The question took Alfred by surprise. The man's tone stung, but he let it fall to the floorboards. His voice was quieter as he replied.

"I'm not sure how else to think of people."

"And if you found out that someone wasn't what he had led you to believe? What would you think of him then?"

Alfred considered the question before giving an honest answer. "That not all lies are created equal."

Mathias nodded. "Sometimes we lie for others."

"For others. For ourselves. A lie of love is not necessarily the same as a lie for gain, is it? I believe we can lie for good reason."

Mathias looked past Alfred at the package on the desk, and his eyes brimmed with tears. Alfred leaned his elbows onto his knees and closed the space between them.

"Whatever this is, Mathias—"

"It's why I can't go on like this."

"Like what?"

"Like this!" His tone was sharp. "I've deceived you and Mrs. Poplar. I've been stupid to think I could carry on like this and make something of myself in this city." He sniffled and tossed the rag onto the bed. When he caught sight of Alfred's expression, he shook his head and let out a frustrated laugh. "I hope you stay this kind, Alfred. This believing, this trusting of others."

"Try me." Mathias crumbled at the remark, and Alfred felt a small sense of relief with having taken control of the conversation for once. He shrugged. "If you think I'm as kind-hearted as you say, try it on me."

"Try what?"

"The truth."

Mathias looked away, and Alfred watched the man breathe. He knotted his fingers until he'd reddened the skin at the knuckles. When

Mathias turned back, his eyes were red-rimmed and a trail of hot tears cut through the bruises at his cheek and jawline.

"This is not an easy thing."

Alfred nodded, not wanting to discomfort him, but he felt the unease that had crept into the folds of the walls. When Mathias spoke again, his voice was weak and his breaths were quick as if he were searching for strength in every crevice.

"When I see you speak of Florence," he started, "it's a sort of honest love. Your love for her is so genuine. It's something I want so desperately for myself that I oftentimes find myself envious of your good fortune."

He tightened his jaw as a tear fell onto the front of his shirt with a muted thud. His body heaved as he took in a breath, and his voice rose in pitch as the words cascaded out like waves rushing onto sand.

"I know that's a terrible thing to feel, but know that it's from a good place. Because the truth is that I have known a love like that. The sort that makes me feel whole and energized." A small laugh escaped among the tears. "It makes me feel like I can fly with the birds. Like I am who I have always longed to be. Completely me."

He let out a shaky breath before continuing.

"The truth is that I've fallen in love with a man." He let out a big breath as if to settle the air around him, and his voice evened out. "And the worst of it is that it's not even my secret to keep anymore. John knows, and he has threatened to tell the dean of the college." He shook his head, blinking away the tears that had settled in the corners of his eyes. "I'll be out of the university with nothing to my name. And Thomas—Thomas will lose his store. And we'll both be lucky if we're not jailed."

The room grew steadily heavier as the weight of his words settled on Alfred's shoulders. The silence that followed was long and interrupted only by the quick call of a bird at the window. Alfred felt sick to his stomach as he put the pieces together.

"That's why those men attacked you?"

Mathias nodded. He wiped at his cheeks and sniffled before grabbing the rag off the bed and drying his face with a clean corner of cotton.

"All those days sailing with Thomas? The dinners and outings?"

"It is easier to be ourselves when there's no one to see you but the ocean." Alfred nodded with a knitted brow, his eyes on Mathias's shoes. "Thomas is a member of the sailing club," he added, as if some truth had been had in it all.

"Does Mrs. Poplar know?"

"I think she does, in some way or another."

Alfred imagined the woman, saying her evening prayers with Mathias on her lips, but the image was difficult to conjure without her soft eyes and loving tone. It was the only way he imagined she spoke to anyone, God included. Mathias's voice was vulnerable when he spoke next.

"Do you think me sick?"

The question surprised Alfred, and he snapped his head up to look at Mathias. His face was bruised and his eyes red. His shirt was torn, and his hair was disheveled. He looked the part of a well-trodden man, nothing like the respectable doctor in training that had greeted him in the spring, but more than anything Alfred thought he looked like a man with very little left to lose. But what he did have, Alfred knew, was very valuable.

Alfred softened his brow and shook his head slowly. "No, Mathias. I don't think that at all." His friend's chin quivered as he nodded, tears brimming. "But I do think you've done a poor job at cleaning your cuts."

They shared a small laugh, and Alfred scooted forward a few inches on his chair. He reached up and gently turned Mathias's face for a better look.

"I think Mrs. Poplar has some ointment in the wash room. Why don't I get a fresh bowl and rag and you can change out of your clothes?"

Mathias nodded as he wiped away the last tears before they reached his cheeks. Both men stood without another word, and Alfred returned the chair to the desk. He left Mathias to change before procuring a bowl and clean towel from the kitchen. When he returned, he set up the station at the desk and Mathias sat by the lamp so he could see his work better. When they were finished, Mathias's situation was made clear: two bruises on his left side, a gash along his brow, a busted lip, and a swollen jaw, but his eyes told more than the bruises.

Alfred brought him a plate of ham, beets, and rolls, and they ate in his room, Mathias in the bed and Alfred at the desk. John returned at some point, taking the stairs loudly, and Mrs. Poplar arrived after dark, but neither of them intruded on the conversation that followed between the men. It was well after midnight before Alfred returned to his room, his voice worn out by such a long stay, but he had left his friend resting and safe.

He sat at his desk and pulled the bottle of amaretto out of the opened package that Thomas had left with him on the porch. Mathias had smiled at the gift and kept the note for himself, but he'd happily sent the bottle off with Alfred, saying he didn't need any help sleeping. Alfred felt the same way, but he opened the bottle with a pop and poured himself a small drink anyway. The smooth taste helped settle the night a little more quickly and, whether he believed his eyes or not, made the stars glisten a little more brightly than they had before.

Chapter Forty-Five

Clouds moved across the island like sails of invisible ships pushed by a tropical breeze. The morning broke across Alfred's windowsill in a shatter of golden light, and he found himself feeling the pang of the late night. The amaretto had been a sweet lullaby that had sent him drifting into a deep sleep a little after one o'clock, but the few hours in bed and full glass of liquor had taken their toll. He washed quickly over the sink and did his best to give himself a clean shave before hurrying down the stairs and into the dining room where Mrs. Poplar was settling into her seat at the head of the table.

"Good morning, dear," she called, setting a bowl of melon beside his empty plate. "Running a little behind again?"

"That seems to be my luck lately."

He took his seat across from Mathias's empty chair and gave John a cursory glance before pouring himself a cup of coffee. The aroma of the meal pulled at his stomach, and he took a hearty bite of leftover ham. Mrs. Poplar looked beyond him toward the front of the house.

"Is Mathias coming down this morning?"

"He's not feeling up to it today."

John popped his newspaper as he turned the page and glanced toward Alfred. "Having the hell kicked out of you will do that to you."

Alfred stilled, a mouth full of melon, and stared at John as the man returned to his newspaper. Sensing Mrs. Poplar's eyes on him, he forced himself to tear his eyes away from the man and take a drink of coffee. The woman's voice was hesitant as she cut into her toast.

"Is he not well?"

"Just under the weather," Alfred replied. "I'd give him a little time to sleep it off, and he should be fine."

She nodded, giving a worried glance toward John before continuing with her breakfast. They ate the rest of the meal in quiet conversation of Dr. Cline's upcoming lecture, Alfred's final touches to Hilary's field guide, and Mrs. Poplar's onion plants that had begun to burn up in the late summer heat. When John folded his paper and slid out of his seat, Alfred hurriedly chewed the last of his morning roll and took a quick drink of coffee. Mrs. Poplar waved him off as he offered to clean up his mess, and he leaned down to give her a kiss on the cheek, which she returned with a broad smile.

John was pulling the door to when Alfred took hold and yanked it back open. John faltered and turned, glaring at him with dark eyes beneath his bowler.

"What the devil's gotten into you?"

"I should be asking you the same question."

He gave an irritated wave and started down the steps, but Alfred was on his heels. "How did you know that Mathias had been attacked?"

"A lucky guess."

He grabbed John by the arm and spun him around, pulling him close enough to feel his hot breath of surprise on his cheek. At such close proximity, Alfred towered over him, and John's eyes ran his full height before matching Alfred's glare.

"You know more than you're letting on," Alfred hissed. "And I've grown tired of this game."

"Then you picked the wrong city." He leaned an inch closer. "Maybe you should go back to the territory and make friends with your own kind."

Alfred shoved him back and let loose of his jacket. John shook his sleeves and smoothed them out before adjusting his collar. His eyes never left Alfred's face, and it stirred something in Alfred that threatened to take over his senses.

"You'd better watch yourself, John. You'll throw one too many punches and find yourself on the receiving end of something far worse one of these days."

"Wasn't that what your little joke was all about?"

Alfred stared as John finally met his gaze.

"You know, it took me a while to figure it out, but it wasn't too difficult in the end. He only goes three places anymore. The college, Thomas's shop, and sailing. And God knows they aren't out there for the view."

"You sick bastard."

"Once I figured out Thomas had written the letter, I realized what a fool I'd been thinking I was careful in keeping a little romance to myself. I couldn't very well let Mathias do the same." He lifted his chin. "How'd they do anyway? Just a few bruises or did they clean them up well and good?"

Alfred clenched his jaw, but it made no difference. He had no words for the man, only a burning desire to push him into the street and beat every ounce of arrogance out on him. But he stood still, fuming. When John tilted his head and gave him a sympathetic look, he knew he'd lost the upper hand.

"Did you really think you could best me, Alfred? You're a weatherman without a penny to your name. You don't fit here. You never will."

They stared for a second more before John turned and made his way out onto the street. Alfred watched him go, his chest burning with what felt like the offspring of sadness and humiliation, but none of it was his. It all belonged to Mathias. Every syllable had been laced with disdain for the man; Alfred had simply been the messenger, and knowing John, that's what he had likely intended all along.

Alfred returned to the house and made his way upstairs, not wanting Mrs. Poplar to see him in such a state. He washed his face in the cool water of the basin and sat on the side of the tub for several minutes, trying to calm his nerves. When he'd regained his composure, he stepped out into the hall and quietly opened Mathias's door.

His friend was sitting up in bed reading the morning newspaper. He let the paper fall onto his lap.

"Did Mrs. Poplar send up biscuits with you?"

"No." He closed the door. "Was she supposed to?"

"She said she'd send up some food in a bit. I can't say I'll argue much with it. The smell alone is intoxicating."

Alfred leaned against the desk. "She's been up then?"

"Just a few minutes ago. She said you'd mentioned I wasn't well."

"I played it off as a touch of something."

"I think she realized it was a touch of someone's fist," Mathias remarked, gesturing to his jaw. "She's a smart one."

"It doesn't take doctor to diagnose this one, Mathias." The man chuckled and glanced back down at his paper. Alfred chewed on his lip for a moment before speaking again. "Do you remember telling me that John knew?"

Mathias looked up at him with curiosity.

"That John knew about you," Alfred continued. "And that he was going to tell the university." Mathias nodded and pushed himself up, sitting straighter against the headboard. "How did you know that he had intentions of telling anyone?"

"I found a letter he had written to the dean of the university."

"A letter? When?"

"The night he came in and accosted us in the parlor." Alfred thought back to the night and replayed the events in his head. "He must've dropped it in the commotion. I saw it beneath one of the chairs and picked it up on my way out of the house that night."

Alfred nodded as the realization took hold. "While Mrs. Poplar and I were replacing the books."

"I think so." He watched Alfred inquisitively. "Why?"

"Did anything come of it?"

Mathias shook his head and looked about the room as if searching for an answer among the sparse walls.

"Not that I know of. I was rather on edge the rest of the week, thinking I'd be called into the office and dismissed, but no one ever said anything to me."

"You think he dropped it, then?"

"I suppose so." After another moment of contemplation, Mathias pushed again. "Why are you so interested?"

"No reason," Alfred lied, sitting up straighter and lifting his eyebrows as if to brush away the worry that had settled in his mind. "The comment had simply stuck in my mind, and I wondered if you still had fears that he would be acting on it."

Mathias shook his head. "Not to give John much credit, because he can't stick with much of anything except women, but perhaps he simply let it go. Maybe the thought of writing another letter to the dean was too much trouble."

Alfred forced himself to nod as he squeezed his chin between a thumb and forefinger.

"Perhaps."

Mathias returned to his newspaper, and Alfred pushed himself up from the desk. He had an opportunity that he didn't want to take lightly. Confess what was now his and John's secret or keep it buried somewhere that could sustain a fire of that intensity for as long as he could. Watching his friend, a bruise covering the edge of his jaw and a cut digging into his lip, Alfred knew he hadn't the courage to do either, but he had the heart to save the man anymore heartache than what he had already endured. And that was enough for him.

He opened the door and took a step into the hallway before turning back into the room.

"I'm out for most of the day."

Mathias looked up. "Off to see Florence?"

"And attend the lecture tonight."

"Oh." Mathias frowned. "I'll miss out on it."

"Florence has agreed to go," Alfred replied with a grin. "Her aunt's friend was delayed in her travels."

"She's a good one, Alfred."

"I know," he remarked. "Listen, I know it's rushed, but I thought a day trip might be worth the trouble. We could get away and go to the mainland."

Mathias smiled. "Just the two of us?"

"Why not? Take the train up to Houston and have a keg in Mudville."

"I think that's a lovely idea."

"Tomorrow then?"

"I'll wear my best suit."

Alfred shut the door and left the man to his newspaper, adding one more errand to his day full of tasks and thinking it ironic that his first trip back off the island should be to help another man escape his troubles when it was something similar that had brought him onto the island in the first place.

———•●•———

The streets were crowded as men and women walked the city. It was the end of August, something that resembled the heavy pull of an undertow as summer held on. Alfred fanned his face with his hat as he entered the train station. A clock in the center of the station showed he was running behind, and he hurried toward the teller's counter. He purchased two coach tickets to Houston for the following morning and tucked them into his pocket as he made his way back out onto the street.

Florence was waiting for him on a bench on the corner of Strand and 24th Street, her pale blue dress dancing a ballet at her feet in the breeze. A tumble of auburn hair fell from beneath her hat, and something about the color of her dress, a bright ray against the red stone of the bank building, and the way she sat on the bench with her ankles crossed and her chin lifted at just the right angle, made him slow his pace.

"A penny for the lady's thoughts."

She looked up with a knowing smile, holding her hat in place with a light touch. "That I could use a gentleman to keep me company." She slid her arm through his as she stood and let her skirt fall in a waterfall of blues.

"I believe the lady wanted taffy?"

They walked the Strand, letting their conversation give them escape from the crowd that bustled around them. At 25th Street they moved in and out of coaches until they reached the steps of Bloomberg's Bakery & Sweets. A small crowd was gathered at the back of the store, and Florence led Alfred through the crowd and up to the railing. Muscular hands pulled at taffy, stretching the thick texture until it began to tear into thinner sheets. They folded the ends back together, wrapping the taffy in on itself on a work table before beginning the process again. Dark red diluted into a pale pink, the air becoming sickly sweet. A worker molded the taffy into a brick and began cutting small pieces that he set aside to be wrapped.

Florence pulled Alfred closer to the bakery case where a table of wooden crates were neatly labeled and filled to the brim with pieces of wrapped taffy. Children pushed their way up to the crates and buried their arms up to the elbows before pulling out their prizes. Alfred reached into the first crate and pulled out a piece of pink taffy in a white wrapper.

"Cherry," Florence announced.

Alfred scanned the crates of orange, yellow, green, and blue taffy. "Which one is your favorite?" he asked as he sniffed a yellow piece.

"All of them."

"A bit of a sweet tooth?"

She nodded as a young boy came up behind the crates. He looked from Alfred to Florence with a tired smile.

"Would you like to try the taffy?"

"Oh, no need," Alfred replied, pointing to the stack of paper bags behind the boy. "The lady says she likes them all, so we'll take two of each flavor."

Florence helped the boy fill the bag, sneaking a piece into his pocket as a thank you, and led Alfred to an empty table at the center of the store. She picked a piece out of the bag and unwrapped it, and he did the same. He dug around until he found the one that matched her color.

"Oh, it's quite tough," he announced as he bit into it. "And sticky."

"It's taffy."

"Yes, but it's very—"

He chewed in an exaggerated motion and felt his teeth pull at the candy, his nose scrunching up at the texture.

"Chewy," he finally finished.

She gave a laugh and took a small bite of her taffy as he removed his hat, thankful for the breeze blowing through the store from the front windows. After smaller bite of his taffy, he watched her chew on her own candy.

"Florence?"

"Hm?" She pulled another piece from the paper bag and began unwrapping it.

"I've the mind to visit the bank this coming week to apply for a loan."

"Oh?"

"To buy a house."

She looked up and met his eyes. Her mouth continued to chew heavily on the candy, and the contrast of her well-made dress and fashionable hat with the cheerful way she chewed made him snicker. She covered her mouth as she tried to quickly finish the candy, but a smirk crossed her lips and lifted her cheeks from behind her hand.

"Stop it!"

"What? Admiring how beautifully you chew taffy? I'd rather not."

She swallowed the piece and neatly folded the wrapper. "A house then?"

"I thought perhaps in a neighborhood near the boardinghouse. The houses are a bit smaller toward the edge of the city, but they're nearer the beach. It might not have many rooms, but you would have enough space to paint. And we might be able to afford a piano after a while."

She laid her hand on his, and his thoughts froze in mid-formation.

"A room to play for you would be luxurious." Her eyes twinkled. "But a small house near the beach sounds even better."

He grinned and resisted the urge to lean in and kiss her on the cheek. He took her hand in his instead and gave it a squeeze. She looked about the room, her face hinting at their impropriety, and slid her hand back across the table. They both reached into the bag and retrieved more taffy.

"Have you spoken again with Mathias?"

He nibbled a small piece from the orange taffy. "We spoke last night."

"Are things better?"

"I believe so." He was quiet a moment before continuing. "Do you think there is a good enough reason to keep a secret from someone?"

She considered his words as she spun a bite of taffy around her mouth.

"I suppose if you have good intentions. Why?"

He nodded, keeping his eyes on the taffy wrapper. She was watching him when he looked up. "John made a comment about Mathias, and I haven't said anything to him about it yet."

"Will you?" He bit his lower lip as she folded another wrapper and laid it with their stack on the table. "What's stopping you?"

"I don't want to upset him. He's had a lot of worry and stress lately. This will only add to it."

"No good can come from telling him?"

Alfred made a pensive expression that she studied intently as she waited. Finally, he shook his head. "Not today."

"It seems like you've already made your decision then."

He nodded as he watched a set of twin boys reach into the taffy crates and pull out handfuls of wrappers. A shadow crossed their table, and Alfred glanced up as a familiar voice reached his ears.

"Well, aren't you two sharing quite the feast?"

Evelyn's frame was exaggerated in a fitted blue blouse and darker skirt that met her boots at the ankles. She tugged at her gloves to reveal pale hands as she looked down at the taffy wrappers on the table.

"Really, darling," she said with a lower voice, "you should consider what others will think."

Florence's face tightened as she shifted in her chair. "Pardon?"

"The taffy, dear," Evelyn cooed with a glance at Alfred. "A woman indulging so publicly is bound to start gossip."

Alfred moved his chair a few inches away to face both women. "Evelyn," he commented, unwrapping the last piece of taffy, "to what do we owe the pleasure?"

"Dining at the Tremont House before heading to the beach. A heat wave is heading our way so I thought it prudent to get a few trips in before the heat took over." She glanced at Alfred. "But I'm sure you knew that already, what with being a weatherman."

Alfred narrowed his eyes and felt a familiar heat grow in his stomach.

"Climatologist," Florence corrected.

"Oh, of course. How silly of me!" She flapped her gloves against her open palm. "Listen, I am just getting a few pieces of candy for mother's friends who are visiting later this week. Care to join me at the pull counter?"

"I've had my fill," Florence replied with a smile.

"Are you here all alone?" Alfred asked.

Both women looked at him with wide eyes. He'd broken social decorum but didn't care. The woman had seized an opportunity to make her mark on a perfectly good day out, and he wasn't in the mood to let it slide. He glanced about the store as if searching for someone to assign to her and then back to her with an expectant expression.

"Alfred." Florence lowered her voice in embarrassment, but he gave her a small smile before letting his eyes come back to rest on Evelyn, who pursed her lips.

"Not at all. A lady doesn't make her way around town alone if she intends to keep her reputation."

"Of course not." He let the silence sit; she let a smile cross her lips. "If you must know, I'm attending a small event at the beach at the invitation of a suitor. A man I think you know very well."

"Is that so?"

"Mr. John Briggs."

Alfred's smile fell as Evelyn let out a small laugh that grew into a head tilt.

"Yes, he's quite humorous and very intelligent. Refined and well-respected, just the sort a lady looks for in today's society."

"How lovely," Florence replied, keeping her eyes on the woman as Alfred shifted in his seat. "He's studying to be a doctor, isn't he?"

"He is." She nodded. "Top in his class."

Alfred cleared his throat. "That's not quite the accomplishment one would think when he buys his way in."

Florence closed her eyes at his comment while Evelyn let out a snort.

"Well, aren't we in a mood today."

"Please forgive him, Evelyn," Florence commented. "It's been a long week."

"Indeed." She began replacing her gloves on her hands. "I must be off then. Florence, darling, do call on me soon. It's been far too long since we've had tea."

"Of course."

Evelyn looked down at Alfred as she slid her fingers into her second glove.

"Good day, Mr. Ridgeway."

Alfred kept quiet and waited for her to leave before letting out a puff of air. Florence turned to him with a sharp expression.

"What has gotten into you?"

"John."

"What has he to do with any of it?"

He shook his head, recognizing their proximity to a sensitive topic that was not his own to divulge. He reached out a hand and let it rest on her arm.

"I'm sorry. I let my frustrations get the better of me."

"I should say so."

Her eyes softened and she laid a hand on top of his so that their limbs made a small stack of silk and cotton. She leaned forward so that their faces were closer together and looked up into his eyes.

"What flares your temper so when it comes to John?"

"He's an outright ass."

"Well, there's no denying that, but surely that can't be the whole of it."

"I just don't like the idea of him being in company with the likes of Evelyn. Nothing good can come of that. For you or me."

She waved off his comment with his hand. "Oh, Evelyn is all talk. She's harmless deep down. Easily manipulated, the poor girl, and not terribly bright on her own."

"That's my worry."

She stared at him before letting a smile take over her face. She patted his hand and made a motion to stand up. "Come on, then. Let's get you in a better mood before this lecture. Now, if I'm not mistaken, you promised me a fine dinner before this talk of Dr. Cline's."

"I haven't ruined your appetite with sweets and distasteful comments?"

"Oh, was that the plan? Fill me up with the cheaper sweets and petty arguments to avoid the finer foods?"

She smiled, and his sense of peace returned. The issue of Evelyn and John was a figment of his imagination, nothing to be concerned about until it presented itself rightly as a problem. Moreover, Mathias was healing in many ways, already shades lighter in his mood than the previous night, and John had a habit of being full of threats for nearly everyone he encountered. Granted, he had carried one out, but Alfred had plans to be more present for Mathias if that was what was needed. He wasn't going to let John get the upper hand again, whether he let Mathias know or not. He joined her and offered his arm once more.

"To the Tremont House, my lady?"

"Oh, yes! Their shrimp coquets are divine this time of year."

He gave her a mocking nod and guided her toward the door, leaving room for her to step out ahead of him. "You know," he started, "I think I might have something to introduce you to for once."

"Oh?"

"A drink called a mint julep."

"What's a julep?"

"I have no idea," he admitted, "but it tastes very similarly to whiskey and gin."

CHAPTER FORTY-SIX

*T*he YMCA filled the corner of 23rd Street and Winnie Street. A first floor of gray stone with three floors of red brick, the building with its arched windows on the third floor and a cornice that spread out over the street reminded Alfred of the Levy Building. A steady line of people walked through the door, some younger men heading toward the locker rooms and others businessmen searching for the lecture hall. Alfred held the door for Florence and took a last breath of fresh air before stepping into the lobby.

The hall was already bustling with conversation, and Alfred was taken back to the DWC meeting the week before. It had been especially embarrassing when Mr. Runge had interrupted his passing out of the brochures, but perhaps more than anything it had been frustrating to hear how easily the committee had convinced the attendees of the necessity of the channel expansion. Alfred had bicycled by the Lyceum the next day only to find several of their pamphlets along the sidewalk, and he'd saved them, slipping them into his sack, for opportune moments when the expansion made its way into conversation as it had a habit of doing. He and Florence took two seats off to the side of the room where they wouldn't find themselves directly in Dr. Cline's view.

Florence's hand rested on his arm. "Are you alright?"

His throat scratched as he swallowed. "What do you mean?"

"Your leg won't sit still, and I don't think I've ever seen you so fidgety."
He glanced around the room.

"I need to speak with Dr. Cline before the lecture, but I don't see him.
I wonder if he's somewhere preparing." He leaned over to whisper. "I'm
going to step outside for a moment."

"Are you sure everything is alright?"

"It's fine," he mouthed with a grin and took off toward the back of
the room.

In the hallway, men had gathered to share their gossip of the day
before taking their seats. The sound of hard-skinned balls hitting walls
somewhere nearby echoed down the hallway as Alfred slid in and out
and around groups of people. Finally, toward the back of the hallway near
the men's locker room, he spotted the familiar pensive expression and
thin-framed glasses of his mentor.

"Dr. Cline?"

The man kept his eyes on his manuscript as he mouthed the words to
an invisible audience. Alfred came to a stop a few feet away.

"Isaac?"

He looked up, his eyes shifting from annoyance to recognition. "Oh,
Alfred. What a relief that you've come. And, good, you've worn a tie."

Alfred instinctively touched the knot at his throat.

"Is that particularly curious?"

"Not usually, but I'm in a bind. It seems a loose thread in my tie has
had its last go-around. I went to straighten it a few moments ago, and it
came loose." He lifted his chin. "It only stays together if I keep my neck
facing forward and don't look to either side."

Alfred scrutinized the tie. It seemed to be staying in place quite well,
but he was keenly aware of the man's insistent attention to detail. A loose
thread or not, a crooked tie was likely disastrous in the man's mind.

"What can I do?"

"May I borrow your tie?"

Alfred glanced back at the growing volume of the room behind him.
He needed desperately to speak with him about his lecture and the chan-

nel expansion, but giving up his tie had not been on the drawing board of ideas. He bit his lip and looked back at Isaac, who was waving at an elderly gentleman as he passed toward the restroom. He began untying the knot and slid the material loose of his collar.

"Thank you. My wife would have it out with me if I gave a lecture in such a shabby state."

He turned to a small mirror that hung on the wall and began tying a knot at his collar. Alfred unbuttoned his own collar and felt his body relax a smidge with the fresh air washing over the nape of his throat.

"Sir, I have a pressing question regarding your lecture."

"Yes?" The man knitted his brow as he fumbled with the material.

"You're aware of the Deep Water Committee's intent to expand the shipping channel for a third time?"

"Any man with an address south of the mainland knows something of the project, I'd imagine."

He gave up on the knot and pulled the tie loose again to start over.

"Are you going to discuss the expansion at all in tonight's lecture?"

"Why would I do that?" He folded one side of the tie and began looping the other. "The lecture is about the natural position of the island and its weather phenomena, not that political mess."

"There seems to be a consensus among the committee that you'll be supporting their belief that the channel expansion will have no effect on the island should a hurricane make landfall."

Dr. Cline finished the knot and pulled at the ends of the tie to straighten it out. He gave the front of his shirt a smoothing before turning back to Alfred with a furrowed brow.

"Who told you that?"

"Colonel Moody made a statement to that effect at the last Deep Water Committee meeting."

"You attended a DWC meeting?"

Alfred felt the judgment in the man's gaze in the silence that followed.

"I was passing out pamphlets against the expansion," he admitted.

"Ah." His usual demeanor returned. "Well, I've no intention of making this a political evening. I'm simply here to give the facts. If those happen to coincide with the efforts of the DWC, that is beyond my control."

The hallway began to empty out, and he picked up his manuscript to give it one last glance. Alfred took a step closer.

"Sir, I believe in presenting the science to the people as well as you do, but if people were to believe that you are in support of the expansion—"

"Dr. Cline?" Both men looked up to find a well-dressed gentleman with a flamboyant tie at his throat. He made a small gesture to bring the climatologist forward and gave a nod toward the lecture hall. "Shall we introduce you?"

"Ah, yes." He nodded toward Alfred as he closed his manuscript and set the pages together in his hands. "Thank you again for the tie, Alfred. I'll return it with interest on Monday."

"But, sir, the expansion."

Dr. Cline turned and leaned forward, his voice dropping to a whisper as if pressuring a child.

"Facts, Alfred. That's all we're discussing tonight. Remember that we cannot control what people do with what we tell them."

He turned and shook hands with the event host before following him into the talkative room. Alfred stood in the hallway for another minute, his collar loose and his shoulders tense, as he collected his thoughts. If he'd done what Hilary asked, he had no way of knowing it. When the room began to quiet down, he slid up the side aisle to where Florence sat. In his seat was Hilary's short, old frame, a walking stick leaned against his knee. Alfred looked from Florence to Hilary with exasperated eyes.

"Oh, Alfred, my boy," Hilary started. "Here, we saved you a seat." He gestured past Florence, who smiled up at him and patted the empty seat on the other side of her.

"I have a seat. You're sitting in it."

"Don't be such a wart. Come on. He's about to start."

Alfred pushed past the man and carefully made his way past Florence before taking the seat next to her. She looked him over.

"Are you missing your tie?"

"Dr. Cline needed it more than I did."

She gave him a puzzled look. Hilary leaned forward and gazed down the row at him.

"Did you speak with him?"

"I tried."

"And?"

"I lost my seat and my tie."

Hilary scrunched his face at Alfred's sarcasm and leaned back in his chair. Florence's hand was warm on his arm, and he focused on the comfort of her presence next to him. For the first forty minutes or so, the lecture was rather basic: an explanation of certain phenomena, what sounded like tall tales of Dr. Cline's misadventures before arriving in Galveston, and a solid explanation of how storms form and how waves are affected by the moon. Until then, Alfred had let himself relax and fall into the role of the observer rather than the scientist, but when a man in the audience took an opportunity to inquire about the threat storms posed to the harbor, Alfred's stomach tightened.

"An excellent question," Dr. Cline answered, "and an easy one to address. First, it is important that you understand that our island is naturally in a beneficial position being surrounded by much shallower waters than many other islands. The mainland has sloped down and eroded over time at a very mild angle. From one side of the island to the other is less than four feet of difference in elevation."

He slid one hand into his pocket and moved the other casually in front of him as he spoke.

"This shallow water means that the heat, which strengthens storms in the gulf, is lost at a gradual rate the closer they come to land. Rather than intensifying, they begin to weaken until they have lost their veracity, almost like a balloon that has been deflated."

He waited for members of the audience to nod along with him before continuing.

"Now, it is reasonable to assume that even a weaker storm holds the potential to bring floods and strong winds onto land, which we have seen them do before. However, you must remember that we already have a barrier for the harbor in place against such threats. The jetties. Our engineering not only creates an entryway into the shipping channel between Galveston and Pelican Islands but redirects the current and keeps silt and sand from settling in the channel. It also protects the channel from the intense surge that can accompany a storm. That, gentlemen, is the what convinces me that our harbor is not as vulnerable to such monster storms as what other islands experience."

"But a cyclone is a very real possibility for Galveston, is it not?" The same man stood from his seat, and Isaac slipped both hands into his pockets to give the man time to expound on his question. "Not to insult your work, Dr. Cline, but It seems a bit prudish for us to think that we are immune to such a threat."

"It might appear that way to many people," Isaac replied with a warm smile, "but to get more at your question, it might seem prudish to assume that we are immune to what others experience. However, the truth lies in the potential of a storm to actually produce the winds and surges that are often claimed when stories travel into Galveston. I hear stories of winds in excess of one-hundred and fifty miles per hour, mature trees uprooted, surges that overtake islands and wash inhabitants clear off the other side."

The room erupted in a quiet murmur of discontent, and he held up his hands to quiet the crowd. Florence fidgeted in her seat, looking to Alfred, who patted her hand gently.

"I say these things only to explain that storms simply do not grow to be that severe here. Because of the island's location within the gulf, its shallow waters and proximity to the mainland, storms of that severity have to not only enter the gulf mainly unobstructed but cross the waters while continuing to intensify and then manage to keep a path that puts them directly in front of our island. Assuming that were to happen, the storm would need to be in such a strong state that it could survive the shallower, cooler waters as it neared the island. Only then could it succeed in running ashore and barreling over us in the same way that sailors are said to have witnessed on singular islands out beyond the gulf."

Alfred shifted in his seat and glanced to Hilary, who was leaning forward on his walking stick. His eyes were locked on the climatologist, his face taut with thought.

"I suppose," Isaac continued, "that some of you have heard of Cuba's close call with a storm less than a week ago." A few members of the audience nodded, and Isaac mirrored their motions. "Your worry is that if Cuba can find itself so vulnerable to a cyclone, what protection can we afford Galveston? Well, ladies and gentlemen, you can put your worries to rest. I'll end tonight's lecture with a simple fact that I have found often alleviates the unfounded fears of many residents who hear of far-away storms ravaging islands. Galveston is a unique city, engineered and laid out with forethought, and it is for this reason that its chances of survival are stacked in its favor."

He returned slowly back to his lectern as he spoke.

"It will do you well to remember that it is not the winds, but the storm surges that often do the most damage when hurricanes strike shorelines. Simply put, the pressure drops as the storm approaches, allowing the water to rise. The greater the storm, the less the pressure, and the more water that rises up beyond sea level. While it might not be terribly difficult to imagine water rising over the beach, imagine for a moment the tremendous force that would be required to not only raise enough water to flood the entirety of the island but to wash away its structures, its foundation. A storm of that level is simply beyond comprehension. It would be impossible for any hurricane to create a storm wave which could materially injure our city given our location."

He fell silent a moment, letting the statement sink into their minds, and then he gave a curt nod.

"I want to thank you for your attendance this evening. It has been most pleasurable for me, and I do hope you have found some enjoyment in it as well."

An applause started at the front of the room and spread through the crowd until several gentlemen at the front of the audience stood. Alfred followed suit and waited for the applause to die down before turning back to Hilary, who continued to lean on his cane and stare pensively at the front of the room. He glanced up as Alfred gestured for Florence to trade him seats.

"Well," Hilary started, "that was an entertaining show."

"You don't believe him?"

"Believe him?" He scoffed. "He's the Chief Climatologist. Of course, I believe him. The problem is that I think he's wrong."

Alfred shook his head as he watched a group of men gather around Isaac, each taking their turn to introduce themselves before asking a question.

"In the end it has very little to do with the channel," Alfred commented. "Convincing people that the harbor is protected from hurricanes is a moot point if Isaac believes hurricanes of that magnitude will never reach the island. He just solved their biggest problem for them."

Hilary straightened his neck and knitted his brow. He looked at Alfred with a hard stare. "You're right."

Alfred met his gaze. "I know."

"No, I mean, what if you're right about all of it? You've told me on more than one occasional that he and his brother disagree on the potential of a severe hurricane making landfall, but the Deep Water Committee was leaning on Dr. Cline's opinion to get more investors to buy into the channel expansion."

"I don't follow where you're going with this."

"Why did they want to boast Cline's statements if they didn't need them? They could have simply used his logic in their meeting, brought up his previous argument against a sea wall and said the jetties protected the harbor."

When Alfred looked up at his mentor, the crowd had thinned, but conversations were being had all around the room. Joseph stood off to the side of the hall, his hat flapping anxiously behind his back, while a few men busied themselves engaging him in conversation. Alfred contemplated the scene—the lesser brother playing second violin to the more prominent researcher. The contrast was sharp but disturbing. He let his eyes drift back to Isaac.

"They needed supporters to hear it straight from him."

Hilary let his eyes settle on Joseph. His mouth tightened as he leaned on his cane. "If the naysayers won't speak up here, they won't speak up later on. They needed that sort of problem squelched early on."

"Who?"

Both men turned to see Florence leaning in at the edge of their circle. She fanned herself lightly and gave them a single raised eyebrow. Alfred leaned back to grant her more room to hear them.

"The Deep Water Committee. They believe Dr. Cline is right about the chances of a severe hurricane striking Galveston."

"Is he not?"

"I don't know. That's the problem."

Florence glanced at Joseph before giving the men a sideways glance of concern.

"You said it was Isaac who rebutted the call for a sea wall to build the island up against a storm surge," Alfred continued.

"Yes. The funding was being collected, but the committee felt it was unnecessary and a waste of money. He was called in as an expert and said the project was unfounded."

"On what grounds?" Florence asked.

Hilary gestured toward the front of the lecture hall with a wild expression. Florence and Alfred both nodded.

"Do you think he knows he is being used to testify to their investments?" Florence whispered.

"Isaac is a sharp man," Alfred replied.

"Oh, no doubt," Hilary added, "but not every man can see past his own praise."

"You think he's blind to it?"

All three looked across the room, first to Isaac and then to Joseph, who now stood alone, the men around him having taken their places in line to speak with Isaac. He fingered his hat before glancing up and holding Alfred's gaze a moment longer than was expected. His gait was unhurried as he moved toward the back the room, leaving Isaac to his crowd of admirers. Hilary watched the man leave before looking back toward the front of the room.

"It wouldn't be the first thing he was blind to."

CHAPTER FORTY-SEVEN

*S*unday was a bright day. Large clouds rose miles into the sky like white thunderheads, moving off the horizon and over the water as the start of the heat wave settled in. Despite the lecture the evening before, Alfred awoke in a pleasant mood. The breeze that blew through his window smelled of oleanders, and his day promised to be an adventure that he had needed. The train was pulling away from the station at a quarter to nine, and he'd been able to arrange for Joseph to take the remaining measurements for the day. It had only cost him a day's worth of cleaning instruments, something Alfred felt was worth the trouble. But Joseph was already in the office when Alfred stepped through the door.

"Catching up on work?"

"Not quite. We've received a telegram from the D.C. office that a tropical storm is forming in the Atlantic northeast of the Caribbean."

"Where's it headed?"

"South of Florida, I presume, but one never knows."

The map Alfred had drawn for Isaac was spread out on the table with red, blue, and yellow lines showing the paths of various storms that had crossed the gulf over the past thirty years. Joseph had marked the ones that had seared the Texas coast and was tracing their lines back to their origins in the Atlantic.

"It has a good chance of entering the gulf if it crosses Cuba," Joseph thought aloud.

"Is that the criteria?"

"Seems to be."

Both men inspected the map until Alfred checked his pocket watch. It was half past six. He snapped it shut and headed toward the door, log-book in hand. What little bit of the morning remained in the office flew by with the wind and he was out the door by half past eight.

Mathias was waiting for him at that station when he arrived, leaning against the clock pole and jingling the change in his pockets. The bruises on his face had darkened at the center, now splotched with purple and green along their edges, and the relaxed swelling in his lip had revealed a thin cut. The brim of his straw hat shaded the upper half of his face, but Alfred could see the outline of his mouth twist into a grin.

"Ready for an adventure," Alfred asked.

"I think I'd be a tad less nervous if I knew what sort of adventure this was going to be."

"I was thinking a gambling den before dinner, mud oysters and drinks at the first pub we can find, and the horse races before heading back."

Mathias gave a hearty laugh as the train whistle blew, announcing its arrival. The two made their way into the station and found their seats at the back of the last car.

"Did we get the last tickets on the train?"

"Not quite."

Alfred slid his window open. The smell of coal dust and the harbor wafted in like a mechanical blend with the steam of the train engine. People bustled along the platform as the rumble of the engine vibrated beneath the car. The platform slid by in slow motion, and buildings gave way to the edge of the island and Galveston Bay. The water glistened like diamonds buoyed on the surface as the wind whipped across the wide expanse of ocean. Alfred tugged on Mathias's sleeve.

"Come on."

Mathias glanced about the train before following him. Alfred unlatched the door that led to the platform at the back of the car and unhinged the door.

"What are we doing?" Mathias asked.

"Trust me. And leave your hat."

Alfred stepped outside and held the door open. Mathias hesitated, glancing back at the other passengers in the car, only a handful of whom were intrigued by the open door. Turning back to the platform, he stepped out of the car and felt the rush of the air on his face. The wooden boards of the trestle flew beneath them at a speed that both struggled to comprehend, and Mathias gripped the railing with white knuckles. Alfred pulled on his sleeve and slid him into the corner of the platform, which met the side of the train car.

"Look around the car!" Alfred pointed as he yelled over the clack of the train wheels. "Toward the front!"

"What am I looking for?"

Alfred pulled him closer to speak in his ear. "The birds. Watch the birds."

Alfred patted his shoulder as he leaned around the car. Mathias was met with a rush of wind. It took away his breath and he stepped back to look at Alfred, who was settling in on the other side of the platform. He watched as Alfred pointed up to the figures overhead. Looking up, Mathias leaned against the railing to see a flock of Brown Pelicans soaring overhead. The birds were gigantic, flying only feet above the train with wingspans that stretched over six feet from tip to tip. Mathias opened his mouth in amazement, a joyous noise escaping his lungs.

Alfred got his attention and stepped up onto the first rung of the railing, leaning his shins and knees against it to balance himself. The bumps of the train track were hard but rhythmic and allowed him to keep his weight where it needed to be. He motioned to Mathias, who followed suit, though more slowly, until both men stood on each side of the car, their feet on the bottom rungs and their hands gripping the handles on the sides of the car tightly.

With a nod, Alfred let loose of the handle and spread his arms out, leaning slightly outward so that the winds alongside the car washed beneath his wings and flapped his jacket wildly behind him. The smell that rushed his senses reminded him of summers back home, and he was overcome with the sensations of the day—the warmth of the air, the shine of the water, the color of the sky. It was beautifully and overwhelmingly delicate. He glanced over at Mathias, who was slowly spreading his arms. Alfred felt a noise rise in his throat, and he let it erupt like a child. The train barreled along the bridge and carried the men, arms out, jackets flapping, and eyes open to the world, over the bay and toward the mainland. A newfound freedom rushed over Alfred as they spread their wings and flew with the pelicans over the water of Galveston Bay, summer giving birth to September in the warmth of the gulf as clouds gathered out over the horizon.

SEPTEMBER

Chapter Forty-Eight

September 5th
Temperature: 86 degrees
Winds: 4 MPH
Pressure: 29.84 bars
Rain: 0 inches

The forecast for Monday night had been dead wrong, and Isaac had been hearing about it for two days. When a low-pressure system had moved in off the water, the resulting storm came with rain and wind that knocked out power across the island. Alfred had woken up to a landscape of trees swaying in the dark and the faint glow of lamps through windows down the street, only to find Mrs. Poplar cooking breakfast in the kitchen with an oil lamp at her side. The city grumbled about the loss as if they had never lived without the vaporous glow of electric lights, and Alfred wondered if anyone longed for the simpler days of dark evenings like he did. When Wednesday morning arrived, the city seemed to be in better spirits. Power had been restored, the streets had begun to dry out, and peddlers had their carts in the street and along the sidewalks to sell roasted peanuts and salted meat to passersby who were in too much of a hurry to gossip at the local deli on their way into work. Alfred was thankful for the return to normalcy and said as much when he returned from taking the morning's observations on the rooftop.

"It won't last," Isaac announced. "It never seems to."

"The weather?"

"The people. Correct forecasts are our job, but incorrect ones—and they will always exist—bring out the worst in people."

Alfred opened the logbook on the table as Isaac handed him the morning's telegram from headquarters. He felt his shoulders slump at the message.

"The heat is returning?"

"Seems that way." Isaac rested his palms on the table and looked out the window, letting out a puff of air. "Not a thing we can do about it."

Alfred began translating his observations for a telegram to the D.C. office. Northerly winds had moved onto the island after the storm, dropping the temperature the day before to nearly eighty degrees, making for a nice reprieve after a day of fussing without electricity. As he neared the end of his notes, the phone filled the room with a metallic echo. Isaac rolled his shoulders to stretch his back as he lifted the receiver.

"Captain Ellison. Yes, good morning." The room was silent a moment but for Alfred's shuffling of papers. "No, no word yet. I'm sure there will be an update tomorrow, but the bureau is quite confident the storm will be moving north along the eastern coast."

Alfred began noting the upcoming forecast for the newspaper when Isaac hung up the receiver.

"This storm already has a reputation preceding it," Isaac commented, returning to his desk.

Alfred tapped his pencil on his desk. "A few storms have disobeyed traditional behavior before, though. You can't blame them for being unnerved by the thought."

"True, though the entire scenario is so unlikely that it hardly warrants the worry. More than anything, our greatest fear should be of unnecessary panic by a storm warning."

Confidence laced Isaac's words, and Alfred felt the air thicken between them. As the man returned to his manuscript, Alfred gathered the notes. Buttons was as bright-eyed as he could manage and took the notes without question. Alfred scanned the room for the well-built assistant that had escorted him to the back of Lyceum, but the print shop was empty.

"I'm running another errand. I'll be back to pick it up before seven-thirty."

"A quarter to eight," Buttons corrected.

"Pardon?"

"I'm running the presses alone this morning."

Alfred lowered his voice and glanced about the room as he spoke. "Where's your assistant?"

"Jailed."

Alfred straightened. "What for?"

Buttons shrugged. "I would put my money on brawling, though disorderly drunkedness is just as likely. Either way, my arms don't work as quickly as his."

Alfred watched the old man shuffled toward the back of the room and called after him.

"Can you operate all of these presses by yourself?"

"Not likely," he called back without turning around. "But I've got a step stool to give me height and glasses to give me sight. That's all I can really ask for at my age."

Alfred was reminded of Hilary by the comment and a thought popped into his mind.

"Do you take dinner?"

Buttons looked back at him with magnified eyes and a quizzical expression. "Are you asking if I eat?"

"No, sorry." Alfred shook his head to clear the air of his words. "Your assistant, did you allow him to take breaks for dinner and supper?"

"Of course." He gave a large huff. "And I paid him a dime more than he was worth. I might be old, but I like to think I understand what people need nowadays."

Alfred tapped the counter as he nodded. "Are you posting to fill the job?"

"Going in the paper tomorrow."

"Hold off on the advertisement. I have a man for you. I'll have him come by this evening."

"At seven," Buttons replied, leaning down to read Alfred's notes. "I'll need assistance with a pamphlet."

"At seven," Alfred repeated.

He was out the door and in a jog back toward Postoffice Street in one swift motion, aware of how tight it would be for him make it back after running the extra errand, retrieving the map, and dropping it off with the newspaper office before he was expected back in the office at 8:30. The morning air was refreshing as he rounded the corner and headed toward the post office. A few stray clouds floated overhead, but the mostly empty sky gave the illusion of a globe that was bright blue at the center and faded into a light peach on the rooftops. It was a deception, he knew: the heat was already settling back onto the island despite a slight reprieve overnight. He pulled the package from his sack as he entered the building and felt its weight in his hands.

When he had finished the last sketch for the field guide, Alfred had been surprised to find he felt a touch of sadness. So much of his time had been spent on outings with Hilary, taking notes about their observations and sketching birds in flight or feeding on the water when the man's fingers failed to move fast enough, while the last month had been little more than painting in Hilary's study and finalizing the draft. Now the final product, a one-hundred and seventy-three-page manuscript of detailed observations of native island birds, was bound together with nearly sixty-five pages of watercolor paintings. All of their work had come to this—a neat package tied with string and addressed to Philadelphia.

Alfred hesitated to hand over the bundle to the clerk. He fought the urge to take the package back and hold it close to his chest. So much work being sent off to someone he'd never met at the hands of an unknown team of messengers. The package would travel cross-country by train before being transferred and delivered to Philadelphia, perhaps even carried to a building downtown where it would sit in an office for weeks before being reviewed. The publication was a certain result; Hilary had known that from the start after talking with the same publisher that had worked on his previous field guide. But that didn't ease Alfred's uneasiness.

The clerk began writing up a receipt, double-checking the delivery address and routes.

"It's a very important package," Alfred noted.

"They all are, sir."

Alfred paid the man with cash that Hilary had given him. He slid the change into his pocket as he stepped back out into the heavy air of the island. It seemed to have doubled in weight, but it did little to dispel the island's energy. The streets were overflowing with activity as people walked along the sidewalks and drays carted goods across the city. A light breeze blew from the east over the bay, pushing smoke inward, and gave the illusion of clouds, but no one seemed to mind the extra shade or smell of coal as they made their way into the business district.

Having set the appointment with Buttons at seven o'clock and finished his errands, Alfred retrieved the forecast map, deposited it with the newspaper, and returned to the office. When Joseph arrived a little after noon from taking field observations, he was followed in by a Western Union messenger. Isaac took the telegram and passed it to Joseph after giving it a quick read.

"The storm will likely be felt as far north as Norfolk by Thursday evening," he read, "and will extend over the Atlantic and South New England states by early Friday afternoon."

Alfred stopped his review of the logbook to listen.

"The storm, which has not intensified since leaving Cuba, has been attended only by heavy rains, which are likely to cause flooding and moderate winds. Its effects will end the period of high temperature that has prevailed east of the Mississippi."

Joseph slid the telegram across the table and returned to his work, and Isaac did the same. Alfred quietly read the telegram to himself. It was good news for the island, for the bureau when he thought about it. There would be no storm warning or raised flags, no preparations to be made, no panic to be had. But the confidence in the telegram, the same confidence Isaac had had earlier, tugged at his senses. They had no way of tracking storms at sea. Ships could not wire or cable their reports while out in the water. But surely the bureau had verified the storm's location before sending the update. Alfred nodded as he dropped the telegram back onto the table where it caught a stray ray of sunlight through the window. It seemed the only thing in store for Galveston was the potential for cooler weather once the storm had passed. And no one could complain about that.

Chapter Forty-Nine

September 6th
Temperature: 80 degrees
Winds: 5 MPH
Pressure: 29.974 bars
Rain: 0 inches

Joseph was already in the office when Alfred arrived Thursday morning and had the notes along with the D.C. office's regional forecasts set aside on the table. Both men were in genial moods despite the early hour. The island had transformed overnight with the start of a cool front that had dropped the temperature to nearly eighty degrees. Whatever it was—the start of autumn, a confluence of fronts, the effects of the storm on the eastern coast—it was a tease to the end of a blistering summer and had eased the island's suffering a touch.

"We're due to take observations at Pelican Island," Joseph announced, "but I was hoping to visit Captain Gregory this afternoon."

"Is he well?"

Joseph shook his head. "Quite the opposite. Mrs. Gregory was hoping a visit might cheer him up."

"I can do the observations," Alfred offered.

Joseph nodded, awkward in the ensuing silence until he found his voice once more.

"You're doing well here." He paused for a long moment. "Isaac is not the most practiced at acknowledging progress. He was initially sent here to assist in cleaning up the office's lenient practices, and I think he's become accustomed to looking for ways to sharpen others' abilities."

Alfred recognized that the comment was not entirely a professional observation. He thought back through the summer and tried to identify a moment when Isaac had uttered a comment that could be construed as legitimate praise for Joseph but failed to find one. To be fair, he came to the same conclusion when he tried to remember Joseph praising Isaac for his prowess in understanding the weather. While Isaac may have been unpracticed in praising others, Joseph was just as inexperienced when it came to seeing his brother for the expert that he was.

"What I mean to say," he continued, "is that your work has contributed a good deal to our continued efficiency. That is something we have needed. Good assistants are difficult to come by nowadays."

"Thank you."

Alfred wondered if that was the extent of a probationary assessment. Joseph hadn't outright stated it, but being implied to be a good assistant was likely as high of praise as Alfred could hope for from the two men given their conflicting personalities and incongruent perspectives. Whatever Joseph meant by it, he took it as a vote of confidence.

"You'll take the evening observations?" Joseph asked as Isaac came into the office.

Both men glanced his way before returning to their conversation.

"Yes, I'll be here."

"Thank you."

His last words were quiet, nearly whispered, and Alfred returned to his coding of the observations with the understanding that Isaac would not be aware of Joseph's absence, justified as it was.

"Have we received the national map yet?" Isaac asked.

Joseph gestured toward the paper next to Alfred's translation notes.

Isaac pulled it aside and reviewed it.

"Cool fronts west of Florida and heavy rain," Isaac noted. "Looks like the storm is on track for the east coast. It's not reaching the mid-Atlantic until tomorrow evening."

"It must be going slower than they anticipated," Alfred commented.

Isaac made a noise of agreement. "It's possible that it's weakening before making landfall."

"Could it have missed Florida altogether?"

"That's unlikely with its previous path," Isaac reminded him. "That would have been a tight turn, even for a smaller storm." He slid the map back toward Alfred. "Tell me when you've finished the telegram. I'd like to look over the notes before finalizing the forecast."

Learning the art of forecasting was no small feat in a bureau that suffered from more than the occasional misinterpretation of the weather, but Isaac took his duty to heart. He reminded Alfred regularly of the danger of becoming a fortune teller when winds could shift so quickly.

"Cooler weather might very well be on the way," Isaac admitted, crossing out words in the draft. "But the clouds are scattered today, meaning there's little to keep us cool without a straight north or northeasterly wind."

As his mentor had forecasted, the day grew hotter well into the early evening, but the streets took on a blend of greys as streaked clouds settled overhead. Jogging down 23rd Street, the wharves drifting in the steely haze of a late summer evening, Alfred worked through the crowd as the steamy shorefront worked at his collar. Summer, it seemed, had no intentions of letting go no matter what was on the horizon.

Ritter's Café and Saloon took up the first floor of a four-story brick building just off of 21st Street on the Strand. A printing press claimed the second story, but it was the smell of tenderloin trout that brought islanders through the doors. Competing with the aroma of soaps, oils, and perfumes from down the row and the odor of coal blowing from the harbor, the warmth of butter-soaked fish with capers and the sting of mixed drinks welcomed Alfred into the cool space. Hilary sat in the center of the bustling restaurant, his frame frail and face taut. Alfred lowered his voice as he took his seat.

"What is it?"

Hilary spun his nearly empty whiskey glass. "What's the word in your office?"

Alfred drank gratefully from his glass of water as the room became a murmur of voices punctuated with occasional laughter. He wiped at the sweat on his lip.

"It's clearing Florida today and moving north. It should be in the mid-Atlantic by tomorrow morning, and we'll be getting the benefit of cooler weather."

"You're certain?"

"The report came from D.C. this morning."

Hilary was silent as he gazed out the window at the front of the restaurant. Passersby swept back and forth across the panes as the evening grew darker than usual.

"What if it's wrong?" Hilary asked.

"About the cool front? It'll come as an effect of the hurricane."

"I don't think that's the only thing heading our way." The man's eyes unnerved Alfred as he spoke. "I won't pretend to know more about weather than Dr. Cline, but I have lived on this island longer than he's been watching the clouds. Something is amiss in the water."

The waiter arrived and set down two plates of fish filets with roasted corn and potato cakes.

"I ordered for you," Hilary commented without a change in his mood.

The waiter poured a white wine sauce over the fish and left without a word. The scent of cooked mushrooms wafted up from the plate. Alfred was tempted to shove a heaping forkful into his mouth but waited for Hilary to begin cutting into his own filet before following suit. Hilary continued his thoughts as he chewed on a bite of potato cake dipped in the wine sauce.

"I went to the east end looking for Sanderlings. They're nearing the start of their migration season."

Alfred nodded as he chewed, distracted momentarily by a roar of laughter at the bar. Hilary's voice faded slightly before returning in full force to his ears.

"The tide is too high and the surf is too rough. It's as if a storm were moving in, but there's nothing on the horizon."

"Perhaps it's just the offshoot of a smaller thunderstorm pushing the tide in."

Hilary shook his head. "Not at this rate. I've only ever seen this when a storm is on the shore. It's more than a simple wind. Something is knocking the water off its balance."

"What would do something like that if not a storm?"

Hilary stared at him, his jaw rotating like a cow working at cud. Alfred stopped cutting his fish and shook his head in a single, confident shake.

"No."

"How can you know?"

"It's the one thing they are certain of."

Hilary waved off the comment with his hand, and Alfred let his fork fall onto his plate.

"What?"

"You're so trusting."

"Of science?" It was the first time Alfred had felt so frustrated with the man. He was brilliant with birds and plants, but he distrusted every other field that studied the natural world, as if he were the only one who could understand the inner workings of life around them. "Science is only as good as its interpretation."

Alfred let out a sigh and leaned onto his elbows. He blinked heavily at the passersby in the street. A produce store across the Strand welcomed visitors with open arches as they came and went with bags of goods. A dray backed up to the raised curb to let two young boys load the driver's wares from the upper level. Alfred returned to the meal, his muscles tense at the conversation.

"Fine. Let's say you're right and the storm is entering the gulf and that the United States Weather Bureau has completely misidentified the location of the storm and is sending inaccurate reports nationwide."

"Sarcasm rarely catches its prey."

"That's what you are implying, yes?"

Hilary acquiesced and nodded as he gestured to the waiter for another drink.

"If that were the case," Alfred continued, "that would mean that the storm has the entire southern coast as its target. There is no reason to assume it is heading for Galveston."

"I wasn't suggesting such a thing. That's not only unknowable, that's the less of the concerns."

Alfred shut his eyes as he shook his head, his voice betraying his irritation. "Less of the concerns?"

"If the storm has cleared Florida and is anywhere in the gulf, anyone living on the ocean is a potential victim when it makes landfall. It's in God's hands as to who faces that horror."

The waiter set a drink down on the table as he passed by to another table. Alfred lowered his voice, suddenly aware that their conversation could bring about a misunderstanding that would quickly turn into an unmanageable panic.

"What could possibly be worse of a concern than a hurricane making landfall in Galveston?"

Hilary leaned closer and matched his whisper.

"That the Weather Bureau was so arrogant that it let a storm hundreds of miles wide escape its detection because it refused to believe that nature knew better."

Hilary straightened as he took another bite of potato cake, and Alfred felt his stomach churn. He entertained Hilary's suggestion and felt as if the doors had been opened onto the street. He was warm beneath his shirt and took a long drink of water, his mint julep hardly touched. After several minutes of Hilary cutting into and eating the last of his fish, Alfred loosened his jaw and met the man's gaze. It wasn't the same expression Alfred faced in the office—there was no arrogance, no expectation.

Hilary simply waited to hear Alfred's assessment. When he finally gave it, he felt his heart grow heavy.

"Alright. Let's say that's the case. How do we know?"

"Can you spare another hour?"

Hilary snapped at the waiter to get his attention and handed him payment for the meal. Alfred checked his pocket watch.

"If we leave now. I have to be back in the office in an hour."

"My Motorwagen is in the alley." He threw his napkin onto the plate of leftover capers and fish.

"Where are we going?"

"To show you a view of the island you'll never forget."

——•••——

Temperature: 90 degrees
Winds: 14 MPH
Pressure: 29.818 bars
Rain: 0 inches

The drive to the east end was windy. Gusts blew in off the water, intensified by the speed of the Motorwagen. Alfred had ridden in it four or five times but was still uncomfortable with how crudely it handled on the roads, especially beyond the city where they turned to little more than dirt trails. The sky had become darker with clouds blocking out a good deal of the sun, leaving only a sliver of tangerine light peering through a slit above the horizon. The light was reflected as a winding splash of color on the otherwise gray ocean.

Hilary slowed as they neared the section he had visited earlier in the day. Alfred could see that the water was unusually rough. The winds were out of the south such that the change in surf was not surprising, but something about the way they moved made him stare as he watched the waves peak beyond the sand and then rush onto the sand. When Hilary brought the car to a stop, he had to tear his eyes away from the water to wrangle himself out of the sidecar.

The air was frightfully heavy. He rolled up his sleeves as he followed Hilary through the dunes and waist-high grasses that bowed frantically in the winds. They slowed as they reached the edge of the grasses, and Alfred peeked around the stands of dancing stalks to see a group of Sanderlings on the edge of the dunes, their white belly feathers ruffling in the wind.

"They're restless," Hilary observed. "And fewer than before. Nearly half have already gone."

"Where?"

"South, I would presume, but I don't think that's the case today." He motioned toward the waves. "Do you see?"

Alfred pushed a stand of grass out of his way, careful to stay partially in the cover of the dunes so as not to spook the birds. The waves tossed as if pushed by invisible fingers and then heaved onto the beach. Something about the surf made him uneasy in the way it disobeyed the wind, as if it were thinking for itself. He stepped out of the dunes and slid a few inches onto more stable sand. The birds called out at the movement, and a few took flight, moving farther down the beach. He reached the tide sooner than he expected. All down the length of the empty beach the water had pushed several feet inland, much closer to the dunes than was normal. Hilary's voice fought against the wind from behind a mound of sand crowned with cordgrass.

"Do you agree?"

Hilary's words were short, but there was little to say when it all seemed so odd. Alfred nodded as he stood on the edge of the dunes and looked back toward the water.

"Something seems amiss." He glanced at Hilary. "Have you seen this before?"

"No, but I wasn't the naturalist in 1875 that I am today."

His mention of the year made Alfred close his eyes as he listened to the wind blow off the water. Could he hear the beginnings of a hurricane if he listened closely enough? The spray carried on the wind and was warm against his arms and face as he thought about the implications. If this was truly a hurricane moving in from the gulf, then the bureau had it all wrong. Every single report. But how could they have reported it so inaccurately? Surely someone had reported the storm as coming inland in Florida if they had released a report saying so.

The beach had taken on a haze, as if a mist had moved beyond the water and begun to soak the air around the city. It resembled the blur that a flame takes when a hurricane glass has been left to collect the soot of the nights before. The world had lost its definition, leaving his mind to orient itself.

"It doesn't look right," Hilary commented. "That's all I know."

Alfred nodded, unsure he could add anything useful, but it was the birds that gave a reply. They took up together, a collection of feathers in the mist, and flew over the dunes, passing over the men as they flapped their wings in an effort to gain lift with the wind at their tails. Both men followed their paths with their chins lifted and making an arc in the sky as their eyes were pulled back toward the city. Alfred felt the significance of the moment as he watched the birds work against Hilary's knowledge of their behavior and move away from the water, but the thought grew a thousand times in weight with Hilary's words.

"It looks like they're not the only ones deserting us."

Alfred's eyes left the Sanderlings and skimmed the sky. Flocks of birds were erupting from the island in nearly every quadrant of the sky he could see. Collections of black dots moved like waves in the gray sky, but their calls were drowned out by the rush of the ocean in his ears. He attempted to count the birds, but it was an impossible task. Over the island, hundreds if not thousands of birds were taking flight and moving away from the water. Those closest to them flew northeast toward Bolivar Peninsula, the offshoot that worked with Galveston Island to nearly close off Galveston Bay from the ocean, while those farther inland seemed to be moving northwest to the other side of the bay. The sky took on the darker hue of collected wings and rattled Alfred.

"Where are they going?"

"North. West. Anywhere but here."

Alfred couldn't take his eyes off the birds as they made the wind visible with their rehearsed movements, waves across the sky.

"Why?"

Only the wind tickled his ears in reply. When Hilary didn't answer, he looked over at the man and read the answer on his face. For the first time since keeping his company, Alfred was thankful he hadn't answered a question. He looked back at the scene, watching the birds fly inland by the thousands as the waves continued to roar behind them in the heat of a late summer wind.

CHAPTER FIFTY

September 7th, 6:22 AM
Temperature: 88 degrees
Winds: 7 MPH
Pressure: 29.948 bars
Rain: 0 inches

Alfred slept poorly that night, unable to shake the image of birds flocking from the island. Much to his relief, Isaac and Joseph were huddled over the storm map when he burst into the office the next morning. He threw his sack onto his desk without taking his eyes off the men.

"I think the storm is in the gulf," he blurted.

Isaac watched him momentarily and returned to the map as Joseph drew in a breath.

"We agree."

"You've seen the tides?"

Alfred stepped up to the table, and Joseph furrowed his brow.

"The tides? No, New Orleans sent a telegram early this morning that they are experiencing rough seas and increased winds. They believe it could be the effect of the storm, but it doesn't match what the D.C. office is telling us."

Isaac was sketching lines and marks on the map with a pencil.

"The telegram said they noticed a slight drop in barometric pressure overnight," Isaac commented, "but nothing too concerning. The waves, however, cannot be the result of the storm in its present location."

"According to the bureau," Joseph commented.

Alfred glanced down at the map. "But they wouldn't announce its location without having confirmed its course, would they?"

Isaac removed his glasses and rubbed at the bridge of his nose.

"It is common practice to confirm a storm's location on land before reporting it, but that isn't always followed as well as it should be. And impossible if the storm hasn't made landfall yet."

Joseph shot Alfred a glance and raised his eyebrows. Isaac looked up and acknowledged Alfred's physical presence with a knitted brow.

"How did you come to the conclusion that the storm was in the gulf?"

"The waves. They were quite rough yesterday evening along the beach, unusually so despite the wind. It was as if they were working against it."

Isaac narrowed his eyes as if scrutinizing small print. "That's not a good deal of evidence. Not enough to sound an alarm anyway."

Alfred licked his lips. "Hilary Carson took me to the beach to see the water. He's convinced the weather is taking an odd turn and believes the water is a sign that the storm is nearby."

"Ah," Isaac replied with a nod. "Mr. Carson has quite a few strong opinions when it comes to how nature portrays itself."

"I believe he's right."

"I hope you will pardon my criticism, Alfred, but you do not know the waters like we do."

"No, but I know weather." Both men turned to face him. The air thickened as he drew in a breath and tried to calm his nerves. "And it doesn't just come out of nowhere. It was the same back home. The skies change and the winds stop dead when a tornado is on the horizon. Even the animals, sir. They disappear. I know nature fleeing when I see it."

Joseph pushed himself up off the table as Isaac crossed his arms and left his glasses dangling from two fingers.

"How do you mean?"

"Birds are flocking off the island by the hundreds. They are literally fleeing the island."

Isaac digested the observation for a long moment before shaking his head. "I've never heard of such a thing."

"That's beside the point."

Isaac's brow raised in a quick motion, and Alfred stumbled to recover.

"What I mean is that they are fleeing something. If it's the storm, it could mean that we are nearer than we have come to appreciate."

Joseph's chin glided across the office as he looked at his brother with skeptical eyes, but it took only a second for Alfred to realize that he was not the target of the man's doubt.

"We can't wait, Isaac. If the storm has entered the gulf, we must notify headquarters and sound the alarm. It will take hours for the island to evacuate."

"Evacuate?" Isaac shook his head. "Even if the storm were in the gulf, an evacuation is completely unnecessary. The panic that would ensue as some forty-thousand people fought over the bridge to the mainland would crumble the structure."

"Waiting is too dangerous."

Joseph's voice rose in pitch, and Alfred concluded that this conversation was not starting anew. It had been roiling earlier, and he had simply stepped into the calm of it as they looked at the map.

"What would you have me do, Joseph? The D.C. office has given strict orders not to sound storm warnings without their permission. Even if we thought the storm were in the gulf or anywhere nearby, we do not have the authority to raise the flags."

"Then wire D.C. and tell them what we believe to be the case."

"What you two believe to be the case," Isaac parried. "And tell them what? That the water was especially rough and a local birdwatcher noticed flocks of birds leaving the island? We are scientists. You need something much more conclusive if you are going to make such a weighty assertion as to raise storm warnings without a storm in sight."

The room fell silent. The early hour found the streets nearly empty, and only the rush of the wind sounded in the office as the occasional gust pushed against the window panes. Isaac slid his glasses back on and stepped up to the map.

"Without the wires to Cuba, we've no way of knowing what they experienced. Flooding, winds, it's all likely, but D.C. won't buy it. What we know is unofficial."

He looked down at the map and slid a pencil across the table. Sketching faint lines, he drew an arc from the tip of Florida to the shore of Louisiana and then another in a wider angle from Cuba to northern Mexico.

"It could have sidestepped Florida and remained undisturbed, or it could have been pulled farther south, moving it closer to Texas." He straightened. "If your theory is correct, either arc will carry the storm away from us, to our east into New Orleans or past us to the west of Corpus Christi."

"Either way, it will cross the open gulf," Joseph added.

"And the deepest, warmest waters," Alfred commented, finishing the thought.

Isaac's face was tense, his eyes concentrated, crafting tension out of the lines on the map at the center of their triangle about the table.

"Then we wait. If the storm is truly heading into the gulf, headquarters will know about it in due time. If it is pushing up the Atlantic coast as they predicted, then we've nothing with which to worry our minds in the end."

"And if no one encounters the storm in the gulf? If no one knows its course?" Joseph tightened his jaw between questions. "What then?"

Isaac held his gaze before letting his arms fall away from his chest. "We wait."

He turned back to his desk, leaving Joseph with the map and Alfred to search for the logbook as daybreak broke the edges of the windows.

—•●•—

September 7th, 7:33 AM
Temperature: 91 degrees
Winds: 9 MPH
Pressure: 29.945 bars
Rain: 0 inches

The morning dragged on sluggishly. The heat continued to surge, reaching over ninety degrees as mid-morning approached, leaving the island steaming along the streets and in the buildings. Alfred had already begun to sweat through his shirt when he returned with the morning's rooftop observations, and the shade of the office did little to relieve him of the sticky sensation as the cotton clung to his skin. He carried on with his work, delivering his notes and the morning report to Buttons but without the formality of a jacket and with the added color of sleepless eyes.

When Buttons called to the back of the shop, keeping to himself at a small cutting station, a short, squat man rounded the corner. A grin of large teeth took over his face as he approached the counter.

"Edwin!" Alfred returned the smile as he set the notes and map onto the counter. "It's a pleasure to see you again. I trust you're liking your new post."

"Oh, yes, sir. I gotta learn a good bit when it comes to the machines but nothing I can't handle when I put my mind to it."

Alfred glanced toward the back. "Buttons is treating you well, then?"

"He's a good man," Edwin replied, leaning forward to lower his voice. "He lets me have a full hour at lunch and closes shop at eight o'clock every day."

Alfred nodded as he straightened. "Quite a change?"

"For the good, sir. For the good."

"Excellent. Well, I've got the daily notes here for the map. Has Buttons explained the bureau's printing or shall I instruct you?"

"No need," Edwin replied, sliding it all across the table to review. "He's a good teacher. Much better than old Mr. Jeffries."

He gave Alfred a wink and carried the materials to the back. Buttons gave a small wave as he glanced up from his stack of newly cut pamphlets. The day was continuing to melt as Alfred made his way to the office. When he joined the two brothers, Isaac was speaking to a captain who had stopped by before putting out that afternoon while Joseph dug through the stack of maps along the wall.

The telephone's metallic call carried from the wall, and Joseph pulled himself away from the shelf of maps to lift the receiver.

"Galveston Weather Office."

Alfred eavesdropped on Isaac's comments to the captain but heard only snippets as the climatologist walked him out the door. Joseph's bass carried through the otherwise empty office.

"Delivery, please. Yes, thank you." The receiver resumed its rest on the side of the box, and Joseph looked up to see Isaac returning to the office. "Western Union has an urgent telegram. They're sending a carrier to deliver it."

"Did they say who sent it?"

"The D.C. office."

Isaac nodded as Joseph glanced at Alfred. "Likely an update to the forecast." He settled back into his chair. "Too late now. Alfred's already taken the map to print."

The carrier, a boy of no more than twelve, was at the door in less than five minutes. He handed the telegram to Alfred and was already racing back down the hallway before he could properly thank him. Giving in to prudence, he looked to Isaac, who gave him a nod, before pulling at the lip and opening the telegram. His breath caught somewhere deep in his lungs.

"Sir?"

Joseph looked up from the stack of maps as Isaac turned in his chair. "What is it?"

"Previous reports found to be inconsistent. Storm now tracking in the south of the Gulf of Mexico heading north by northwest. Rough water, high winds, and potential for high tides. Order to issue storm warning until further notice."

Alfred looked up to where Isaac had risen at his desk. His figure was framed by the daylight in the window beyond him. His posture was sincere and attentive, but his face was partially shaded by the angle. Alfred squinted to better see his expression, but his voice communicated more than his eyes ever would.

"Joseph, the flags." His brother was across the room in four wide strides and pulled down a wooden box from atop the instrument shelf. "Alfred, you'll assist us to learn the protocol in the event that neither of us is available when a storm warning must be issued."

They marched up the stairs to the roof, where the wind whipped at their hair, thin wisps of clouds spreading across the sky above them like stretched taffy.

"The clouds," Joseph commented.

Isaac nodded and looked up in all directions with a pensive mouth. "The storm could still be heading northwest and clear us entirely. Perhaps simply a change in cloud cover."

Isaac opened the latch for the flag rope and threaded it through the holes along the edge of the first flag while Joseph held it taut against the wind.

"Remember," Isaac commented, "this is only a warning. It's not a certainty. That's our official stance."

Alfred nodded as he watched the flags whip in the wind, popping with each new gust as they bent and unfurled in rhythm. The bottom flag, maroon with a black square at the center, was the storm flag. Alfred knew the severity that it could bring if it turned out to be necessary, but it was the top flag that carried the most sentiment in the moment. The white pendant told locals that the storm was heading northwest, coming from the southeast. Alfred had read enough reports and listened to enough of Isaac's discussions to know that the west side of a hurricane was preferred.

The winds would be strong, but the rain and flooding, the most severe of the impact, was always to the east of the storm's focus, its central circle where the winds died down. If they could trust this prediction, Galveston would be spared.

An hour later, the same Western Union carrier knocked at the door and handed Joseph another telegram. Sent only to southern regional offices, the telegram was imprecise but informative considering the changes that had occurred in the last twenty-four hours. The storm was south of Louisiana, keeping to the northwest at a slow pace. High northerly winds were predicted throughout the night with heavy rain starting on the following morning and carrying on throughout the day. Alfred was neither surprised nor comfortable with the report. How quickly the D.C. Office had changed the facts. Rather than feeling like an official report, the update was more of an annoyance, and he struggled to decide if it was a good thing that Hilary had been able to identify the storm's path before the national office.

As he made his way to the boardinghouse for dinner, having agreed to return to take observations later in the night, he decided that it didn't matter how he looked at the situation. It was all irrelevant. The D.C. office could have ignored Cuba and missed the storm altogether, and Hilary would have caught on sooner rather than later. It could have perfectly tracked the storm's path, but the Galveston Office couldn't have issued a storm warning before now without permission. None of it mattered, he determined, because it would have played out similarly regardless of how it gotten there.

As he shut the door against the wind and removed his hat, the smell of baked ham leading him on, he realized that their role in the grand scheme had little to do with preemptive actions. Forecasts were right, and forecasts were wrong, just as Isaac had said. The people never remembered the former and tended to focus on the latter, but there was little his office could do on its own. The real control lay with the national office, which had cut ties with Cuban climatologists, ignored tropical storm warnings in the Caribbean, and was more interested in saving a nickel than funding proper equipment. In the end, his role in all of it was much smaller than he had imagined.

Much, much smaller.

CHAPTER FIFTY-ONE

September 7th, 8:29 PM
Temperature: 90 degrees
Winds: 17 MPH
Pressure: 29.926 bars
Rain: 0 inches

*I*t's blowing like a nor'easter out there."

Mrs. Poplar's voice carried from the dining room followed by her boots on the floorboard as she carried a tray through the house. John was absent at dinner, leaving the three to a meal of baked ham with an apricot preserve and roasted potatoes. Mathias had been in an agreeable mood for days, something Alfred had come to miss in the last few weeks, but he was less talkative at dinner. Mrs. Poplar, however, was keen on keeping company well into the evening. When she had insisted on having drinks in the parlor, she had shooed them out of the dining room and sent them to clean up.

"One thing I've never liked about the island is the wind," she continued as she set the tray down on the table between the two parlor chairs, "It seems to come off the water like it has a mind of its own."

Alfred took a glass of amaretto from the tray and stood next to the empty fireplace, leaning against the mantle.

"That's not entirely inaccurate," he commented.

"Oh, don't make it worse! Personifying the world around us does little more than scare us into thinking we have no control over our lives."

Mathias fell into one of the chairs. "Such heavy conversation for so late in the evening."

"Says the doctor," Alfred joked.

Mathias smiled and lifted his drink in a toast. Mrs. Poplar took the empty chair and let out a sigh as she settled her skirt about her legs. She scrunched her face as she fell back against the cushion.

"This hip is getting stiff."

"Too much activity," Mathias announced.

She swirled the amaretto, watching it slide around the sides of her glass.

"Well, it does me no good to wallow inside the house." She looked up at the empty fireplace. "I've got to do something with my time."

"That's not what I meant."

She gave him a small smile and sipped on her drink. "Next you'll be telling me to mind my drinks."

"That's not a bad suggestion given your conditions, but isn't it rather informal for a proprietor to be having drinks with boarders in the first place?"

"Oh, hush. None of us is what God intended."

All three murmured agreement and tilted their glasses. Alfred preferred the smooth texture of the drink as it slid down his throat, but he was still growing accustomed to the flavor, a cherry essence with a slightly nutty aftertaste. The more he drank it, the more he preferred whiskey.

"I heard the Weather Bureau raised the storm flag today," Mathias commented.

Mrs. Poplar gazed up with big eyes. "Is that so?"

Alfred nodded as he took another drink. His nerves sparked with anticipation of worry, and the liquor cooled the sensation. But the heat and tension of the day weighed on his mind. Hilary had been proven right when Isaac and the bureau had been proved wrong—but no comments had been made to this effect. No recognition given, no apology offered. More concerning was the lack of updates from the national office.

"The storm that was expected to move up the eastern coast has moved into the gulf," Alfred explained. "The bureau has asked southern offices to issue storm warnings to alert locals and ships in preparation."

"It's standard protocol?" Mathias asked.

"Somewhat."

A gust of wind rushed the windows behind him. The day was catching up with him, tempting his legs to march up the stairs and straight into bed.

"But is it?" Mrs. Poplar watched him with scrutinizing eyes. "I haven't seen a storm flag but two, maybe three times since moving to the island. That seems a bit of a serious matter to consider it standard protocol."

"The truth is we don't know the storm's exact path, so all cities that could lie in its path are on alert."

"In other words," Mathias replied, settling further into his chair, "it's the next step when they don't really know if we're in danger or not."

Mrs. Poplar looked from one boarder to the other while Alfred eyed Mathias. When he caught the woman's questioning expression, he nodded and looked down into his glass. "We're not certain where it is exactly or where it is heading, but we do know it's in the gulf and it's heading toward the shoreline."

Mathias pursed his lips. Mrs. Poplar took another sip of amaretto.

"Well, I suppose it's good to know something is rumbling about, even if it doesn't hit us," she mused. "Flooding is nothing to go on about anymore. It's practically its own season on the island."

"A little wind and rain never hurt," Mathias commented.

"It would be more than a little wind and rain." Alfred finished his drink and set the glass on the mantle next to his elbow. "The bureau doesn't like us to say what it is, but a hurricane is no small matter on an island like this."

"What do you mean?" Mrs. Poplar asked.

"Simply that Dr. Cline might have his notions of how Galveston geography makes it a harbor against high storm flooding, but I have my doubts." The amaretto was reading his script for him, but he didn't care. "I fear that a severe hurricane has the potential to flood the island at a much greater height than its experienced before."

"It can't flood that severely," Mathias argued. "We're surrounded by ocean. The water can't accelerate so quickly. It would simply wash back out into the bay or the surf."

"I'm not convinced that would be case. With the intense winds pushing northward, I think the surf would be pushed inland. The bay could absorb some of it, but if the water rose faster than it drained, the island would be submerged." He rubbed at his forehead, pushing away the start of a headache. "With a hurricane dumping inches of rain, I don't think it's inconceivable that such a scenario could become a dangerous reality."

Mathias chuckled. "I thought the bureau's business was to keep us calm and assured when severe weather was heading our way."

Alfred returned the humor and pushed off the mantle, crossing his arms. "I'm afraid my dance card is full this late in the game. I'll work on softening the forecast for you next week."

All three gave quiet laughs, and Mrs. Poplar pushed herself up onto her feet. She made a pained face with the movement.

"Are you using the cream I gave you?" Mathias inquired.

"Yes, dear." She huffed as she started around the chair, her weight unevenly distributed as she went. "It smells horribly and is too oily for my liking."

"But it's working?"

She waited until she was nearly out of the parlor before replying. "Yes."

Mathias shook his head and reached for the bottle on the table. He refilled his glass as Alfred took Mrs. Poplar's chair. The two sat in silence as the sounds of her cleaning carried from the kitchen and the occasional gust of wind came from the porch. Soon her boots came back through the house and started up the stairs before giving way to a silent house.

Mathias spoke to the empty fireplace.

"A child came into the hospital today." Alfred looked over at him and noted his empty gaze as if the room had lost its light. "He works at the dock unloading the ships. One of the crates they were moving by rope and pulley, and the rope snapped. He was beneath it when it fell."

"The crate hit him?"

The flatness of Mathias's voice left Alfred's stomach in knots. "It crushed his leg from the knee down."

"Dear God."

Mathias took a long drink and let his head fall back onto the chair before continuing.

"Do you ever wonder if you make a difference in what you do?" He glanced up with big eyes. "I don't mean your work isn't significant. Don't get me wrong. I just mean to ask if you ever doubt how the world works. Some days it feels like none of it makes a difference."

"Like it goes on without you." Mathias nodded, glancing toward Alfred before taking another drink. "Some days," Alfred continued, "I wonder how anything I do changes any of it. I'm the least experienced in my office and still burning through books and manuscripts. I give forecasts that have to be verified, take observations that have to be checked, clean instruments that others are using. And then something like this storm comes along."

"How does that play in?"

Alfred shook his head in frustration.

"I thought something was off, that the storm might be moving our way. Joseph agreed, but Isaac ignored us. He refused to take it seriously until the bureau issued a storm warning."

"It's not like they didn't issue it in time," Mathias assured him. "People will know. If it comes our way, they can prepare."

"I know, but I find the entire situation infuriating. The bureau was certain it knew the storm was heading north, away from the gulf, when it was moving into the gulf. If it was wrong about that, something so significant, what else is it blind to?"

Mathias took another drink, and Alfred let out a deep breath.

"What happened to the boy?"

"He lost his leg at the knee. I assisted with the surgery this afternoon."

Alfred felt a sting in his stomach as he considered their roles in the world. He had no room to complain when he sat beside Mathias, but he wasn't certain how to apologize when he owed the sentiment to the boy more than his boarding mate.

"At least he survived."

"Yeah." He drained his drink and set the glass down on the table as he stood. "He survived today, but I'm not so sure about the night." He gestured toward the bottle. "Keep the rest. I'll sleep well enough as is."

Alfred nodded, and Mathias started toward the stairs. His steps were slow and purposeful, leading Alfred to glance at the bottle. He had drunk nearly half of it on his own. Alfred felt the world squeeze in around him as he stood and walked toward the coat rack by the door. He had so little about which to complain when he looked at those around him—Mrs. Poplar's health, Mathias's work, Hilary's loneliness—but the unease that had settled into his mind since the bureau's telegram earlier in the day felt like an anchor pulling at his mind regardless of the company he kept.

The winds had picked up and mixed with the heat of the oncoming night to make for an uncomfortable atmosphere. He was sweating by the time he arrived at the office. He climbed to the rooftop with his collar unbuttoned and his sleeves rolled up to his elbows. As he sat on the rooftop and watched the city turn in for the night, he was struck by how vulnerable it all seemed in the quiet of the darkness. Ships were moored and floating, their wood softly moaning, while the clack of horses became rare the later the night wore on. When he took the last reading of the day at midnight, an extra observation in preparation for the potential storm, the city was sound asleep but the weather was alive and changing. The anemometer read nineteen miles per hour as the half-shaped moon slid quietly behind a scatter of clouds over the water.

CHAPTER FIFTY-TWO

September 8th, 5:08 AM
Temperature: 84 degrees
Winds: 26 MPH
Pressure: 29.731 bars
Rain: 0 inches

The last glass of amaretto had done its job well and sent Alfred off to sleep just after one o'clock, erasing the worry of the preceding day and washing away the heaviness that had ridden in his chest. Its effect had been stronger than he had anticipated and he woke up disoriented in the darkness of his room. Something pulled him out of the weightlessness of his dreams. It was only a few seconds before he made sense of his surroundings and heard the knock at his door. Mrs. Poplar's voice was adamant, if not a little weary, as it carried from the hall. He threw off the blanket, his skin sweating against the cool wind that blew through the cracked window across the room, and found the floorboards with his feet.

"Just a moment," he called out, his voice cracking in confession of the early hour.

He slipped into his pants and pulled an undershirt over his torso. Thoughts ran through his mind of what he would find on the other side of the door and urged him to take larger steps as he reached for the door-knob. Mrs. Poplar stood in her nightgown with a robe cinched tightly at her waist. The few strands of gray hair that hung about her face were lit up by the oil lamp in her hand. His eyes instinctively searched the hall behind her.

"What is it?"

"A message boy is downstairs for you."

He glanced toward the dark stairs as his mind switched gears and Florence flashed across his mind.

"What's happened?"

She swallowed as she shook her head. "I'm not certain. He said Joseph Cline sent him to wake you."

"He's downstairs?"

She nodded and began to lead him to the first floor. He was thankful for her slow pace as he tried to clear his mind of the anxieties that had so quickly arisen at the sound of her voice. The lower level of the house welcomed him with cooler air. A messenger of no more than fourteen stood in front of the door in baggy pants and a shirt rolled up past his elbows. His hat was too large and threatened to lose its precarious balance and drop over his eyes. He removed it as Alfred took the last step and glanced at Mrs. Poplar.

"This is Mr. Ridgeway," she commented with a soft voice.

The boy held out a handwritten notecard that had been folded in half. Alfred flipped it open and read the message twice to be sure.

"Did he pay you to return a reply?"

"Yes, sir."

The boy offered him a pencil, and Alfred wrote on the back of the note in a quick scrawl before handing it back. "You'll be a good twenty minutes ahead of me."

The boy pocketed the note and pulled his hat onto his head before turning toward the door. Alfred turned and started up the stairs.

"I'm afraid I'm needed at the bureau, Mrs. Poplar."

"Here, dear," she called after him. "Take the lamp. I'll light another one and pack you some food."

He reached down and took the lamp. Taking the stairs two at a time, he was in his room within seconds and hurriedly dressed in fresh clothes. Mrs. Poplar had a sack of leftover rolls and sugar cookies waiting for him by the door when he came down a few minutes later.

"Be careful, dear. The wind is still blowing."

"Will you be home today?" he asked as he slid the food into his sack.

"Until the afternoon. I had planned on calling on Mrs. Roshman for a game of bridge."

"I'd prefer you wait to leave. If the weather proves to be severe, it's better you are caught at home than out."

He stepped out into the darkness of the morning and felt the wind push against his hair. The coolness shocked his system awake, and he pulled his hat down tightly on his head.

"Is the storm moving in?" she asked timidly, closing the door slightly to block the wind.

"I'm not certain, but I will message you if it looks to be that way. Promise me you'll keep to the house until I've sent you word that it will be safe."

"I will."

"And please let Mathias know. He has obligations today."

She nodded, and he jogged down the steps. The door was closed when he looked back as he rounded the house. The bicycle was leaning against the back of the house where an oleander bush flailed in the wind and beat its petals against the rusted metal. He walked it to the street and began pedaling his way toward the office. The trip proved more difficult than he anticipated with the wind, but he was pulling the bicycle into the lobby of the stairwell at half past five and took the stairs at a steady pace to give himself time to catch his breath. Only Joseph was in the office when he opened the door, but the man's expression laid another layer of worry on the air.

"You made better time than you expected," Joseph announced. "The messenger left only a few minutes ago."

Alfred set aside his sack and jacket, dropping them into his chair as he crossed the room "Your message was vague. What's the development?"

"We believe the storm is much closer than we anticipated."

"How much closer?"

Joseph pointed to the map on the table. The lines Isaac had drawn the day before still ran through the gulf and toward the southern coastline.

"Closer than Isaac predicted. The winds have picked up. It's a northern wind, but the drop in pressure has me unsettled. Nearly two-tenths since your last record."

Alfred focused on the map. A number of factors could have brought about the drop, none of which had to do with a tropical storm or hurricane, but that didn't negate the possibility. "What does Isaac say?"

Joseph let out a breath and leaned against his desk with crossed arms.

"That we must control the potential for panic. He's speaking the bureau's words and ignoring what is right in front of him."

"We can't fault him too greatly for it. That's is his job." Joseph narrowed his eyes at him, and Alfred shook his head. "I apologize. That sounded argumentative." He rubbed his forehead in agitation. "I'm very tired."

The silence that followed was long but light, as if each man were giving the other room to organize his thoughts. When Alfred spoke again, his voice was soft and measured.

"What drew you into the office?"

"The tide woke me."

"The tide?"

Joseph gave a quick nod. "It vibrated the house as it hit the stilts and made the wood moan with each oscillation. I've never felt it grab at the foundation like that before."

Alfred did the math quickly. "But Isaac's house is nearly two blocks off the beach."

"Precisely."

A small pebble of anxiety dropped into Alfred's chest. "How deep was the water?"

"Only a few inches. Nothing to cause concern were it raining, but that is uncommon to occur on its own."

"I don't understand."

Joseph pushed off his desk. "Neither do I. Isaac admits that it could be an indication of the storm moving closer, but he's not certain." He crossed the office and began weighing down the papers on Isaac's desk with books and ink wells. After securing everything, he pushed up on the window and opened it a few inches. "And this cooler temperature is not common for hurricanes. So Isaac is skeptical."

"What does the bureau say?"

"Aside from their forecast for the weekend?" Joseph cracked a grin and tossed Alfred the early edition of the paper. "Bottom right of the seventh page."

Alfred flipped to the page and skimmed until he found the official forecast that had come through late the day before. Indications were that the storm would strike somewhere east of Texas and continue west. No considerable disturbances were expected, but it was the admission, either by the newspaper or the bureau—though it was unclear which had made it—that made Alfred's mouth run dry.

"The Weather Bureau," Alfred read out loud, "is unable to determine at this point in time what degree the storm will reach or develop when it makes landfall in Texas." He looked up at Joseph. "What does that mean?"

Joseph's eyes were dark and his face pulled down at his mouth. Alfred saw the man's weariness for the first time and regretted having been so defensive of Isaac in the earlier moments of arriving. Joseph's worry was heavier than his own. Alfred seemed to be ignoring those around him for the sake of his own pettiness. Joseph, he now knew, had been carrying the weight of this storm more heavily than Alfred.

"It means they do not know where it is or what it looks like." His jaw tightened as he looked out the open window at the start of the morning's dawn. "It means they have no idea what is heading our way."

———•●•———

8:27 AM
Temperature: 82 degrees
Winds: 29 MPH
Pressure: 29.706 bars
Rain: 0 inches

The telephone began ringing just before seven o'clock. The first call was from Isaac. Joseph later explained that they had gone separate ways around four-thirty, half an hour after Joseph had woken his brother with concerns about the unusually high tide. Isaac was calling from his house after monitoring the water. The waves were slow but abnormally large, pushing onto the sand in a fatigued sort of manner that Isaac had never seen. He was checking on his wife before coming into the office to assist with the day's work and would observe the water again in an hour. Alfred assured him that all would be well until he was able to make it to the Levy Building.

However, he had underestimated the spice that the cold weather, northerly winds, and odd water would add to an otherwise bland day. The telephone's metallic clang continued for nearly an hour before Isaac arrived. Captains and seamen pushing out from the harbor inquired about conditions on the water and residents along the southern beaches reported unusually high tides, but no call came from the bureau—and not a single call spoke of conditions elsewhere along the coast. Galveston, for all it knew, was alone in the unfamiliar beauty of early September, and it had the island bustling as people flooded the streets, many appearing to head south toward the oceanfront. By the time Isaac arrived a little before nine o'clock, Alfred had spent more time talking on the telephone and comforting concerned residents than he had spent taking observations or preparing the day's forecast, which was officially late reaching the newspaper office.

"The waves are oddly slow," Isaac explained after Alfred hung up from one of the bathhouses along the beach. "Their caps are larger than I've seen, but I can't understand why a northerly wind would create that effect."

Isaac glanced out his window. The view stretched across the roofs of three blocks of buildings and gave him a perched bird's view of the wharves. Ships were tied to the harbor and rocking gently in the waves, their masts ducked beneath the rooflines.

"A blowout," he observed.

Alfred looked out the window from behind Isaac. "What's a blowout?"

"The northern wind pushes the water south out of the bay and lowers the tide on the bay side."

"Could that be affecting the waves?"

"Potentially," Joseph added. "But we have blowouts throughout the year, and we've never seen the waves behave like this."

A hearty knock at the door took them all by surprise. Isaac called out, and a burly man of nearly six feet stepped into the office. He was dressed in a well-fitted suit but had replaced the jacket with a naval-style coat that snapped at the neck and buttoned on the far side of the torso to keep the wind out. His beard was a thick gray that, Alfred decided, mistakenly aged him.

"Good morning, Dr. Cline," he announced with a gruff tone.

"Captain Hix, it's a pleasure to see you."

The two shook hands, and Alfred couldn't help but be amused at the contrast in their statures, Isaac a stiff man with a focused brow and the seaman broad-shouldered with a high chin. The captain gave a nod to Joseph and Alfred before gesturing beyond the window.

"I hear a storm is brewing in the gulf, and I fear this is more than a squall that's tipping my ship from side to side."

Isaac nodded as he crossed his arms. "The bureau has confirmed that a storm is moving through the gulf, but it's likely nothing more than an off-spur of the storm that struck Florida earlier this week."

Alfred glanced from Isaac to Joseph, snapping his mouth shut at the explanation, but Captain Hix appeared to be less trusting than Isaac had assessed.

"Are you certain of that?"

"Fairly certain. Our reports show that the storm is expected to hit eastern Texas and bring in some rain and wind with it. We'll likely see localized flooding, but I wouldn't expect much more."

"How far west will it land?"

Isaac shook his head and glanced toward the window as if to make his case. "That's difficult to say without a clear spotting of where it lies at the moment. Somewhere along the Texas and Louisiana border I would guess."

"I've no reason to be concerned, then, pushing off this morning to head southwest?"

"I don't see any."

The man nodded and smoothed his hair before returning his hat to his head. He paused in his reach for the doorknob.

"You've been taking readings this morning, I presume, with a storm so close to shore."

"Naturally."

"I see. Perhaps my barometer is in need of repair, then."

He opened the door and stepped into the hallway. Isaac followed, stopping in the doorway "Why's that?"

"Well, it seems to have dropped substantially in the past six hours. Rather unlike it, even at sea where the conditions change considerably day to day."

"We've observed the same, but nothing to worry us. It will likely be little more than our usual rains and street flooding."

"That's a comfort," Captain Hix said with a smile and a nod. The captain's footfalls carried down the hallway as Isaac shut the door. A storm brewed in Joseph's eyes as he watched him cross the room.

"What the hell was that?"

"We don't want a panic, Joseph."

"Or deaths at sea for God's sake! He's going to put out into the gulf and could run right into the storm."

Isaac ignored the comment as he gathered a few items from his desk. When he turned back toward the door, his pace carried a little more urgency than before, and Alfred felt the tension grow. Isaac lifted his jacket from the coat rack and slid his arms into it.

"I'm going to walk the Strand and advise merchants to raise their goods off the ground before the rain arrives."

"Isaac," Joseph protested, "we need to warn people. If this storm hits without warning, the consequences could be devastating."

"That's precisely what I'm doing."

Joseph took a few steps toward the door. "No, you're advising them to take precautions against flooding. We both know that is not the gravest concern here."

"Joseph, I have had it." Isaac's face flamed at the temples as he turned toward his brother. "Our positions are not to create an uproar over every change in weather. We are scientists. We observe and study and feed our findings to D.C. That is all. Now, if you believe that your role warrants more responsibility, then I recommend you have that out with the head office, but I am quite certain you'll find yourself back to selling insurance before being the first climatologist granted permission to issue hurricane warnings without a D.C. official overseeing his every move. I will not disobey our orders to wait for permission to issue a hurricane warning and send this island into a mass panic."

He pulled at his jacket to straighten the shoulders, his eyes sharp when he met his brother's gaze. "And neither will you."

Isaac left the office to the echoes of his footfalls down the hall. Joseph stood in silence as Alfred looked out the window at the wind. It blew consistently against the panes and whistled between open sections of the seal, cooling the office. The sudden sound of the telephone jolted Alfred from his seat. He answered it quickly, his heart pumping so thunderously that his hands took a slight tremble as he lifted the receiver.

"Yes." Joseph watched him, his hands in his pockets and a blank expression on his face. "Yes, thank you. Yes, I would advise it."

He hung up the receiver with a click and turned to Joseph. The words came flatly, but he knew their weight was more than he could communicate.

"The Midway is flooding and two buildings have already suffered damage from the waves."

Joseph scarcely had time to react before the door to the office opened, and the same messenger that Joseph had sent to fetch Alfred in the early morning hours fell into the room. His face was rosy with exertion as he huffed for breath.

"The trestle over the beach is impassable," he shouted, his excitement taking over. "They say part of it collapsed into the ocean!"

CHAPTER FIFTY-THREE

10:02 AM
Temperature: 82 degrees
Winds: 31 MPH
Pressure: 29.646 bars
Rain: 0 inches

When Isaac returned to the office, a note of worry had settled in his eyes. The man who was known for being steady and reserved had an urgency in his mannerisms that unsettled Alfred and vindicated Joseph. His voice, however, never wavered.

"The bay side has the ships pitching, and they say the beach has nearly two feet of water covering it up onto the road."

"We're aware," Joseph replied mildly. "The telephone has been ringing since you left. The Midway is flooded, and the beach trestle is impassable because of the waves."

Isaac turned with a tight brow. "The trestle?"

Alfred watched Isaac's face as it began to unravel. His eyes searched the window over his desk for answers. When he came up empty-handed, he glanced between the two men.

"What were the last observations?"

"Winds up twelve at thirty miles per hour," Alfred replied. "Pressure at twenty-nine point six-four-six. Almost a full tenth lower."

Alfred watched him lean against his palms on the table. His face was clouded over, and Alfred felt like they were perched atop the building, waiting to see if the wind would push them over the ledge.

"Joseph, I want you to go topside and take readings of current conditions. I'm going to telephone Murdochs and ask for an update on the beach and then telephone my house to evaluate the south side."

Joseph did as he was told without comment. Alfred waited to be told what to do, but Isaac lifted the receiver and spoke into the telephone without giving further instructions. He could do nothing but listen to one side of the conversation.

"Henry? Isaac Cline here. Yes, we are aware. I'm calling about the tide. Can you look outside and tell me how high it looks to be along the beach. Yes, I'll wait."

He looked over to Alfred but remained quiet. During his first weeks at his post, Alfred would have found the man's silence intimidating, worrying at how he was coming up short of expectations, but now, with the wind shaking the windows and the flags flapping mercilessly on the rooftop, he recognized something new in Isaac's silence. Fear. And it tilted the entire office off-balance.

"Yes, I'm here. I see. All underwater, then? And the street? I understand. Yes, I would advise you to consider closing shop for the day. We do anticipate rain later on and the flooding might continue into the afternoon."

The office door opened and Joseph stepped in, his hair wind-whipped. Isaac hung up the receiver. "Henry says the tide looks to be nearly two and a half feet and beyond the street now." He looked to Joseph. "What of the conditions?"

"I need Alfred's assistance. The wind is too strong for me to read and hold the logbook steady."

Isaac motioned for Alfred to follow. "Attend to the instruments with Joseph. I'm going to send a telegram to D.C. to alert them of the flooding."

"What will you tell them?" Joseph asked, stepping aside for Alfred to move into the hall.

"That we are experiencing high water with opposing winds in anticipation of the storm's landfall. Perhaps that will assist them in determining if it appropriate for us to issue a hurricane warning."

Joseph left the door open as he guided Alfred down the hall and up the stairs. He paused just before reaching the access to the roof.

"Brace yourself," he advised, gesturing toward the logbook. "Keep it close or it'll rip the pages."

Alfred nodded, and Joseph pushed the door open against the wind. A vortex of air spilled into the stairwell, and Alfred nearly lost his balance, finding it a few feet forward as he leaned into the force. Stepping out onto the roof, he found the world to be a whirlwind of cold air. It swirled around him like a tornado, pushing at his chest as it hit him from one direction and then pulling at his back as it moved around the buildings and up the sides from another direction. He mimicked Joseph and ducked down to walk into the wind. When they reached the instruments, the anemometer was spinning at a furious speed, and Alfred knew the winds had picked up since the previous observation less than an hour earlier. Joseph bent down to read the instrument's needle.

"Thirty-four," he yelled over the wind.

Alfred hunched down behind him and carefully opened the logbook, exposing just enough paper to make the notation. He closed it and waited as Joseph moved to the barometer.

"Twenty-nine point six-three-eight."

Alfred made the notation, and they continued this way through the remaining instruments. It took nearly ten minutes for them to finish the observations, and they were exhausted from the effort by the time they returned to the office. Isaac soon returned as well, his hair windblown and the hems of his pants wet.

"The Strand is flooding," he announced in agitation, "and the ships are having to start their boilers to stay aloft in the high water."

Joseph and Alfred crossed the room and looked out the window over Isaac's desk that peered onto the harbor. Stacks of steam and black smoke gushed up from the harbor and blew south over the city in the strong wind. From the angle of the window, Alfred noticed that the ships appeared taller than they had earlier in the morning, and he imagined them tugging at their tethers as the water continued to rock them in the strong winds.

"I don't understand it," Isaac continued as he joined them. "The wind should be pushing the water out, but I can't figure out why the water is building so high in the bay and on the shore."

"Could the storm be pushing water ashore in advance of its arrival?" Alfred offered.

Isaac shook his head. "Not with a northern wind like this. It should push it back out nonetheless. That aside, the majority of flooding on the west side of a hurricane comes from rainfall, not rising tide."

Market Street was below them, but rather than its usual bustle of businessmen and weekend shoppers, shallow water filled the street and propelled wooden boards from the Strand and lost goods from one end to the other. Two small children had commandeered crates and were floating down the street like shipwrecked captains much to the amusement of their parents. They watched the scene unfold this way for nearly an hour as the ships' stacks continued to rise and the street water deepened until men were rolling up their pant legs to cross from one raised sidewalk to another. The sky began to darken as a result of the ongoing boilers and new clouds that began rolling in from somewhere to the east. Just before twelve-thirty, the rain began to fall.

Isaac's mannerisms became distressed, or perhaps nervous, though Alfred was unable to tell, and he announced he was calling Murdochs again to check on the tide. But when he tried the line, he was unable to reach the bathhouse. Alfred and Joseph listened as he tried to telephone Murdochs again before trying another bathhouse and finally a local doctor's office. None of the calls went through, and he hung up the receiver quietly before telephoning his own house. When it brought about the same result, he looked back at the men and swallowed.

"There's been no word from D.C. and it appears telephones are inoperable along the beach. I fear we are on our own, gentlemen."

"What are we to do?"

Joseph looked ready to act, and Alfred wondered how long he had been harboring his anticipation of this very situation. He would give Isaac the credit that the older brother was steadier in his emotions, but he now wondered if it would have been better if Isaac had heeded his brother's concerns earlier in the day. They couldn't very well wait around for D.C. to realize how dire of a situation was unfolding halfway across the country before they could issue a hurricane warning. And the longer they waited, the more likely it was that the weather would worsen.

His mind settled on Florence, and his gut tightened as he remembered his negligence to send her a message to stay indoors. She would be unaware of the oncoming storm, just like the rest of the island. Mrs. Poplar would be safe at home if she'd kept her word to wait for him to give her the all-clear. Mathias, he knew, would be at the hospital. He would be able to relay a message to him with a warning of the oncoming storm, but Hilary was another story. He knew the old man was weary of the weather from the start, but where he would be at a time like this was a different issue altogether. Likely on the beach observing the weather, but that didn't make Alfred feel any better about his safety.

When Isaac did not immediately answer Joseph's question, Alfred posed a new one.

"How do we warn people?"

Isaac's face was expressionless. His eyes were blank as the situation dawned on him. They had an island of nearly forty thousand people to alert of what he was increasingly coming to believe was a hurricane heading straight for them, and they had no other means outside of rooftop flags and their own voices. With the telephones down on the south beaches, those who needed warning the most were unreachable from their office. The thought was settling in each man's mind when the air erupted with a monstrous roar that sounded like the thunder of a canon.

All three turned and looked out the window to see a large cloud of smoke and dust rushing skyward from the Strand as the northern wind caught the particles and began moving them into the city.

CHAPTER FIFTY-FOUR

12:48 PM
Temperature: 81 degrees
Winds: 34 MPH
Pressure: 29.426 bars
Rain: 0.42 inches

The wind whipped around the corners and picked up speed as it barreled down 23rd Street, throwing rain against their faces. The three men leaned into it as they sloshed across the flooded street and made their way to the Strand. Despite the weather, a crowd had already begun to gather at the intersection. Isaac pushed through, leading his assistants around the corner and toward the west. When they broke through the crowd, Alfred froze. Bricks and pieces of molded cornice were scattered along the sidewalk and had built a small dam of shrapnel in the street that was now being pelted by cold drops of rain. Pieces of shattered glass littered the sidewalk around their feet. Joseph's voice broke through the roar of the wind.

"It collapsed!"

They moved closer as the wind cleared the air of the dust, searching for a safe passage into the rubble. It took Alfred a moment to piece together the scene. The restaurant was in shambles. Beams stuck up from the collection of fallen material, and he recognized a section of the wooden bar. It was Ritter's Café and Saloon. He searched the open gouge between the buildings for the table where he had met Hilary less than twenty-four hours before, but it was gone. In its place was a hulking piece of black machinery. It lay on its side but looked strangely familiar.

"The printing press has fallen through," a man shouted from behind them.

Alfred peered up, struggling to remember how the structure had looked the night before. Four stories were now torn down and heaped on the ground. From somewhere deep inside, voices began to call out. All of the men jumped into action, a few instructing their wives to seek shelter in a store across the street, and began traversing the rubble. Several individuals, mostly staff, were making their way out of the kitchen in the back of the building, but a few stood over the middle of where the dining room had been, lifting away bricks and pieces of collapsed roofing.

"The room exploded," a waiter shouted to Alfred as they assessed the scene. "There was a horrendous noise somewhere on the floor above us, and then the room simply shattered."

Joseph leaned closer and pointed up. "The roof."

Alfred looked up into the falling rain. It was gone. The printing shop hadn't fallen through the floor; the building had collapsed because the roof had been blown off by the winds. He turned back toward the street and felt the sting of the wind on his face. It burned like pinpricks on his cheeks, but he imagined the force it would take to rip a roof from a building. And he was fairly certain they were close to what was needed.

"The room would have exploded with a decompression like that," Isaac shouted over the noise. "It would have caused the building to burst outward and taken the floors down with it."

Joseph nodded. "And the printing presses."

A group of men pushed their way closer to the rubble and began lifting sections of the building that had landed atop the tables, but Alfred's attention was drawn elsewhere when he felt a contrast in his body. The cold wind was made worse by the rain and made his legs prickle where his pants had taken on water crossing the street, but now his feet felt the slightly warmer temperatures of the water once more. He looked down and saw that the water had capped the sidewalk and was now rising into the building. Joseph made the same observation, and pulled Isaac away from the rubble. They saved their conversation until they had reached the safety of the office, but it was a short one nonetheless.

"We're sending a telegram to D.C.," Isaac stated as he burst into the office. "We've waited long enough."

Joseph was close behind him as Alfred shut the door. The office provided warmth simply by keeping the wind and rain at bay, and Alfred shivered as he tried to work out the cold that had settled in him. The other two men were too distracted to either contend with the cold or notice it altogether.

"How will we warn people?" Joseph asked, bringing them back full circle to Alfred's question.

"Let me compose a telegram. Alfred, I'll ask you to take it Western Union. They should understand the significance of delivering it quickly." Alfred nodded, as Isaac found his pen. "Joseph, I want you to try to telephone whomever you can contact, anyone on the island with open lines, and tell them to move toward the center of the island." He paused in thought. "And to shelter in stronger houses."

"And what will you do?" Joseph inquired.

"I'm going to check on Cora and then ride to the beach. Everyone along the beach must evacuate as far inland as they can."

Alfred took a step closer. "Inland? You mean off the island?"

Isaac's expression was sympathetic despite his tone. "No, I'm afraid we are past that point. We need to get everyone to the center of the island on this side of Broadway."

Alfred glanced to Joseph, who was already talking to the operator in an attempt to contact anyone along the beach. His voice was steady, despite the urgency, and Alfred found comfort in knowing they were more experienced. He was not expected to have all the answers. They would tell him what to do. He was not on his own.

When Isaac finished writing the telegram, he passed it to Alfred and hurried across the office to retrieve his jacket. "Tell them it is a government telegram and is of the utmost urgency." He pulled his hat tightly onto his head as the panes rattled in a deep vibration. "It is unlikely that I'll be back to the office until the wind dies down."

He glanced at Joseph.

"He will instruct you on anything further that needs to be done here, but you should not stay longer than required. Either of you."

Joseph let out a frustrated noise as he called up the operator again to request another line. They were all taken, the operator had explained, by residents calling about the flooded beaches. Isaac gave them both a last glance before closing the door. Alfred unfolded the telegram and read the message. The climatologist reported impassable streets with rising waters, high winds, and the fear that the hurricane's intensity would be more severe than anticipated.

Against all his strict adherence to protocol, Isaac Cline, esteemed climatologist, had gone against the bureau's order and declared it a hurricane. He was no longer waiting, nor was he testing the waters. The most experienced man on the island was about to tell the bureau what they refused to admit: a hurricane was making landfall on Galveston Island.

And practically no one outside of the three of them had any idea what was coming their way.

———•●•———

2:22 PM
Temperature: 79 degrees
Winds: 39 MPH
Pressure: 29.399 bars
Rain: 0.83 inches

Alfred left Joseph at the telephone and made his way down to the street. Dr. Cline's horse was already gone, but the streets were anything but bare. People waded through the water in all directions. Men in suits, women in waterlogged dresses, children waist deep or, for the littlest ones, in their fathers' arms. He pushed his hat down tightly onto his head and stepped down into the street with them. The water had turned colder, and the rain bit at his hands and face. He pushed his way across Market Street and fought a tight crowd of businessmen to make his way back up onto the covered sidewalk where the water was only a few inches deep. The trip would have been much faster if it hadn't been for the wind blowing incessantly down the street, made worse as the buildings acted as a tunnel. It pushed debris along the water's surface and made what little room there was to navigate those fleeing the business district all the more constricted. When he finally reached the Western Union office on the Strand, his legs ached from the exertion and his fingers felt ice cold.

The office was packed. A crowd had pushed their way in, some seeking shelter from the rain and flood as they debated the best course of action while others barked messages or waited impatiently to pass their telegrams over the counter to a clerk. But the message was all the same—the telegraph lines were down. No messages were coming in or going out of Galveston. Alfred pushed his way to the front of the counter and hailed a younger clerk who was watching the crowd with alarm.

"You there!"

The young man glanced his way with wide eyes, and Alfred motioned for him to come closer. He did so cautiously, keeping his distance. Alfred thrust the telegram across the counter.

"This is an urgent message for the United States Weather Bureau. It must go out immediately."

"The lines are down, sir."

Alfred looked down the counter at the dozens of other men and women who argued with the remaining clerks. Judging by the tone of their voices and the way their pitch rose like the tide on the beach, panic had set in, and there was nothing to be done. He looked back at the young man.

"All of them?" The man nodded, and Alfred felt fear creep in. "How else can I get a message off the island?"

"By telephone if the lines are still up."

Alfred closed his eyes with frustration. The answer had been in front of him in the office, and he'd left it to trudge through flooding waters to a dead end. He spun around and began pushing his way back toward the door.

"I'd hurry, sir," the young man called after him. "I hear the lines on the south side are all down."

Alfred emerged from the telegraph office and back onto the street. The cold air was a stark contrast to the warmth of the gathered bodies that had surrounded him only moments before. In the street a man struggled to guide his horse through the water as his dray continued to catch on debris and the uneven street below the water. Alfred pocketed the telegram and hopped off the sidewalk and into the water, the splash soaking his shirt. He wiped at his face as he called out.

"Leave the dray!" The man turned and squinted at him as he pulled on the horse's reins. Alfred stepped closer and reached out to calm the animal as it pulled against the man's efforts. "You'll have to leave it."

"I need to get it out of the flood waters!"

The wind made conversation difficult, and Alfred leaned closer to speak into the man's ear.

"The whole island is flooded. Leave the dray and save your horse!"

The man looked at him with bewilderment before nodding and hastening his motions to unhook the horse. Alfred helped him loosen the straps and unhook the animal before making his way back toward the office. When he turned onto 23rd Street, the situation was dire. Hundreds of people were now flooding the street with the rising bay. The water was nearly at his thigh in the stret, higher still for men of less height and women, but they all crammed beneath the covered walkways along buildings and struggled to pass through the streets. The quickest passage, he determined, was the center of the street. He started south.

The wind gusted as he made his way, knocking women off balance and lifting lighter debris from the water. Papers let loose by open doors flew in the air and clung to torsos and the occasional horse as the lucky few on horseback made a faster journey away from the bay. Behind him a woman screamed as her child slipped off the walkway and splashed into the water. He came up crying as a man lifted the soaked child back up to his mother. When Alfred finally made it to the Levy Building, he yanked the door open against the wind and slid through the opening with a huff. The door slammed shut and sealed him in the lobby.

Joseph was still on the telephone when he returned, but his mood had shifted. He asked for another line and tossed Alfred a tight-jawed glance as he entered the office. Alfred did not remove his dripping jacket or hesitate at the door. He crossed the office and held out his hand.

"I need the line."

"Are you mad?"

"The telegraph lines are down. We'll have to make a long-distance call to get the message out."

Joseph's face fell. What anger he had built up let out like a deflated balloon. His voice took on its softer tone when the operator returned, and he held up a finger to Alfred.

"Yes. Yes, I'm here." He leaned closer into the telephone. "We have an urgent message for the Western Union Office in Houston." The woman's voice was muffled but obviously overwhelmed. Joseph's words took on a similar manner. "I understand there are callers ahead of me, but this is an urgent government message. We must inform our office of the approaching storm."

When the woman insisted there was nothing to be done, he leaned closer to the machine.

"Find Tom Powell," he growled. "Yes, Mr. Powell. I must speak with him immediately."

A thud came from overhead, and both men looked up. Joseph met Alfred's gaze and motioned toward the ceiling.

"I'm not sure how much longer the instruments will last," he admitted. "Can you see what the measurements are before we lose them?"

Alfred handed Joseph the telegram and shed his wet jacket. It would do him no good and was weighing him down tremendously. The last thing he wanted on the rooftop, where there was very little shelter from the wind, was something to act as a sail and drag him over the edge. He grabbed the logbook and searched for a pencil.

"Yes. Tom, this is Joseph Cline from the Galveston Weather Bureau Office."

Alfred found a pencil tucked away in his desk and slammed the drawer shut as he marched toward the door, the wind taunting him from the windows.

"I have an urgent message that I need your office to deliver. Our telegraph lines are down."

Alfred left the door open, knowing that the building was vacant but for the two of them, and heard a touch of relief in Joseph's voice as he made his way down the hall, someone finally agreeing to send word to D.C. When he reached the roof, the access door wouldn't open. He pushed against it with his shoulder and felt it give, but a gust slammed it back against him. He tossed the logbook a few steps down, knowing he would be unable to record anything while standing in the wind, covered or not, and gave the door a hard shove. It broke loose of its jamb and swung open. The force reversed as the wind caught the open door and threatened to pull it out of his hand. He wrestled with it until he was able to pull it back toward the building and let the wind slam it shut.

The city was a torrent of rain, cold wind, and clouds, but very little could be seen from the rooftop. The usual view of lofty clouds floating over the harbor and peach-crested sunsets was now a haze of water and gray skies. He leaned into the wind and glanced back toward the gulf. The skies were darkening off the horizon, and he knew his eyes were seeing the fate of the island as it rounded the bend. He ducked down, taking big, slow steps toward the instruments.

The anemometer spun wildly, reading forty-four miles per hour, as the rain gauge rocked violently in the wind. The wind had turned—it now blew from the northeast. He committed the recording to memory—an inch and nearly three-tenths. He gripped the pole of the platform and leaned in toward the barometer, shielding his eyes with his other hand. Twenty-nine point one-six-five. The number erased all doubt. The storm was arriving on Galveston. Hilary's intuitions, Joseph's calculations, Captain Hix's barometric readings—they were all confirmed by the floating curve of bottled mercury atop the Levy Building. A hurricane had crossed the Gulf of Mexico, ignoring what climatologists thought they knew about weather, and was making landfall on an island with no escape.

He knew there was little else he could do and made his way back toward the door. Opening it proved much more difficult than closing it had been, and he struggled for nearly two minutes in the rain, his fingers slick on the doorknob, before he was able to inch it open enough to wedge his arm between the door and the jamb. He slid through the opening and pushed the door away with his shoulder as he made his way back into the stairwell.

As he did, a peculiar noise caught his attention. Small but distinct, separate from the roar of the rain and howl of the wind, it was a sudden snap behind him. He paused long enough to glance back across the roof. There among the platform, just below the spinning anemometer and dropping barometer, was the bare attachment of the rain gauge. The metal tube was gone, now blowing somewhere over the buildings in the wild wind of the oncoming storm, and Alfred could do nothing more than take the last step into the building and let the door slam shut behind him.

CHAPTER FIFTY-FIVE

3:41 PM
Temperature: 76 degrees
Winds: 44 MPH
Pressure: 29.165 bars
Rain: 1.27 inches

Joseph was at the window watching the streets below when Alfred returned, dripping and chilled. Alfred tossed the logbook onto the table along with the pencil and fell onto a stool. Joseph handed him a hand towel from his personal sack.

"Well?"

"Winds at forty-four," he reported, wiping his face dry. "Pressure at twenty-nine point one-six-five."

Joseph stiffened. "One-six-five?"

Alfred nodded as he wiped at his hair. "Total rain was nearly an inch and three-tenths, but you'll not be taking any more measurements—"

Joseph gripped the logbook and slid it wildly across the table. Alfred jerked at the motion.

"What are you doing?"

Joseph opened the logbook and skimmed the entries until he found what he was looking for. He mumbled to himself as he made notations in the margin of the paper. When he looked up at Alfred, his lips were parted but silent.

"What is it?"

"The pressure was twenty-nine point seven-three-one when I arrived this morning." Alfred glanced down at the scribbles on the paper and then back at Joseph with a shake of his head. Joseph's tone took on a sharp edge. "That means the pressure has dropped over half an inch in less than twelve hours. That's nearly a full bar every other hour."

He fell onto the stool beside him as Alfred contemplated the math. Pressure fell as hurricanes neared. It was the low pressure that allowed storms to form at all, but pressure dropped progressively, picking up speed as a storm neared and reaching its lowest measurement when the storm was overhead.

"But the winds are only at forty-four miles per hour," Alfred stated.

"Exactly." It came together in Alfred's mind, and he saw the threat for what it truly was. "I was too distracted with the telephone," Joseph explained. "I wasn't checking the log, watching the pattern."

"The storm is not even fully on land yet," Alfred replied, ignoring his comment. "That means this is only a precursor to what is still over the water." Joseph nodded solemnly, but Alfred wouldn't let him stay quiet. "How large is this storm going to be?"

Joseph shook his head, his expression knotted and tight.

"I have no idea. We have nothing to compare it to. No way to know. That was the danger all along, wasn't it?" He looked up at Alfred. "But if these measurements are correct, this storm will be larger and stronger than anything we've ever seen."

"What do we do?"

That was the question of the day. Every one of them had thought it, and he knew thousands of people were speaking the same words in the flooded streets as they made their way to higher ground. He imagined people along the beaches as Isaac rode by the Midway and along the flooded sections, asking him what they should do. He wondered what the Chief Climatologist would say, where he would direct them as the water began to flood the island on all sides. The bridges were no doubt impassable by now, the trolleys inoperable, the tracks flooded. What to do would be the question of the century come tomorrow.

"Nothing."

Alfred held Joseph in his stare, and the man simply shook his head.

"We've waited too late, Alfred. There's nothing we can do."

The lights flickered around them, and a cold set into the room. Alfred was certain he could feel a draft coming from the windows, but he glanced instead about the office, searching for something to draw his attention to, an answer of some kind. There had to be something they could do for themselves and those flocking in the streets, but nothing surfaced. The lights flickered again, and Joseph rose from his stool. His motions were to the point, and Alfred knew his intentions. The two men gathered their jackets and sacks without speaking, and Joseph gave the office a quick dressing down. He slid the logbook onto the shelf and shelved the maps before nodding at Alfred.

"The streets should be easier to pass as you near the center of the island," Joseph explained. "Broadway is one of the highest points on the island. It has never flooded before now."

"I need to get to Nineteenth Street and Avenue M."

They took the stairs quickly as they descended into the colder air of the stairwell.

"You'll do better at higher ground. I suggest staying around Broadway."

"No." They stopped inside the lobby. "I must get across town."

The bulb overhead let out a pop and the room fell into darkness that was broken only by the faint light beyond the door. Joseph glanced up before bracing himself against the door.

"We've both a long walk ahead of us, then. God speed."

He pushed open the door and let it catch in the wind. Water was already crawling over the threshold and into the lobby. A few people sought the open door, cramming into the lobby to get out of the wind, but Alfred left them alone as he stepped out onto the sidewalk. The water had risen still but looked to be no more than waist-deep. If Joseph was right, the water would recede the closer he got to Broadway, but that did little to sharpen Alfred's courage. The winds had continued to build, and he was certain they had grown to well over fifty miles per hour in the short time since his last observation.

He navigated the flooded steps down into the street and began to walk south along 23rd Street. The skies had darkened tremendously since he had been on the roof and bought a premature evening that filtered the cityscape in the low light of a summer storm. He ducked his head as he walked, keeping a hand on his hat, but he made it only a few feet before he lost his grip. His bowler whipped off his head and flew skyward. He kept his eyes ahead and let it go, clutching his sack tightly as he went.

When he reached Postoffice Street, Alfred found the roadway jammed with refugees seeking the same solace from the storm. Families with bags over their shoulders and businessmen with papers held high out of the water had converged on the intersection as they headed south. Alfred glanced down Postoffice and wondered about Mrs. Poplar. The house was sturdy and she had a second floor to escape the water. As he slowed at the back of the crowd, he contemplated detouring to check on her, but his mind wrestled with the scene in front of him. Hundreds were fleeing their homes, pushing away from the water's edge. The wind grabbed and yanked loose clothing and papers from their hands as abandoned sentimentalities became flotsam and buoyed between bodies as the crowd crept forward en masse.

His mind sharpened as he looked back. More people trudged toward him like a never-ending river of torsos, and he realized the predicament had taken a turn for the worse. Soon they would pack the streets too thickly, and no one would make progress. But did they know they were seeking shelter closer to the storm? He doubted it and looked about frantically for an escape. The wind stung at his face as it blended with the shouting voices of frantic men and women. He caught sight of a man on a horse and pushed his way toward him, taking the corner of a suitcase to his chin. He rubbed it angrily as he waved at the man.

"Ho, there!"

The man continued to stare toward the front of the crowd, and Alfred grabbed hold of his leg. The man shook it instinctively and nearly caught Alfred in the face. He recoiled before stepping closer and shouting up at the man.

"What's the trouble?"

The man raised up and looked forward. He bent down to yell closer to Alfred, sending the horse into a sidestep as it whined.

"Looks to be two horses caught in some debris."

"Is there a way around?"

"Very little!"

Alfred glanced about at the frightened faces and turned back toward the horseman and away from the wind. His jacket was wet, but money of any sort was good. He pulled out his wallet.

"Can you offer a ride beyond the crowd?"

The horse shook nervously as the water lapped at its legs. Alfred held up a bill, and the man took it tightly as the wind tried to claim it as its own. Alfred stepped up onto the nearby sidewalk and mounted the horse behind the man in a quick motion. The horse was slow to move and unsure of its footing, and the mass of people that had formed a wall behind the tangled horses made it difficult to pass. What people had managed to squeeze through on the street or walk up the sidewalk stepped aside as much as they could manage as the man guided the horse through the water. Once they were past Postoffice Street, the man turned back and shouted, but his voice was almost inaudible over the wind.

"How far are you going?"

Alfred leaned in to answer but caught sight of a short-statured man a few hundred yards ahead of them. He waved off the horseman and slid back into the water. With renewed vigor, he trudged through the water by kicking up his knees as if to jump with each step. The crowd still lingered behind him as men worked to untangle the horses, which left the street much less crowded as he navigated the covered street.

"Edwin!"

His voice was lost on the wind, and he wondered how anyone could hear themselves speak in such a state. He repeated the call nonetheless until the man glanced up and saw him approaching. Edwin veered his course and met him in the middle of the street. They huddled closer to block the rain.

"Quite a storm," Edwin commented, his eyes darting about them.

"You need to seek higher ground. Go south."

He shook his head. "My wife and daughter are with her sister." He leaned closer. "Off of Merchant in a warehouse."

"Are you certain?"

"They sent a messenger."

Alfred pointed behind them. "The crowd's too thick. Head a block over to get to them, but go higher. This is only going to rise as the storm comes through."

Edwin nodded and clapped him on the shoulder. "I knew there was good in knowing a weatherman." He gave his bright smile before letting it fade in a tight expression. He pulled his collar up higher over his face and gave a nod toward the south. "The water's better that way."

The two men parted, but Alfred couldn't help but look back. The wind had shifted a bit more and now stung only his left cheek, though the rain felt as if it was coming from all directions. Edwin's frame sank lower into the water as he neared the now-untangled horses and walked head-strong into the crowd of oncoming refugees. Alfred knew he would not detour. No man would when in search for his family. Straight down 23rd Street would be the fastest route. He couldn't blame him for it, but he felt a sting deep in his chest that emanated down his spine as he watched the man shove against the flow of people and water until he disappeared in the throng of bodies. His mind told him it was the cold taking over his senses, but his heart told him it was grief, as if he were watching a man walk headlong into his own demise.

He returned to his trek southward, leaving behind the panic that now encompassed the business district as the remaining rooftop instruments continued to monitor the storm without attention, the anemometer creeping over sixty miles per hour and the barometer falling to twenty-nine point zero-five.

CHAPTER FIFTY-SIX

4:02 PM
Temperature: 78 degrees
Winds: 64 MPH
Pressure: 29.05 bars
Rain: 2.06 inches

Alfred gave up on his sack when he reached Winnie Street. It pulled in the water and weighed him down once it had cleared the surface. It only took him a second to debate his options before he simply lifted it overhead and tossed it over a fence into a deserted yard to keep it from falling underfoot in the flooded street. When he reached Broadway, his thighs were burning from his walk, and his clothes were soaked through. The avenue was not dry as Joseph had anticipated; inches of water collected against the curbs and on either side of the palm-lined median.

All around him people marched in the water, some just beginning their treks home while others fled the southern half where passersby shouted the water had reached nearly four feet along the beaches. Alfred was unsure what to believe as the city evacuated to the safest point on the island. He frantically looked up and down Broadway as he began to run through the crowd. Men pushed against him and warned him to stay. He relived the warnings he had just given Edwin but in reverse, and the frustration at his slow going grew until he found himself splashing into knee high waters again, the shift in floodwaters taking him by surprise.

The wind was tremendous as he turned east with the hope that moving off 23rd Street would grant him a less-traveled road. His steps grew slower as the water deepened, and he realized his mistake too late. The elevation fell slightly as he moved east and led him into deeper waters. As he turned at 19th Street, the water reached his waist. Fewer people now traveled the streets, but his mind began to wonder at what lie ahead. The island was submerged in nearly every direction he looked, and the wind blew the water up in sprays that painted his face in saltwater as he lifted his head. The water was thick as a lake and muddy from the sand and muck it carried ashore with it. He glanced desperately about him, seeing only a few others traversing the neighborhood with him, and became momentarily absorbed in the panic that began to creep into his chest.

The water continued to rise, and he struggled to breath from the cold that was settling into his nerves. His bones ached; his muscles cried out. But it was when his foot found a discarded bicycle that lay hidden beneath the water that he lost his courage to the waters. He fell forward as a cry left his lips and was submerged fully beneath the water. The salt stung at his eyes and burned as it traveled up his nose. He came up sputtering and shouting at the pain in his ankle, but there was no one to hear him. Cold and afraid, the intensity of the moment taking hold, he made his way toward the side of the street and wrapped an arm around the narrow trunk of a palm tree.

The wind gusted at tremendous speeds, and he leaned his cheek against it to catch his breath. The force of the ocean pushed him backward while the wind ran past him and held him against the tree. It was a disorienting sensation that he struggled to understand, but he held on tightly as he opened his eyes narrowly to the south and scanned the distance. There was nothing but water and sky and houses floating in a waveless sea. The ocean had claimed the island.

A cry split the air, and he glanced back painfully into the wind to see a child splashing in the water. His father let go of the bag that had been balanced on his shoulder to take hold of the child's arm before he was torn out of reach. The bag fell into the water with a triumphant spray of water before beginning its journey as a tumbling load of cloth along the current. The child came up screaming while the mother gave a single attempt to catch the bag as it passed. It was no use. It was out of reach within seconds.

Alfred took a deep breath before letting go of the tree and continuing his journey. His ankle throbbed with the weight of each step, leading him to move along the side of the street where trees blocked a portion of the current if he walked between them. When he reached the next corner, he saw a man with a similar idea who had attached himself to a tree across the intersection. When Alfred reached him, he realized a horse was tied about the tree as well.

"You've got to head north," Alfred shouted, the wind stealing his words before they could leave his lips.

The man shook his head, and Alfred gripped the tree before leaning over to yell closer to his ear. The man held on to the reins with white knuckles.

"I can't leave the horse!"

"You can't stay! The water will continue to rise!"

He glanced toward the ocean and noticed the sky darkening at a steady pace. Soon it would be an artificial night that nothing could pierce, and any man caught outside would be the worse for it. He wondered how many blocks he had walked since leaving Broadway.

"The owner paid me five dollars to keep this horse alive! I have to keep his head above water!"

Alfred shook his head once more and pleaded with the man, but he held strong to the tree and wrapped the reins about his hands to fasten himself to the trunk with the horse. The water was at Alfred's chest, nearing the man's shoulders, and it was easy to see that the man would drown before the horse. He leaned forward once more, ready to argue, when a shattering noise sounded overhead. Both men ducked instinctively, the other man hitting the water with his face. When Alfred glanced about, the world spun with tremendous force. The fronds of the palms bowed and pitched like ships tossed at sea until they threatened to break off entirely. Giant oaks twisted as their boughs were brushed by the rising water and bent to the wind. But something moved in the air on a different trajectory. When he realized the origin, he covered his head and ducked once more as the sound came again like a gunshot blasting against the tree.

Broken bits of ceramic fell around them and knocked against Alfred's hand. He glanced up before lifting his head to see roof tiles flying in the wind. The force, he knew, had already reached hurricane strength, and the tiles were simply no match for the wind. Another tile pierced the air and struck the tree trunk above him. He looked up at the tile where it had lodged into the wood like a knife and felt the blood in his veins pulse frantically. He leaned forward as much as he could to flatten his opposition to the wind and reduce his surface area. His ankle screamed as he moved and his heart beat wildly in his chest as the world around him began to turn upside-down.

The wind roared as rain pummeled his face and shoulders. Ceramic tiles flew through the air with broken pieces of wood and debris as he stumbled onto a fence and gripped its wrought-iron posts for support. When he looked over the fence, the familiar facade of Florence's house stood bravely over the water, and he felt a surge of hope. He pulled himself along the fence and felt the wind shift slightly as he turned the corner. When he had crossed the street, he found the gate to her yard ripped fully from the fence posts.

He took the steps one at a time until he was out of the water and leaned against a pillar on her porch. The wind howled angrily as he shook from the cold. It took all his strength to reach up and pound against the door, shouting out her name. He prayed she was home but knew in his heart that there was very little that could survive what was nearly upon them. As he took a final glance out at the flooding street, he felt the door give way beneath his hand.

Chapter Fifty-Seven

6:01 PM
Temperature: 76 degrees
Winds: 89 MPH
Pressure: 28.93 bars
Rain: 2.43 inches

*F*lorence's arms were warm as she helped him into the house. She struggled to shut the door, and he let his body fall against it as they pushed it back into the door jamb. He let out a rough breath and felt his legs tremble as he used the wall beside him for support. His voice was hoarse when he finally spoke.

"Where is your aunt?"

"She was at bridge when the rain began."

He held her gaze. "You've been alone?"

"Yes," she answered, her eyes brimming with tears.

He stood and held out an arm. She stepped into his embrace, and he held her tightly against him. The warmth of her body eased his trembling, but he did little to suppress her quick breaths that hinged on deep sobs. He rested his chin against her head as he contemplated their situation. The house was dark and an oil lamp burned on the table near the stairs.

Daylight had quickly faded, and he had no sense of time or place. He knew where he stood, but to determine where that was in relation to the rest of the island was impossible. It all sat beneath feet of ocean water that he feared was only a warning of what would now only be yards off shore.

He lifted his head and looked down at her face. "Did your father leave any clothes in the house?"

She swallowed with a nod. "Upstairs in his bureau."

"I need dry clothes."

She stepped back, wiping her eyes, and reached for the lamp. He followed her up to the second floor. When she motioned toward the room at the end of the hall, he took her hand. She grimaced.

"My hands are not at their best today."

"Can you sit here and rest them?"

The wind shook the window pane at the end of the hall, threatening to break it from the housing, and the house creaked with the force. She nodded. He pulled a chair from the nearest room and set it at the top of the stairs against the wall. He took the lamp and set it on the ground at her feet to light the hall.

"I'll only be a moment," he assured her. "Then we can figure out how to ride out the rest of the storm."

"The rest of it?" Her eyes searched his, and he realized his error. He had meant to reassure her, to protect her in whatever way he could, but he had not been prepared for what the day had promised. "What more could there be?"

He let out a deep breath and knelt down. "I honestly don't know how much more there is, but I do know that this storm is far more disastrous than we anticipated. We need to be prepared for it to worsen."

She stiffened, and he took her hands gently in his, careful not to bend her fingers.

"I know this is unnerving, and I am just as frightened as you are. But we will come out of this storm together. I'm not leaving you."

Her eyes softened but held his gaze with intensity.

"Trust me, Florence."

She nodded, and he rose. The wind gusted against the house as he closed the door to the bedroom. In the bureau he found a pair of pants and a cotton shirt. He rolled up the sleeves and tucked in the shirt to clear his hips for what he knew was coming next. Against the threatening pop of the windows, a gentle ticking came from a valet stand beneath the shirts. He glanced at the pocket watch and felt his head begin to ache. It was after six o'clock. It had taken him nearly two hours to cross the city.

He opened the bedroom door to find Florence in her chair. She gave him a weary smile as he approached.

"What must we do?" she asked.

"Does your father keep tools in the house?"

She shook her head. "They're all in the stable."

"Damn." He ran through the lower level in his mind, taking an inventory of the house. "I need something big and sharp."

"Sharp?"

He nodded. "Like a blade."

"I can't think of anything in the house that would have a blade." She lifted her eyebrows as a thought came to her. "Cook was using a hatchet yesterday to break up bones for her dog."

"Is it in the house?"

"Downstairs. She forgot to take it out with her."

He carried the lamp as they moved down the staircase. He held out his hand for her to balance as she took them slowly. He didn't need to ask. Her stiff gait gave away her injuries, so much more than her hands. Her arthritis was reawakening throughout her body. She stood in the doorway and held the lamp with both hands as he lifted the hatchet from the counter in the kitchen. He walked past her without a word, and she followed him into the front room. A small scream left her throat as she watched him squat onto one knee, lift the hatchet overhead, and slam it down into the floorboards.

"What are you doing?"

He lifted the hatchet skyward and brought it down again on the floor as the boards split beneath the blade. He looked back at her through the dark house with scattered breaths.

"Trying to save your house."

"By chopping holes in the floor?"

Her voice verged on incredulity as he let the hatchet fall a third time through the wood. A larger hole appeared and he turned back to her. "When the water comes in, it will need somewhere to go." He walked past her and into the hallway. "If it can't go down below the house, it will push through it. With enough force and nothing to ground the house, it will pull it off its foundation."

He stopped beyond the stairs near the entrance to her music room and knelt onto one knee before bringing the hatchet down again. She jolted at the noise and looked away as he chopped another hole into the floorboards. When he had finished, she stepped closer to peer into it.

"This will hold the house in place?"

"That's my hope."

He continued into the parlor and chopped another hole before moving into the dining room. By the time he returned the hatchet to the kitchen, he had cleared holes in the floor of every room and was sweating about his brow and arms. He took the lamp from her and helped her settle into a chair in the parlor. Her hands still trembled.

"Are you cold?" She nodded, and he settled the lamp on a side table. "Where do you keep the blankets?"

"There is a quilt on my bed upstairs. The second room to the right."

He leaned forward and kissed her forehead.

"I'll be right back."

He took the stairs slowly, keeping most of his weight on his left ankle as he navigated each step. His entire body ached as he moved across the hall to her room. It was dark, but he could make out the outline of her bed. Mosquito netting hung from both sides like a pale shadow. A bureau rested along one wall while a mirror took up a corner against the other wall. He felt the foot of the bed until he found the quilt neatly folded on one side. He stuffed it beneath his arm and turned to go.

A sparkle caught his attention along the wall, and he turned and looked out the window. Beyond the glass was a sea of darkness dotted with the warm glow of oil lamps. Houses were alight all along the street like ships lost at sea calling for a savior. The blackness of the water looked impenetrable, devouring the light, a dark void where land had once been. It felt like he was looking out on a world that was something other than what he had known, like a story told by old men of days long past. He frowned at the darkness beyond the window pane as the cold returned to his body.

And then he heard Florence scream.

CHAPTER FIFTY-EIGHT

6:38 PM
Temperature: 75 degrees
Winds: 105 MPH
Pressure: 28.89 bars
Rain: 2.79 inches

Alfred ignored the pain in his ankle as he took the stairs as quickly as his legs would carry him. He rounded the corner and practically ran into the doorframe as he stopped at the entrance to the parlor. She held the lamp in shaky hands that sent the light trembling along the walls.

"What is it?"

His heart raced as he waited for her to answer, but all she could do was point at his feet. He looked down. It took a moment for him to make sense of the way the floor shimmered in the lamp light. He spun around toward the door at the front of the house but could only make out the outline of the windows that looked out onto the street. He splashed through the water that was now at the top of his shoes and took the lamp from her hands as he raised her to her feet. The sound of water draining down the hole he had chopped beside the chair filled the air as he helped her toward the stairs.

The water continued to rise more quickly than he could fathom. By the time they reached the stairs, it was at his calves; seconds later, his hips. He focused on Florence's steps, trying desperately not to let her trip as the water began to lap at the hem of her dress. By the time he began taking the first steps behind her, the water was above his waist. The water had risen within seconds. The waiting was done with. The storm had arrived. And there was nowhere to go but up.

Pieces of furniture cried out as the water swept them off their feet: a table near the door slipping against the wall, a wicker chair in the sitting room knocking against the fireplace, the china in the hutch rattling from the vibrations of the rising tide. It called after them as they fumbled to reach the second floor. The water chased them as he followed Florence up the stairs until it was biting at his heels halfway up the staircase. He turned to look down into the water where it had stopped less than three feet below the top stair. It stared back at him silently with black eyes, and he felt a chill take over his body. He spun around to see Florence standing in the middle of the hallway, her face lit by the flickering light of the oil lamp. Her dress hung like a heavy drape and dripped water onto the floor. A crash beyond the window shook them both, and he laid an arm around her as he tried to make sense of the world as they now knew it. Rain beat at the window panes while the wind screamed along the outside of the walls. Everything below them—the entirety of the island they called home—was now below more than ten feet of water, the last half of which had risen in less than a minute.

A shift had occurred, that much he knew. He strained to listen and thought he heard the wind blowing more steadily against the south side of the house, but he couldn't be certain. Not with the roar of the wind and the knocking from downstairs. He took the lamp from Florence, careful to keep one arm behind her, and lifted it over the staircase. The side of one of the armchairs from the parlor buoyed just below the surface of the water. It was caught in the banister, its legs tangled beneath the thick mahogany, and called out to him like a drowning man preaching to the shore. A voluminous thud beat against the floor beneath their feet and reverberated through the floorboards. He stepped back and pulled her closer.

"It's the furniture," he whispered into her hair. "The water is knocking it about against the ceiling."

She nodded, and he knew the question that was on her mind. He prayed she wouldn't ask it. The water only needed a few more feet to reach the second floor, and they had nowhere else to go. He glanced about the hallway.

"I think the wind is from the south. Let's move to the back bedroom." He glanced down at her face where she leaned against his shoulder. "It'll be quieter back there." He stepped back to lead her, but she pulled against him, her hand in his. He turned to see her staring down the stairs into the darkness.

"Our lives are underwater," she spoke to the ocean. "My paintings. My piano. My mother's silver. It's taken it all."

"It hasn't taken anything yet. It will all be there when the water recedes."

She took a long moment to look away from the water and back to him. When he saw the sadness in her eyes, his chest grew heavy, and he tugged her away from the edge of the stairs. The back bedroom was the largest of the three, where he had changed only a short while before, and despite having two windows was somewhat quieter than the hall. The rain did not beat so heavily against the walls on the north side of the house. Thunder echoed somewhere out over the island, the first he had heard, and he reckoned that was a good sign.

"The storm must be nearly centered over us now." He helped her sit on the edge of the bed, and she began ringing the water out from the bottom of her skirt. Her movements were intentional and lacked the quick motion of a young woman's hands.

"How long will it last?"

"Perhaps a few more hours."

She nodded as he settled the lamp on the side table. He opened the bureau and reached up above her father's shirts to pull down a quilt. When she had given up on wrestling the water from the material, she sat back on the bed, and he covered her with the blanket. She reached out for his hand.

"Sit with me."

"I need to keep an eye on the water."

Her mouth turned down at the corners. "We'll know if it rises."

He understood her meaning and was thankful she hadn't needed him to say it. He walked around the bed and pulled himself up onto the mattress. It gave with his weight, but she leaned into him as he wrapped an arm around her and pulled her closer. The house creaked in the wind, but most of the air around them was a consistent roar of weather, interrupted by the occasional bump or knock from downstairs. After several minutes, the sounds came more often and in higher pitches. He imagined the water meeting the last step before it spread across the floor.

"Where shall we be married?" he asked.

She looked up at him with narrow eyes and read his expression. A small laugh escaped her lips. "The church, I suppose."

"You wouldn't rather the beach?"

She let her cheek fall back against his shoulder. "On the beach? Why would one want to have a wedding on the beach?"

Two hard knocks came at the floorboard in quick succession. He glanced over her and toward the floor by the door.

"Imagine it," he suggested, speaking a little louder to compete with the wind. "A sunset over the water with birds overhead. The dunes behind us with the water lapping at our feet." The house gave a creak that stretched into a moan. He held his breath to listen and let it out slowly. If she noticed, she didn't let on.

"And the smell of saltwater on the air," she added.

"Perhaps a bouquet of oleanders in your hands."

She let out a long breath as another knock came, muffled and soft. Her hands were resting open-palmed and face up in her lap. The knuckles were noticeably swollen, and he took one gently. She looked down at them.

"What will be left of the island?"

He breathed in the question and let it settle. "I'm not certain."

The window pane rattled ferociously, and he pulled her closer. The warmth of their bodies had soothed her trembling, but he couldn't help but feel how small she was in his arms. He loved her for her confidence, her beauty, the way her laugh filled his heart with peace, but as they sat together on the bed with the storm raging just beyond walls of wood and plaster, he felt how vulnerable she was. He saw how weak her body had become. And he cursed the universe as he shut his eyes.

"Will it be worse closer to the beach?"

"Yes. They sit a little lower." His voice fell into a whisper. "The water will be higher."

As another clap of thunder barreled over the roof, he thought of Hilary in his mansion. His house was well-suited for the winds, though the water would be higher in his lot. If he had stayed at home, he would be luckier in the end having a fortress between him and the ocean.

"And the people caught in the flood?"

He knew it was no longer a flood. It was the ocean swallowing the island. It had raged in the gulf until it could no longer contain its own strength and surged inland, devouring everything in its path. He thought of how the streets must look now—oil lamps glowing only in the second-story windows as families gathered in the last shelter from the rising waters. What would become of those left in the elements? The man with the horse. The people rushing northward from the Strand. Edwin. His mind drifted to Mrs. Poplar alone in her house, her husband's picture beside her bed as she prayed to the sound of the wind. Then Mathias came to mind. And the young boy in the east wing. What would become of all of them?

For a moment his mind stilled as he began to wonder what would become of him and Florence. He opened his mouth to say something comforting, but the words were cut short by another creak of the wood followed by a pop. It took them by surprise, and they looked toward the wall. The wallpaper, a deep mauve with thick golden stripes, revealed a giant tear in the fabric. He leaned forward as Florence sat upright. Water dripped down the paper and onto the floor, sparkling like a fountain in the lamp light.

He walked slowly, his heavy footsteps muffled by the water below. His fingers met wet paper as he rubbed at the wall. His eyes caught sight of movement near his feet, and he spotted a bubble in the wallpaper. It grew almost imperceptibly until it was the size of a child's ball and bulged with a thin, round skin. He took a step back as he watched it like a snake on the hunt. His muscles stiffened, ready to act, as another muffled knock came from below and the bubble burst, spraying water along the wall.

Florence yelped, and he held up a hand to calm her. The wall behind where the bubble had formed was water-logged plaster and soaked wood.

"What is it?"

The window rattled as a tremendous gust shook the floorboards.

"The walls are soaking up the water from downstairs."

She glanced instinctively toward the door and back to him. "What does that mean?"

"I don't know. It could be—"

A long moan erupted in the air and howled beneath the water. He listened, trying to pinpoint its origin, but it seemed to be coming from somewhere deep within the house. A tremor went through the structure, and he felt his balance shift. Florence looked at him with wide eyes, and his muscles went into action as he threw the quilt off her legs and pulled her onto her feet.

"Was that something outside?" Her voice shook with her hands, and he pulled her close, protecting her from something unseen.

"No, I think that was the house."

"You mean water moving through it?"

He swallowed as he tried to hear anything other than the rain beating against the roof and the wind threatening the windows, but the world had turned silent elsewhere.

"No. I mean the house shifting off its foundation."

He was still holding her against his chest when the world erupted around them.

CHAPTER FIFTY-NINE

7:42 PM
Temperature: 77 degrees
Winds: 111 MPH
Pressure: 28.87 bars
Rain: 3.06 inches

The shudder that ran through the house might as well have been an earthquake beneath their feet. The world slid as if on ice, and they leaned into each other as the ground pitched beneath them. It was a slow pull at first, smooth like glass, but stuttered as it grew in intensity, until a great vibration echoed along the floorboards and up their legs. Alfred looked about them frantically. There was nothing to do. They had nowhere to go. If the house slipped from its foundation, it would fall into the water, and nothing would be carried far before colliding with the rest of the world. If they survived the taking of the house, he knew they wouldn't survive its desecration at the hands of the ocean. He made a split-second decision.

"How well can you swim?"

The floor shook again as the wind grew in volume.

"Swim?"

"We're going into the water. Can you swim on your own?"

"Yes, but—"

Another shudder, stronger, deeper within the house, cascaded up the walls and into the bedroom as light flickered around them. The lamp on the side table shook violently. He considered the wind and how the current would pull. The house was likely to go into the water heading north. They wanted to be anywhere but on the north side when they went into the water. He took her by the arm and pulled her closer to the east window.

"When the house breaks free, it won't last long in the water before it begins to tear apart. We have to get out of the house before we're pulled under with it." He looked her square in the eye. "Do you understand?"

She nodded.

"The winds will be worse than you can imagine, and there will debris everywhere. We have to find something to use as an anchor, something to hang on to until the water recedes."

"But how?"

"Grab for whatever you can. Anything that doesn't seem to be moving in the water."

The house began to shudder without end, and he felt his legs struggle to keep their balance. But when he heard her next words, he felt like his entire body would give out.

"I can't, Alfred."

He leaned closer. "What do you mean?"

She lifted her hands between them, and he looked down at her swollen knuckles. Her voice was soft in his ears.

"I can't hold on to anything."

The floor trembled, and he felt a fire grow within him. His eyes searched the room as the house began to slide. He could feel the water push at the foundation, and he knew he was running out of time. He reached up and yanked a curtain from above the window. The rod fell to the floor with a crash and he pulled at the material until the rope that had held the curtain back broke free. Pulling her against him, he tied one end around her waist and the other around his own. He stepped up to her until there was nothing between them but their breath and their heartbeats.

A roar bellowed from the first floor, and she let out a small sob.

"I can't, Alfred! This won't work."

He wrapped his arms around her as tightly as he could as he put his shoulder against the cold glass of the window.

"It will, Florence. It has to. This is the only way we make it to the beach."

She kept her eyes on his, her strength returning, and gave a strong nod. He returned it as the house let out a final cry. The sound of wood being bent beyond its strength split the air. Somewhere down below the staircase cracked with the weight of the house, and the hall was filled with the sound of intricately carved branches breaking from their roots. Her voice quivered as she let her head fall onto her shoulder.

"What do we do?"

He squeezed her tightly as he whispered in her ear. "Don't let go."

And all at once the world he had fought so vigorously to keep outside erupted into the room around them. The floorboards splintered as the lower half of the house shifted fully from its banks and the upper floor was pulled with the current. The lamp fell to the floor and shattered, plunging them into darkness, as he leaned against the glass. He had to only wait a few seconds before the wall pulled away, and everything he knew was plunged into the cold water of the gulf.

He could feel Florence's form in his arms as the water overtook them, and he opened his eyes to nothingness. It was a deep blackness, a void that engulfed everything that had once been beautiful and bright. He kicked with his legs against the weight of the ocean and felt Florence doing the same. The torrent pulled at them until he felt the rope around his waist grow taut, but he could still feel her against his hands. She was there. That was all he knew. That was all he needed to know.

He kicked until he found purchase on something. It tumbled beneath his feet like unsteady earth but gave him enough weight to propel him forward. As the cold water took hold of his senses, he struggled to keep a grip on Florence's arm. A flash somewhere in the water drew his attention, and he focused on its source. His lungs burned for air, but he kicked frantically, willing the water to carry them skyward. Another flash burned momentarily like a photograph bulb through glass. Lightning. He had found his way.

His fingers ached and his lungs burned for oxygen. They were feet, maybe yards, from the surface. The house had pulled north as he had anticipated, but the weight had likely pulled them under farther than he had realized. Six more feet. He thrashed wildly, pulling both of their bodies toward the night sky. Five feet. Another flash took over the water. Four feet. As it crackled over the island, it lit the water around him, giving him a momentary view of the carnage into which they had been thrown. The outline of a tree was below him—he was swimming in the sky. A wall of darkness was to his right, likely the house as it unfurled in the current, and a large shadow was above them. Three feet. And as he neared the surface, so close he felt like he could reach out and grasp the wind with his fingers, the shadow moved over him and blocked the flash of light overhead.

His hand slammed into it, but it held fast. It was solid and buoyed like a water-logged barrel, bouncing just beyond the surface. The water was dark again as he wrestled with it, trying desperately to move around it. The current pulled them all to the north, and he fought to free them from its cover. He let go of Florence's hand and reached as far as he could, searching the smooth wood for its edge. When he found it, he gripped the ledge and pulled with every fiber in his body. The water resisted, but the bureau gave way. He felt the weight of the rope as he surfaced. A cough erupted from his lungs as it joined the scream of the wind that battered the surface of the water. He reached out and gripped whatever would hold his weight on the bureau as his body was freed of the water's grasp and he buoyed farther up onto the surface. He gasped for a breath and felt his lungs set on fire as the air filled them with saltwater and wind. He reached into the water and gripped the rope. His eyes burned as he held on to the bureau as it rocked back and forth on the violent sea. He pulled the rope up, and it came with very little effort. He didn't need the world lit up with lightning to know that the rope was empty. It came out of the water still tied in a tight knot

But Florence was gone.

CHAPTER SIXTY

7:54 PM
Temperature: 78 degrees
Winds: 114 MPH
Pressure: 28.85 bars
Rain: 3.19 inches

Alfred screamed her name into the wind. The water tossed him blindly in the dark as the world seemed to come undone. When the lightning returned, it lit up a scene he could not recognize. A few houses peaked through the surface like rocks along a shore, but the water was otherwise uninterrupted. Where homes had once been, now there were none. Debris raked along his body as he held onto the bureau, unable to climb it as it threatened to tumble back into the ocean. His voice cracked as he shouted into the storm. When the bureau caught the trunk of a giant oak tree, it pushed into his ribs and knocked the wind out of him as it rolled on end. He fought it as he caught his breath and came out on top of it with his arms stretched fully across the wood. He lifted his head, unsure of where he had traveled. Were the remnants of the house nearby? He drew in a deep breath to scream once more as a crack of lightning lit up the sky and sent an electric charge through the air. He felt it pull at the water, the world painted in a blinding white, and it was in this moment of forgiving light that he saw her.

Her figure was small in the water and clung to what looked like a broken section of wall. His heart leapt at her sight, but the wall would not hold against anything that came in its path. His time was limited, as was his ability. She was more than twenty feet away in raging waters that hid an immeasurable amount of dangers. He took as deep of a breath as he could muster and lifted his feet up until they were against the bureau. With one swift motion he propelled himself into the water and toward where he had lost her in the darkness. The water was stronger than he anticipated. It gripped his limbs and pulled him down into the depths. Keeping above the surface was difficult, and the wind made it all the more unbearable. His sight was lost in the darkness as his ears struggled to distinguish any sound over the roar of the wind. It blew at a speed that he hadn't thought possible. His muscles ached as he fought the current. His mind began to doubt. He should have reached her by now. Was he going the right direction? Had the wind blown him off course?

He felt his legs begin to slow as he kept his eyes straight ahead. He struggled to keep his mind where it needed to be, and as if in slow motion, he felt his muscles begin to seize. He practically paddled in the water, moving nowhere it seemed as the darkness encapsulated him, but he thrashed nonetheless. It was a numbed state of pure determination—his mind racing as his body began to give up the fight—that let him see more clearly when he had finally reached the edge of the broken wall.

He gripped it tightly and fumbled along the edge. She was there. She had to be. The water pulled at his legs as he slid himself along the edge. Finally, as a distant flash of lightning streaked over the island, he saw her faint outline just a few feet away. He reached out and felt the cold skin of her arm, and his body erupted in a sob.

She didn't let go of the wall, but he could hear her voice as he neared. He reached up and took a better grip of the wall where a window had been and pulled himself closer to her. When he felt her face against his own, he finally let himself breath fully. He had found her. That was all that mattered.

"Can you climb?" he shouted.

He felt her arms move next to his body, but she stayed in place. He leaned closer to yell into her ear.

"I'm going to help you up!"

Alfred had one hand at her lower back when the wall slammed against them and broke in half. The front half bent and crumbled into the water, pitching their half up more than a foot into the air before slamming it back down against the water. He felt her pull away when they hit the water and instinctively let go of the wall to keep a hold of her. One hand grabbed her by the waist while the other took a fistful of dress as he struggled to keep her by his side. If she was going into the water, he was going with her.

The wall slammed into an obstacle again and caught him on the temple. Pain radiated though his scalp as he went under. He kicked against the current and came back up to the wind with a sputter of saltwater. Florence had managed to turn and was now in his arms, her skirt floating around them. He yanked her toward him as his back hit something solid and anchored in the water, and he felt her weight push into his. His body was bitten by sharp needles as he shifted so that she was between him and the object. The darkness made his imagination run wild as he felt around them. Leaves. He felt leaves.

"Climb!"

She gripped what she could and pulled with what strength she had as he let himself fall a foot or so below her, one hand gripping a branch tightly, as he pushed her up into the tree. When she was more than half out of the water, he found another branch and hoisted himself up beside her.

"Higher," he shouted. "We have to get higher!"

The wind made the climb perilous as the branches began to thin out nearer the top of the tree. When they found a thick enough bough for her to grip with her back against the trunk, he found another one beside her and stood, his boots sliding on the wet wood, one arm tangled up in the branches and the other wrapped tightly around her body to strap her in place.

The world looked enormous from their pedestal high above the city. When the thunder roared, it echoed across an empty desert of ocean, and the lightning lit up what was left of the island. Tree tops looked like stands of grass in the tide as debris buoyed and bounced with the current down streets, through alleys, and across now-empty lots. Alfred searched for a landmark, anything to give him a sense of direction or of where they were, but he found none. They were in the middle of the ocean as far it mattered. The ocean had erased their lives and everything in them with so little warning.

He balanced himself on the oak tree, his muscles screaming for rest as the world swirled beneath them, and gazed up at Florence's face. Her eyes were closed against the storm as stray strands of hair whipped around her face. Without opening her eyes, one hand crept up Alfred's back until it found his neck and wrapped around it as tightly as she could manage. The wind blew and the sea raged. The water rose until it reached his feet while the winds swirled the world around them in dramatic contrast to what they had known. And when cries came from the water, Alfred searched the surface for a hand to take hold, but nothing ever materialized. After nearly three hours of holding each other in the branches, the wind began to ease its course as the rain lightened to a steady shower. And as the sun began to rise, Alfred dared to turn and look back toward the beach.

It was nothing but sand and water, a barren landscape wiped clean by the ocean's mighty waves. The world as they had known it was gone.

Chapter Sixty-One

September 9th, 6:14 AM
Temperature: 82 degrees
Winds: 7 MPH
Pressure: 29.23 bars
Rain: 3.78 inches

The breeze carried with it the scent of days spent in the ocean, of lighthearted summers beneath the palms in the warm afternoon, but it was a false image that held reality in stark contrast to what the island had been. When the water finally began to recede, Alfred felt certain that little more than solitary trees jutting up from the sand would be left beneath the surface. However, his first glimpses of the wreckage left behind the tide struck more sharply at his stomach than he had anticipated.

The sun rose cleanly over the ocean and shattered the remnants of the gray sky with a disorienting canvas of tangerine and raspberry hues. As he helped Florence down from the tree, a trying and painful task, Alfred noted how crisp the air had become with the cooler temperatures and so much of the moisture now to the north. The first scent was of the fresh water, and it gave him hope that the island was not as it seemed from so high above the streets; his eyes betrayed the security he had found on the wind, however, when he began leading them away from the tree.

What had once been streets were now indistinguishable among the debris. Houses had been torn from their foundations and ripped apart in the water before being scattered along the storm's path. Where there were no walls or doors or shingles, there were belongings, people's possessions, tossed haphazardly in piles of timber and broken tree limbs. A few feet in front of them lay the discarded remnants of a woman's bureau tangled in the splintered boards of a home. A bit farther was a chandelier resting neatly atop a broken piece of wall, the decorative paper torn but still attached. Beneath it jutted out the bruised and bloated arm of a man.

Alfred turned and pulled Florence to him as he kept her eyes on the distance. She focused on the sun and let the cool breeze push her hair away from her face. He noted how she rested one arm against her torso.

"Can you walk?"

She nodded.

"We'll have to traverse the debris." He took her arm gently. "Try to step where I step."

"Where are we going?"

He stared at her before looking back towards the tree. "There's nothing left near the beach. It's all been shoved inland. I suppose it's best to head north and see if we can find somewhere to rest."

"And have you looked after," she replied, reaching up to touch the cut on his forehead.

He leaned down and kissed her forehead. She gave a weak smile. He hated what he knew they would see on their way across the island, but he knew of nothing else to do but move on. That seemed like the most logical answer for them. It seemed like the only answer anyone could give with the world in pieces as it was.

He led her through the wreckage, over hills of debris, through small clearings, and around damaged homes that had clung to their foundations but leaned at incredible angles that defied gravity. They saw people's lives strewn out before them and left to dry in the sun, but it was the evidence of lives lost that gave the strongest blow. Florence jerked away from his grasp when she saw the first of many bodies left by the water, and he comforted her each time she made her way, her feet uneven on the rubble and her hands weak, to try to aid what life remained. But there was never any to be found. Like bottles drained of lightning, the bodies littered the piles of debris until they began to see them in every direction they looked.

Less than a block from the oak tree, they encountered a house that had survived the flood. It stood straight and tall like a proud soldier. The windows were smashed, the door ripped from its hinges, and bald patches along the roof where shingles had been ripped from their attachments, but it stood nonetheless. Several people were gathered on the porch pushing debris from the steps to make way into the street. They looked up at Alfred and Florence and gave nods before carrying on their way. Farther down as they neared Broadway, more houses began to dot the horizon where it had been only debris and sky before. Alfred had little sense of location without something to use as a compass, but some survivors who had ridden out the storm in their houses offered their addresses. In an hour's time, they had barely made it two blocks, and Florence needed to rest.

The remainder of the morning went much in the same way. Alfred helped where he could, pulling debris from the front of houses and moving the injured out of the rubble when they were found. Florence watched from afar, unable to add any strength of her own, but Alfred turned after lifting a broken dining room table from atop a pile that had once been a house and found Florence had gone. He called out to her and mounted the nearest hill of wood and debris only to see her several yards down, sitting on a crate. He jogged toward her and slowed as he heard her singing softly. The scene came into view, and he stopped several feet from her.

A child, no more than eight years old, was beside her, his head in her lap. A wound on the side of his head bled onto her skirt, and his breathing was labored, but he looked out at the sun with big brown eyes. Florence's voice carried on the breeze like a birdsong as she smoothed the child's hair back away from his face and rocked him gently from side to side. Alfred felt his body weaken as he stood, unable to move. The horror of it all had finally reached them. He had not been able to protect her as he thought he could. He had kept his composure as they passed bodies buried in the deep recesses of the storm's damage, but this was pain of a different sort.

As he watched the child's eyes close, he felt his legs give way and he took heavy steps toward her. The wood creaked as he sat next to Florence. He took her hand, leaving the other to soothe the child as best she could, and together they cried for the first time since the winds had brought the storm into their lives. He sobbed for the people all around them that were buried in their houses and for the life he had planned, a life that would be far different now. And when he took the child from her lap and carried him to the nearest house where they had begun to gather the dead in a make-shift morgue, he cried for the innocence that was lost in his arms and the innocence that had been lost in the night.

———•●•———

9:22 AM
Temperature: 83 degrees
Winds: 6 MPH
Pressure: 29.41 bars
Rain: 3.78 inches

When they reached Broadway, they found that it had fared better than the southern side of the island but had not escaped the wrath by any means. It's only saving grace had been the wealth that had built their homes along the street. Built of large stones rather than wood, several houses shimmered in the morning light and cast long shadows to the west over flattened ground where other homes and gardens had once been. The height and peak of the Gresham House stood solidly among the wreckage, while St. Joseph's Church bared a wall and steeple that had been catastrophically torn away. Farther down homes appeared as shadows along the horizon, but it was Ashton Villa that brought Alfred comfort. When they reached its steps, he called into the house without a sliver of formality. Ms. Bettie appeared moments later and helped him walk Florence up the stairs and into a chair on the second floor. The room was littered with fine china and the family's silver, all brought up, he later discovered, as the flood waters began to slither across the lower level. He covered Florence with a blanket and turned to Miss Bettie.

"She needs water to drink and something for her arthritis. Hot water bottles or a heated rag."

"The kitchen was flooded," she replied, a fierceness in her eyes. "But I'll see what we can do. The cistern on the roof is still drinkable, but it won't last long."

Her boots were heavy on the hollow boards as she left the room, and Alfred turned back to Florence. Her eyelids drooped as exhaustion finally took hold. He caressed her cheek.

"I need to get to the office to try to get a message out and see if I can make it to the boardinghouse."

"You'll come back?"

"As soon as I can. I promise."

The staircase was beginning to warp, creaking beneath his weight as he made his way down. The floorboards of the first floor were coated in mud, and silt clung to the walls of the grand house. It was an unfathomable transformation, a stark contrast to the luxury he'd seen there just months earlier. He started toward the open doorway, the stench of the city creeping into the house, and stopped short. Sidestepping the crudely cut hole that had been chopped into the floorboards of the villa, he couldn't help but feel a little relief. At least one house he knew had made it through.

The walk toward the Strand was less painful. The water had not gotten quite as high nearer the bay, and the structures in the business district were more sound. But that did little to alleviate the atmosphere. Wreckage still blocked streets, and, as people came out of hiding and began to wander the island, the finality of the situation had settled among the dust. People wept for those missing, parents sought news of their children, and men, some injured but walking, began moving debris to search for survivors. Most, he knew, were doing it out of the sheer confusion of having survived, but the hope that they held onto was bright and contagious. He spent nearly three hours digging among the rubble with other men, pulling bodies from the piles and rescuing at least six injured people. When he was finally relieved by a set of younger men, he continued toward the harbor until he reached the Levy Building.

The door was open when he reached the fifth floor, and he didn't knock as he stepped into the room. Isaac stood in the center, looking toward his desk. Every window was a gaping hole through which the wind carried a new scent that now permeated across the island. The floorboards were warped from the rain and the room littered with papers. The maps were thrown about, sopped in rainwater. Loose papers had been blown in every direction and stuck to the walls, desks, table, and floor. Isaac's desk was bare; his manuscript, his second attempt at the book, was missing, no doubt scattered all about the office and Market Street below.

Alfred cleared his throat, and the man turned. His face was hollow and pale. He had a cut on his cheek and his hair stood in all directions as if dried in the wind. Alfred ran a hand through his own hair, wondering at his appearance.

"I can come back at a later time."

"No," Isaac contested quietly. "It's fine."

Alfred took a few steps closer and picked up a book off the floor. He remembered his sack, discarded at an address he could no longer recall, but he knew that it was now somewhere at the bottom of the bay. He set the book down on the table.

"You fared alright?" Alfred asked.

Isaac was silent as he looked out the window toward the harbor. Beyond the open window, Alfred could see that the wharf had been victimized more than anyone could have expected. Ships had been tossed violently, their rigging tangled with one another and broken masts leaning into the air. He wondered about those who had pushed out into the gulf the morning before.

"I survived," Isaac replied, his voice dropping as he continued. "But my wife is missing."

Alfred's stomach lurched, and he wished he had stayed with Florence in the comfort of the house on Broadway. He closed his eyes as he shook his head.

"I'm so sorry, Isaac."

The man turned and nodded, his jaw tight. He looked around the office with his hands in his pockets. After a long moment, he took a few steps toward the toppled bookcase.

"I had hoped some part of my life had survived the storm, but it seems very little of anyone's life survived." He nudged a book with the toe of his shoe. "There will be little to return to when it comes time, but I fear it will be a while before I am able."

Alfred watched the man, words failing him. He had cried just hours before as he carried the body of a child he hadn't known. He couldn't imagine the pain of losing his closest companion. Isaac drew in a deep breath and turned toward him.

"There's little here to salvage. I simply wanted to see for myself."

"I can work on saving what can be saved."

Isaac nodded. "In due time." He started toward the door in a painful gait that gave away more injuries hidden beneath his clothing. "But not today, Alfred." He took a final look about the room as he headed toward the door. "Not today."

Alfred searched the room after Isaac left, but the man had been right. There was very little worth saving in the end. A few books that had been sheltered by the turned-over shelf, two instruments that had been designed for high winds and rain, a pair of old field boots—little pieces of their world that had meant nothing the day before but now were priceless in the aftermath. When Alfred made it to the roof, he found it bare. Every instrument had been blown clean off the rooftop; only brackets now sat in their place. The storm flags were gone and the flag pole bent.

But it was the scene from up high that leveled Alfred, the final scene that broke his composure. From the rooftop of the Levy Building he could clearly see the island as it now was, devastated and vulnerable. The streets were non-existent, and he could not determine where one neighborhood ended and another began. Were it not for the few homes that had survived, he would have had no landmark but the shore. The roofline of Ashton Villa sparkled in the sun miles away as the obelisk of the war monument cleared the sky above the flattened land around it. The beach was nearly indistinguishable from where houses had once been, and the western end of the island was bare. He let out a breath as he looked to where the orphanage had once stood; it was nothing but rubble and sand.

He tried to assess the damage from the roof, but, when he had finally had enough, he let his legs carry him back down to the street. More people were walking around, some shifting debris while others appeared lost and disoriented. Alfred watched them for a moment as he considered what their life had become.

He and Florence had survived.

Isaac had in all likelihood lost his wife and unborn child, though his three daughters were safe. Joseph, he assumed, had ridden out the storm with them as well.

He was uncertain of Hilary.

He prayed Mrs. Poplar's home still stood and knew he could make it there before sundown if he left soon. Mathias, he knew, was at the hospital, less than a mile from the boardinghouse. Whether or not it had survived, he would have to learn after he traversed the rubble.

He stepped down onto what was left of 23rd Street and joined a group of men who were clearing out a path for horses and drays. The horses moved slowly as they worked to carry larger pieces out of the way and into alleys, and Alfred found their somber gait to be appropriate as the sun began to lower itself in the sky. As the evening settled onto the island, Alfred made his way east toward the boardinghouse, stopping every now and again to offer an extra set of hands. When he reached the corner where he had first seen the boardinghouse nearly four months earlier, he couldn't help but let out a small sob as he lifted a bruised and tired hand up to the bushes along the fence and breathed in the smell of what he would always remember as an island that glistened in the sun like a pearl on the ocean.

The emerald green leaves surrounded his face as he let his senses fall back into the life he had known and remember the innocent beauty of the Galveston he had known.

*S*ummer had settled on the island like a thick coat of honey. The oleanders were in bloom along the fenceposts where Florence had trimmed them back, and the porch was surrounded with honeysuckle. The breeze carried the scent of the island through the windows and into the house where it mingled with fresh bread and apple jam. From above the sitting room, the sound of heavy footfalls carried across the floor and down the stairs. Alfred turned just in time to grab the boy under the arms and lift him up into the air. He squealed with delight as Alfred spun him in circles before setting him down and patting him on the back, sending him out the front door and into the yard. He sat back down on the sofa and returned to his book. The pages rippled at the edges with a stiffened spine, a piece of the storm's legacy. As Alfred caressed a wrinkled page, he thought about what his life had become in the past nine months.

When Isaac finally returned to his duties two weeks after the storm, Alfred had found him quiet and withdrawn. He had not yet found his wife's body. That would come a week a later, but the toll of caring for his three daughters in her absence had taken its toll. The conflict in the office was subtler than before, but the tension had remained. Joseph was reassigned by the national office to a Puerto Rico station, and Isaac had left in May to lead a regional weather office in New Orleans. Alfred took over the Galveston duties barely a year after arriving on the island.

The devastation at the hands of the storm was unthinkable, edging the months in a brutality that seemed to ebb and flow throughout the city. Debris had filled the streets for weeks. Working parties of volunteers had worked to clear paths and eventually lots, but the severity had been more than anyone could have predicted. And the death toll had quickly colored the island a pale shade of its previous glory.

Buildings on the Strand had been emptied of their goods as the street became a makeshift morgue. Mothers, fathers, spouses, and friends had lined up on the sidewalks to shuffle through the shops and warehouses and search for their missing loved ones, many leaving as forlorn as when they had arrived. That was how most people were left—without closure. A small shake of the head and downcast eyes became the norm when names were brought up, and it hadn't taken long for Alfred to intimately learn the pain of missing someone.

He had volunteered with the burying brigade, but the work proved to be too much for most men. There had simply been too many bodies and too few workers. As the numbers had grown, burying them became impossible. Two days after the storm, the city had begun strapping bodies to barges and sending them out to sea, weighting them down with debris before laying them to rest in the ocean. It had seemed fitting to bury them in the very water that had taken their lives, but life has a way of smearing good intentions. When bodies had begun floating back up on shore, the city became desperate. For months afterward, pyres had lit up street corners well into the night as they burned the victims of the storm, and the city had smelled of ungodly smoke as an ash had settled on the trees and sand.

Mrs. Poplar had been most disturbed by the constant glow about the city, reminders of the friends and neighbors she had lost. She had braved the storm on her own in the darkness of her bedroom with nothing more than an oil lamp and a stiff hip. The first floor had been flooded but fared better than most houses on the island. After clearing out the mud that had caked the floor and putting her husband's waterlogged library into the yard, she had opened her house to more than sixty-eight souls who had lost their homes. Food and clean water had been in short supply for weeks, but she had made the most of the situation and made good use of her store of pickled beets and potatoes, which had been spared from the flood waters by high pantry shelves.

John had returned to the boardinghouse the day after the storm without a word. He'd had a cut on his hand, a bruised shoulder, and what turned into pneumonia, but he'd taken to his room immediately and avoided conversation as much as possible. His brusque nature seemed to have waned, though his arrogance remained, and he had grown tired of the families seeking shelter in the boardinghouse by the second meal at Mrs. Poplar's warped dining table. As soon as he had recovered, he had found accommodations elsewhere, no doubt paying a pretty penny in the scarce market. Mrs. Poplar had wished him well as she shut the door behind him before moving a family of five into his room. Alfred later heard that John had assisted with the tremendous number of patients that flooded the hospital during the weeks after the storm, but his presence proved ill-fitting. He'd been dismissed and moved to Dallas shortly afterward.

When the last family left the house to start anew, Mrs. Poplar opened it again to women who had lost their husbands and soon found a new purpose for her cooking. She played bridge with the women every Tuesday in the sitting room and turned her husband's parlor into a school room.

After two days of no word from Mathias, Alfred had made his way to the hospital. The debris had built up against the building, and windows had been blown out of their frames. When he had found a staff member, he was met with a quick wave of the hand and directed to take the injured to the east wing where there was a clear path.

"I'm looking for someone, a doctor by the name of Mathias Ortiz."

The man had had a bandage about his head and one arm in a sling, and he had spoken softly as patients were carried in.

"Mathias was caring for a young boy when the water began to rise." He had set his eyes on Alfred as if to ensure he understood the weight of his words. "He was a very brave man for what he did, never leaving the boy's side."

Mrs. Poplar had cried when he sat her down and told her of the man's words. They were the tears of a mother. Alfred had helped her gather up what they could of Mathias's belongings before families arrived in need of shelter. Later in the silence of the washroom, Alfred had finally let the overwhelming emotions take hold. He'd sat on the side of the tub and sobbed like a child until he could only gasp for air.

Thomas had been difficult to find, having been holed up in a warehouse on the Strand when the water rose and then left with hundreds of people pushing their way out of the district, but Alfred had visited his shop daily until he had found him in the store. The man had been difficult to read and kept quiet as Alfred had helped him clean up the glass from the broken window. Neither had needed conversation as they'd worked on the task, an understanding between them that they shared their grief but lacked the words to heal it.

It was Buttons who had come to Alfred with the news of Edwin. His body had been discovered beneath the rubble of a collapsed building on Market Street. He had never made it to his wife and children, stopping instead to assist a stranded woman where her coach had become stuck in the flooded streets. His family was taken into the boardinghouse, where an envelope with money was delivered a few weeks later. Mrs. Poplar never let on to the origin of the money, but she had happily recounted the story when Buttons had visited the following week to bring books to the boarders.

Florence's Aunt Katherine had escaped the storm entirely unscathed, finding herself in the part of the city that suffered the least damage, but the Goodman family had not been so lucky. Evelyn had been at home and rode out the storm with her mother, while William had been caught in flood waters while making his way across the city to comfort the two women. The coach had been swept off its wheels and overturned as the ocean surged onto the island. Alfred preferred to believe that William managed to escape the coach before he drowned, but no one could not say for certain. William's body had been found less than a hundred feet away from his mother's house, resting against a tree trunk.

It took weeks to pull together the stories of those Alfred knew, and each new piece realigned his life in a different way. But it was Hilary's piece that had shattered his world so completely.

When Alfred had finally found a path down 25th Street the day after the storm, it had been wiped clean on the southern end. Hilary's mansion with its dark stone and sharp rooflines had become little more than a collection of broken trees and debris. Searching the rubble proved dangerous, but he had managed to pull together a search party by the afternoon. They had worked to clear the rubble for hours, but it became apparent that sections of the house had been carried away. As the last of the search party moved to the lot next door, Alfred had felt his legs give out. The entire world had turned inside out in less than a day, and the weight of it pulled at his lungs, stealing his breath. He had cried as he sat on the steps of Hilary's crumbled home and watched the world move by at a glacial pace. A glint had caught his eye near his foot where a copper mug sat in a puddle of muddy water beneath the remnants of a window frame. He'd taken it back with him as the last vestige of a house that had once been part of his life.

For months the newspaper printed the names of those identified as deceased and those who had survived, but Hilary's name never appeared. After a week of silence, Alfred reported Hilary as missing to the *Galveston Daily News*, but no one ever came forward with his whereabouts. His house was cleared with the debris, leaving an empty lot by the start of the new year, and January brought a telegram from Houston declaring Alfred the executor of Hilary's estate. The birdwatcher had been wealthy and childless, something the two men had never discussed. Every cent had been transferred into Alfred's name.

A survey of the shipping channel had been published in October and plans went forward with the expansion of the channel and subsequent joining of the islands despite the damage to Galveston. Pelican Spit would be no more, and the bureau was prepared to lose their observation station. In an attempt to bring the city together as their future began to brighten, the Deep Water Committee had asked Alfred to join their efforts to impress on residents the significance of the expansion for Galveston's recovery. He had respectfully declined. The field guide had been published in late March, and Alfred had made a habit of taking it with him to every public meeting he attended where the expansion was the topic of discussion, much to Julius Runge's annoyance.

A noise on the front porch pulled Alfred from his thoughts and back into the sitting room.

"Daddy, look!"

The boy ran back into the house and held up a large white blossom. A smile overtook his face as he proudly displayed it for Alfred to see. A smaller girl ran in behind him. She laughed as Alfred placed the flower in her hair and lifted her up into his lap as the boy ran back outside. Footsteps came from the back of the house, and Alfred smiled at how much steadier Florence's gait was now that her hip had healed.

"Well, what are you two doing?"

She beamed down at them, her face framed by auburn locks that tumbled over her shoulders.

"Daddy made me look pretty."

"He certainly did!"

She caressed the girl's face before letting her hand wander to Alfred's shoulder. The sound of laughter came from the yard, and both of them looked out to see Mrs. Poplar tickling the boy. He ran around the house as she made her way up the stairs. Her gray skirt billowed in the breeze as she came in, her cheeks rosy from the warmth of the day.

"Oh, look at you, Rose!" She straightened as if admiring a painting. "What a beautiful woman you're becoming."

The girl slipped from Alfred's lap and took Mrs. Poplar by the hand before leading her into the kitchen, Florence close behind them. Their wedding had been a small affair with the city in such a state. It had not been on the beach but in the Methodist church where she wore a white gown with lace about the neck. It hadn't taken long for them to realize she was unable to bear children, but neither of them had counted it as a loss. Not when there were so many children in need of homes. Mrs. Poplar had known Daniel's mother, who perished in the flood, and Rose had been discovered alone in the street, barely three-years-old. She had no story to tell, but Alfred preferred it that way. If her earliest memories were of love, then it suited her all the more.

"Dinner's ready!"

Alfred called to Daniel, and the boy giggled as he made his way to the porch, bouncing a stick along the ground as he climbed the steps.

Daniel ran in and took his seat at the table where Rose was already poised on the edge of her chair. Mrs. Poplar set a basket of rolls on the table and took a seat next to Daniel as Florence settled in next to Rose. Two seats sat empty. Alfred took the one nearest the kitchen; the last was reserved for Mathias, the man who had introduced him to the love of his life, dared him to be brave, and taught him that a real man was true to who he is. He felt a small sting for the life they had lived together before the storm, however short. He breathed in the scent of the summer and let out a breath.

A warm hand came down on his shoulders as the women talked amongst themselves, and he let a smile take over his cheeks. He looked back to see Mathias standing behind him.

"Sorry I'm late." He gave a grin. "Work never stops."

"We're just glad to have you."

He nodded and made his way to the table. He took his seat slowly, a habit he had learned after losing sight in his left eye. It had been days before they had been able to visit him in the hospital, but they had simply been happy to see him. The water had rushed into the hospital without warning, the same surge that had sent Alfred and Florence rushing up the stairs that night, but Mathias had had more than himself to think of. With an amputated leg, the boy Mathias had been looking after had been unable to flee, and so Mathias had carried him up the stairs and secured him on the third floor before returning to help other patients to safety. It had all been unfortunate timing in the end. The window had shattered, its frame splintering as the elements burst into the hospital, and Mathias had been front and center. Debris had struck him as he trudged through the flood waters, blinding him in one eye and shattering his arm. The doctor's words to Alfred had not been an exaggeration—Mathias had bravely faced the storm to save others. And the hospital had recognized his dedication. After more than three weeks of care, he'd joined the hospital as a practicing physician.

Laughter radiated in the air as the scent of oleanders wafted into the room. Alfred sometimes yearned for the simplicity of the life before the storm, but he was quickly reminded of the beauty of the life he had gained. Of the life he loved. As he bowed his head, letting Mrs. Poplar say grace, he thanked God for his wife, his family, and the most beautiful love letter anyone had ever written.

He thanked God for oleanders in June.

AUTHOR'S NOTE

While the Great Storm of 1900 is a historic event, I have taken some fictional liberties in this novel. I have tried as best I can to keep true to what is known about those characters who lived through this catastrophic hurricane, including their lives before and their actions during the storm. I have altered some aspects of history, such as who performed an action or having certain characters interact, to move the story along at a faster pace and allow Alfred to remain the focus of the novel. In this way, I hope I have given those who lived through the storm a voice and represented their stories in such a way as to show not only their tremendous strength but the harrowing experience they shared.

THE PEOPLE

Many characters in this novel experienced the Great Storm of 1900 in reality, including Dr. Isaac Cline, Joseph Cline, Julius Runge, Colonel Moody, Ike Kempner, and Bettie Brown, while several characters were the product of inspiration and my imagination—Alfred, Florence, Mrs. Poplar, Mathias, John, and Hilary among others. Those characters who truly lived had their own impact on the island and were included in an effort to capture the city as it was during that time.

Dr. Isaac Cline is perhaps the most associated name when it comes to the Great Storm of 1900. He is well-known for his intellectual prowess as well as his role on the island during the storm. He survived the storm along with his three children; his wife, Cora, pregnant with their fourth child, drowned when their house broke apart in the storm surge. She is buried on Galveston Island. Written in history as a stoic man who held his duty above all things, he took time away from his post as he settled the children into their new life after the storm and grieved his wife, returning to the bureau a few weeks later. Isaac went on to lead the first regional U.S. Weather Bureau office in the south, heading up research in New Orleans and finally completing the manuscript that became his life's work.

Joseph Cline rode out the storm with Isaac's family and the nearly fifty neighbors who had gathered in the climatologist's house. He is credited with rescuing two of Isaac's children. Joseph went on to work in Puerto Rico before returning to the U.S. Both men published memoirs that discuss their careers in climatology and briefly mention their experiences with the storm, but neither gives much reference to the other. Historians theorize that their relationship continued to erode after the storm, perhaps made all the less repairable by their shared experience.

Julius Runge was a store owner and importer with intimate ties to the German nation state. In addition to importing European goods that were often collected by wealthy Galveston residents, Julius used his position as consul to the German Empire and his importing ships to bring European immigrants to Galveston, assisting the island in becoming the busiest port of entry in the south in the late nineteenth century. A large portion of immigrants who entered through Galveston's port were of German heritage, in addition to the thousands of Jewish immigrants, and Julius worked to help them establish new lives in the city and beyond, occasionally hiring them while providing others with means to move into northern Texas or beyond to find work and establish communities. While I could find no evidence that he was part of the DWC, I chose to incorporate his character to highlight the European influence that was associated with the higher echelons of Galveston at the time.

Colonel W. L. Moody, Sr. was a wealthy patron of the city and led many ventures that brought exporting opportunities to Galveston. Most well-known for his work in the cotton exchange, Colonel Moody was a founding member of the DWC and worked to expand the wharves and shipping channel. As with all businessmen, some of his practices have been questioned by historians; however, the legacy that he left on the island is by no means small. The Moody Foundation has reaches throughout Galveston and well into Houston, supporting the arts and humanities. The home that Colonel Moody bought only weeks after the storm is still recognized on the island as The Moody Mansion and provides a deeper understanding of how the Moody Family continues to support local programs and education today.

Ike Kempner was the son of Harris Kempner, a founding member of the DWC. While Ike had regular dealings with members of the DWC after he took over the family companies with his father's death, his exact involvement with the committee was not a clear membership. I chose to have him continue his father's role within the DWC because of his prominence in the city's business thread. As a noteworthy member of society, Ike was well-liked and helped develop the city into the exporting force it became, even after the storm. The family business expanded as the Kempner name matured, and by the middle of the twentieth century, the Kempners were involved in exporting, cotton, banking, and more, eventually founding the Imperial Sugar Corporation and co-founding with William Lewis Moody, Jr. the American National Insurance Company. Their family's influence and generosity has endured in the island's history and is visible in many aspects of the island, including Kemper Park and the renaming of 22nd Street as Kempner Street. As with the Moody family, the Kempner's support of the island's culture and growth cannot be overstated and continues to ring true today.

Ms. Bettie Brown was a real character in every sense of the word. Raised lavishly in Ashton Villa, the first mansion built on Broadway and a structure that survives to this day, Miss Bettie inherited a great deal of wealth and was known to flaunt it as she traveled the world. She was a skilled painter, and several of her canvases still hang in Ashton Villa. The upper balcony of Ashton Villa was used occasionally to cool off from the summer heat, taking advantage of the winds that carried over the houses, and I like to imagine that she hosted entertaining guests such as Hilary and Buttons when she was alive, leaving neighbors to speculate about her inviting men to keep her company unchaperoned. She was also known to race a chariot down Broadway at sunset, a fact that I knew had to be included in this story. Ms. Bettie was with her mother and grandmother in Ashton Villa when the storm arrived in 1900, and she worked with her housemaid to take the silver and household items to the second story as the storm surge made its way into the house. The water rose to nearly halfway up the staircase, and the structure's survival is partially credited to her opening the grand windows along the first floor, which allowed the water to flow through the house without taking it with the current.

The Deep Water Committee was created in the 1870s to gain funding for the initial expansion of the island's shipping channel and was still in existence when the Great Storm of 1900 struck the island. It consisted of several businessmen who comprised the majority of the city's wealth. As with many aspects of Galveston business, the wealthiest of the lot tended to make decisions, and this was true of the Deep Water Committee as well. The shipping channel was initially expanded in 1888 and then again in 1896, which should not have been a surprise given that a large portion of Deep Water Committee members were involved in cotton export and gained financially from the expansions. This is not to discredit their efforts, as the expansions no doubt had a strong effect on the island's industry and growth; however, the Great Storm of 1900 caused tremendous damage to the island and the wharves, which slowed the island's progress. Houston eventually surpassed the recovering port to become the primary import and export location in Texas. The Deep Water Committee continued their efforts after the storm and assisted with gaining funding for the grade raising and construction of the seawall, adding to the men's list of projects that propelled the island forward.

The Locations

Among the locations mentioned in the novel, many of them have been preserved and are open on the island today while a few were inspired by other structures. The Levy Building can be found on the corner of 23rd and Market Streets with lofts on the upper floors where the Galveston Weather Office resided in 1900. The weather office experienced wind damage due to its height. Windows were blown out, water drenched the interior, and Isaac Cline lost his second attempt at a manuscript.

Ashton Villa, as mentioned above, was home to the Browns and was recently purchased by the Galveston Historical Foundation; its tell-tale green shutters can be seen by tourists as they drive down Broadway. Those who stop along the sidewalk will not only see the original wrought-iron fence buried half in the ground as a result of the island raising but the second-floor balcony where Miss Bettie entertained visitors.

The Tremont House was in its second iteration during the 1900 storm and had minimal damage from the storm; however, it fell into disrepair and was condemned a few decades later. The current Tremont House is the third version of the hotel but has retained a good deal of the hotel's original charm, including an old wooden bar that dates back to before the storm.

The Garten Verein ("Garden Club" in German) was built in 1880 and became a popular location for sports, events, and walks in its extensive gardens. Unfortunately, the dance pavilion where Alfred and Florence have their first dance was the only structure that survived the hurricane in 1900. The storm piled debris over five feet high throughout the grounds, decimating the lush gardens. The pavilion has required wide-ranging renovations over the years, and the Galveston Historical Foundation opens the venue for weddings and events. The Garten Verein currently sits in Kempner Park, joined through the back windows by aged oaks that shade the few remaining paths.

The Lyceum was originally a wooden building that was eventually renovated with a stone façade. However, many aspects remain original to the building, including the stained-glass windows that look out onto 24th Street. The structure survived the Great Storm of 1900, experiencing only interior damage, and provided shelter to homeless families for weeks afterward.

Old Red, also known as the Ashbel Smith Building, was the inaugural building of the state's first medical college, which opened in 1891. The building suffered extensive damage to its roof during the storm, but the remainder of the structure fared well enough to be renovated and eventually preserved. It still operates as part of the university.

Offat's Bayou still offers a beautiful view of the bay on the west side of the island, just beyond the causeway that connects to the mainland, and has been used by the local university's crew team for morning practice. Old maps of the island before the grade raising show bayous and waterways that no longer exist, and some of these bayous were reimagined for the novel as I experienced Galveston Island as my characters would have experienced it.

THE U.S. WEATHER BUREAU IN 1900

One of the biggest liberties that I took with the story was the replacement of John Blagden, an assistant observer assigned to Galveston during the storm, with a fictional character. Blagden joined the Galveston Weather Bureau office only weeks before the storm and assisted the Clines in their day-to-day observations and field work. Blagden is known to have stayed at the Levy Building until the winds breached 100 miles per hour and ripped the anemometer from the rooftop, proving perhaps to be the most dutiful in taking measurements nearly every ten minutes until the storm became too powerful. Blagden provides insight into the days leading up to the storm in a letter dated September 10, 1900, stating that "we had warning of the storm and many saved themselves by seeking safety before the storm reached here. We were busy all day Thursday answering telephone calls about it and advising people to prepare for danger. But the storm was more severe than we expected."

History shows that Blagden and the citizens of Galveston had a better understanding of what was heading their way than the U.S. Weather Bureau's office in Washington, D.C. In 1956, the Forecasts and Synoptic Division of the bureau sent a letter in response to a citizen's inquiry in which it stated they could find "no reference to the issuance of hurricane warnings for the Texas or Louisiana coasts" for the Great Storm of 1900. Rather, the only references that can be found are tropical storm warnings "from Pensacola to Galveston" on the evening of September 7th and a shift in location on the following morning from "Galveston to Brownsville." A report stating that Galveston was in imminent danger or acknowledgement that a hurricane had entered the gulf never came.

Isaac Cline was likely one of the first on the island to identify that something was amiss with the weather regardless of what official reports were saying. On September 7th, he noted that the waves were not ebbing and flowing at their usual tempo and that a heavy swell had reached the island and continued through the night. He also made note of the tide rising and beginning to flood the beach despite the wind being from the north, which he expected would have blown the water back out into the gulf. However, this was made all the more confusing for Isaac due to climatology's misunderstandings of storm behavior. Isaac kept his eyes on the horizon, watching for the brick red color that the sky was known to take on before a hurricane arrived. It never appeared and left the man questioning what could be driving the odd behavior in the water if it were not a hurricane.

The theories behind storm behavior were also a complicating factor for how the U.S. Weather Bureau approached the forecasting of hurricanes. As an accepted theory of storm behavior, climatologists believed that hurricanes that made their way across the Atlantic and crossed north of Cuba would turn and follow the eastern seaboard of the U.S. So certain was the Weather Bureau in this behavior, that it was likely the reason they forecasted that the storm would move up to the Carolinas after drenching Florida rather than taking its actual course into the Gulf of Mexico.

They were so confident in their prediction that the bureau was hesitant to change its forecast after the expected rains and winds did not appear in the southeastern states. It was only after weather patterns were identified along the southern coast, as the storm began to track toward Louisiana before shifting toward Galveston, that the bureau finally issued a forecast stating that the storm had entered the gulf. It was labeled a tropical storm rather than a hurricane, most likely because it was thought the storm had exhausted its strength. By the time Galveston was recognized as a potential for landfall, the hurricane was less than 24 hours away from shore.

Details regarding communications within the U.S. Weather Bureau and actions on the part of the local Galveston office during and following the storm are blurry, even in first-hand accounts. Isaac Cline, in a report from late-September 1900, stated that, not only were warnings received and distributed in Galveston two days before the storm's arrival, but the storm was announced in the newspaper. He credits this early warning with saving thousands of lives after residents in lower-lying areas were able to move to higher ground before dangerous conditions arrived. While he states that nearly "12,000 people moved out prior to the crisis," it is not clear if he means they sought higher ground—of which there was only eight feet to be found on the island—or if he believed that many evacuated the island in advance of the hurricane's landfall. Regardless, the sincerity of the warnings Cline references are debatable, as many survivor accounts carry a theme of shock at not only the arrival of a hurricane but its severity.

A post-storm review of September's weather activities according to the U.S. Weather Bureau asserts that warnings of the hurricane's advancement "were timely and received a wide distribution not only in Galveston but throughout the coast region." However, records show that issued storm warnings were inaccurate. Galveston was not noted as a potential path for the storm until less than 24 hours before flooding would begin, and the two warnings that were issued were for a tropical storm that was assumed to have started to run its course. No matter the attempts made to warn locals, Galveston was unprepared for the storm that ravaged its coast. To the U.S. Weather Bureau's credit, modern analysis by the National Oceanic and Atmospheric Administration (NOAA) reveals that one of the island's greatest weaknesses in 1900 was unavoidable: identifying the exact location and path of the storm was impossible while it moved through the Gulf of Mexico. Wireless communication for ship-to-shore messages was in its infancy and was not yet available to Weather Bureau offices. When combined with the assumption that the storm would move along the east coast, the Galveston Office had no way to know what was crossing the gulf and turning toward their shores.

Perhaps one of the most damning events for Galveston during the summer of 1900 was the U.S. Weather Bureau's decision to cut ties with Cuba regarding weather-related communications. The political climate of the bureau was the result of tight funding and unrealistic expectations, which was threatened further by Cuba's ability to not only forecast hurricanes earlier but more accurately. Because of the island's location, Cuba's history of hurricanes provided meteorologists with plenty of data and experience to forecast storms well before they were seen just by changes in the tides and skies. The U.S. Weather Bureau's administration in 1900 determined that their methods, which were often scientifically based but not explained in such terms, were not on par with the U.S. offices, resulting in a moratorium on weather-related communications from Cuba. Had the lines from Cuba not been scrutinized and eventually cut, it is likely that Galveston would have had advance notice of the storm's path and known days earlier that precautions were needed.

THE GREAT STORM OF 1900

The Great Storm of 1900, so named because the protocol of giving hurricanes names had not yet been adopted, was a category 4 hurricane. Wind speeds reached over 130 miles per hour and flooding was inconceivable, leaving the entire 209 square miles of Galveston Island submerged in ocean waters. Many survivors accounted how treacherous the roads became by mid-day when the rain had just begun to fall, thanks to the rise in tides as the storm approached. What likely confused Isaac Cline the most was how the flooding continued despite the wind being out of the north, which should have blown the water out of the bay. The morning started with low water in the bay because of the winds, but even a front moving down from Oklahoma Territory was no match for the storm's strength. When the storm approached, pressure continued to drop, though slowly at first, which pushed the water inland. By the time Isaac Cline realized the severity of what was happening, the worst of the storm was only hours away.

Many homes and buildings might have been sturdy enough to withstand the flooding and winds if it had not been for one unknown danger that lurked in the water. A railway trestle that carried trains around the island and toward the mainland had been built near the beach, no doubt giving passengers the view of a lifetime as they traveled above the ocean and watched the sunset over the Gulf of Mexico. When water began flooding the beach the afternoon of September 8th, it took very little time for the water to reach the base of the wooden scaffolding. The storm surge arrived hours later and rose with tremendous speed as the pressure dropped drastically. Several survivor accounts describe the initial storm surge as rising feet within seconds, carrying with it the force of over 130-mile-per-hour winds.

The trestle could not withstand the 15-foot surge and collapsed. But rather than breaking it apart, the storm surge carried the mess of mangled wood and metal onto the island where it acted like a battering ram, slamming into structures and pushing them off their foundations. As the trestle moved northward with the water, it thickened as it collected debris until it resembled a wall being pushed across the island by the storm's force. This is the wall of debris that Isaac Cline believed slammed into the side of his house, which otherwise would have likely been able to survive the flooding waters atop its stilts. When the wall of debris came to a stop, the island that was left in its trail was wiped clean of standing structures and resembled a beach of nothing more than downed trees and wooden planks from splintered houses.

CLINE FAMILY

Isaac Cline returned home around 2:00 PM the day the storm arrived. He found his pregnant wife and three children at home along with several neighbors who were seeking shelter from the beach. The number of refugees that knocked at their door grew as the day wore on, in part because people felt safe in the presence of the Chief Climatologist and in the house he believed could survive any flooding the island experienced. After flood waters chased everyone to their second floor, the island now submerged in darkness, it took only another hour before the trestle and wall of debris struck the house. Joseph held on to two of the three Cline children, while Isaac recovered the third. Together, the five drifted on debris throughout the night, but there was no sign of Isaac's wife, Cora, when the sun came up.

A letter written by John Blagden tells the story of him returning to the office after the storm had passed in which he "found a note from the younger [Joseph] Cline telling me of the safety of all except the Dr.'s wife." The number of victims surpassed anything the city could have prepared themselves to experience, leaving the newspaper to simply report names and, if known, relationships to others. Cora Cline's line read simply: CLINE, Mrs. Isaac M. (wife of Local Forecast Official). She was interred in Galveston's Lakeview Cemetery.

AFTER THE STORM

John Blagden describes the scene following the storm as one in which bodies were constantly pulled from the wreckage and carted down streets to morgues. People had lost clothes and were only in what they had worn through the storm. Electricity was completely out, returning the city to candlelight, while a lack of food and water caused a fear of a famine. Military rule took over in lieu of an active city government, giving rise to rumors, which Blagden admits might have been true, that anyone caught pilfering bodies was shot on sight.

It is likely that, even with military rule enacted, the city was in a constant state of disorganization for days after the storm. A letter written to the mayor of Galveston accounts for horses lost in the storm and requests the purchase of four more to assist in a more efficient fire department. Edwin N. Ketchum, the Chief of Police, wrote and signed a pass to identify a man as a special Clerk of the Galveston Police Department in lieu of proper identification or an office during relief efforts. The city was far from being in an operable state and faced a dramatic feat of providing a sanitary environment for survivors.

The city's recovery efforts were an arduous process that started with simply clearing paths for horses, carts, and people to move about the city. A report dated September 15, 1900 and submitted by the Foreman of the Streets and Alley Department to the Acting City Engineer details the department's efforts in a line-by-line account of what far surpassed their daily responsibilities. The first line states that they had "opened [a] passage on Tremont Street [23rd Street] from Avenue M to Avenue O" while line six notes that, during their work to clear the way on 31st Street from Avenue O to Avenue P½, they buried 12 bodies and 22 animals. A note later in the report, which was written on a scrap of ledger paper, states that men dug ditches to drain stagnant water that was as deep as two feet in some central areas of the island.

Relief efforts came from near and far with donations pouring in from around the country and organizations such as the Red Cross setting up camps to assist residences in their struggle to return to normalcy. Clara Barton, the President of the Red Cross, described her arrival in Galveston in a letter to President McKinley as beyond exaggeration:

"It was one of those monstrosities of nature which defied exaggeration and fiendishly laughed at all...attempts of words to picture the scene it had prepared. The churches, the great business houses, the elegant residences of the cultured and opulent, the modest little homes of laborers of a city of nearly forty thousand people; the center of foreign

shipping and railroad traffic lay in splinters and debris piled twenty feet above the surface, and the crushed bodies, sad and dying, of nearly ten thousand of its citizens lay under them."

The *Galveston News* became the primary source of information for people seeking aid or the whereabouts of their loved ones. A notice from September 1900 lists the locations of ward chairmen to whom people could apply if they required supplies, while the newspaper ran daily lists of those who were known to have survived and those whose bodies had been identified among the dead. After several people were reported as dead only to be found alive, the newspaper kindly asked that all reports be verified before being submitted to print to avoid undue stress on surviving family members.

The effects of the storm continued well after the flood waters receded. While thousands drowned in the storm surge that overtook the island, many survived only to succumb to their injuries hours, days, or weeks later. With the unsanitary conditions of the city that followed for weeks afterward, survivors faced the threat of disease, with many dying from dysentery, tuberculosis, malarial fever, and pneumonia for months after the storm. It was impossible to know how many had perished in the storm or calculate how many died afterward, leaving officials to only estimate the total number of deaths. Conservative estimates say at least 5,000 victims died because of the storm, while historians have said that the number is likely to be closer to 8,000 deaths.

LOSS AND DAMAGE

On October 9, 1900, the Galveston Relief Committee completed a census of the city to better assess total loss and damages. Twelve wards are reported with a total surviving population of 25,639, noting 3,406 deaths. While it is not clear if the deaths are meant to be associated solely with the storm or since the last census, the number is now understood to be generously low. Modern estimates attribute at least 5,000 deaths to the storm with the potential of more than 6,000 fatalities with some estimating near 8,000 deaths. Through their efforts to gather and preserve information pertaining to the storm, the Galveston and Texas History Center at the Rosenberg Library has digitized a list of those reported through various sources as having died during the storm by drowning or from injuries sustained during the hurricane. Their list includes 5,132 names of known victims as of the original publication of this book. It is likely that many people, having lost their homes, possessions, money, and immediate family, left Galveston to return to their families or start fresh in a town that was not facing such tremendous recovery. Unfortunately, as a result, an accurate number of deaths caused by the storm and its aftermath will never be known.

The same census estimates that more than $7.5 million dollars in property damage occurred over the month between the storm and the report filing, equating more than $225 million in today's currency. A single note at the bottom of the page states that the estimate does not include public buildings, stocks of merchandise and inventory, and mortgages. A more realistic property loss was likely more than $9 million with the damage suffered by businesses on the wharves, which had exported nearly $90 million in cotton the previous year and were left to clean up the harbor and damaged inventory before shipping could resume.

REBUILDING GALVESTON

One of the most respectable traits of Galveston citizens is their persistence and determination, which has been evident after several hurricanes that have ravaged the island since 1900. Those that stayed behind after the Great Storm of 1900, however, not only worked to rebuild the city but to protect it against what had proved to be a very deadly opponent. Through an unbelievable feat of engineering, the city set out to literally raise the island to gain more height above the ocean. While the height would provide a new level of safety, more was needed, and the city also began work on building a seawall—a structure that would stretch along the southern edge of the island and would deflect strong swells back into the ocean. The hope was that these two defenses would work together to not only limit the amount of flooding that would occur if another hurricane were to make landfall but the damage that could result with what water managed to make it on land. Given the storm surge of the Great Storm of 1900 was just over 15 feet, the city decided that a 17-foot wall was a necessity.

The grade raise was 17 feet on the beach and gradually tapered to meet the island's natural height toward the north. Jackscrews were used to raise structures that had survived and could be salvaged. This included tremendous stone mansions and churches along Broadway. Utility lines were raised, but surviving trolley tracks were buried and rebuilt on the new surface as sections were completed. The raising was done by dredging sand from the shipping channel, pumping the slurry mixture into a blocked section, and draining the water to leave sand behind. It took nearly a decade for 500 blocks of the city to be raised. Evidence of the raising can still be seen today throughout the island, such as Ashton Villa's half-buried metal fence attesting to the Brown family's decision to bury the lowest level of their home rather than raise the house up to the new ground level.

The seawall took nearly two years to complete and cost more than $1.5 million. The structure is a concrete wall that is 16 feet wide at its base, rises up to meet the island level, and concaves to absorb the shock of the waves and push the water back out to sea. Riprap was placed in front of it to help slow the water before it impacted the wall. As the city entered its second decade of the twentieth century, it was much more prepared for what the ocean would bring its way, and it didn't have to wait long to see if its investment had been worth the effort. In 1915, a hurricane made landfall just southwest of the city and rammed the seawall for nearly 40 hours, much longer than the Great Storm of 1900 would have. To the credit of engineers, the storm surge did not breach the wall, though some waves topped the structure due to high winds and intensified flooding. The seawall did experience some erosion due to the extended length of time that water pounded against its embankment, and the greatest damage came at the hands of a four-masted schooner that was tossed onto the seawall and caught the edge of the structure with its anchor.

The seawall proved successful in protecting the island from the storm, and it was later funded for expansion in 1918 and again in 1950. The extensions protected the island against Hurricane Carla, a category 5 storm, in 1961; there were no homes destroyed or deaths at the hand of storm surges. When Hurricane Ike, a category 4 storm, hit Galveston in 2008, the seawall held but the damage was more extensive than with previous storms. The U.S. Army Corps of Engineers completed its first major repair to the seawall in 2009 and it remains a landmark of the island's resilience to this day, protecting 10 miles of the island from oncoming storms.

ACKNOWLEDGEMENTS

This book involved so many moving pieces that I would not have fully understood without the assistance of those at The Self Publishing Agency. My sincere thanks to Megan Williams for her guidance and continued support throughout the publication process. Thanks also go to Laura Wrubleski for her work on the book interior and to Liana Moisescu for her beautiful cover design.

I owe a good deal of gratitude to the Galveston Historical Foundation, Moody Foundation, and Mitchell Historic Properties, all of which have contributed to the preservation of Galveston's history and provided me with a plethora of resources for inspiration during the writing of this novel. I would not have been able to experience such history firsthand without their conservation of the island's buildings and educational programs. Special thanks also go to the Rosenberg Library for their support of my book release event and their continued research of the Great Storm of 1900.

And lastly but by no means least, I owe the most thanks and gratitude to my family. To my parents for encouragement and support as well as for telling nearly everyone they knew about my book. And to August for reading more drafts than my editor, talking me through doubt and tears, and supporting me even when my characters became an obsession—I couldn't have finished this book without your love.

Author Interview

What drew you to write a novel centered around the Great Storm of 1900?

When I first visited Galveston, I was immediately taken with how much history was preserved on the island. A walk down the Strand offers a stroll through the city's Victorian heyday, not to mention the mansions that dot Broadway, and I soon found myself reading as many books I could on the city's history. The Great Storm of 1900 was the island's pivotal moment; it fell from prominence in a matter of hours, going from the Wall Street of the South to devastation overnight, and the significance of that image stuck with me. On top of its impact to the southern export business, the severity of the storm was unthinkable at that time, and the Galveston weather office was unprepared for what was heading their way. Once I understood the elements that were at play when the hurricane made landfall, the story began to weave itself together and allowed me to indulge my obsession with Galveston history at the same time.

Why did you focus on the meteorological aspect of the storm through your characters' lives?

The politics surrounding the weather bureau at the time of the storm felt the most disastrous when I looked at the whole picture. The science behind a hurricane was rather simple when I got down to it, which is what made the story all the more intriguing. The Galveston weather office couldn't communicate with Cuba and so didn't know what was heading their way. They misunderstood how hurricanes would behave in the gulf and had a notion that the island was safe for various reasons. It all added up to the perfect storm, and the best way to highlight those behind-the-scenes moments was through the eyes of the Galveston climatologists.

Nature features throughout the novel. Why was that important for you to emphasize?

Galveston Island is home to a wide range of bird life and is a key location for migrating birds. Historical accounts say that the island was so thick with birds that they would blot out the sun when they took to the skies, but American society had yet to understand the effects of exploitation, especially for fashion trends, in 1900. The Migratory Bird Treaty Act wasn't signed into law until 1918, at which point several species of birds were on the verge of extinction or had already been eradicated due to hunting and industrialization. Because the novel centers on the force that nature can exhibit, especially when taken for granted, I wanted to emphasize humankind's role in destruction as well rather than only exhibiting how we became victims of the storm. Giving my protagonist the conflict between not only understanding nature as it affects the island's safety but his role in the destruction of natural habitats felt like a relevant move given today's political climate.

What are the difficulties of writing historical fiction?

The most difficult aspect for me in writing historical fiction is the need to be as historically accurate as possible. Even when writing about things I know, there are pieces that have to be put together well in a scene to pull it off. It can be something simple, like the food that was served for breakfast at that time in that region, or something more complex such as how the upper class socialized in Galveston, but part of what makes historical fiction such an enjoyable experience for me is having a story that simmers in historical accuracy. That research can also be a joy for me as well when it's something I'm interested in learning—historical fiction authors learn so much in the writing process!

What did research look like for you for this novel?

Initially, it was reading for pleasure, and I like to think it continued that way but with a more narrowed objective. I was lucky enough to live within driving distance of Galveston, so some of my research was conducted in person. I toured the Garten Verein, the Ashton Villa, the Lyceum, and the Bishop's Palace, and we've spent our summer weekends walking the Strand and 23rd Street for the past several years. I also have the good fortune of marrying a naturalist who not only took me out to the bayous but is a constant resource about local wildlife. Between those resources, I read as much as I could get my hands on about the island and influential people of the time and combed through the Rosenberg Library's online archive to see how the city and its buildings look in 1900 before and after the storm. Because the storm is such a well-documented disaster, there are a lot of resources available if you know where to look.

What is it like publishing your own book rather than working with a trade publisher?

Independently publishing a book is an eye-opening experience. There are so many pieces that have to fit together and in a short amount of time, but the rewards are well worth the effort! As this is my first novel, everything was a learning process. From the book design and formatting to registering ISBNs and creating publication platform accounts, I was constantly researching the best way to go about it all. But it allowed me to have control over how my book developed and how it was being released into the world. While trade publishers can offer benefits with publicity, indie authors and publishers are developing a presence on platforms to market their books in similar ways. Learning everything about how to get a book from draft to publication has been an entertaining experience that I'm looking forward to repeating!